INVASION!
"Drop cloak!"

Captain Benjamin Sisko said as the three alien ships on the viewscreen swung in on the attack. The toneless curtness of Sisko's voice told Dax just how grim the situation must be. "Divert all power to shields and weapons."

"Damage to forward shield generators," O'Brien's voice reported. "Diverting power from rear shields to compensate."

"Return fire!" Sisko leapt from his command chair and went to join Dax at the helm. "Starting evasive manuevers, program delta!"

Alien phaser fire washed the Defiant's bridge in a fierce white light. . . .

Look for STAR TREK Fiction from Pocket Books

Star Trek: The Original Series

Star Trek: The Next Generation

Star Trek: Deep Space Nine

Star Trek: Voyager

STAR TREK
DEEP SPACE NINE®
INVASION!

BOOK THREE

TIME'S ENEMY

L.A. GRAF

INVASION! concept by John J. Ordover and Diane Carey

POCKET BOOKS
New York   London   Toronto   Sydney   Tokyo   Singapore

An *Original* Publication of POCKET BOOKS

POCKET BOOKS, a division of Simon & Schuster Inc.
1230 Avenue of the Americas, New York, NY 10020

STAR TREK is a Registered Trademark of
Paramount Pictures.

A VIACOM COMPANY

This book is published by Pocket Books, a division of
Simon & Schuster Inc., under exclusive license from
Paramount Pictures.

ISBN: 0-671-54150-1

First Pocket Books printing August 1996

10 9 8 7 6 5 4 3 2 1

POCKET and colophon are registered trademarks of
Simon & Schuster Inc.

Printed in the U.S.A.

Before

Out here where sunlight was a faraway glimmer in the blackness of space, ice lasted a long time. Dark masses of it littered a wide orbital ring, all that remained of the spinning nebula that had birthed this planet-rich system. The cold outer dark sheltered each fragment in safety, unless some chance grazing of neighbors ejected one of them into the unyielding pull of solar gravity. Then the mass of dirty ice would begin its long journey toward the distant sun, past the captured ninth planet, past the four gas giants, past the ring of rocky fragments that memorialized a planet never born. By that point it would have begun to glow, brushed into brilliance by the gathering heat of the sun's nuclear furnace. When it passed the cold red desert planet and approached the cloud-feathered planet that harbored life, it would be brighter than any star. Its flare would pierce that planet's blue sky, stirring brief wonder from the primitive tribes who hunted and gathered and scratched at the earth with sticks to grow their food. In a few days, the comet's borrowed light would fade, and the tumbling ice would start its long journey back to the outer dark.

One fragment had escaped that fate, although it shouldn't have. It carried a burden of steel and empty space, buried just deep enough in its icy heart to send it spinning back into the cloud of fellow comets after its near-collision with another. For centuries afterward, it danced an erratic path through the *ice-littered darkness before it settled into a stable orbit in the shadow of the tiny ninth planet. More centuries passed while dim fires glowed on the night side of the bluish globe that harbored life. The fires slowly brightened and spread, leaping across its vast oceans. They brightened faster after that, merging to form huge networks of light that outlined every coast and lake and river. Then the fires leaped into the ocean of space. Out to the planet's single moon at first, then later to its cold, red neighbor, then to the moons of the gas giants, and finally out beyond all of them to the stars. In all those long centuries, nothing disturbed the comet and its anomalous burden. No one saw the tiny, wavering light that lived inside.*

Until a fierce blast of phaser fire ripped the icy shroud open, and exposed what lay within.

CHAPTER
1

"IT LOOKS LIKE they're preparing for an invasion," Jadzia Dax said.

Sisko grunted, gazing out at the expanse of dark-crusted cometary ice that formed the natural hull of Starbase One. Above the curving ice horizon, the blackness of Earth's Oort cloud should have glittered with bright stars and the barely brighter glow of the distant sun. Instead, what it glittered with were the docking lights of a dozen short-range attack ships—older and more angular versions of the *Defiant*—as well as the looming bulk of two Galaxy-class starships, the *Mukaikubo* and the *Breedlove*. One glance had told Sisko that such a gathering of force couldn't have been the random result of ship refittings and shore leaves. Starfleet was preparing for a major encounter with someone. He just wished he knew who.

"I thought we came here to deal with a *non*military emergency." In the sweep of transparent aluminum windows, Sisko could see Julian Bashir's dark reflection glance up from the chair he'd sprawled in after a glance at the view. Beyond the doctor, the huge conference room was as empty as it had been ten minutes ago when they'd first been escorted into it. "Otherwise, wouldn't Admiral Hayman have asked us to come in the *Defiant* instead of a high-speed courier?"

Sisko snorted. "Admirals never *ask* anything, Doctor.

And they never tell you any more than you need to know to carry out their orders efficiently."

"Especially this admiral," Dax added, an unexpected note of humor creeping into her voice. Sisko raised an eyebrow at her, then heard a gravelly snort and the simultaneous hiss of the conference-room door opening. He swung around to see a rangy, long-boned figure in ordinary Starfleet coveralls crossing the room toward them. Dax surprised her by promptly stepping forward, hands outstretched in welcome.

"How have you been, Judith?"

"Promoted." The silver-haired woman's angular face lit with something approaching a sparkle. "It almost makes up for getting this old." She clasped Dax's hands warmly for a moment, then turned her attention to Sisko. "So this is the Benjamin Sisko Curzon told me so much about. It's a pleasure to finally meet you, Captain."

Sisko slanted a wary glance at his Science Officer. "Um—likewise, I'm sure. Dax?"

The Trill cleared her throat. "Benjamin, allow me to introduce you to Rear Admiral Judith Hayman. She and I—well, she and Curzon, actually—got to know each other on Vulcan during the Klingon peace negotiations several years ago. Judith, this is Captain Benjamin Sisko of *Deep Space Nine,* and our station's chief medical officer, Dr. Julian Bashir."

"Admiral." Bashir nodded crisply.

"Our orders said this was a Priority One Emergency," Sisko said. "I assume that means whatever you brought us here to do is urgent."

Hayman's strong face lost its smile. "Possibly," she said. "Although perhaps not urgent in the way we usually think of it."

Sisko scowled. "Forgive my bluntness, Admiral, but I've been dragged from my command station without explanation, ordered not to use my own ship under any circumstances, brought to the oldest and least useful starbase in the Federation—" He made a gesture of reined-in impatience at the bleak cometary landscape outside the windows. "—and you're telling me you're not sure how *urgent* this problem is?"

"No one is sure, Captain. That's part of the reason we brought you here." The admiral's voice chilled into something between grimness and exasperation. "What we *are* sure of is that we could be facing potential disaster." She reached into the front pocket of her coveralls and tossed two ordinary-looking data chips onto the conference table. "The first thing I need you and your medical officer to do is review these data records."

"Data records," Sisko repeated, trying for the noncommittal tone he'd perfected over years of trying to deal with the equally high-handed and inexplicable behavior of Kai Winn.

"Admiral, forgive us, but we assumed this actually *was* an emergency." Julian Bashir broke in with such polite bafflement that Sisko guessed he must be emulating Garak's unctous demeanor. "If so, we could have reviewed your data records ten hours ago. All you had to do was send them to *Deep Space Nine* through subspace channels."

"Too dangerous, even using our most secure codes." The bleak certainty in Hayman's voice made Sisko blink in surprise. "And if you were listening, young man, you'd have noticed that I said this was the *first* thing I needed you to do. Now, would you please sit down, Captain?"

Sisko took the place she indicated at one of the conference table's inset data stations, then waited while she settled Bashir at the station on the opposite side. He noticed she made no attempt to seat Dax, although there were other empty stations available.

"This review procedure is not a standard one," Hayman said, without further preliminaries. "As a control on the validity of some data we've recently received, we're going to ask you to examine ship's logs and medical records without knowing their origin. We'd like your analysis of them. Computer, start data-review programs Sisko-One and Bashir-One."

Sisko's monitor flashed to life, not with pictures but with a thick ribbon of multilayered symbols and abbreviated words, slowly scrolling from left to right. He stared at it for a long, blank moment before a whisper of memory turned it familiar instead of alien. One of the things Starfleet Academy asked cadets to do was determine the last three days of a starship's voyage when its main computer memory had failed. The solution was to reconstruct computer records from each of the ship's individual system buffers—records that looked exactly like these.

"These are multiple logs of buffer output from individual ship systems, written in standard Starfleet machine code," he said. Dax made an interested noise and came to stand behind him. "It looks like someone downloaded the last commands given to life-support, shields, helm, and phaser-bank control. There's another system here, too, but I can't identify it."

"Photon-torpedo control?" Dax suggested, leaning over his shoulder to scrutinize it.

"I don't think so. It might be a sensor buffer." Sisko scanned the lines of code intently while they scrolled by. He could recognize more of the symbols now, although most of the abbreviations on the fifth line still baffled him. "There's no sign of navigations, either—the command buffers in those systems may have been destroyed by whatever took out the ship's main computer." Sisko grunted as four of the five logs recorded wild fluctuations and then degenerated into solid black lines. "And there goes everything else. Whatever hit this ship crippled it beyond repair."

Dax nodded. "It looks like some kind of EM pulse took out all of the ship's circuits—everything lost power except for life-support, and that had to switch to auxiliary circuits." She glanced up at the admiral. "Is that all the record we have, Admiral? Just those few minutes?"

"It's all the record we *trust,*" Hayman said enigmatically. "There are some visual bridge logs that I'll show you in a minute, but those could have been tampered with. We're fairly sure the buffer outputs weren't." She glanced up at Bashir, whose usual restless energy had focused down to a silent intensity of concentration on his own data screen. "The medical logs we found were much more extensive. You have time to review the buffer outputs again, if you'd like."

"Please," Sisko and Dax said in unison.

"Computer, repeat data program Sisko-One."

Machine code crawled across the screen again, and this time Sisko stopped trying to identify the individual symbols in it. He vaguely remembered one of his Academy professors saying that reconstructing a starship's movements from the individual buffer outputs of its systems was a lot like reading a symphony score. The trick was not to analyze each line individually, but to get a sense of how all of them were functioning in tandem.

"This ship was in a battle," he said at last. "But I think it was trying to escape, not fight. The phaser banks all show discharge immediately after power fluctuations are recorded for the shields."

"Defensive action," Dax agreed, and pointed at the screen. "And look at how much power they had to divert from life-support to keep the shields going. Whatever was after them was big."

"They're trying some evasive actions now—" Sisko broke off, seeing something he'd missed the first time in that mysterious fifth line of code. Something that froze his stomach. It was the same Romulan symbol that appeared on his command board every time the cloaking device was engaged on the *Defiant.*

"This was a cloaked Starfleet vessel!" He swung around to fix the admiral with a fierce look. "My understanding was that only the *Defiant* had been sanctioned to carry a Romulan cloaking device!"

Hayman met his stare without a ripple showing in her calm competence. "I can assure you that Starfleet isn't running any unauthorized cloaking devices. Watch the log again, Captain Sisko."

He swung back to his monitor. "Computer, rerun data program Sisko-One at one-quarter speed," he said. The five concurrent logs crawled across the screen in slow motion, and this time Sisko focused on the coordinated interactions between the helm and the phaser banks. If he had any hope of identifying the class and generation of this starship, it would be from the tactical maneuvers it could perform.

"Time the helm changes versus the phaser bursts," Dax suggested from behind him in an unusually quiet voice. Sisko wondered if she was beginning to harbor the same ominous suspicion he was.

"I know." For the past hundred years, the speed of helm shift versus the speed of phaser refocus had been the basic determining factor of battle tactics. Sisko's gaze flickered from top line to third, counting off milliseconds by the ticks along the edge of the data record. The phaser refocus rates he found were startlingly fast, but far more chilling was the almost instantaneous response of this starship's helm in its tactical runs. There was only one ship he knew of that had the kind of overpowered warp engines needed to bring it so dangerously close to the edge of survivable maneuvers. And there was only one commander who had used his spare time to perfect the art of skimming along the edge of that envelope, the way the logs told him this ship's commander had done.

This time when Sisko swung around to confront Judith Hayman, his concern had condensed into cold, sure knowledge. "Where did you find these records, Admiral?"

She shook her head. "Your analysis first, Captain. I need your unbiased opinion before I answer any questions or show you the visual logs. Otherwise, we'll never know for sure if this data can be trusted."

Sisko blew out a breath, trying to find words for conclusions he wasn't even sure he believed. "This ship—it wasn't just cloaked like the *Defiant*. It actually *was* the *Defiant.*" He heard Dax's indrawn breath. "And when it was destroyed in battle, the man commanding it was me."

"Captain Sisko would let me."

It occurred to Kira that if she had a strip of latinum for every time someone had said that to her in the last forty-eight hours, she could probably buy this station and every slavering Ferengi troll on board. Not that the prospect of owning a dozen wrinkled, bat-eared larcenists filled her with any particular glee. But at least Ferengi were predictable, and they didn't act all affronted every time you refused to jump at their comm calls or told them their problems were trivial. After all, they were Ferengi—any aspect of their lives not directly related to money was trivial, and they did everything in their power to keep things that way.

Humans, on the other hand, thought the galaxy revolved around their wants and worries, and tended to get their fragile little egos bruised when you implied that they might be wrong. With that in mind, Kira had spent the better part of her first day in command—a good two or three hours, at least—placating, compromising, making every sympathetic noise Dax had ever taught her, in the theory that a little stroking (no matter how insincere) was all the crew needed to carry them through the captain's absence. Somewhere around lunchtime, though, she'd elbowed that damned leather sphere off Sisko's desk for the fourth damned time, and the fifth trivial work-schedule dispute let himself into the office while she was under the desk patting about for it, and the sixth subspace call from Bajor—or Starfleet, or some other damned place—started chirping for immediate attention, and it became suddenly, vitally important that she conduct the EV inspection of weapons sail two herself. She fled Ops with the ball still lost in the wilds of Sisko's office furniture, hopeful that shuffling the whining crewman off to Personnel and playing ten minutes of yes-man with a Bajoran minister would buy her enough time to get safely suited up and out into vacuum. O'Brien, bless his soul, only stammered a little with surprise when she plucked the repair order from his hands on her way to the turbolift.

Next time, she'd just have to leave the station without the environmental suit. It would make everything so much easier.

"Well?" Quark hadn't quite progressed to petulance yet, but there was something about having a Ferengi voice whining right in your ear that made even an overlarge radiation hardsuit seem small and strangling. "I'm telling you, this is exactly the sort of thing Sisko would endorse with all his heart."

Kira couldn't help blowing a disgusted snort, although it blasted an irritating film of steam across the inside of her suit's faceplate. She locked the magnetic soles of her boots onto the skin of the sail while she waited for the hardsuit's atmosphere adjusters to clear out the excess humidity. "Quark, Captain Sisko won't even let you in Ops." Which was why he'd wasted no time weaseling onto a comm channel Kira couldn't escape, no doubt. "I don't know why he lets you stay on the station at all."

She could just make out his squat Ferengi silhouette scuttling back and forth in the observation port above his bar. "Because the captain has a fine sense of the market, for a hu-man. But not so fine a sense of how to extract profit from opportunity." Kira flexed her feet, breaking contact with the station and letting the momentum of that slight movement swing her around to the front of the sail's arc, out of Quark's line of sight. *I really am out here to do work,* she told herself as she passed a diagnostic scanner slowly down the length of one seam. The fact that she enjoyed a certain cruel satisfaction every time Quark grumbled with frustration and ran down the corridor to the next unobstructed window was really just a perk.

"I'm still picking up some residual leakage," she reported to O'Brien. The rad counter on the far right of her helmet display barely hovered at the bottom of its range, and she scowled around a renewed twist of annoyance. "Not enough to warrant lugging out this twice-damned hardsuit, but . . ."

"Sorry, Major—Starfleet regulations." His blunt Irish brogue managed to sound honestly sympathetic for all that Kira suspected he never much considered resenting Starfleet protocol. "Anytime you send personnel to inspect a first-stage radiation hazard, you've got to send them in ISHA-approved protective gear."

"And in my case, that means a hardsuit built to fit a guy like Sisko."

"Well, they are sort of one-size-fits-all."

Kira stopped herself just before she snorted again and fogged her faceplate. "One size fits all humans over two meters tall."

"Yes, ma'am," O'Brien admitted. "Something like that."

"Major, I really don't think you're giving my proposal the attention that courtesy requires."

Kira pulled herself hand-over-hand down the outside of the sail, dreaming wistfully of pushing off toward the wormhole and letting it whisk her far away from even the slightest whiff of Ferengi. "O'Brien, isn't there some way you can cut Quark out of this channel?"

"Not without cutting you off from the station, too, ma'am. Sorry."

She wondered whether she should tell him how much that concept appealed to her.

"It's just that Captain Sisko doesn't appreciate the *spiritual* importance of recreation the way—"

"No, Quark!"

The squeak of pained indignation in her ear couldn't have been more poignant if someone had gone fishing for the barkeep's nonexistent heart with a spoon. "Major, you have my word that everyone will stay to my back three Dabo rooms."

"That's what you promised the *last* time you organized a gambling tournament." She planted her feet again with a *clang* that she felt through her suit but couldn't hear, and pushed open the access door to the inner sail with as much violence as the microgravity would allow. "Instead, the Bajoran Trade Commission wrote up a four-page complaint about increased shoplifting on the Promenade, and Morn filed sexual-harassment charges against no less than six of your players."

The ragged puffing of another sprint along the Promenade balcony was followed by distinctive slap of Quark plastering himself to yet another window. "But *this* year—" Kira could just imagine the sweet-sour smell of his snaggle-toothed grin. "—I've hired an Elasian cohort to serve as exclusive door guards."

"No!" Kira watched her radiation gauge soar to an almost alarming level, and punched one fist against the interior lighting panel to brighten the room. "Now, which word of that didn't you understand?"

"Most likely the declarative negative. It's a recurrent problem with the Ferengi, I'm afraid." Even if Kira hadn't recognized the security officer's gruff sarcasm, the growl of naked animosity in Quark's muttering would have told her it was Odo who had walked in on the Ferengi's noxious attempts at charm. "Apparently the Ferengi don't have a word in their language for 'no.'"

Quark sniffed with what Kira suspected was supposed to be indignation, somehow managing to sound both obsequious and offended at the same time. "That's not true," the Ferengi countered. "We have several, depending on how much negotiation it will take to change your mind."

"Tell me you're taking the whole tournament to the Gamma Quadrant," Kira suggested.

"And never coming back," the constable added.

"—then I might consider giving you permission to use

the station as a jumping-off point. Until then . . ." The diagnostic scanner flashed brilliant white, warning that enough first-stage radiation soaked the weapons sail to light most small cities for a year. Kira barely took the time to fold up the scanner before stepping backward out the door. "Chief, did you see that reading?"

"I saw it." O'Brien sounded more frustrated than upset. Kira suspected he was wishing he were here now instead of her. "I could have sworn we checked all the power units in those phaser batteries on our last external inspection. One of them must have gone bad."

"Should that be throwing off so much first-stage radiation?"

"Not usually," he admitted. "But whatever's gone wrong in there, Major, it's not something you should be tracking down with a handheld scanner and a trouble light. Now that we know where the problem is, I can have my boys start working on it."

"Leaving you more time to consider my proposal," Quark said brightly.

"*No,* Quark."

She'd never heard a Ferengi hiss like that before. "Fine." Out on the surface of the habitat ring again, Kira saw Quark make a short, frustrated gesture with his arms in the distant window, then pointedly return his hands to his sides with the same finality a Bajoran would have used when dusting herself of someone else's dirt. "Fine! I took you to be a generous, understanding woman with a clear sense of your duties to the people on this station." He angled a petulant glare up at the slim figure towering behind him. "Obviously, I was wrong. So if you'll excuse me, I'll go back to salvaging the economy on my own." He lifted his chin with an indignant sniff, and stalked out of sight beyond the window's frame as though he hadn't been the one trespassing on her comm channel in the first place.

"I don't know how Sisko ever gets any work done around here," she complained—mostly to herself—as she pulled the access door closed behind her.

"By staying in his office, I suspect."

Kira glanced over toward the window as though she could have seen any real expression on Odo's wax-smooth features even if he weren't so far away. She didn't always know how to take the constable's remarks when he wasn't being overtly sarcastic. Did he state the blatantly obvious because he meant some kind of veiled criticism, or just because it was the truth? With Odo, sometimes an answer was just an answer—refreshing after the labyrinthine politics of the Federation and Bajor, but not always any easier to take.

"What can I do for you, Odo?" She turned to push off for the airlock, ready to shed this cumbersome, too-hot carapace and take a private meal in her quarters before falling into bed. "Please tell me Sisko called and said he'd be home for a late dinner."

"Unfortunately, no." And he sounded truly apologetic, as though Kira's lighter teasing were just as heartfelt as anything he ever said. "Although you wouldn't be the only one glad for his return." A data inset sprang to life at the bottom of her suit display, scrolling information past her chin as she walked. Kira glanced a frown toward the window, then chided herself for the uselessness of the gesture and looked away.

"So what's this?" she asked.

"Read it."

Security reports, dating back to seven days ago, all with Odo's blunt, clear signature in the corner. The first three entries looked like a hundred others that had come across Sisko's desk while Kira sat there—the late-night break-in of a store catering to tourists who wanted to backpack their way around Bajor, a discrepancy between goods received and the bill of lading for a shipment of computer components on their way to Andor, the theft of—

Kira paused, cocking her head inside the big helmet as she glanced down at the fourth item on Odo's list, then blinked back up through the other three. "Robberies." She looked ahead, at the station laid out before her, at the wormhole, at the stars. "All of these are robberies of some kind, and all within the last week. A crime syndicate, trying to set up shop on *Deep Space Nine?*" In so many ways, it was the ideal location: The wormhole made for a perfect escape route, and there were no extradition treaties with the Gamma Quadrant.

Odo grunted in his version of grim amusement. "There

really isn't room here for any more organized crime than what Quark already controls. Besides . . ." He must have touched something on his own padd to brightly highlight the item currently on Kira's display. ". . . there isn't much of a black market for household power matrices, much less for portable thermal storage containers." A few flashes of data brought up another report from farther down on the list. "Unfortunately, tactical plasma warheads still bring a healthy profit, no matter where you plan to sell them."

Kira didn't immediately recognize the style of paperwork in front of her, but what it said was clear enough. "Six liters of weapons-grade liquid plasma, missing from a shipment to the starship yards at Okana." A little thrill of almost-panic whispered through her. "That's on Bajor."

"Which is only three hours by shuttle from *Deep Space Nine.*" With only Odo's gravelly voice for company, Kira suddenly felt very vulnerable out here in the open. She made herself start walking again, heading straight for the airlock's neon fluorescent striping. "Anyone with this list of materials," the constable went on, "could spend a few hours in a Federation library and easily construct an explosive device powerful enough to destroy this entire station."

Not to mention vaporize a small starship, or depopulate any province on Bajor. Kira spat an angry curse, and keyed open the airlock on runabout pad F with awkward gloved fingers. "Any guess as to their intended target?" How could the Federation make this kind of information just *available* to any psychotic who asked? Didn't they realize that Bajor wasn't some population of doe-eyed pacifists, but, rather, a roil of scarred soldiers and ex-resistance operatives who had perfected filching the innards for bombs years before the Federation wandered onto the scene?

"That would depend on several factors," Odo said. "We don't even know who 'they' are yet."

"No . . ." Kira drummed one foot impatiently inside its ill-fitting boot, watching the atmosphere readings bloom inside the airlock even as she heard the hiss and rumble of air pressure gathering around her. "But I'll bet we can guess."

She could almost read Odo's thoughts in his grim silence. The constable knew as well as Kira that the paramilitary

cells who'd begun shaking their fists in the northern prov-
inces these last few months were little more than old
resistance fighters with a new bone to chew. "Oppression is
oppression!" was their cry—they claimed little difference
between the Cardassians' iron bootheels and the Federation's paternal "control by example" from their lofty space-
station pedestal. As far as Kira was concerned, all you had
to do was look at their respective medical facilities to
appreciate how unrelated their motives toward Bajor were.
Still, zealots had a habit of ignoring opinions not directly in
support of their cause of the week, and this latest batch
seemed just as unyielding as any other; they might not have
posted any official threats yet, but Kira knew these sorts of
people almost as well as she knew herself. It was really just a
matter of time.

"I thought that was supposed to be the difference between
democracy and dictatorship," she said aloud, stepping
sideways to squeeze through the airlock door as it rolled
aside. "You don't have to blow up things just to have your
voice heard."

Odo looked up from the other side of the bay, stroking
one hand thoughtfully across the nose of an as-yet-unnamed
runabout. "The humans say old habits die hard."

Which meant that humans and Bajorans had something
in common, although perhaps not the best attributes of
either.

A chirp from inside the hardsuit's helmet saved her from
having to contemplate the question further. "Ops to Major
Kira."

She popped the seals on the helmet anyway, dragging it
off her head and tucking it under one arm rather than get
trapped inside this suit for any longer than she had to be.
"Go ahead, Chief."

"We've just picked up a neutrino flux from the wormhole,
Major. It looks like someone's coming through."

Kira glanced a startled look at Odo. "Are there are any
ships due back from the Gamma Quadrant?"

Odo shook his head in silent answer even as the human's
voice replied, "No, sir. Nobody's due in or out for at least
another three days."

She curled one hand over the rim of the helmet to muffle

L. A. GRAF

the comm pickup there as she commented softly to Odo, "I suppose it's too much to ask that our bomb builders chose just this moment to relocate their materials."

He scowled down at her in fatherly disapproval for such a naive suggestion, taking her comment just as seriously as he seemed to take everything. Kira decided it wasn't worth trying to explain her admittedly weary sense of humor right now, and instead withdrew her hand from the helmet and set it on the floor so she could crack the chest on the suit and squirm herself free.

"Chief, I'm still down in Runabout Pad F getting out of this damned suit. Put the station's defense systems on standby, then transfer an outside view to the runabout's viewscreen." Stepping free of the bulky trousers, she motioned Odo to follow as she let herself into the small ship's hatch. "I want to see what's going on."

"Aye-aye, Major."

The inside of this runabout was as identical to every other such craft as a Starfleet shipyard could build it. Oh, the floor plates were too bright and unscuffed, and milky sheets of protective sheeting still draped the four seats and all the stations, but the number of steps from the hatch to the helm were exactly the same, the shadows that fell across her eyes as they walked through the cabin came in exactly the sequence she expected, and the clearance between panel and seat when she slipped into the pilot's chair was so familiar that she barely even noticed the crinkle of sheeting under her hands. She certainly didn't feel any need to pull her eyes away from the newly awakened viewscreen and what it had to show.

Light swirled against the cold backdrop, a spiral blossom of energy and quantum probability far too lovely to deserve its inelegant human name—wormhole. From the moment she'd first seen the gateway twist into being, Kira accepted that this was something more wonderful and significant than merely what the Federation's mathematics justified. That science could touch the tip of this iceberg didn't bother her—understanding the parts of a thing granted you no special insight into its nature, just as a meticulous description of all the biological systems making up a Bajoran gave you no true idea of the person living inside

16

that shell. Four years of watching spaceships come and go through the wormhole's flaming mouth had done nothing to dim her convictions: the phenomenon's very existence proved there was more to life than simply what met the eye.

This time, the wormhole's gift was little more than a twinkle of reflected light, tumbling, spinning, flashing in and out just at the portal's edge, too small to really be seen. When the petals of radiant energy finally folded back in on the singularity and retreated into invisibility, only the tiny glitter of movement remained, drifting lazily, darkly toward Bajor.

"It isn't powered." Odo leaned over the console to peer at the viewscreen, his colorless eyes intent on the tumbling mite. "It's either lost its engine, or it never had one."

Kira nodded with a thoughtful frown, and tapped at her comm badge to reconnect with O'Brien in Ops. "Any idea what that is, Chief?"

He was quiet for a moment, no doubt conferring with his equipment. Kira drummed her fingers on the sheeting covering the panel and willed herself not to hurry him, even when Odo speared her with an intensely irritated glare for the noise she made.

"Iron . . ." O'Brien said at last, his voice distracted and thoughtful. "Nickel . . . traces of duranium and methane ice . . ." He gave a little grunt of surprise that sounded ever so slightly disappointed. "My guess is a cometary nucleus. Maybe an asteroid fragment."

Nothing interesting, in other words. Kira sat back with a satisfied nod and pulled her hands away from the panel. Just as well. She didn't think she could stand much more "interest" around the station just now.

"Major?" O'Brien caught her while only half standing, mere moments before she would have thanked him for his time and gone back to her runabout inventory. "Major, the computer's listing that fragment's course as being right through Bajor's main ore-shipping lanes. We might want to take care of it before it passes out of phaser range."

With the wormhole's location, just about anything that came through under free momentum had to cross a Bajoran shipping lane eventually. "Anything in the fragment that'll react badly to our weapons?"

"No, sir. The minerals are pretty evenly distributed, through and through. It should vaporize nicely."

She straightened the covering on her chair with a flick of her hand, and suppressed a grin when Odo echoed her gesture on the draping he'd disturbed on the console. "Then go ahead, Chief. Minimum burst, though—I don't want—"

Movement shimmered across the still-active viewscreen, and she felt a momentary sting of anger at the thought that O'Brien had opened fire without waiting for her command. Then her brain registered that there'd been no streak of phaser light even as she ducked around the pilot's chair to relocate the newly arrived fragment. The single hard spark of light was gone, replaced by a glittering cloud that drifted away from itself like puff-flower seeds when shattered by a single quick breath. What once was one was now many, and dissipating rapidly.

Kira didn't even get a chance to question O'Brien before his voice volunteered, "So much for weapons practice. It broke up."

"Broke up?" Odo parroted. He frowned a question at Kira that she wasn't sure how to answer while O'Brien confirmed, "Broke up. We've got about ten dozen pieces floating out there right now, none of them bigger than three meters across." Easily small enough to be handled by the screens on any sublight shipping vessel Bajor put out.

The constable didn't look particularly enheartened as he watched the last of the cloud evaporate. "It's deep space on the other side of the wormhole," Kira explained, personally just as glad not to have one more thing to worry about. "The methane ice probably sublimated in the solar wind from Bajor's sun, and it didn't have enough left to hold it together." She reached between the seats to clap him on the shoulder. "It happens all the time."

Odo's face thinned the way it sometimes did when he let his attention get absorbed in something outside himself. "Then why is the wormhole doing that?"

She followed his gaze to where a faint, amber corona misted the void right where the mouth of the wormhole cast its brilliant whirlpool when it appeared. The rippling haze looked like gold dust, floated on a celestial pool.

Pushing aside a corner of the material cloaking the panel,

she woke up the science station and made a brief query back to the Ops computer and its adjacent sensor array. Even if the runabout's sensors were on-line, they couldn't have told her anything from inside the docking pad. What the Ops sensors told her was as elegantly unromantic as all of science's purported truths. "Minor fluctuations in the subspace membrane." She flashed Odo what was meant to be a reassuring smile as she shut down the panel again. "Probably didn't like the taste of that asteroid fragment. It'll settle down in an hour or two, you'll see."

Odo only grunted, his eyes darkened with suspicion even as he let Kira turn him away from the viewscreen and lead him out of the runabout. "Constable," she sighed, "we've got Sisko gone for who knows how many days while the Bajoran Resistance builds a bomb right under our noses, and you're worried about an asteroid fragment that destroyed itself when it entered the star system." She shook her head and switched off the bay's lights. "All of our problems should be so simple."

CHAPTER
2

THE ADVANTAGE OF having several lifetimes of experience to draw on, Jadzia Dax often thought, was that there wasn't much left in the universe that could surprise you. The disadvantage was that you no longer remembered how to cope with surprise. In particular, she'd forgotten the sensation of facing a reality so improbable that logic insisted it could not exist while all your senses told you it did.

Like finding out that the mechanical death throes you had just seen were those of your very own starship.

"Thank you, Captain Sisko," Admiral Hayman said. "That confirms what we suspected."

"But how can it?" Dax straightened to frown at the older woman. "Admiral, if these records are real and not computer constructs—then they must have somehow come from our future!"

"Or from an alternate reality," Sisko pointed out. He swung the chair of his data station around with the kind of controlled force he usually reserved for the command chair of the *Defiant*. "Just where in space were these transmissions picked up, Admiral?"

Hayman's mouth quirked, an expression Jadzia found unreadable but which Curzon's memories interpreted as rueful. "They weren't—at least not as transmissions. What you're seeing there, Captain, are—"

"—actual records."

It took Dax a moment to realize that those unexpected words had been spoken by Julian Bashir. The elegant human accent was unmistakably his, but the grim tone was not.

"What are you talking about, Doctor?" Sisko demanded.

"These are actual records, taken directly from the *Defiant*." From here, all Dax could see of him was the intent curve of his head and neck as he leaned over his data station. "Medical logs in my own style, made for my own personal use. There's no reason to transmit medical data in this form."

The unfamiliar numbness of surprise was fading at last, and Dax found it replaced by an equally strong curiosity. She skirted the table to join him. "What kind of medical data is it, Julian?"

He threw her a startled upward glance, almost as if he'd forgotten she was there, then scrambled out of his chair to face her. "Confidential patient records," he said, blocking her view of the screen. "I don't think you should see them."

The Dax symbiont might have accepted that explanation, but Jadzia knew the young human doctor too well. The troubled expression on his face wasn't put there by professional ethics. "Are they my records?" she asked, then patted his arm when he winced. "I expected you to find them, Julian. If this was our *Defiant*, then we were probably all on it when it was—I mean, when it *will be*—destroyed."

"What I don't understand," Sisko said with crisp impatience, "is how we can have actual records preserved from an event that hasn't happened yet."

Admiral Hayman snorted. "No one understands that, Captain Sisko—which is why Starfleet Command thought this might be an elaborate forgery." Her piercing gaze slid to Bashir. "Doctor, are you convinced that the man who wrote those medical logs was a *future* you? They're not pastiches put together from bits and pieces of your old records, in order to fool us?"

Bashir shook his head, vehemently. "What these medical logs say that I did—no past records of mine could have been altered enough to mimic that. They have to have been written by a future me." He gave Dax another distressed look. "Although it's a future I hope to hell never comes true."

"That's a wish the entire Federation is going to share, now that we know these records are genuine." Hayman thumped herself into the head chair at the conference table, and touched the control panel in front of it. One of the windows on the opposite wall obediently blanked into a viewscreen. "Let me show you why."

The screen flickered blue and then condensed into a familiar wide-screen scan of the *Defiant*'s bridge. It was the viewing angle Dax had gotten used to watching in postmission analyses, the one recorded by the official logging sensor at the back of the deck. In this frozen still picture, she could see the outline of Sisko's shoulders and head above the back of his chair, and the top of her own head beyond him, at the helm. The *Defiant*'s viewscreen showed darkness spattered with distant fires that looked a little too large and bright to be stars. The edges of the picture were frayed and spangled with blank blue patches, obscuring the figures at the weapons and engineering consoles. Dax thought she could just catch the flash of Kira's earring through the static.

"The record's even worse than it looks here," Hayman said bluntly. "What you're seeing is a computer reconstruction of the scattered bytes we managed to download from the sensor's memory buffer. All we've got is the five-minute run it recorded just before the bridge lost power. Any record it dumped to the main computer before that was lost."

Sisko nodded, acknowledging the warning buried in her dry words. "So we're going to see the *Defiant*'s final battle."

"That's right." Hayman tapped at her control panel again, and the conference room filled with the sound of Kira's tense voice.

"Three alien vessels coming up fast on vector oh-nine-seven. We can't outrun them." The fires on the viewscreen blossomed into the unmistakable red-orange explosions of warp cores breaching under attack. Dax tried to count them, but there were too many, scattered over too wide a sector of space to keep track of. Her stomach roiled in fierce and utter disbelief. How could so many starships be destroyed this quickly? Had all of Starfleet rallied to fight this hopeless future battle?

"They're also moving too fast to track with our quantum torpedoes." The sound of her own voice coming from the image startled her. It sounded impossibly calm to Dax under the circumstances. She saw her future self glance up at the carnage on the viewscreen, but from the back there was no way to tell what she thought of it. "Our course change didn't throw them off. They must be tracking our thermal output."

"Drop cloak." The toneless curtness of Sisko's recorded voice told Dax just how grim the situation must be. "Divert all power to shields and phasers."

The sensor image flickered blue and silent for a moment as a power surge ran through it, then returned to its normal tattered state. Now, however, there were three distinct patches of blue looming closer on the future *Defiant*'s viewscreen.

"What's that?" Bashir asked Hayman, pointing.

The admiral grunted and froze the image while she answered him. "That's the computer's way of saying it couldn't match a known image to the visual bytes it got there."

"The three alien spaceships," Dax guessed. "They're not Klingon or Romulan then."

"Or Cardassian or Jem'Hadar," Bashir added quietly.

"As far as we can tell, they don't match any known spacefaring ship design," Hayman said. "That's what worries us."

Sisko leaned both elbows on the table, frowning at the stilled image intently. "You think we're going be attacked by some unknown force from the Gamma Quadrant?"

"Or worse." The admiral cleared her throat, as if her dramatic words had embarrassed her. "You may have heard rumors about the alien invaders Captain Picard and the *Enterprise* drove off from Brundage Station. From the spectrum of the energy discharges you're going to see when the alien ships fire their phasers at you, the computer thinks there's more than a slight chance that this could be another invasion force."

Dax repressed a shiver at this casual discussion of their catastrophic future. "You think the *Defiant* is going to be destroyed in a future battle with the Furies?"

"We know they think this region of space once belonged to them," Hayman said crisply. "We know they want it back. And we know we didn't destroy their entire fleet in our last encounter, just the artificial wormhole they used to transport themselves to Furies Point. Given the *Defiant's* posting near the Bajoran wormhole—" She broke off, waving a hand irritably at the screen. "I'm getting ahead of myself. Watch the rest of the visual log first; then I'll answer your questions." Her mouth jerked downward at one corner. "If I can."

She touched the control panel again to resume the log playback. Almost immediately, the viewscreen flashed with a blast of unusually intense phaser fire.

"Damage to forward shield generators," reported O'Brien's tense voice. "Diverting power from rear shield generators to compensate."

"Return fire!" Sisko's computer-reconstructed figure blurred as he leapt from his captain's chair and went to join Dax at the helm. "Starting evasive maneuvers, program delta!"

More flashes screamed across the viewscreen, obscuring the random jerks and wiggles the stars made during warp-speed maneuvers. The phaser fire washed the *Defiant's* bridge in such fierce white light that the crew turned into darkly burned silhouettes. An uneasy feeling grew in Dax that she was watching ghosts rather than real people, and she began to understand Starfleet's reluctance to trust that this log was real.

"Evasive maneuvers aren't working!" Kira sounded both fierce and frustrated. "They're firing in all directions, not just at us."

"Their present course vector will take them past us in twelve seconds, point-blank range," Dax warned. "Eleven, ten, nine . . ."

"Forward shields failing!" shouted O'Brien. Behind his voice the ship echoed with the thunderous sound of vacuum breach. "We've lost sectors seventeen and twenty-one—"

"Six, five, four . . ."

"Spin the ship to get maximum coverage from rear shields," Sisko ordered curtly. *"Now!"*

"Two, one . . ."

Another hull breach thundered through the ship, this one louder and closer than before. The sensor image washed

blue and silent again with another power surge. Dax held
her breath, expecting the black fade of ship destruction to
follow it. To her amazement, however, the blue rippled and
condensed back into the familiar unbreached contours of
the bridge. Emergency lights glowed at each station, making
the crew look shadowy and even more unreal.

"Damage reports," Sisko ordered.

"Hull breaches in all sectors below fifteen," O'Brien said
grimly. "We've lost the port nacelle, too, Captain."

"Alien ships are veering off at vector five-sixteen point
nine." Kira sounded suspicious and surprised in equal
measures. Her silhouette turned at the weapons console,
earring glittering. "Sensors report they're still firing phasers
in all directions. And for some reason, their shields appear
to be failing." A distant red starburst lit the viewscreen,
followed by two more. "Captain, you're not going to believe
this, but it looks like they just blew up!"

Dax saw herself turn to look at Kira, and for the first time
caught a dim glimpse of her own features. As far as she could
tell, they looked identical to the ones she'd seen in the mirror
that morning. Whatever this future was, it wasn't far away.

"Maybe our phasers caused as much damage as theirs
did," she suggested hopefully. "Or more."

"I don't think so." O'Brien's voice was even grimmer
now. "I've been trying to put our rear shields back on-line,
but something's not right. Something's draining them from
the outside." His voice scaled upward in disbelief. "Our
main core power's being sucked out right through the shield
generators!"

"A new kind of weapon?" Sisko demanded. "Something
we can neutralize with our phasers?"

The chief engineer made a startled noise. "No, it's not an
energy beam at all. It looks more like—"

At that point, with a suddenness that made Dax's stomach clench, the entire viewscreen went dead. She felt her
shoulder and hand muscles tense in involuntary protest,
and heard Bashir stir uncomfortably beside her. Sisko
cursed beneath his breath.

"I know," Admiral Hayman said dryly. "The main circuits picked the worst possible time to give out. That's all
the information we have."

"No, it's not." Julian Bashir's voice sounded bleak rather than satisfied, and Dax suspected he would rather not have had the additional information to give them. "I haven't had a chance to read the majority of these medical logs, but I have found the ones that deal with the aftermath of the battle."

Hayman's startled look at him contained a great deal more respect than it had a few moments before, Dax noticed. "There were logs that talked about the battle? No one else noticed that."

"That's because no one else knows my personal abbreviations for the names of the crew," Bashir said simply. "I scanned the records for the ones I thought might have been aboard on this trip. Of the six regular crew, Odo wasn't mentioned anywhere. I'm guessing he stayed back on *Deep Space Nine*. My records for Kira and O'Brien indicate they were lost in some kind of shipboard battle, trying to ward off an invading force. Sisko seems to have been injured then and to have died afterward, but I'm not sure exactly when. And Dax—" He stopped to clear his throat, then resumed. "According to my records, Jadzia suffered so much radiation exposure in the final struggle that she only had a few hours to live. Rather than stay aboard, she took a lifepod and created a diversion for the aliens who were attacking us. That's how the ship finally got away."

"Got away?" Sisko demanded in disbelief. "You mean some of the crew survived the battle we just saw?"

Bashir grimaced. "How do you think those medical logs got written up? I not only survived the battle, Captain, I appear to have lived for a considerable time afterward. There are several years' worth of logs here, if not more."

"Several *years?*" It was Dax's turn to sound incredulous. "You stayed on board the *Defiant* for several years after this battle, Julian? And no one came to rescue you?"

"No."

"That can't be true!" The *Defiant*'s captain vaulted from his chair, as if his churning restlessness couldn't be contained in one place any longer. "Even a totally disabled starship can emit an automatic distress call," he growled. "If no one from Starfleet was alive to respond to it, some other Federation ship should have. *Was our entire civilization destroyed?*"

"No," Hayman said soberly. "The reason's much simpler than that, and much worse. Come with me, and I'll show you."

Cold mist ghosted out at them when the fusion-bay doors opened, making Dax shiver and stop on the threshold. Beside her, she could see Sisko eye the interior with a mixture of foreboding and awe. This immense dark space held a special place in human history, Dax knew. It was the first place where interstellar fusion engines had been fired, the necessary step that eventually led to this solar system's entry into the federation of spacefaring races. She peered through the interior fog of subliming carbon dioxide and water droplets, but aside from a distant tangle of gantry lights, all she could see was the mist.

"Sorry about the condensate," Admiral Hayman said briskly. "We never bothered to seal off the walls, since we usually keep this bay at zero P and T." She palmed open a locker beside the ring doors and handed them belt jets, then launched herself into the mist-filled bay with the graceful arc of a diver. Sisko rolled into the hold with less grace but equal efficiency, followed by the slender sliver of movement that was Bashir. Dax took a deep breath and vaulted after them, feeling the familiar interior lurch of the symbiont in its pouch as their bodies adjusted to the lack of gravitational acceleration.

"This way." The delayed echo of Hayman's voice told Dax that the old fusion bay was widening as they moved farther into the mist, although she could no longer see its ice-carved sides. She fired her belt jets to follow the sound of the admiral's graveled voice, feeling the exposed freckles on her face and neck prickle with cold in the zero-Centigrade air. Three silent shadows loomed in the fog ahead of her, backlit by the approaching gantry lights. She jetted into an athletic arc calculated to bring her up beside them.

"So, Admiral, what have you—"

Her voice broke off abruptly when she saw what filled the space in front of her. The heat of the work lights had driven back the mist, making a halo of clear space around the dark object that was their focus. At first, all she saw was a huge lump of cometary ice, black-crusted over glacial-blue gleaming. Then her eye caught a skeletal feathering of old metal buried in that ice, and followed it around an oddly familiar curve until it met another, more definite sweep of metal. Beyond that lay a stubby wing, gashed through with ice-filled fractures. She took in a deep, icy breath as the realization hit her.

"That's the *Defiant*!"

"Or what's left of her." Sisko's voice rang grim echoes off the distant walls of the hold. Now that she had recognized the ship's odd angle in the ice, Dax could see that he was right. The port nacelle was sheared off entirely, and a huge torpedo-impact crater had exploded into most of the starboard hull and decking. Phaser burns streaked the *Defiant*'s flanks, and odd, unfamiliar gashes had sliced her to vacuum in several places.

She glanced across at Hayman. "Where was this found, Admiral?"

"Right here in Earth's Oort cloud," the admiral said, without taking her eyes from the half-buried starship. "A mining expedition from the Pluto LaGrangian colonies, out prospecting for water-cored comets, found it two days ago after a trial phaser blast. They recognized the Starfleet markings and called us, but it was too fragile to free with phasers out there. We had to bring it in and let the cometary matrix melt around it."

"But if it was that fragile—" Dax frowned, her scientist's brain automatically calculating metal fatigue under deep-space conditions, while her emotions kept insisting that what she was seeing was impossible. "It must have been buried inside that comet for thousands of years!"

"Almost five millennia," Hayman agreed. "According to thermal spectroscopy of the ice around it, and radiometric dating of the—er—the organic contents of the ship."

"You mean, the bodies," Bashir said, breaking his stark silence at last.

"Yes." Hayman jetted toward the far side of the ice-sheathed ship, where a brighter arc of lights was trained on the *Defiant*'s main hatch. "There's a slight discrepancy between the individual radiocarbon ages of the two survivors, apparently as a result of—"

"—differential survival times." The doctor finished the sentence so decisively that Dax suspected he'd already known that from his medical logs. She glanced at him as they followed Hayman toward the ship, puzzled by the sudden urgency in his voice. "How much of a discrepancy in ages was there? More than a hundred years?"

"No, about half that." The admiral glanced over her shoulder, the quizzical look back in her eyes. "Humans don't generally live long enough to survive each other by more than a hundred years, Doctor."

Dax heard the quick intake of Bashir's breath that told her he was startled. "Both bodies you found were human?"

"Yes." Hayman paused in front of the open hatch, blocking it with one long arm when Sisko would have jetted past her. "I'd better warn you that, aside from microsampling for radiocarbon dates, we've left the remains just as they were found in the medical bay. One was in stasis, but the other—wasn't."

"Understood." Sisko pushed past her into the dim hatchway, the cold control of his voice telling Dax how much he hated seeing the wreckage of the first ship he'd ever commanded. She let Bashir enter next, sensing the doctor's fierce impatience from the way his fingers had whitened around his tricorder. When she would have jetted after him, Hayman touched her shoulder and made her pause.

"I know your new host is a scientist, Dax. Does that mean you've already guessed what happened here?"

Dax gave the older woman a curious look. "It seems fairly self-evident, Admiral. In some future timeline, the *Defiant* is going to be destroyed in a battle so enormous that it will get thrown back in time and halfway across the galaxy. That's why no one could come to rescue Julian."

Hayman nodded, her voice deepening a little. "I just want you to know before you go in—right now, Starfleet's highest priority is to avoid entering that timeline. At all costs." She gave Dax's shoulder a final squeeze, then released her. "Remember that."

"I will." Although she managed to keep her tone as level as always, somewhere inside Dax a tendril of doubt curled from symbiont to host. Curzon's stored memories told

Jadzia that when he knew her, this silver-haired admiral had been one of Starfleet's most pragmatic and imperturbable starship captains. Any future that could put that kind of intensity into Hayman's voice wasn't one Dax wanted to think about.

Now she was going to see it.

Inside the *Defiant*, stasis generators made a trail of red lights up the main turbolift shaft, and Dax suspected the half-visible glimmer of their fields was all that kept its crumbling metal walls intact. It looked as though this part of the ship had suffered one of the hull breaches O'Brien had reported, or some even bigger explosion. The turbolift car was a collapsed cage of oxidized steel resin and ceramic planks. Dax eased herself into the open shaft above it, careful not to touch anything as she jetted upward.

"Captain?" she called up into the echoing darkness.

"On the bridge." Sisko's voice echoed oddly off the muffling silence of the stasis fields. Dax boosted herself to the top of the turbolift shaft and then angled her jets to push through the shattered lift doors. Heat lamps had been set up here to melt away the ice still engulfing the *Defiant*'s navigations and science stations. The powerful buzz of their filaments and the constant drip and sizzle of melting water filled the bridge with noise. Sisko stood alone in the midst of it, his face set in stony lines. She guessed that Bashir had headed immediately for the starship's tiny medical bay.

"It's hard to believe it's really five thousand years old," Dax said, hearing the catch in her own voice. The familiar black panels and data stations of the bridge had suffered less damage than the rest of the ship. Except for the sparkle of condensation off their dead screens, they looked as if all they needed was an influx of power to take up their jobs again. She glanced toward the ice-sheathed science station and shivered. Only two days ago, she'd helped O'Brien install a new sensor array in that console. She could still see the red gleam of its readouts beneath the ice—brand-new sensors that were now far older than her own internal symbiont.

Dax shook off the unreality of it and went to join Sisko at the command chair. Seeing the new sensor array had given her an idea. "Can you tell if there are any unfamiliar modifications on the bridge?" she asked the captain, knowing he had probably memorized the contours of his ship in a way she hadn't. "If so, they may indicate how far in our future this *Defiant* was when it got thrown back in time."

Sisko swung in a slow arc, his jets hissing. "I don't see anything unfamiliar. This could be the exact ship we left back at *Deep Space Nine*. If the Furies are going to invade, I'd guess it's going to be soon."

Hayman grunted from the doorway. "That's exactly the kind of information we needed you to give us, Captain. Now all we need to know is where and when they'll come, so we can be prepared to meet them."

"And this—this ghost from the future." Sisko reached out a hand as if to touch the *Defiant*'s dead helm, then dropped it again when it only stirred up the warning luminescence of a stasis field. "You think this can somehow help us find out—"

The chirp of his comm badge interrupted him. "Bashir to Sisko."

The captain frowned and palmed his badge. "Sisko here. Have you identified the bodies, Doctor?"

"Yes, sir." There was a decidedly odd note in Bashir's voice, Dax thought. Of course, it couldn't be easy examining your own corpse, or those of your closest friends. "The one in the ship's morgue sustained severe trauma before it hit stasis, but it's still recognizable as yours. There wasn't much left of the other, but based on preliminary genetic analysis of some bone fragments, I'll hazard a guess that it used to be me." Dax heard the sound of a slightly unsteady breath. "There's something else down here, Captain. Something I think you and—and Jadzia ought to see."

She exchanged speculative looks with Sisko. For all his youth, there wasn't much that could shatter Julian Bashir's composure when it came to medical matters. "We're on our way," the captain told him. "Sisko out."

Diving back into the shattered darkness of the main turbolift, with the strong lights of the bridge now behind her, Dax could see what she'd missed on the way up—the pale, distant quiver of emergency lights from the *Defiant*'s tiny sickbay on the next deck down. She frowned and followed Sisko down the clammy service corridor toward it.

"Is the ship's original power still on down here?" she demanded incredulously.

From the darkness behind her, she could hear Hayman snort. "Thanks to the size of the warp core on this overpowered attack ship of yours, yes. With all the other systems shut down except for life-support, the power drain was reduced to a trickle. Our engineers think the lights and equipment in here could have run for another thousand years." She drifted to a gentle stop beside Dax and Sisko in the doorway of the tiny medical bay. "A tribute to Starfleet engineering. And to you too, apparently, Doctor Bashir."

The young physician looked up with a start from where he leaned over one of his two sickbay stasis units, as if he'd already forgotten that he'd summoned them here. The glow of thin green emergency lighting showed Dax the unaccustomed mixture of helplessness and self-reproach on his face.

"Right now, I'm not sure that's anything to be proud of," he said, sounding almost angry. His gesture indicated the stasis unit below him, which Dax now saw had been remodeled into an odd mass of pumps and power generators topped with a glass box. A fierce shiver of apprehension climbed up the freckles on her spine and made her head ache. "Why haven't you people done anything about this?"

Admiral Hayman's steady glance traveled from him to Dax, and then back again. "Because we were waiting for you."

That was all the confirmation Dax needed. She pushed past Sisko, and was startled to find herself dropped abruptly to the floor when the sickbay's artificial gravity caught her. Just a little under one Earth standard, she guessed from the feel of it—she felt oddly light and off-balance as she joined Bashir on the other side of that carefully remodeled medical station.

"Julian, is it . . . ?"

His clear brown eyes met hers across the misted top of the box. "I'm afraid so," he said softly, and moved his hand. Below where the warmth of his skin had penetrated the stasis-fogged glass, the mist had cleared a little. It was enough to show Dax what Bashir had already seen—the unmistakable gray-white mass of a naked Trill symbiont, immersed in brine that held a frozen glitter of bioelectric activity.

She had to take a deep breath before she located her voice, but this time her symbiont's long years of experience stood her in good stead. "Well," she said slowly, gazing down at the part of herself that was now immeasurably older. "Now I know why I'm here."

CHAPTER
3

YR1, DY6, 2340
Patient immobile + unresponsive. Limited contact + manipulation of subject due to fragile physical state and possible radiation damage, no invasive px/tx until vitals, Tokal-Benar's stabilize. Fluid isoboramine values <47%, biospectral scan=cortical activity < prev. observed norm, ion concentration still unstable. (see lab/chem results, atta) No waste products yet; adjusted nutrient mix +10% in hopes of improving uptake. Am beginning to fear I can't really keep it alive after all.

Staring down into the milky shadows of the suspension tank, Julian Bashir blinked away the image of those old medical records and trailed a hand across the invisible barrier separating the two realities. The stasis field pricked at his palm like a swarm of sleepy bees. "I guess I was wrong."

"Does that mean you don't think it's still alive?"

Bashir jerked his head up, embarrassment at being overheard smothering under a flush of guilt as soon as the meaning of Hayman's words sank in. He pulled his hand away from the forcefield, then ended up clenching it at his side when he could find nothing else to do with it. "No, I'm fairly certain it's still living." At least, that was what the readouts frozen beneath the stasis field's glow seemed to indicate. "It was alive when the field was activated five thousand years ago, at any rate. I can't tell anything else about its condition without examining it in real time." Although the thought of holding the orphaned symbiont in his hands made his throat hurt.

Across the table from him, Hayman folded her arms and frowned down at the shimmering box. The watery green of the emergency lights turned her eyes an emotionless bronze, and painted her hair with neon streaks where there should have been silver. "Assuming it's in fairly stable condition, what equipment would you need to transfer this symbiont into a Trill host?"

The question struck him like a blow to the stomach. "You can't be serious!" But he knew she was, knew it the very moment she asked. "Admiral, you can't just change Trill symbionts the way you would a pair of socks! There are enormous risks unless very specific compatibility requirements are met—"

"What risks?" Hayman freed one hand to wave at Dax, standing silently beside her. "It's the same symbiont she has inside her right now!"

It occurred to Bashir, not for the first time, that he didn't like this woman very much. He couldn't imagine what Curzon Dax had ever seen in her. "It's a genetically identical symbiont that is *five thousand years* out of balance with Jadzia! For all we know, the physiological similarities between the two Daxes could make it even harder for Jadzia to adjust to the psychological differences." Dax herself had withdrawn from the discussion almost from the beginning. She'd turned her attention instead toward the naked symbiont in its stasis-blurred coffin, and Bashir wondered which of her many personalities was responsible for the eerie blend of affection and grief he could read in her expression. He wished he could make Hayman understand the implications of toying with a creature that was truly legion. "These are *lives* we're talking about, Admiral, not inconveniences. Any one of the three could die if we attempt what you're suggesting."

Hayman glared at him with that chill superiority Bashir had learned to recognize as a line officer's way of saying that doctors only earned their MDs because they hadn't the stomach for regular military. "If we don't find out who carved up the *Defiant* and pitched her back into prehistory," she told him coldly, "millions of people could die."

He clenched his jaw, but said nothing. *That's the difference between us,* he thought with sudden clarity. As regular Starfleet, Hayman had the luxury of viewing sentient lives in terms of numbers and abstractions—saving one million mattered more than saving one, and whoever ended the war with the most survivors won. As a doctor, he had only the patient, and even a million patients came down to a single patient, handled over and over again. No amount of arithmetic comparison could make him disregard that duty. And thank God for that.

Hayman made a little noise of annoyance at his silence, and shifted her weight to a more threatening stance. "Do I have to make this an order, Dr. Bashir?"

He lifted his chin defiantly. "As the senior medical officer present, sir, Starfleet regulations allow me to countermand any order you give that I feel is not in the best interests of my patient." He flicked a stiff nod at the stasis chamber. "This is one of those orders."

Surprise and anger flashed scarlet across her cheeks. For one certain, anguished moment, Bashir saw himself slammed into a Starfleet brig for insubordination while Hayman did whatever she damn well pleased with the symbiont. It wasn't how he wanted things to go, but it also wasn't the first time that a clear vision of the consequences came several seconds behind his words. He opened his mouth to recant them—at least in part—just as the admiral turned to scowl at Sisko. "Captain, would you like to speak with your doctor?"

The captain lifted his eyebrows in deceptively mild inquiry. "Why?" He moved a few steps away from the second examining bed, the one that held the delicate tumble of bones that Bashir had scrupulously not dealt with after identifying whose they were. "He seems to be doing just fine to me."

Hayman blew an exasperated breath, and her frustration froze into a cloud of vapor on the air. Like dragon's breath. "Do I have to remind you people that you were brought here so Starfleet could help you avert your own deaths?"

"Not if it means treating Jadzia or either of the Daxes as a sacrifice," Bashir insisted.

Dax stirred at the foot of the examining table. "May I say something?"

Bashir kept his eyes locked on Hayman's, refusing the admiral even that small retreat. "Please do."

"Julian, I appreciate your concern for my welfare, and for everything you must have gone through to keep the symbiont alive all this time . . ." Dax reached out to spread her cool hand over his, and Bashir realized with a start that he'd slipped his hand onto the stasis field again. "But I don't think this is really your decision to make."

He felt his heart seize into a fist. "Jadzia—"

"Dax." She joggled his wrist gently as though trying to gain his attention. "I'm *Dax*, Julian. *This*—" She patted his hand on the top of the tank, and he looked where she wanted despite himself. *"This* is Dax, too." The pale gray blur was nestled in its bed of liquid like a just-formed infant in its mother's womb. "I trust you enough to be certain you didn't do this as some sort of academic exercise. Preserving the symbiont must have been something you knew for a fact that I wanted—that *Dax* wanted. And the only reason I can think of that I'd be willing to live in a tank like this for so many hundreds of years is the chance to warn us about what happened—to prevent it in any way I can."

Sisko came across the room, stopping behind Dax as though wanting to take her by the shoulders even though he didn't reach out. "We don't know that for certain, old man. And if we lose both you *and* the symbionts testing out a theory . . ." His voice trailed off, and Bashir found he wasn't reassured to know that Sisko was just afraid of failure as he was.

"We're only talking about a temporary exchange," Dax persisted. "Julian has obviously managed to re-create a symbiont breeding pool well enough to sustain my current symbiont for the hour or two we'll need."

But being correct about the time frame didn't mean she was correct about the procedure. "There's still the psychological aspect," Bashir said softly. "We don't know what the isolation has done to the symbiont's mental stability." His hand stiffened unwillingly on the top of the tank. "Or what that might do to yours."

Dax caught up his gaze with hers, the barest hint of a shared secret coloring her smile as she took his arms to hold him square in front of her, like a mother reassuring her child. "I know for a fact that even six months of exposure to mental instability can't destroy a Trill with seven lifetimes of good foundation. Six hours with some other aspect of myself isn't going to unhinge me." She let her smile widen, and it did nothing to calm the churning in his stomach. "You'll see."

"If you're not willing to perform the procedure, Doctor, I'm sure there are other physicians aboard this starbase who will."

Anger flared in him as though Hayman had thrown gasoline across a spark. Dax's hands tightened on his elbows, startling him into silence as she whirled to snap, "Judith, don't! I won't have him blackmailed into doing this."

The admiral's eyes widened, more surprised than irritated by the outburst, but she crossed her arms without commenting. A more insecure gesture than before, Bashir noticed. He was secretly glad. He didn't like being the only one unsure of himself at a time like this.

"What if there were some other way?" he asked Dax. She opened her mouth to answer, and he pushed on quickly, "Symbionts can communicate with one another without sharing a host, can't they? When they're in the breeding pools back on Trill—when you're in the breeding pools with them?"

The thought had apparently never occurred to her. One elegant eyebrow lifted, and Dax's focus shifted to somewhere invisible while she considered. "It doesn't transfer all the symbiont's knowledge the way a joining does," she acknowledged after a moment, "but, yes, direct communication is possible."

A little pulse of hope pushed at his heart. "And in a true joining, Jadzia wouldn't retain any of the symbiont's memories, anyway, once the symbiont was removed."

Dax nodded thoughtfully. "That's true."

"So what harm is there in trying this first?"

"Trying what first?" Hayman's confidence must not have been too badly damaged, because the impatient edge to her voice returned easily enough. "What are you two talking about?"

Bashir looked over Dax's shoulder at the admiral, schooling the dislike from his voice in an effort to sound more professional. "When they aren't inside a host, Trill symbionts use electrochemical signals to communicate with one another through the liquid they live in. Even a hosted symbiont can make contact with the others, if its host is first submerged in the fluid pool." He glanced aside at the tank while his thoughts raced a dozen steps ahead. "If we can replicate the nutrient mixture that's been supporting the symbiont, and fill a large enough receptacle, I think the Daxes should be able to . . ." He hesitated slightly, then fell back on the easiest word. ". . . talk to each other without having to remove Jadzia's current symbiont."

Hayman chewed the inside of her lip. "We could question this unhosted symbiont that way? It could talk to us through Dax?"

"Through Jadzia," Bashir corrected automatically, then felt heat flash into his cheeks at Hayman's reproving scowl. "Yes, we could."

"Julian's right." Dax saved him from the rest of the admiral's disapproval. "I think this will work."

"And if it doesn't work?" Hayman fixed Bashir with a suspicious glare, as if expecting him to lie to her. "What are our chances of losing the symbiont?"

"I don't know," he admitted. He wished the truth weren't so unhelpful. "I don't know how fragile it is, how much radiation damage it may have sustained back then. It may not live beyond removal of the stasis field, and I don't know what effect physically moving it from one tank to another might have." He looked into Dax's eyes so that she could see he was being absolutely honest, as a doctor and as her friend. "I do know it will be less traumatic than trying to accomplish a joining under these conditions."

Dax nodded her understanding with a little smile, then squeezed his arms once before releasing him to fold her own hands behind her back. "I think this will be our best option."

L. A. GRAF

"All right, then." Hayman flashed Bashir an appreciative grin, all his sins just that quickly forgiven now that she had what she wanted. Bashir wondered if that was supposed to make him feel as guilty as it did. "Let's give this a try. Lieutenant—" She gathered both Dax and Sisko to her side with a wave of one hand. "—you and the captain can tell me how much fluid and what size tank we'll need, then help me get it all down here. Doctor, wake up the symbiont." She leaned across the tank to clap him manfully on the shoulder, and Bashir found he didn't like the contact. "Looks like it's time to finish what you started."

"Oh, this is so exciting! My brother has snoopers installed all over his bar, but this is the first time I've ever had a chance to see *legal* surveillance equipment!"

Ferengi. In the last few days, Kira had come to realize that the Prophets had obviously chosen to punish her for all past sins by stranding her on board a space station stuffed to bursting with obsequious Ferengi. It was the only explanation that sat right with her sense of justice, because she just couldn't bear the thought that she'd ended up here by random chance, with no hope of ever changing or avoiding this destiny.

Still, as she stared down into Rom's flat face with its vapid, snaggletoothed grin, all she could think was that she'd never in all her life done anything bad enough to deserve this.

"Move along, Rom," O'Brien suggested from where he lay twisted onto one hip inside the open panel. "The major and I have got work to do."

She was impressed by the chief's casual brush-off, as though they weren't doing anything more unusual than patching a leaky data conduit. She'd almost have thought he'd spent his years in the Resistance, too. Although maybe Starfleet wasn't all that different. It would have been a nearly perfect dodge if Rom possessed any ability to pick up on tone of voice or other such social cues.

"That's an EM snooper, isn't it?" He clutched his little tool kit excitedly against his stomach, squatting to cock his head into O'Brien's workspace. "Who are you monitoring?

Is it on this deck?" Eager grinning gave way to a stunted, breathless laugh. "I guess it would have to be—you'll never home in on a power source from more than a few hundred meters away with that thing."

O'Brien endangered his status as de facto Resistance by angling a questioning look up at Kira. She shrugged behind Rom's back, then spun away from the chief's pursed lips to pace an irritable circle.

She could probably just chase Rom away with threats of physical violence, but that wouldn't do much to preserve their cover as a routine maintenance team. He'd probably go sniveling back to Quark about how Kira was so rude she wouldn't even let him talk to O'Brien about spy devices, and that would land a genuinely intelligent Ferengi on Kira's tail—the last thing she needed. How could something that was supposed to be so simple and discreet swell so rapidly into a quasar-sized pain in the butt?

It had been Kira's idea. She could be honest about that, because she still thought it was a pretty good one. Accepting the assumption that there were militia members on the station trying to construct a plasma device, they sure as hell couldn't be using the station replicators to make their parts. If nothing else, the standard station replicators had governors preventing the manufacture of certain items—like detonators and targeting devices—which meant the militia must have brought their own replicator with them, one that had already had its governing circuits chopped out. Her first thought had been to search for an off-grid power source with the station's sensors. O'Brien, however, had pointed out quite patiently that a scan of that magnitude would probably register on even the cheapest black-market protection box. The militia would have to wonder why Starfleet was scanning its own station. A discussion on what *wouldn't* register had finally led to the palm-sized device O'Brien was struggling so valiantly to install—a hypersensitive sensor shunt that would tingle at the first sign of a nonsystem power flux, letting Kira monitor any off-grid replicator activity from the privacy of Sisko's office. It had seemed like such a perfectly elegant solution by which to locate their would-be terrorists.

At least, right up until Rom came along.

"So can I guess what level EM field you're scanning for?" The Ferengi snorted with an almost endearing humility, admitting, "I may not have good lobes for business, but I've always been good at guessing games."

"Rom . . ." Kira reached down to haul him to his full dwarfish height. "Has it occurred to you that surveillance implies a certain amount of discretion?"

He seemed shocked that she felt the need to remind him. "I won't tell anyone!"

"If we stand here having this discussion much longer, there won't be many people on the station who don't already know!" His shoulders felt thin and without padding, as though stingy Ferengi couldn't tolerate surplus even in regards to the muscles of their own bodies. Kira resisted gripping him too tightly for fear she'd dent his narrow bones. "This is classified Starfleet business, Rom. I could have Odo lock you up until this is all over if I decide you're too much of a security risk. Do you understand?"

Mouth shut, one crooked tooth peeking out past petulant lips, Rom nodded mutely.

"Good. Now go back to work, and don't breathe a *word* of this to Quark unless you want to spend the rest of your fertile years in a jail cell."

"But—"

Kira clapped her hand over his mouth; the skin felt leathery and cool. "Not. A. Word."

The grumble of unhappiness he breathed against her hand almost made her feel sorry for depriving him of what had to be one of his few honest pleasures. It couldn't be easy living under Quark's shadow. Fidgeting as though no longer certain what he was supposed to do with his time, Rom hugged his tool kit even tighter and stepped over O'Brien to scurry back toward the Promenade.

Then he paused, shuffled in nervous indecision, and turned around to scuttle past them again on his way back into the habitat ring.

Kira turned to watch him disappear around the bend. "Rom!"

His lumpy, bat-eared head popped back into view.

"The bar's that way," she said with a jerk of her thumb.

He grinned, nodded, looked abruptly serious again as he pointed back around the corner behind him. "But the job I'm supposed to be doing is that way."

Kira frowned. "That way is the guest quarters."

"I know." He danced forward a few steps, caught up in his own enthusiasm. "I've been doing repair work for guests on the side so that I can send extra money to Nog. He likes to go out with his hu-man friends when he isn't in engineering classes." A look of startled realization cringed across his wrinkled face, and he pleaded suddenly, "But don't tell my brother! If he knew I was using my job at the bar to meet customers, he'd insist on taking half my profit!"

O'Brien pushed himself out of the panel he'd been patiently bugging. "I'm not sure you ought to be doing that."

"It's completely ethical," Rom objected. Then he bobbed uncertainly from foot to foot, grumbling. "Basically. Sort of. Don't hu-mans have a Rule of Acquisition that says 'What your brother doesn't know, he can't keep'?"

"I mean fixing the equipment." O'Brien stooped to lift the access cover back into place, tossing Kira a smooth, expressionless nod as he spoke to Rom. "You're not licensed to do repairs on Starfleet machinery, and I'm not keen on having to follow behind whatever it is you do."

Rom brightened and waved the chief's concerns aside. "Oh, I don't touch the Starfleet equipment. Just the things people bring with them. Data-conversion cubicles, holo-plates, portable replicators, gum massagers—"

"Replicators?" The word snapped at Kira's attention like an electric shock. "Somebody on the station brought their own replicator?"

Rom nodded dramatically. "And I don't know *what* they've been making with it, but I've been up here to fix it four times!"

Catching hold of his elbow, Kira shook him impatiently before he could lapse into vivid descriptions of his work. "Can you show us where it is?"

To her surprise, Rom squinted with as much cunning as she'd ever seen him attempt to display, and asked, "Will you show me how your sensing equipment works if I do?"

There was some of Quark's bloodline in there after all.

"Yes," Kira growled, "I'll show you the equipment. Now, where's this portable replicator?"

With the resilience of a springball, he bounced back to cheerfulness and waved for them to follow. "They're very good customers," he explained in a confidential whisper, as though this might help excuse whatever it was they turned out to be doing. "So please try not to look too shocked when you see how they keep their quarters. I never want to offend them, since they pay in cash and all, but I don't understand how Bajorans could live in a place like that. It looks like a bomb went off in there!"

Kira had been thinking a lot about bombs of late, and one look at the cluttered, disarranged stateroom only brought her fears more sharply into focus. Although not for the reasons Rom would credit her for, she was sure.

It was the clothes, more than anything else. The room's inhabitants had shoved everything about—a table over here, the bed lifted up against the wall, the chairs impatiently stacked out of the way in one corner—but nothing was broken, nothing blasted apart into splinters too tiny to see. It was the random, wandering piles of clothes that looked as though they'd just dropped off the people wherever they happened to stand that burned through Kira's conscious thoughts and dragged her back through the decades to when she'd camped with her resistance cell on the edge of Veska Province.

She'd been very young then, not even twenty. Her cell's leader, Shakaar, had volunteered them to help clean up what was left of a farm community after another group of so-called freedom fighters accidentally detonated a fusion bomb in the valley nearby. There hadn't been much left worth salvaging—buildings and trees and fences all lay pushed flat to the ground, as though toppled over by a violent wind; even the blackened ground still felt hot through the soles of her borrowed radiation suit. When they came across bodies, they were blistered and mummy-dry, but it was their nakedness that gnawed at Kira with its insensibility.

"What did they do?" she remembered demanding with

youthful indignation. "Blow up the place, then come through and loot them for their clothes?"

The look of surprised sympathy on Shakaar's face had made her feel immediately foolish and ignorant for having asked. "Nobody looted anything," he said sorrowfully. "The ones who were building this bomb didn't even leave bodies." His eyes lingered painfully on the spread-eagled body of what might have once been a woman, her head burned all bald and shiny. "It was the force of the blast that blew their clothes off. Seams on clothing aren't as strong as skin and bone."

But then where had all the clothing *gone*?

It was an image that had haunted Kira for months after the horrible event, filling her with an aversion to radiation suits that she knew was stupid, but which she'd never been able to completely overcome. The hiss of the air pumps and the inside staleness of breathing her own sweat always took her back to that woman on the street and the maddening question of what had happened to her clothes.

The hardsuit walk this morning had been bad enough. Following it up with Odo's revelation that someone on board the station might be planning to build a plasma bomb had reawakened those old memories with a clarity that nearly made her sick. She almost dreaded going back to her quarters tonight; she had a feeling she wouldn't get much sleeping done.

The clack of O'Brien's fingers on the keyboard of a data terminal drew her back into the moment, and she was shamefully glad for the distraction. Off to one side, Rom wandered nervously around the carnage as though it really were radioactive, picking up things in no discernible order, sorting the pieces into illogical piles in a pointless Ferengi attempt to be helpful. Kira left him to his scavenging to stand beside O'Brien at the terminal. "What have you got?"

"Nothing," he grumped in brusque frustration. He tapped the side of the terminal, where a tangle of technical patchwork marred the casing before bleeding over into the wall. "They used a security bypass to override the lockouts and access the main computer. I thought maybe I could backtrack their work and figure out what they'd been looking at, but they wiped the volatile buffer when they were finished."

A ridiculously haughty snort made Kira turn, and Rom took her shift of attention as some sort of invitation to stump through the piles of litter and join them. "You Bajorans!" he muttered with a shake of his head. "You never listen! I *told* them they'd have to disconnect the bypass, *then* wipe the volatile buffer." He squinted critically at the bypass, clucking with disapproval. "Otherwise, the backwash from the buffer imprints the last few megs of its memory onto the bypass circuit."

Kira fisted her hands behind her back to keep from dragging Rom away by one giant ear as O'Brien leaned around to start disconnecting the bypass. "Anything else about this group you want to tell us?" she asked.

"Uh . . ." Rom's face went slack with thought. "They're irritable about people being in their room when they're not here?"

That sort of went without saying.

"Major . . . ?"

Pushing Rom behind her, Kira moved should-to-shoulder with O'Brien in the hopes she might be able to block at least part of the Ferengi's view with her own body. The chief had patched the bypass through his engineering tricorder, and the little screen now flickered and rolled with the reflection of whatever had last passed through the data terminal. The grim set of the human's jaw told her he wasn't happy with what he'd seen. Taking it from him, Kira turned the little device to face her, and watched a moving schematic of the station tumble by in fading blue and white.

The view stopped, backed up, and froze on a close-up of the station's underbelly. A hand-scrawled circle looped into being around the station's lowermost reactor bays, and the words "Dro—Good location if we want a chain explosion" appeared beside the circle as though penciled in by a ghost.

"Oh, my god . . . !" She lifted her head to meet O'Brien's stark, unhappy eyes. "They're not building it for export," she whispered. "They're planning on using the bomb right here."

CHAPTER
4

REVIVING THE SYMBIONT took longer than replicating the nutrient bath. Bashir crawled under and around every inch of the modified examining bed, tracing circuits, studying connections, wishing he could reach the workings still locked inside the stasis field. He wanted to be sure of what the symbiont's tank was designed to do, wanted to have some vague idea what would happen when he touched *this* switch, irised *that* valve—wanted, more than anything, to reconstruct whatever he was thinking back when this seemed like a good idea five thousand years ago.

They'd hauled in two banks of brilliant floodlights, and suspended them from opposite walls near the ceiling so that they burned every trace of shadows away. The ambient temperature in the medical bay responded by creeping up a handful of degrees. Hands and fingers still felt thin and cold, but words no longer smoked when people talked. It somehow made the room feel even smaller and more fragile than before.

While Sisko guided a grav sled of spun siding into one corner of the tiny bay, Bashir slipped his arm behind the bed's main diagnostic panel and verified that it wasn't included in the stasis field—but it had been deactivated by the simple expedient of a laser scalpel through its primary data conduit. His future/past self must have deemed the power drain not worth leaving the symbiont a

47

panel display it couldn't even read. His current self was forced to agree.

As the first vial of the symbiont's support medium was passed through a tricorder to determine its suitability, he finally realized that what he'd taken as a fluid-drainage shunt was actually part of the coolant system for the tank. The CV pump soldered to the bottom of the table must be how he'd kept the N_2 up to pressure, although he couldn't figure out how it had been tied into the power grid. What could he possibly have planned to use as a replacement if one of those fragile tubes had ruptured?

When Dax finally arrived in an embarrassingly brief hospital gown to confer with Hayman and Sisko, Bashir had just noticed that the symbiont's transparent tank had been built from a single large sheet of hull-grade aluminum. The fourteen-digit part code that had been stamped across its middle was now divided into snippets of three and four, reflecting and re-reflecting each other from all six sides of the container. The last two numbers stared back at Bashir from the bottom of the tank, turned upside down and backward under ninety liters of cloudy fluid. He obviously hadn't thought about the positioning when he fitted that piece into place. He wished he had. Staring at those switched-around numbers every day for more than half a century must have driven him crazy.

"Julian?"

Turning his back on the tank was a little harder than he expected. He clenched the engineering probe he'd been using a bit more tightly in his fist, and tried on a smile for Dax's behalf. Judging from the softening of her already gentle expression, the attempt failed miserably.

"I'm ready whenever you are," she said, patting his arm in reassurance.

He hadn't even heard them fill the pool. "Let's get started, then."

Replacing the probe on the engineering cart, Bashir did his best to push his emotions as far away from him as he could. Now was a time for accuracy, not sentiment; he had a better chance of making Hayman do what he said if she thought he was speaking from the head, not the heart. Still, he'd never been very good at concealing his feelings. This was a hell of a time to have to start.

"I'd prefer to bring the patient out of stasis slowly," he said, moving toward the head of the table so that Sisko and Hayman could join them. Dax stayed close to his shoulder. He was grateful for her nearness. "Judging from my medical logs, the symbiont's condition prior to suspension wasn't good, and I'm afraid of losing it to revival shock."

Hayman scowled down at the waiting tank, drumming her fingers against her leg. "How slowly are we talking?" As though impatience didn't show clearly enough in her stance.

Bashir sighed and shook his head. "I said I'd *like* to bring it out slowly. But I apparently salvaged this stasis field from one of the morgue drawers, and it's strictly binary, either on or off." He meant to look up at Hayman, but found himself facing Dax's cool gray eyes instead. "I just want you to understand that this isn't a simple matter of switching off the field and scooping the symbiont out of the medium. We'll have to proceed very carefully."

Hayman made a face, as though planning to say something cutting, then tossed a sharp glance at Dax—and another at Bashir—before nodding with a half-muffled sigh. "I understand."

Dax answered Bashir's worried look with a smile. "Just do the best you can."

That much had never been in doubt.

The main switch for the stasis field was a small ceramic toggle underneath the lip of the table. When Bashir first examined the tank, he'd found an on-off capacitor patched into a data padd and epoxied to the inside of the tank. For one horrible moment he thought he'd been stupid enough to lock the only controls inside the field with the symbiont. It wasn't until he found the ceramic switch a few minutes later that he realized what he'd left inside for the symbiont: an escape hatch, a way to remove itself from the agonizing centuries of aloneness that must have crawled by between then and now. A kind of temporal euthanasia. As he fingered the switch, poised to catapult the past into the present, he only hoped the creature inside would forgive him both roles he'd played in its long interment.

"Well . . . here goes nothing."

49

A spark and flash of disruptive energy swept the stasis field away, and the sweet, sharp smell of five-thousand-year-old symbiont billowed out like a sigh.

Bashir had his tricorder open before the field's lingering static charge had faded. Readings leaped into life as though startled, then settled, and sank to an easy throb as they identified the symbiont's biochemistry. A slight climb in cortical activity and a sudden dump of neurotransmitter into the fluid, but otherwise remarkably stable. He breathed a silent prayer of thanks. Inside the tank, a bracelet of ripples patterned the water's surface as the symbiont shuddered, and a weak lightning bolt of energy spattered the side closest to Bashir. He pressed his palm against the tank in unconscious reply.

A thin chill ached against his palm. Bashir blinked his attention downward, suddenly aware of what he'd done. "Dax, how warm is the medium in the pool?"

Retrieving one of the engineering tricorders from the cart behind her, Dax crossed the room to scan the larger fluid bath. Bashir noticed for the first time that it steamed gently, a pale wisp of vapor skating about on its surface. "Thirty-four degrees," she reported.

Steam, he realized. That's what had misled him. A pebblework of condensation studded the underside of the stasis tank's lid, making him assume the interior was warm as well as humid. But his hand on the side registered coolness despite the chilly temperatures in the bay, and his tricorder confirmed that they'd heated the larger pool a good ten degrees warmer than they should have. "We have to bring the fluid temperature down to twenty-one degrees." Then, as another reading leveled out at a different value than he'd detected through the stasis field, "And increase the salinity by another eleven percent." He shook his head in a spasm of self-anger. "God, what was I thinking when I put this together? Why didn't I leave myself notes?"

Correctly assuming that those last two comments didn't require a response, Sisko excused himself with a nod. "I'll get the salination equipment."

Still trailing her hand in the water, Dax looked up at Bashir with a frown. "Julian, the breeding pools on Trill are warmer than this."

Bashir nodded distractedly, keying another request into his tricorder. "But the tank isn't. I don't want to shock the symbiont's system by raising its body temperature too rapidly." Satisfied that the pumps could handle a brief loss of humidity, he felt along the seam between lid and sides for an opening.

"I have to get in this pool, too," Dax grumbled. But she stood to help Sisko lower the salinating infuser into the fluid without questioning the doctor's decision.

Hayman, on the other hand, snorted as Bashir fitted a finger under the edge of the lid and pried it upward. "That tub has almost two thousand cubic liters of liquid in it," she pointed out. "Do you really expect me to wait another twenty-four hours while it cools ten degrees?"

Bashir bit back the first angry words that came to mind and handed Hayman the lid as he eased it out of its fittings. "How you do it is not really my concern," he said stiffly. "I'm telling you that *not* doing it could endanger my patient, and end your precious interrogation before it starts." He snatched a pair of surgical gloves from the kit beside him, pointedly not shying from her distrustful glare. "This is not negotiable, Admiral. If you want me to be your medical officer, you have to do as I say."

Whatever emotion flashed through her pale eyes never really made it to her face, and Dax's hand on her shoulder halted any words before they formed. "Come on, Judith." The Trill cast Bashir a half-amused, half-reproving glance. "I'm sure there must be superconducting coil around here somewhere. We'll work something out."

Hayman startled the doctor with a quick, cryptic smile, then let Dax lead her away toward the exit. Bashir watched them until they disappeared into the unpowered areas of the ship, telling himself he wasn't jealous.

"Antagonizing a Starfleet admiral isn't what most people would consider a wise career move, Doctor."

Bashir shot a quick look toward his captain, surprised to find him already returned to the end of the table. Sisko smiled in response to Bashir's self-conscious blush. "Eleven percent." He gestured back toward the nutrient pool behind him. "Just like the doctor ordered."

Bashir nodded, just as grateful for an excuse to turn his

attention back to business. "I'm not trying to antagonize her," he admitted uncomfortably as he snapped on the skin-hugging gloves. "I just . . ." *Don't like her attitude? Wish she showed more care about a nonhuman species? Didn't sound so willing to sacrifice both Jadzia and Dax to her imaginary time frame?* He set about tugging the gloves up over his sleeves with a great deal more attention than was really necessary. "She's obviously very used to getting what she wants."

"She's a rear admiral," Sisko said dryly. "There aren't many people in Starfleet who can say no to her."

He didn't add "except you," but Bashir heard the words anyway. He felt his face tighten in renewed embarrassment, and bent his head over the symbiont's tank to hide it.

Dax and Hayman returned only a few minutes later with a heat diffusion coil from the *Defiant*'s engine room, and Sisko went to help them wrestle it into place. Balancing his tricorder carefully on the corner of the tank, Bashir busied himself with a hands-on exam of the symbiont while the others unfolded the paper-thin heat deflectors. The fluid in the tank was eerily cold. Not so much so that he lost the feeling in his fingers, but enough to make him sympathize with Jadzia's unhappiness about being immersed in it. He slipped one hand under the symbiont without actually touching it at first, just letting himself adjust to the feel of the medium, letting the symbiont adjust to the presence of his hands. It stirred blindly at the surface of the liquid.

"It's all right . . ." Bashir whispered, wanting to comfort it but not sure what to do. "You know me, Dax, don't you?" He thought again of the bony clutter that was the extent of his organic legacy in this timeline, and smiled wryly. "We spent a lot of time together, you and I."

A snap of chemical lightning lashed out and bit at his hand.

Bashir jerked out of the tank with a startled gasp, sloshing water across the front of his uniform and splashing a milky puddle onto the floor. The symbiont sparked a few more times as it bobbed in the newly turbulent fluid, and Bashir called "It's all right—I'm fine!" before the others could do more than whirl in alarm at the commotion.

"What happened?" Dax's voice had dropped into the

deeper, more serious tone that Bashir always assumed she'd inherited from some previous host.

"Nothing," he assured her, fighting down his embarrassment with a self-deprecating smile. He lifted his hand to show her the small hole burned through his glove by the symbiont's thinking. "It—*you* are just a little more active than I expected, that's all."

Dax smiled back at him, her eyes crinkling with unexpected mischief. "Never underestimate the staying power of a Trill."

"This is a good sign?" Hayman pressed. "Right?"

Bashir peeled off the ruined glove and tossed it back into his kit. "Yes, Admiral Hayman, this is a good sign."

Armed with a fresh glove, he let the others go back to their cooling, and eased his hand back into the fluid. This time the symbiont's electrochemical tendril brushed against his wrist so lightly he couldn't even feel it through the latex.

"That's all right. . . ." It nuzzled into his palm as he came up under it, smaller than he remembered, more wrinkled. "It's my fault—I overreacted. I'm sorry if I startled you." Some odd, detached part of his brain made a mental note to log more clinical hours with Trill symbionts—on his next leave, perhaps, if the Symbiosis Commission on Trill could be convinced. He was the only Starfleet medical doctor within parsecs of *Deep Space Nine,* after all, and he owed it to the station's personnel to be as knowledgeable as possible about all their medical needs. That Jadzia Dax was the only Trill on DS9 didn't absolve him of that duty to her. Besides, he'd have to know a good deal more about unhosted symbionts than he currently did if he was going to take care of Dax for seventy years after—

No. He shook his thoughts back to the present with a scowl. Best not to dwell on that. The whole point of being here was to avoid that timeline, even if their very presence at the starbase said that so far they hadn't. His next leave, then. For no other reason than Jadzia and the present, he would visit the Trill homeworld on his very next leave.

"Twenty-one degrees, Doctor." Hayman's voice jumped suddenly louder, but this time Bashir was careful not to make any sudden moves for fear of upsetting the creature in his hands. "We're ready."

He took a deep breath that still somehow felt not quite deep enough, and lifted the symbiont from the water.

It broke surface with a dainty splash, but didn't spark or struggle. Bashir wasn't sure it could, really. From both his reading and his conversations with Jadzia, he knew that symbionts slipped into a kind of torpor once they bonded with a host, never moving again after their initial nestling for position among the internal organs. He wasn't sure how motile they became after long periods of separation.

—*must get to the Trill homeworld*—

But, if anything, the symbiont relaxed into his grip as though welcoming the touch. It hung more flaccid than he remembered from the one other time he'd handled it—over five thousand years in its own past—and its skin felt as though the slightest intemperate squeeze would sink fingers right into its vitals. He'd handled brain tissue that felt less fragile. Bashir crossed the tiny medical bay with his eyes on the patient every inch of the way, afraid to do more than cup his hands beneath it, afraid to jar it with the force of his footsteps, afraid the frigid air would sere its delicate tissues beyond any hope of repairing. He only knew he'd reached the pool because Sisko stretched out an arm to stop him before he could bump into the side.

"Please bring me my tricorder." His voice felt dry; he couldn't talk above a whisper. As Sisko obediently retrieved the device, Bashir eased down to one knee to lower the symbiont over the side.

The fluid felt startlingly tepid after the chilly air.

He supported its weight at first, absurdly worried that it would sink to the bottom and drown. But, of course, symbionts didn't breathe, that job being more suited to their hosts or an oxygenated liquid. Still, as Dax stepped carefully into the pool, he glanced up at her and said, "You might have to hold it near the surface. I'm not sure how well it can swim just now."

She nodded seriously, then ruined the image a moment later with a theatrical wince as she slid, chest-deep, into the bath. "Julian, I'm going to cut off your hot-water rations for a *week* for this!"

He smiled despite himself. "I guess I'll just have to shower at your place."

She flicked a handful of water at him, but he was already wet, so he didn't mind.

Dax reached out to accept the symbiont as gently as a mother would receive her newborn child. It stirred spastically at her touch, more a shiver than a movement. Bashir opened his mouth to tell Jadzia to stay still for a moment— just until the ancient Dax had adjusted to her presence— but she was already frozen, her eyes locked on the small gray creature. After a long, silent minute, Bashir gently withdrew his hands from between Jadzia's and the symbiont, and let her cradle its whole eiderdown weight. A smile as odd and fleeting as the symbiont's thoughts ghosted across her face. Bashir wondered what she was thinking as she slowly repositioned her hands, and whether or not the damaged symbiont was thinking it, too.

A crooked platter of lightning flashed across the surface of the water. It dissipated long before it reached the sides, and Bashir realized that it was feeling out its boundaries. It knew it was somewhere different from its stasis tank, but hadn't yet figured out where, or with whom. Bashir sank back on his heels and took the tricorder Sisko silently held in front of his face, quietly unfolding it just as a pale, exploratory tendril brushed against Jadzia's forearm. She twitched with a little gasp.

Bashir glanced up briefly from the first scroll of readings. "Are you all right?"

A snap of energy, strong enough to crackle the water, leapt from symbiont to host. Jadzia stiffened as coils of light flashed up her torso, flickered across her face. Bashir had to quell an urge to drag her out of the pool. Instead, he tightened his grip on his tricorder, and focused grimly on its readings as Jadzia's hands dropped slowly beneath the surface, slipping the symbiont out of sight.

Then, eyes closed and chin bowed almost to her chest, she started to cry.

"What?" Hayman took two urgent steps forward to lean on the side of the tub. "What's the matter? What's happening?"

"Nothing." At least, he hoped it was nothing. Bashir watched the values for both Jadzia and the ancient symbiont as they intersected, overshot each other, then settled fitfully into a parallel rhythm. "I think they're communicating," he said, more to Sisko than Hayman. "I . . ." The symbiont's readings veered upward for a moment, only to slowly rebound and rejoin the others. "What we're seeing is most likely Dax—*old* Dax—and not specifically Jadzia." He turned an apprehensive look up at his captain. "You should be able to talk with it. But be careful."

Sisko's easy nod said the warning was unnecessary, but it had been more for Hayman's sake, anyway.

"Jadzia?" The captain's voice was gentler than Bashir had ever thought it could be. Sisko knelt at the head of the tub as though talking with a child. "Jadzia, can you hear me?"

When her sobbing continued unabated, Bashir suggested, "Talk to Dax," and Sisko nodded again.

"Dax . . ." This time he touched her shoulder lightly. "Old man, it's Benjamin."

The eyes she opened on them seemed darker than before, glossy and opaque. Not Jadzia's eyes, but the time-cracked glass of a much older Dax, one who hadn't seen the world in far too long. When Jadzia turned her head to look around the ruined medical bay, her neck moved in uneven jerks, like a misaligned gear. Those dark doll's eyes never focused on anything. Not really.

". . . same so same and cold stay alive out the back out the first stay alive oh point nine not even that much when surviving all alive stay alive please stay alive not much longer . . ."

"She's rambling." Hayman squatted into Bashir's field of vision on the other side of the pool. "What's she saying?"

Bashir assumed she wanted something more coherent than a direct translation of the Trill's mumbled words. "Give her some time to orient herself . . . itself. . . ." The symbiont's cortical activity jittered like a fibrillating cardiogram at the sound of his voice, and the surface of the medium heaved in response to Jadzia's sudden spastic movement.

"Julian . . . ?"

Her whisper reached straight through him, chilling him to the base of his spine. "I'm here." It was all he could think of to say.

A little ghost glimmer of lightning moved beneath the surface of the fluid, and Jadzia leaned so far forward in the bath that she submerged herself nearly to the chin. ". . . It *is* . . . you . . ." Lifting one unsteady hand from the milky brine, she stopped just short of stroking his face. ". . . so beautiful . . . so *young* . . . Julian, you did it . . . !"

The new flood of tears was too much for him. "We should stop this—"

Sisko clamped a hand firmly on the doctor's shoulder, and bore down hard when Bashir tried to push himself to his feet. "As you were, Doctor."

"But, Captain—" He knew what Sisko would say: Both Dax and Jadzia knew what they were getting into, and neither one would thank Bashir if they failed to avert the temporal disaster because he got cold feet. Clenching his jaw against a new confusion of guilt and anxiety, he shrugged off Sisko's hand and fixed his attention on the tricorder in his hands. "Neurotransmitter levels are up twenty-three percent, and both Jadzia and the medium are exhibiting dangerous isoboromine imbalances."

He didn't have to detail for Sisko what those readings could mean. "We'll pull them out before rejection sets in," the captain assured him with an easy confidence Bashir couldn't share. "Don't worry."

Too late for that.

"Dax . . ." Hayman tugged at the Trill's shoulder from behind. Jadzia responded like a blind man who's heard a distant noise—by lifting her chin attentively into the air, but not moving any other part of her body in response to the admiral's summons. "Dax, it's Judith. You've got to tell us what happened to the *Defiant.* Who attacked you? Where did it happen?"

When did it happen? Bashir thought, but didn't ask. This unorthodox communion was under enough stress already. Cortical activity inside the cloudy pool crept up a stair-step of readings until it froze at a single manic value; the Dax buried inside Jadzia answered its twin only faintly, and the woman caught between them began to shiver. This time when she reached for Bashir across the fluid, he took her hand and held it tightly.

"Tell them," he whispered. *Tell them and get out of there, before we lose you all!*

"Don't go through the wormhole." She spoke the words slowly, with the same careful precision a child might use when reciting something in a language she didn't really understand. Bashir wondered how much of its incarceration the symbiont had spent memorizing this message in order to keep the words even this coherent and clear. "If we don't go through the wormhole, we won't go back in time. If we don't go through, the battle will happen without us. We won't go back in time, and they'll all stay where they were, where they are, back in time."

Hayman scowled. *"They* who?"

Dax didn't seem to hear her. "You have to stop it before it starts. This time can be different. This time I'll be there. Make sure you capture one."

Bashir felt Sisko and Hayman stir uneasily above him, both of them taking breath to ask for details, press for specifics. But he knew it was pointless—this was little more than a recording, and the playback had started. Jadzia's eyes danced across Bashir's face with frantic attentiveness. He recognized with a chill that Dax was telling this to *him*—and only him—after more than five thousand years of painful waiting. For the first time, he wondered precisely who this message was from.

"Capture one. Capture one and talk to it. All you have to do is ask!" She clutched Bashir's hand between both of hers as though desperate to make him understand. "Capture one take it alive *talk to it . . . !"*

"Take what alive?" Hayman grumbled impatiently. "One of the Furies?" Sisko shushed her with a hiss.

". . . capture one talk to it talk to what it's eaten talk to it ask it . . ."

"Jadzia, ask what?" Bashir didn't mean to get drawn into her fugue—didn't want to encourage this to go on any longer than absolutely necessary—but he couldn't turn away from the broken anguish in her plea. "I don't understand!"

". . . the first time they're too many but this time I'll be there and if I just stay alive we can just stay alive it won't be too late because there's no time—" Squeezing her eyes shut against a future-past that only her orphaned symbiont could see, Jadzia bowed her head over the tangle of their fingers, and light flashed scattershot across the surface of the pool. "—too early to leave her to keep it to wait I don't want to I can't help it I never liked the cold—!"

Bashir felt the seizure of her hands around his, and knew what had happened even before his tricorder shrilled its alarm. "Get her out of the pool!"

A single fierce convulsion jerked her upright, almost toppling her back into the fluid as Sisko lunged forward and Bashir clawed at the front of her gown to try and keep her head above water. The captain crashed into the brine, fountaining a great surge of fluid over the sides to splash against the deck. But he had her, one arm across her chest, the other cinched around her middle, heaving himself and Jadzia back over the side and away from the tank while Hayman rushed to intercept them with a too-small towel to serve as a blanket. Bashir registered only that Jadzia was in trusted hands, safe for the moment, then gulped a deep breath and plunged both arms shoulder-deep into the churning bath.

Milky brine splashed against his chest and face, stinging his eyes and making his lips taste like tears. He twisted his head to one side and tried to blink his vision clear, then gave up when some angry instinct reminded him that he couldn't see under the opaque brine anyway. In a strange sense, the sudden darkness helped. The frigid medical bay receded, Sisko's grim, calm voice and Jadzia's ragged gasping both dropping away to some point outside the range of his attention. There was only the pressure of the pool's lip beneath his rib cage, the salty wetness of the fluid soaking the sides and front of his uniform, and the thick, yeasty stench of the turbulent bath. He slid his hands about the bottom of the tank, acutely conscious of how easily he could crush the fragile occupant. Then one wrist bumped something soft and yielding—too much the same temperature as the medium in which it hid to feel entirely real to cold-clumsy human hands—and Bashir rotated awkwardly to cup the slippery mass in both palms, lifting it rapidly to the surface.

The murky liquid shattered under chaotic slashes of

lightning—a symbiont's screams. Bashir felt the electro-magnetic seizure through the membrane of his gloves, a prickling itch that made his fingers twitch involuntarily against the symbiont's paper-thin sides. *Don't!* he thought desperately. *I don't want to drop you!* Immediately on the tail of that fear he heard the gentle splash of his footsteps in the puddle ringing the pool, and deliberately focused his attention on walking quickly but carefully across the bay to the empty stasis tank.

It seemed ludicrously still and small after the turmoil at the larger pool. Bashir wondered fleetingly if the symbiont noticed or cared about the size of its confinement, but thrust the thought away as he hunched over to resubmerge it in the five-thousand-year-old liquid. Visible tendrils lashed out to all sides. When he released the symbiont and whisked his hands away, it sank without a struggle, slowly, weakly. The ceramic switch on the bottom of the tank clicked loudly when Bashir slapped it with his hand, and a rainbow meniscus swept across the tank and its occupant. They froze into a silent bubble, the fluid pausing with the waves of Bashir's withdrawal splashing at the lip of the tank, the symbiont haloed by its own outcries like a lightning rod in the center of a storm.

With an almost physical jolt, Bashir's awareness leapt back to the rest of the room. He spun, reaching behind him for the tricorder he remembered leaving on the engineering cart, then flashed on the image of Sisko holding it out to him while he knelt beside the now empty pool. It was easier to find than the symbiont—it lay on the bottom right where he'd dropped it, waiting patiently for him to rush over and scoop it out on his way past. It woke to his touch with a chirp, and was already compiling a report on Jadzia's life signs when he skidded to his knees beside her.

"Ten cc's of diazradol."

A quick clatter of movement, and Sisko pressed the hypospray into Bashir's outstretched hand. Jadzia's skin felt cold and clammy as he felt out the large vein on the side of her throat, but he remembered with a flush of almost-anger that it was his own hands which were wet and chilled, so nothing they told him could be trusted. He delivered half the neurostimulant without pause, then flipped back the towel covering her torso to hike up the hem of her gown and inject the remainder directly into the symbiont's carry pouch. Almost immediately, she took a great breath, stirring groggily, and the tricorder's screen flashed through a series of reports, each glimpse more encouraging than the last. Bashir draped the towel to cover as much of his patient as possible, then sank back on his heels with an unsteady sigh. "We need real blankets, and a warmer place for her to rest until she wakes up." It wasn't until he tried to peel his hands out of his gloves that he realized he was shaking too badly to grab hold. "I'll need a gurney."

Sisko climbed to his feet without needing to be asked, and Hayman reached across Dax to catch at Bashir's wrist when the doctor leaned to retrieve another hypo from the open medikit. "Is Dax going to be okay?"

He'd learned in his first year of medical school never to say "I told you so" to a superior. But, as a result, he'd perfected the precise set of jaw and eyes to say just as much without speaking. "Her vitals have stabilized, although it's too soon to tell what effect this might have on the host-symbiont relationship. I'll know more in the morning."

An expression that was almost amusement wisped across the admiral's face, and her gray eyes flicked toward some point beyond Bashir's shoulder before she released his wrist and sat upright. "Actually, I was asking about *Dax*. The symbiont." She jerked her chin toward the stasis tank again. "Is it going to live?"

He swallowed a surge of anger, and dug once more at the cuff of his gloves. "I don't know." This time, a glove came off with a whiplike snap, and he threw it to one side before starting just as furiously on the other. "We certainly can't risk any more such experiments and expect it to survive."

She grunted unhappily, then settled into a long moment of silence. "Not right now, at least," she finally sighed. He didn't look up at her, afraid he'd see the cold indifference on her face and forget that she outranked him. "You'll let me know when you've got it stabilized and ready to thaw out again?"

"Of course, Admiral." It was easy enough to promise. By the time it became an issue, he hoped to be too far away for Hayman's orders to matter.

CHAPTER
5

LIKE ANY STARFLEET officer in a frontier quadrant, Benjamin Sisko had heard many of his comrades talk about staring death in the face. For all he knew, he might even have used the phrase himself once or twice. He'd just never expected to really do it.

There was no question that the man in the stasis drawer was him—or would be him, Sisko corrected himself grimly, if they found no way to avert this timeline. Despite the explosion that had shattered his left side and leg to stripped bone and ribboned flesh, the coffee-dark face wore the same thinly carved mustache and beard Sisko had seen in his mirror this morning. He craned his head, peering at the slate-gray collar beneath the stasis shimmer. It might have been his imagination, but he thought one of the four captain's pips shone just a little brighter than the rest. Without meaning to, he lifted a hand to his own collar.

"I've been meaning to order all new ones," he murmured.

"Sir?"

Sisko glanced over at Bashir, who'd been standing so quietly on the other side of the drawer that he'd almost forgotten he was there. To his critical eye, the young doctor looked more tired than a night's lost sleep should account for. When neither he nor Dax had shown up for breakfast with the admiral this morning, Sisko had assumed both were still sleeping after the stress of the night before. His early-morning arrival in the *Defiant*'s medical bay, however, had found the doctor still immersed in his old medical logs. Whatever he'd read there, it didn't seem to have made him any happier than he'd been the night before.

"It's nothing, Doctor." Sisko glanced back at his preserved corpse. "Have you determined an exact cause of death?"

Bashir ran his fingers through already ruffled hair, looking a little harried. "Sorry, Captain. I didn't spend much time examining you when I first came down, and after that—"

"Understood," Sisko said quietly. "But I'd like you to take a few moments now and see what you can find out. We need to know as much as we can about what happened—or will happen—to us, if we're going to prevent it."

"True." Bashir went to fetch his tricorder from the data station he'd been sitting at. He came back frowning. "In order to get a complete scan, Captain, I'm going to have to release the stasis field for a few minutes. Is that going to bother you?"

Sisko shook his head. "Not after having survived a Borg attack, Doctor. Go ahead."

Bashir reached out to toggle the stasis control on the front of the drawer. The shimmer withdrew back into its generating unit, releasing the metallic smell of blood and an even stronger smell of scorched circuits and ozone.

"It was a torpedo hit," Sisko said, before Bashir had even finished his tricorder scan. That particular combination of odors was inescapably linked to his memories of the torpedo blasts that had crippled the *Saratoga*, killing Jennifer and half the crew.

The younger man frowned at his readout. "A torpedo *explosion*," he corrected after a moment. "According to this, the remnant radiation has the frequency you'd expect from one of the *Defiant*'s quantum torpedoes."

"So something triggered a torpedo explosion on board, and I got caught in it." Sisko forced himself to look more closely at the ruin of his left side. "No vacuum damage? This wasn't a hull breach?"

"Apparently not." Bashir frowned and tapped an inquiry into his tricorder, then scanned it across the body again. Whatever it told him made a muscle jerk in his thin face.

"Although there is evidence of partial bone oxidation and secondary trauma to the major blood vessels."

"What does that mean?"

"That you lived at least a short while after the explosion," Bashir said stiffly. "And that I didn't get you into stasis soon enough to save you." He startled Sisko by slamming the morgue stasis field back on with a great deal more force than it required. "I'm starting to wonder just why the hell I did *any* of the things I'm apparently going to do."

Sisko gazed down at his still body with slitted eyes. "If I had to guess, Doctor, I'd say that by the time this happened, we already knew, or guessed, that we'd been thrown too far back in time to be rescued. And that I needed to stay conscious long enough to get the ship to safety."

"But why?" Bashir demanded hotly. "So I could spend the next seventy years making sure Dax stayed alive long enough to go completely around the bend? It would have been better if we'd put you in stasis and lost the ship!"

"No, Julian. Then we'd have had no warning at all that this was going to happen."

Sisko swung around at the sound of that calm voice to see Jadzia Dax levering herself into the sickbay's gravity field. She looked a little pale beneath her spatter of freckles, but her stride was steady when she came to join them.

"Morning, old man," Sisko said, moving aside so she could join him beside the drawer. "How do you feel?"

"Not good enough to be up," Bashir answered before the Trill could. He had angled the tricorder toward her and was watching it with creased brows. "Jadzia, your isoboromine levels are still fluctuating too much. You should be off your feet."

Dax gave him an exasperated glance. "I can't feel any worse than you look," she retorted. "What have you been doing?"

Bashir grimaced in frustration. "Trying to track down any notes I might have made in my medical logs about what happened to us. I can't believe I wrote diary entries for seventy years and never mentioned when or how we got pitched back to prehistoric Earth." He scrubbed a hand through his dark hair again, making it even more disarranged than it already was. "Of course, I also can't believe I never bothered to make an index or catalog of my notes in all that time."

"Knowing you, Julian, you did both of those things, and then put the data chip somewhere for safekeeping," Dax said. "Of course, by the time you got around to doing that—"

"—who knows where I thought the safest place was," he agreed, grimacing again. "In any case, I've found only a few hints so far of what happened to us. It may take me a few weeks to plow through the rest of those records."

"The problem is, we may not have weeks," Sisko said grimly. He gestured at the version of himself that lay inside the stasis drawer. "Dax, how much older do I look to you there?"

She frowned down into the shimmering field. "Not much, Benjamin," she said after a moment. "In fact, I'm not sure you look older at all."

"That's what I thought. That means whatever is going to happen to us could occur anytime between tomorrow and half a year from now." Sisko rubbed a thumb across his captain's pips again, thoughtfully. "Dr. Bashir, is there any way you can narrow down that time estimate?"

"By comparing your current physiology with that of your future self?" Despite the tired lines around his eyes, the doctor hadn't lost any of his keen intelligence. "The trouble is, that will only work if you didn't make any trips through the wormhole between now and then."

"Why is that?"

"Molecular clock reset." Bashir looked up from his tricorder, a trace of his usual mischievous humor returning to his brown eyes. "Don't you remember the paper I submitted to the *Journal of Quantum Medicine* last month, about the submolecular effects of wormhole passage?"

"Uh—vaguely."

Dax gave him a reproving look. "I remember it, Julian. Didn't you conclude that particle-flux effects inside the wormhole introduce small errors into our molecular clocks?"

"Giving rise to apparent time anomalies between our biological and chronological ages," Bashir finished for her. He scanned his tricorder slowly over Sisko, then tapped in an analytical routine. His eyebrows went up abruptly. "According to the random molecular drift of your mitochondrial DNA, Captain, your future self is exactly the same age you are, within the limits of uncertainty imposed by the wormhole."

"And what are those limits, Doctor?"

"Plus or minus about a week, assuming you made at least one trip through the wormhole. Add on two or three days for each additional trip."

"Not good enough," Sisko said bluntly. "If we're going to avoid ending up here, I'll need a better estimate than that."

Bashir shrugged and slid the stasis drawer shut with a definitive clang. "You're not going to get that from medical analysis, I'm afraid."

"But we might get it from the ship's warp core," Dax said. "By looking at the isotopic decay records of the *Defiant*'s dilithium crystals and comparing them with Chief O'Brien's maintenance records back at *Deep Space Nine.*"

Sisko lifted an eyebrow at her. "You think Admiral Hayman will let us talk to him?"

The Trill's gray eyes warmed with amusement. "Oh, I think Curzon can talk her into it."

"You want to know *what?*"

Sisko scowled at his chief engineer. Despite parsecs of distance and the slight buzz of the high-security communications link to *Deep Space Nine,* he could still practically hear the gears clicking over in O'Brien's highly logical brain. It had taken Dax almost an hour to convince Admiral Hayman that the information O'Brien could give them was worth the risk of making this call. The last thing he needed was for his too-brilliant station chief to decipher what must be happening here at Starbase 1, right in front of Kira Nerys.

"Don't worry about why we need the information, Chief," he suggested, stiffening his voice just enough to make it clear that was an order, and not idle conversation. "Just tell us what the isotopic ratios are in the dilithium crystals from the *Defiant*'s warp core right now."

O'Brien's eyebrows rose dubiously, but he made no other protest. "Very well, sir," he said in a carefully neutral voice.

"I don't routinely keep that kind of data in my records, but if you give me a few minutes, I'll run a scan and get it for you."

Sisko's mouth twisted slightly, seeing the impatient way Kira hovered over the engineer's shoulder. "I'm sure my second-in-command can keep me occupied until you get back. Get to work, Chief."

O'Brien nodded and disappeared from the viewscreen. To Sisko's relief, Kira made no comment on the oddly trivial request he'd just made through Starfleet's highest-priority channel. Instead, she leaned both hands on the console in front of her and scowled—not at him, Sisko realized after a startled moment, but at the admiral standing silently at his shoulder.

"Does Starfleet have any idea when we can expect you back at *Deep Space Nine*, Captain?" she demanded.

Sisko exchanged glances with the admiral. "We're still not sure about that, Major. I suspect it will be within the next day or two. Why?"

"Because we have a situation shaping up here that I don't like the looks of," Kira reported. "I think a branch of the Bajoran paramilitary forces is using *Deep Space Nine* to build tactical nuclear weapons. There's a chance—a good chance—that they're planning to blow up the station itself."

Sisko frowned. After a day spent trying to figure out how to reroute the course of time itself, it felt almost nostalgic to be dealing with such a typical Bajoran crisis. He'd done this so many times, he didn't even have to think about his response. "Do you have any idea who's behind it?"

That got him only a fluid Bajoran shrug and a frustrated look. "Not yet. Chief O'Brien and I tracked down an unauthorized replicator they were using in the habitat ring and I have Odo staking it out, but so far no one's sprung the trap."

"Then you don't need me there yet, do you?"

Kira scowled again, this time at him. "Captain, have you considered what Kai Winn's going to do if—when!—she finds out about this? She'll accuse us of giving support to the Bajoran Resistance."

"As I recall, Major," Sisko said quietly, "one of my senior officers has already admitted to doing that."

Kira's face tightened in embarrassment, but she didn't back down. "Which is exactly why we can't give Winn another excuse to sever Bajor's ties with the Federation."

"Agreed," he said. "I suggest you contact Bajor's security forces immediately and enlist their assistance in tracking down this paramilitary cell."

Kira gave him a look of wide-eyed incredulity. "With all the sympathizers the paramilitary has in the regular forces? That would be as good as telling the local cell we're on to them!"

"Precisely, Major." Sisko smiled at her baffled look. "With any luck, that will flush your paramilitary targets out of hiding."

"That might work," she admitted, although a glimmer of doubt still lingered in her dark eyes. "I'll get on it."

"Good." There was still no sign of O'Brien in the viewscreen. "Any other problems since I've been gone?"

Kira glanced down at the ops board in front of her, then shook her head. "Nothing major. One unscheduled wormhole opening due to natural causes, and some minor quantum interference with the communications array. Nothing we can't work around."

"Good." Sisko had already seen the familiar stocky figure of his chief engineer appear behind Kira. "Any luck with those isotopic ratios, Chief?"

"I've got them right here." O'Brien plugged a data chip into the Ops communications console, then tapped in the order to transmit. A scroll of numbers, many of them incorporating the symbol i, promptly rolled across the screen. Sisko glanced at Hayman and got the quick nod that meant they'd been recorded. "That look like what you need, sir?"

"I hope so, Chief. If not—" Sisko paused, realizing he wasn't really sure how to end that sentence. "—well, you'll probably be the first to know. Sisko out."

Admiral Hayman snorted, leaning over to unplug the data chip from her private communications console and toss it at him. "Do you really think this is going to tell us how soon the *Defiant* will run into trouble?" she asked bluntly.

"Dax does," he said, swinging around and heading for the door to Starbase 1's operations center.

"*Jadzia* Dax does." Hayman matched him stride for stride across the busy hum of her command center. "A young science officer on her first tour of duty."

"With a very wise old man inside her." Sisko stepped into the turbolift and waited for her to follow him before he spoke to the computer. "Control room, fusion bay one."

The admiral fell silent, letting the swift whine of the turbolift close around them. "I'll give Jadzia this much," she said at last. "I'm not sure Curzon Dax would have argued quite as strongly for accepting back that old symbiont last night." Her lined face creased with an unexpected hint of humor. "Of course, if it *had* been Curzon, maybe that young medical officer of yours wouldn't have argued so strongly against it."

The turbolift doors opened before Sisko could respond to that, this time on a control room that looked as if it had come straight out of a history book on spaceflight. Walls of monitors and optical circuitry lined three sides of the narrow compartment. The fourth side was made of thick glass panels, turned a gossamer shade of antique gold by the hundreds of fusion blasts they'd weathered. Outside, the condensate inside the huge fusion bay had thinned enough to show them the dark smudge of the ancient *Defiant* floating in its halo of work lights.

Dax swung around from the temporary sensor panel she'd leaned against the central window, gray eyes intent. "Did you get the isotopic ratios I needed from O'Brien?"

"I think so." Sisko handed her the data chip, then went to stand at the window. The exhaled breath of the comet still obscured much of what had been his ship, but the ice had melted enough to show him the gaping crater where a quantum torpedo had exploded far too close to unshielded hull. He frowned. "Was there enough left of the warp core for you to examine?"

"It was completely intact, Benjamin." Dax tapped the chip into its slot with impatient fingers. "That's why Julian's medical bay was still running."

"Of course." Sisko shook his head, annoyed at not remembering that. Seeing the amount of damage the *Defiant* had sustained, that fact amazed him more now than it had the night before. "I had no idea the warp core was that well shielded."

"Me either. It took me a while to get the right range for the sensors." Something beeped on Dax's panel, and she tapped back a response, then glanced out the gold-stained window. Out in the fusion bay, a tiny glitter of floating machinery swung itself into a new position above the shattered ship. "One more scan, and I'll have the current isotopic ratios of the dilithium crystals."

Sisko grunted and turned back to join her. "And that will tell us exactly when we got thrown back in time?"

"No," Dax said promptly. "It will tell us exactly how many times the warp drive was engaged between now and when the ship was crippled." She pointed at the complex numbers pulsing across her sensor screen. "Each time we break the speed of light, Pedone's Law of Imaginary Energy Usage says that the ratio of dilithium isotopes will be altered by a factor of i. By measuring the total change in ratios from our current *Defiant* to the ancient one, we'll get an estimate of how many trips we made before the one that took us here."

Sisko grunted. "Not very helpful, old man, considering the *Defiant* only goes out when she's needed. Three trips might be anything from three days to three weeks."

"True," Dax agreed, not sounding flustered in the least. "But when we're back at *Deep Space Nine,* we'll know exactly how many trips we can safely make in the *Defiant*— and we'll know which one will be the trip that destroys us."

"Assuming you make the same decisions in this timeline that you would have if we hadn't found the *Defiant,*" Admiral Hayman pointed out from the back of the room.

Dax nodded, her eyes never leaving the screen. The complex numbers on it were almost steady now, only a few of their digits wavering to new values as the dilithium scan neared completion. "Fortunately, we'll have Chief O'Brien and Major Kira back at the station to give us their unbiased input about that. If they both agree with Captain Sisko's decisions—"

She broke off, a frown tightening her face to unaccustomed grimness as she ran a finger down the column of numbers on the screen. A quick toggle of her controls brought a second column of complex numbers up beside it. To Sisko's untrained eye, the jumble of numbers and symbols looked nearly identical.

"Then and now?" he demanded, and saw Dax's confirming nod. "How much difference is there?"

"Exactly one factor of i," his science officer said slowly. Her gaze rose to meet his in mutual awareness of what that meant. "That means the next time we take the *Defiant* to warp speed—"

Sisko nodded grimly, his gaze going back to the mist-shrouded comet and the impossible wreck it sheltered. "—we won't be coming back."

A shriek of coruscant energy burned past Kira's cheek, close enough to blind her and powerful enough to warm the chain on her metal earring. *This is the last time I take Sisko's advice!*

"Major, this may not be the best time to mention this . . ."

She shot a glance at Odo on the other side of the corridor. He'd pressed himself to only a few centimeters thick, all but disappearing behind a narrow wall support.

". . . but I don't think contacting Bajoran security forces was a very wise move."

Kira gritted her teeth and flashed a random shot down the corridor just to remind their quarry that she was still there. "It flushed them out for us, didn't it?"

Odo's only response was a wordless grunt.

"Okay, so I didn't exactly plan for them to go on a shooting spree through the station." Another barrage of phaser fire burned the reek of hot ozone through the middle of the hallway, and Kira used the interruption to turn away from Odo and slap at her comm badge. "Kira to Eddington! Where in hell are you people? We could stand a little backup here."

"This is Eddington." Banging and muffled human curses overlapped behind the Starfleet officer's clipped reply. "I'm trapped at the juncture of corridors eleven and six with

Kirich, Glotfelty, and Robb. I'm afraid—" A certain unprofessional impatience snuck into his otherwise self-possessed tone, and Kira could just picture the prim grimace on his narrow face. "The militia crystallized the hydraulics in the bulkhead controls and caught us between sectors. We don't seem to be able to force the manual override, but we might be able to cut our way out."

Odo grunted disdainfully. "In a few hours."

"Yes, sir." Although it sounded like Eddington had to swallow his own tongue to admit it. "I'm afraid that's probably about right."

Kira sighed and drummed the butt of her phaser against one leg. *It's not his fault,* she told herself firmly. *It's not his fault he's human.* Of course, if he'd been Bajoran, this particular little setback would never have occurred. There probably wasn't a Bajoran working on this station who hadn't spent half her young adulthood luring Cardassians into cul de sacs just like the one Eddington and his Starfleet team were trapped in right now. In fact, any resistance fighter worth her salt could recite the specific intersections on *Deep Space Nine* that were best suited for a convenient bulkhead hydraulic failure. Starfleet didn't share that history, and it was probably unfairly racist to be angry with them for that fact. Still, Kira couldn't just turn off the irritation in her voice, no matter how much her head knew she ought to.

"Don't bother, Eddington. Just have Ops send a technician down to replace the hydraulics on those doors." It would be the quickest way to get them out without actually burning down the entire door. "A *Bajoran* technician." Because that would also make the fast way the safest— Bajor had killed a lot of Cardassians through the years with the booby traps left behind in the hydraulic mess.

"Very well, sir." Then, with a somewhat stiff sincerity, "I'm sorry, sir. Eddington out."

His apology left her feeling strangely guilty for having been angry with him, and that only frustrated her more. "You know what Starfleet's problem is?" she asked Odo with a sigh.

"Their officers aren't devious enough?"

She smiled a little, amused by his insight more than by his candor. "Something like that."

72

He nodded very seriously. "It's a good thing we have more than enough Bajoran personnel to make up for that failing, then."

Kira wondered if he was referring to the Bajoran security guards who weren't caught up in the bulkhead trap with Eddington, or to her for having thought up the details of this crazy plan in the first place. As a blur of shouts and gunfire roared down the hall from the cornered terrorists, she decided it would probably be better not to ask.

"You've got squads on the edges of the Promenade?" she said instead. Concentrating on business was always a good way to sidestep conversations you would rather avoid.

"Half-squads," Odo admitted. "That should be enough to keep the militia from breaking through to the public areas."

But only if they keep them moving. "Who's watching beta sector?"

"Sergeant Nes."

A memory of the young Bajoran came easily to Kira—bright, coltish, barely old enough to wear an adult's earring. The first generation who, in a very few years, would have lived more of their lives free of Cardassian rule than as slaves to it. Their very existence was something Kira still reacted to as some sort of magnificent dream, and something that made her intensely proud. "Kira to Nes. How are you holding up down there?"

"We've got them stopped well enough," the younger girl answered promptly, "but I don't think we'll be able to push them back very well."

"That's all right—I want to funnel them down your way, away from the Promenade." She motioned for Odo to get ready, and switched her phaser back over to her right hand. "Once we start pushing from our end, fall back and let them drive you toward the habitat ring—"

Nes hesitated only slightly. "But, Major, if they're trying to reach the docking ring—"

"Precisely." Kira smiled wickedly, even though she knew Nes couldn't see it. "Hold out for about one minute, Sergeant, then cave in. Got that?"

"Yes, sir, Major." Her young voice held all the iron of a veteran resistance fighter. "Nes out."

Slipping around the next arching wall support wasn't

nearly as hard as getting the attention of the security team down the side corridor, but Kira resisted calling them up on the comm—she didn't want the sound of her steady chatter to alert the militia that a well-organized maneuver was in the offing. Across from her, Odo extruded himself through a crack in the wall support and neatly recongealed on the other side. "What if the militia doesn't know about the ore-delivery chute?" he asked while still little more than a glossy sheen on the wall. "If they don't think they can escape, you'll be driving them into the habitat ring."

Kira waved frantically in a frustrated effort to catch the other team's eye, then had to throw herself back against the bulkhead with a curse when the militia, who were paying considerably more attention, rewarded her with a new round of phaser fire. At least that made the security squad look around. "Oh, they know about the chute all right," she said as she flashed the Bajoran in charge a series of quick hand signals. "They've been on this station long enough to steal everything but Quark's bar. They probably know about chutes we haven't even found yet."

Odo grunted and swelled up to his usual height. "Let's just hope they all lead to the docking ring."

The squad from the side corridor was larger than Kira expected, and apparently more than the militia had counted on. What started as a grim push on the part of station personnel deteriorated quickly into shouting and cursing and pounding as the militia crumbled under the new onslaught. Kira heard their frantic voices recede down the curve of the corridor, felt the dull rumble of pounding footsteps through the deckplates as both security and militia broke into a run. The next time phasers shrilled in the distance, there was no return fire from Nes's little group.

"Go! Go! Close on them!" She shouted as loudly as she could while running, half wanting the militia to hear the fierceness in her voice, half wanting Nes to know that she had done just right. When she skated around the corner with her phaser thrust in front of her, though, it was a small sea of startled Bajorans in security brown who jostled to a stop two meters away and not the expected militia ragtag.

"Where are they?" Nes turned almost in a full circle, as though half expecting the quarry to be hidden among her own men. "They didn't come past us, sir, I swear they didn't!"

"They damn well better not have. . . ." She'd have no respect for them at all if they did something so common as simply running. Jamming her phaser back into its holster, she waved Nes impatiently aside and felt along the edges of the closest wall panel from top to bottom. Her hands found the sharp gouges in the metal before her eyes did. It popped off with the first bang from her fist, and the scarred, dirty access hatch beyond it looked as though it had been attacked by a dozen manic laser drills. Crowing with triumph, she threw Odo a smug grin as she straightened and slapped at her combadge. "Heads up, Chief! They're on their way to the docks!"

"I'm with you, Major," O'Brien came back briskly. "I've got an engine start-up on sensors. Pylon two, fourth level." He was silent for a moment, and Kira took the opportunity to disperse Nes and the others to their regular positions before heading for the turbolift with Odo. "They're trying to override traffic control and disengage the docking clamps," O'Brien said at last. "Tell me when you want me to release them."

She swung herself into the lift without slowing down. "Play with them a few times, then pop the clamps." She waited for Odo to slip in behind her before punching the controls for the docking ring. "And get that tracer ready."

"Already up and loaded."

"Good work, Chief." She caught at the rail as the lift heaved into motion, already drumming one foot impatiently in her want to be already parked at the docking ring, setting the next stage in motion.

"You know, Major . . ." True to form, Odo reclined against the other wall of the lift with a cool lack of tension only available to the truly boneless. "If they take their ship through the wormhole, the subspace matrix will erase all signature of the trace."

That was a worry so far from her mind that she almost laughed at the suggestion. "They're not going through the wormhole. They stole those bomb components for Bajor." No matter how misguided, they always thought they were doing it for Bajor. "Either they're running back to their buddies for protection, or they're hoping to pass off the components before they get caught. But either way, they're not going through the wormhole."

Odo pulled his face into a grimace Kira could only assume was one of skepticism. "For all our sakes, I hope you're right."

So did she. But it didn't seem a good idea to reinforce the constable's uncertainties right now.

By the time the lift sighed to a stop just outside the runabout bay, Kira had decided that some glitch in the Cardassian computer system must be responsible for slowing down the station's workings whenever speed was most required. Why else would it take the turbolifts four times longer to get anywhere during an emergency than it did all the rest of the time? And what other explanation could there be for O'Brien taking just as long to announce, "Okay, they've pulled free of the station and are bringing warp engines on-line"? Surely the Ops computers weren't responding with their usual alacrity.

Kira threw herself into the *Rio Grande*'s pilot seat without chastising O'Brien for slowness that was obviously none of his fault. "Mark them, Chief!"

He didn't bother verbally responding, not trusting the equally sluggish comm system to relay his words in time, no doubt. Kira heard the deep whine of the weapons sail next door as its phaser batteries built a charge, and ordered *Rio Grande* lifted to its external launching pad while Odo was still fastening himself into the his own chair. At least the phasers seemed to be operating in normal time—the weapons sail loosed its shot with a short, ripping scream just as the runabout broke vacuum, and Kira saw the brilliant flare of light splashing against the militia ship's unshielded hull without even slowing it down. "Bull's-eye!"

O'Brien sounded significantly less impressed with his own shooting as the familiar blur of warp effect swallowed the militia ship and whisked it away. "Now let's just hope it takes."

"It took." Odo flicked colorless eyes across the runabout's sensor controls. "I'm picking up a faint but steady ionic trace, even after they've gone into warp. We should be able to follow them from several light-minutes' distance with no problem."

"And where are they heading?" Kira asked, trying not to sound too pleased with herself as she eased *Rio Grande* up off its launching pad.

Odo slid her a wry look, his lipless mouth curving into just the faintest hint of a smile. "Bearing oh one seven mark three," he acknowledged gracefully. "Away from the wormhole."

"Of course." It was only slightly better than I-told-you-so, but the least Kira could allow herself. "Chief, you get to mind the store while we're gone."

"I'll try to make sure Quark doesn't run off with too much of the merchandise," he said with a smile in his voice. "Good luck, Major. O'Brien out."

Just finding terrorists on board was the best luck I've had all week. The thought startled her, and she hoped Odo wouldn't notice the heat that washed into her face as she swept the runabout between the huge arching pylons and away from the station proper. It's not that she wanted anything bad to happen to the station, or even that she thought the militia consisted of anything more than the cream of an admittedly demented crop. It was just that activity—almost any kind of activity—would always fit her better than the kind of administrative desk duties Sisko seemed to wear with such ease. It probably said something disturbing about her psyche that she would rather chase a shipload of fugitives with an illegal plasma device than figure out how to display Klingon death icons alongside human menorahs in the Promenade without offending anybody's sensibilities. As she eased the ship through warp one and up to a relatively sedate 2.3, she had to admit that leaving the station and its Ferengi, radiation leaks, and death icons far behind calmed her all out of proportion with the situation she was likely rushing into.

"How are we doing?" she asked Odo, just because this *was* supposed to be a business trip, and not a relaxation cruise.

"The trace is holding strong. Judging from the rate of decay, I'd say they're about eighteen light-minutes ahead of us, proceeding at warp five." He glanced aside at her, one hand resting lightly on whatever reading he'd just been checking. "That's probably their maximum speed, given the age of their ship."

Kira nodded, passing a quick look over Odo's sensor panel more from unconscious habit than because she really needed any verification of the constable's statement. She'd already turned her attention back to the viewscreen, to the soft, computer-corrected blur of stars streaming by the runabout's nose, when something she'd only half-noticed tickled at the back of her awareness. Not quite turning away from her own panel, she tossed a nod at Odo's screen with a frown. "What's that?"

He looked at her, then at the sensor readout as though never having studied it before. "What's what?"

"That!" Kira stabbed a finger at the unidentified ship outline. "That's not the militia, is it?"

He answered with a slight, eloquent cock to his head that Kira always secretly labeled an Odo shrug. "It's some sort of sublight transport. This near the asteroid belt, I'd say an ore carrier, most likely."

An ore carrier. She glanced once, twice at the string of readings as the unknown ship all but rushed up on *Rio Grande* on the sensor screen. "If it's an ore carrier," she asked, "why isn't it moving?"

"Because it's stopped?" His voice held the weary resignation he usually reserved for stubborn Federation officials who refused to acknowledge that the world sometimes moved outside the lines of their little designs. "Major," he said, very carefully, as she leaned over to read the coordinates off his screen, "we technically have no authority over civilian spacecraft inside the Bajoran system. If they choose to stop—"

"Nobody chooses to stop in the middle of nowhere, Constable. Look at them!" She waved at the sensor console, forcing him to look down at his own readings. "The closest moon is thirty light-minutes away."

"And Chief O'Brien's tracer will only last for another three hours."

Yes, she had to admit with a swell of irritation, there was that. She hated it when she couldn't do things exactly as she wanted. "We're not going to be here for three hours. Worst-case scenario, we'll just beam the crew to the runabout." Especially if it was a bulk-ore barge—those almost never crewed more than four people. "That'll take, what? Five minutes? We ought to stay a few thousand klicks behind the militia, anyway."

He didn't reach over and stop her from bringing the ship to sublight, but she could tell that he wanted to by the way he stiffened to a good six centimeters taller than normal. "Major, this is precisely the sort of thing the Bajoran interim patrol is supposed to be responsible for. *We,* on the other hand, are responsible . . ."

She didn't even notice at first when his voice fell silent. Her own thoughts had stopped just as dead, and for the longest time nothing seemed able to get past the visual image of the ore transport hanging lifelessly against the veil of stars. It wasn't even the broken darkness of the ship that first slapped into her consciousness and shivered like ice through all her bones. It was the blossom of frozen gases pluming around the ruptured hull, and the glitter of trailing debris as it painted a slow-motion comet's tail behind the drifting bulk.

"Never mind," Odo said quietly. "The militia can wait."

CHAPTER
6

I T WAS A council of Starfleet's highest-ranking admirals, from the venerable Hajime Shoji to the steely Alynna Necheyev. Even in telepresence, the combined focus of so many piercing stares made Sisko feel like a cadet at his final oral exam. Just as he had then, he folded his hands on the table in front of him to keep his unruly fingers still. This time, however, the emotion he was concealing was a drumming impatience, not nervousness.

"I don't see what the problem is," Necheyev said, voicing Sisko's exasperation for him. It was one of the few times Sisko could remember when his sector commander had been in total agreement with him. "We've discovered that the battle which destroyed the *Defiant* happened on the far side of the time warp, right?"

"Yes," Admiral Hayman said, before Sisko could respond. Sisko settled back into his chair, knowing her gruff voice probably carried more conviction than his own neutral tones. "Our contact with the surviving Trill symbiont gave us very clear evidence of that. The *Defiant* went into the wormhole, was thrown back five thousand years into the past, and *then* encountered the aliens who destroyed it."

Necheyev shrugged, although her razor-blade face lost none of its intensity. "Then whoever destroyed the *Defiant* has been dead for as long as the pharaohs have—and they obviously didn't disturb Earth's history, since we're still here. Why don't we just dry-dock the *Defiant* back at *Deep Space Nine* until it disappears from Starbase One? Then we'll know we averted that timeline."

"And we will also have lost the only stable wormhole known to exist in the galaxy." That voice, as elegantly cold as silk, came not from a wall monitor, but from the third person actually present in Starbase One's small conference room. With her usual curtness, Hayman had introduced the middle-aged Vulcan woman just as T'Kreng, letting Sisko deduce from her civilian robe and platinum medallion that she must be a member of the Vulcan Science Academy. A very high-ranking member indeed, if she had the security clearance to attend a meeting both Dax and Bashir had been barred from. "From either a scientific or a diplomatic viewpoint, I believe that is an outcome we would wish to avoid."

A younger admiral whom Sisko didn't recognize leaned forward, dark eyes intent above his steepled fingers. "But is the loss of the wormhole a certain outcome, Professor T'Kreng? Could the *Defiant* simply have been the victim of a freak quantum fluctuation of the wormhole? One perhaps initiated by some action or accident that occurred while they were traveling through it?"

"The equations governing wormhole physics do allow for that possibility," T'Kreng conceded. "And the spacial displacement created by such a fluctuation could certainly reach as far from Bajor as Earth. However, Admiral Kirschbaum, my calculations indicate that the maximum temporal displacement that could be caused by such a spontaneous quantum event is two hundred standard years, plus or minus ten years." She lifted one graceful hand, in a gesture that somehow managed to convey the enormity of the problem with a minimum of expended effort. "Clearly, we have exceeded the time limits imposed by the wormhole's internal energy sources."

Sisko swung around to frown at her. "You're saying the wormhole *couldn't* have thrown us this far back in time?"

T'Kreng graced him with a frosty look, although he couldn't be sure if it was the blunt question or his scientific illiteracy that irritated her. Unusually for a Vulcan, her eyes were the pale gray of moonstones, making her look even more remote than most of her race. "I made no such statement, Captain Sisko. What I said was that such a massive temporal displacement could not be caused by normal quantum fluctuations in the wormhole. It can be achieved, however, by adding a significant amount of external energy to the singularity matrix."

"And it's the addition of external energy that will destroy the Bajoran wormhole?" Kirschbaum demanded.

"Yes." T'Kreng's icy gaze shifted back to her wall monitor. "The amount of energy needed to produce a temporal displacement of five thousand years is more than a starship could produce with anything short of a total warp-core explosion. I conclude that something other than the *Defiant* caused the disruption of the Bajoran wormhole, and that the temporal displacement experienced by the *Defiant* was a symptom and not a cause of the problem."

"And once it's disrupted, the Bajoran wormhole will stay disrupted?" Hayman asked.

The Vulcan sighed. "The explosion will most likely catapult the wormhole into an indefinite succession of chaotic gravitemporal fluctuations. Even if a ship managed to survive the unstable gravity flux inside the singularity matrix, it could emerge from the other side at any time within the past five thousand years. Or within the next five thousand. The singularity would still exist, but it would be essentially useless."

"Let me ask you a different question, Professor." That polite, grasshopper-thin voice came from the oldest of the admirals, the centenarian Hajime Shoji. "Could this disruption of the Bajoran wormhole have been deliberately induced by some entity trying to subvert the wormhole to its own purposes?"

The Vulcan scientist lifted one eyebrow by so small a degree that Sisko wondered if anyone but he and Hayman could see it. "It is highly unlikely that the temporal displacement in the wormhole was deliberately induced. Not even I can work out the equations required to accomplish that."

Kirschbaum cleared his throat. "I think what Admiral Shoji is suggesting, Professor, is that the time rift may have been caused inadvertently by aliens attempting to take control of the wormhole."

T'Kreng frowned, a minuscule tightening of cheek and forehead muscles. "I am not a diplomatic expert, Admiral, but I believe all the known races have acknowledged Bajor's possession of the singularity."

"Not all of them." Hayman rummaged in one pocket of her coveralls and then startled Sisko by hauling out a small, grotesquely realistic effigy of a horned, yellow-eyed figure. She dangled it in front of her screen, letting reflected light wash across its age-stained but still powerful grimace. "And this one in particular sure hasn't."

"Ah." T'Kreng's pale eyes narrowed to slits. "You suspect that the alien coalition we know as the Furies will tamper with the Bajoran wormhole? Why?"

Hayman glanced up at Shoji, who answered in the slow deliberate tones of someone who'd spent a lot of time considering that question. "Our knowledge of Fury history is incomplete, Professor, but we know that they were driven out of our sector in a war with another alien empire millennia ago." His age-faded eyes slid to regard Sisko thoughtfully. "The five-thousand-year-old battle that the *Defiant* witnessed, just prior to its destruction by one or another of the participants, was undoubtedly part of that war."

Sisko nodded, deliberately keeping his gaze away from the tiny horned devil dangling from Hayman's bony hand. "I suspected as much from the logs, Admiral."

"We also know that the Furies have used artifical wormholes to invade our quadrant twice since then, in an attempt to reclaim what they believe to be their territory." Unlike Sisko's, Kirschbaum's dark gaze seemed to have become glued to the Fury effigy in Hayman's viewscreen. "Now that the *Enterprise* has destroyed that technology in the battle at Furies Point, they may want to coopt the Bajoran wormhole and use it in a similar fashion."

"That is possible," T'Kreng said after a considering pause. "Although I find it a less probable cause of the wormhole's temporal displacement than a natural input of energy from a drifting black hole or cosmic string."

Shoji rubbed his hands together, a paper-dry rustle of ancient skin that carried clearly across the parsecs. "In either case, it's clear that our strategy must be to save the wormhole and prevent the *Defiant*'s fatal trip. Is that feasible, Honored Professor?"

The Vulcan scientist's slim eyebrows lifted again, in the barest of detectable motions. "If you are asking in terms of scientific feasibility, Admiral, the answer is yes. Because the addition of external energy is not a natural part of the wormhole's evolution, no law of science bars us from preventing it."

"But how good are our chances of actually doing it?" Necheyev demanded bluntly. "We don't even know where this energy input is going to come from."

Sisko frowned, remembering Kira's newly discovered paramilitary group and their tactical weapons. He opened his mouth to contradict his sector commander, but T'Kreng's smooth voice had already claimed the monitor's video focus.

"The source of energy is irrelevant, Admiral. By examining the wormhole's current resonance state, I can extrapolate to the precise time and place where the energy input will occur. All you need do is send a starship to that point and order it to destroy whatever energy-producing device or cosmic phenomenon it finds there."

Hayman snorted and set her small totem down on the table with a thump that rattled its contents into an odd, jangling sound. "If you can extrapolate to an event that hasn't occurred yet, Professor T'Kreng, why aren't you out playing Dabo instead of writing four-hundred-page grants to fund your fancy research ship?"

This time the censure in those ice-pale eyes was slanted at the silver-haired admiral. "Because the theory of temporal symmetry applies only to objects outside the Einsteinian frame of gravitational reference. And since a Dabo table is neither a black hole, a wormhole, nor a cosmic string, it is not subject to those equations."

Admiral Shoji cleared his throat diplomatically. "I assume you will need to examine the wormhole at first hand to make this extrapolation, Professor?"

She nodded again. "I will need to make several runs through the singularity matrix itself, to obtain the necessary precision."

"How soon can you leave for Bajor?" Kirschbaum demanded.

T'Kreng made another small gesture, this time one of gracious accommodation. "My research vessel is fully staffed and ready to depart Starbase One within the hour. We can make the run to Bajor in approximately eleven standard hours."

Shoji exchanged consulting looks with his fellow admirals, and got back silent, confirming nods. "Then consider yourself funded at priority research levels for the next week, Professor. You will be working directly under Admiral Necheyev, with onboard liaison provided by Captain Sisko. Are these conditions acceptable?"

"I find them so." T'Kreng gave Sisko a long, measuring glance. "But are you willing to travel on my ship in that limited capacity, Captain?"

Considering that the alternative was to take the *Defiant* on a short trip to a foregone conclusion, Sisko wasn't sure how much choice he had in the matter. Aloud, all he said was "So long as I can bring along my science officer, yes."

T'Kreng's elegant shoulders lifted in the barest of shrugs. "That hardly seems necessary, Captain. Half my shipboard staff hold degrees in either singularity physics or quantum chronodynamics."

Sisko didn't bother arguing with her, since he knew she wasn't the one he had to convince. Instead, he glanced up toward the viewscreen that held the age-crinkled but alert face of Hajime Shoji. "My science officer, Jadzia Dax, is the Trill whose symbiont survived all this time in the *Defiant*," he said quietly. "They communicated at some length this morning. We're not sure yet exactly how much she learned, but she might provide some additional clues that we couldn't get any other way."

Shoji nodded. "In that case, I'm sure Professor T'Kreng will be happy to accommodate both of you." The Vulcan scientist didn't look happy, Sisko thought wryly, but then he wasn't sure she had ever looked that way in her life. "And I suggest you both prepare for an immediate departure. After viewing the visual logs from the *Defiant*, I find myself most troubled by the aspect of this problem that Admiral Necheyev has pointed out."

Necheyev looked puzzled, and for once even T'Kreng's moonstone eyes reflected back incomprehension rather than Vulcan certainty. It was Judith Hayman, however, who had the gruff courage to demand, "What aspect are you talking about, sir?"

Shoji's ruffled white eyebrows rose. "Why, the fact that the aliens who destroyed the *Defiant* five thousand years ago—whether they were the Furies or the unknown conquerors they accuse us of being—had no effect on the ancient Earth. Surely it has occurred to you all why that may be so?"

Sisko took in a deep breath, feeling several disconnected fragments of his daylong uneasiness suddenly congeal to an unwanted conclusion. "Because they didn't stay in that timeline?"

"Precisely, Captain." The rear admiral might be elderly, but he'd been both a tactical and engineering genius in his day. He gave T'Kreng an ironic glance. "I may not hold a degree in quantum chronodynamics, but I've studied the basic equations governing time travel, and there's one thing I'm sure of. Any mechanism that can transport matter backward through time also has the ability to transport it forward."

"Wait! Let me ease it around the replicator—that's it. . . . Now bring it back, straight back—Back! Back! Jadzia, what are you *doing?*"

"Trying to think of a good reason not to hit you."

And she said it through clenched teeth, in the voice Bashir had learned to think of as her "Joran voice." It was the one that showed up right about the time you suspected another sentence or two of argument would get you murdered. She hadn't killed anyone yet—at least so far as he knew—but Bashir had learned long ago not to take anything for granted with an alien life-form, even one that looked so young and lovely. Waving her away from the end of the brine tank, he squeezed himself between the stasis field and the wall to wrestle it into the corner without her. "I'm sorry," he sighed as he leaned his weight into the unit and shoved. "Between sorting through my medical records and pulling together a temporary battery for moving the unit, I didn't get much sleep last night." Actually, he hadn't gotten any sleep at all. But that was a whole other potential conflict that he really didn't want to get into right now. "I guess it's just made me a little cranky."

"Don't apologize." Jadzia crouched to thread the tank's power cable through its tangled workings and under the room's only bunk. "I should have known this would make me edgy." She flushed a little as she handed him the cable at the other end of the bed. "I've never done anything like this before."

Bashir smiled, but accepted the cable and its implied exoneration. "You've never kidnapped yourself?"

"Never done *anything* like this!" She hiked herself up onto the edge of the bunk to give him room to pry open a small access panel on the wall. "Stolen Starfleet equipment, let myself into a science ship's cargo bay, slipped through all sorts of security checkpoints—"

Bashir caught the panel before it clattered against the floor and slipped it up onto the bed beside Jadzia. "Oh, come on! I find it hard to believe Curzon didn't borrow a Starfleet runabout or two in his day."

"Oh, *Curzon* once stole an entire *grakh'rahad* during trade negotiations with the Klingons," she admitted with a smile that wasn't quite memory, and wasn't quite hers. "And *Torias*—" She broke off abruptly, and Bashir wondered if Trill had some code of ethics that discouraged one host from revealing a previous host's indiscretions. Before he could ask, she busied herself handing him a tool he could reach perfectly well by himself. "*Jadzia*'s the one who's never done anything like this." And then, in case this hadn't ever occurred to him before, "She's actually rather proper and dull compared to most of Dax's other hosts."

"Proper, maybe," Bashir allowed, surprised to feel his own face warming, "but never dull." He fitted the tank's power cable against one of the conduit junctions leading to the replicator, and spliced it neatly into the circuit with a few strokes of the welder. "Try thinking of it as an interstellar Academy prank. Instead of moving the Cochran Memorial to the top of Brin Planetarium, we're moving it to Trill." He glanced at the tank as its subliminal purr rose to an audible rumbling with the influx of steady power. "In a five-thousand-year-old stasis tank that weighs only slightly less than the Brin Planetarium."

Dax smiled and rubbed him briskly between the shoulders in motherly support as he rose to sit beside her on the bunk. "How are you going to hide the power draw from ship's sensors?" Apparently, he hadn't been the only one to notice the step-up in the tank's functions.

"It doesn't use as much as you might think," he told her, studying the frozen turbulence of its occupant without quite realizing he did so. "Still, I entered a request for extra replicator time when the captain first told me we'd be taking the *Sreba*. T'Kreng thinks I'm running the tissue reconstruction and cloning experiments Admiral Hayman ordered for the symbiont. The extra mass, of course, is my incredibly sensitive and extensive medical equipment." He pulled his eyes away from one Dax only to face the other with a wry, tired grin. "As long as they only do periodic spot checks on power usage, they shouldn't notice any pattern to my consumption."

Dax returned his smile gently. "You hope."

"Yes," Bashir admitted, sighing. "I hope."

The brisk knock at the cabin door jerked through Bashir like a phaser blast, and he whirled on the bed with a stab of guilt so sharp it almost startled a cry out of him. *I'm not well suited to this,* he thought as he stood, hesitated over what to do about a visitor, and abruptly sat again. He had a tendency to blush and stammer when he knew he'd done something he oughtn't; it had been an unfortunate trait when trying to get away with anything as a child, and it hadn't become any more helpful now that he was an adult. It had a lot to do with why *he'd* never done anything like this during his Academy days, either.

Another knock banged against the door, louder this time, and Bashir looked helplessly at Dax in search of a suggestion.

"It's *your* room!" she hissed, swatting his shoulder on the way toward waving at the door.

Yes, it was. Which probably meant someone was waiting for him to answer before going on their merry way. "Uh . . ." He took a deep breath, straightening himself as though whoever waited on the other side could actually see him. "I'm sorry, but I'm rather busy at the moment. Could you come back later?" Not bad on such short notice. Polite, professional, and appropriately vague. He flashed Dax a relieved grin, pleased to have averted disaster, however temporarily.

"Doctor," Sisko's voice said ominously from the hall, "open this door."

For one suicidal moment, it occurred to Bashir that he could actually refuse—assert his inalienable right to privacy and tell the captain to go away. Then the likely repercussions of that madness cascaded into his rational mind even as Dax was shoving him off the bed to stumble toward the door. He didn't even have time to construct a plausible explanation for what they were doing here before he found himself confronting a handsbreadth view of Sisko's grim, dark face through the barely opened hatchway. "Captain, I'm afraid I'm right in the middle of—"

"Is Dax here?"

Bashir tried not to steal a glance over his shoulder, but it was hard to maintain eye contact with Sisko when he was angry. "I'm here, Benjamin," she called, saving Bashir from having to decide whether or not he should implicate her in his dealings.

The dark burn of Sisko's glare never left Bashir's face as he said, very plainly, "Not you."

The doctor felt as though his stomach would fall straight through into the floor. "Captain—I can explain—"

"I'm sure you can." Sisko reached past with a quick efficiency that startled Bashir into pulling away from the doorway as though expecting the captain to catch him by the collar. Instead, Sisko slapped at the inside door control and keyed the hatch all the way open. "May I?"

Bashir knew a rhetorical question when he heard one. Stepping aside, he granted Sisko access to the rest of the room without trying to stammer any further explanations. On the bunk, Dax returned the captain's scowl with an indignantly raised eyebrow as he stalked past her to glare down at the stasis tank and the frozen creature within.

"Do you two realize that what you've done could get you both court-martialed?" he asked without turning around.

Actually, the thought hadn't occurred to Bashir at all—any concern for his own welfare had drowned under the massive debt owed anything you had kept alive for more than five thousand years. He should have thought about Jadzia, though, he realized. It wasn't fair to drag someone else into his moral dilemmas, no matter how closely they were related to the patient.

Still, Jadzia herself seemed remarkably undisturbed by Sisko's warning. "I'd like to see Judith explain to a board of inquiry how she intends to prosecute us for following the wishes of a sentient life-form who is not *individually* a member of Starfleet."

Sisko turned his stormy frown full on her. "She'll argue that you can't know the wishes of a life-form who is barely conscious."

"*I* can." The ancient certainty in her gray eyes dared anyone to challenge that.

Sisko grunted and turned back to the tank without trying to argue with her. Bashir watched the captain rhythmically bounce one fist against the side of his leg for what felt like several hours before finally risking his voice against the quiet of the room. "How did you find out?" he asked plaintively. "I thought I'd been so careful—"

"I knew," Sisko said, with a sigh so deep it was almost paternal. "I knew the moment you first dropped the stasis field that you wouldn't be able to just walk away. And you, old man . . ." When he finally turned to face them, it was with a resigned fondness Bashir hadn't expected to see after his harsh entrance. "I've never known you to do anything but exactly what you want, no matter which body you're in. I doubted that five thousand years in a fish tank would do much to change that."

Dax flashed the captain one of her many flavors of all-knowing smile, and Sisko surprised Bashir again by laughing softly as he shook his head.

"Then you're not going to tell Admiral Hayman?" Bashir asked.

Sisko glanced up at the doctor's question, and a little of the hardness returned to his tone. "I don't have to. You can cover your tracks from here to *Deep Space Nine*, Doctor, but you can't hide the fact that the *Defiant* at Starbase One is now minus one passenger." He folded his arms and leaned back against the tank to gather both officers under his scowl. "Admiral Hayman went to check on the symbiont's status a few hours after the *Sreba* left dock, and found the medical bay cleaned out—lock, stock, and symbiont."

He wasn't sure which was worse—the disapproval in Sisko's voice or the gape of mute amazement Dax turned up at him. He tried to counter them both with a boyish smile. "I suppose stuffing a pillow under the bedsheets wasn't the most effective strategy in this instance."

Neither of them seemed particularly amused.

"Admiral Hayman called me on a priority Starfleet channel just five minutes ago," Sisko informed him, "demanding that we return to Starbase One—with the symbiont—immediately."

Dax leaned expectantly over her knees. "And you said . . . ?"

"I said," the captain answered smoothly, "that I was a liaison officer and not the captain of this vessel. She has to make her request to Dr. T'Kreng."

Bashir felt as though someone had released a choking band around his chest, and relief burst out of him on a sigh. "Thank you."

Sisko flicked him a hard, unreadable glare. "Don't thank me yet, Doctor. Hayman was still talking to Professor T'Kreng when I left the bridge."

"With as eager as T'Kreng is to get within sensor range of the wormhole?" Jadzia relaxed back onto her elbows with an eloquently dismissive snort. "She'll choose a one-hour detour to Trill over the six hours that obeying Judith's order requires, or I don't know my Vulcans."

"Any change in course is completely unacceptable." T'Kreng stepped around Bashir as though her pronouncement rendered him chronodynamically insignificant, and pointedly sank her attention into one of the many science panels ringing the *Sreba*'s bridge. "We will continue for Bajor at maximum speed."

"But . . ." Bashir pulled his arm away from Sisko's hand before the captain could turn his warning touch into a grip.

91

"Professor T'Kreng," he persisted, following her indifferent back as she moved from station to station, "I don't think you understand. We have an unhosted Trill symbiont—"

"—which has survived without incident for nearly five thousand years. It will survive in stasis a few days longer." She passed her hand across a readout, freezing a string of incomprehensible equations, and turned so abruptly that Bashir almost stepped off the edge of the bridge platform dancing out of her way. She responded to his display of startled emotion by peering down at him with the stoic disdain only Vulcans seemed able to express. "Apply logic to this question, Doctor, not emotion. If we reach the wormhole expeditiously, our actions there will avert the temporal shift which originally brought the symbiont into your possession. Once the temporal shift is removed from our timestream, the symbiont, also, will cease to be part of this reality. Therefore, any efforts to return it to the Trill homeworld are unnecessary."

"Provided," Dax pointed out, "you're successful in preventing the temporal shift."

The Vulcan turned cool eyes on the young science officer. Bashir wondered if T'Kreng would exude such disrespect if she understood that Dax was older than any of them. "My models indicate a 93.789 percent likelihood that I can pinpoint the time and place when the singularity matrix was damaged." She speared Bashir with another glower just on the brink of disgust. "Provided we are not delayed."

He scrubbed a hand through his hair. "Then let me take a shuttle. I can escort the symbiont to Trill by myself, then meet you back at *Deep Space Nine.*"

This time Sisko succeeded in stopping him before he could grab at the physicist's arm. "Doctor—"

"I'm not needed here," he insisted. Torn between appealing to T'Kreng and appealing to his captain, he finally turned to plead with the one he felt most likely to understand. "Whatever's wrong with the wormhole isn't a medical problem," he explained to Sisko. "And unlike Professor T'Kreng, I can't ignore the needs of my patient just because there's a high probability it will be dead soon."

"Do you willfully misunderstand my statements?"

T'Kreng asked in what sounded almost like honest curiosity. "Or is this merely a natural error-generating effect of undisciplined human emotion?"

Bashir swallowed the flash of anger that rushed up on him. "Will you give me a shuttle?" he asked again, more slowly. He refused to dignify her racist elitism with an emotional reply.

Tipping her head infinitesimally, T'Kreng's pupils dilated in response to some subtle shift in her nonexistent mood—intrigue at his persistence, Bashir suspected, or perhaps even honest surprise that he didn't rush to appease her the way everyone else around her had been trained to. "The *Sreba* is a scientific research vessel," she said at last, as though still not quite sure why she needed to explain such a thing to Bashir, "not an exploration craft. We have unpowered lifepods in the event of an accident. We have forty-seven unmanned, self-contained probes for purposes of data collection and sample retrieval. We have seven different configurations of launchable sensor arrays. But we have no long-range shuttles."

Bashir wished there were something he could say, something he could do to make one of those useless payloads substitute. Instead, all he could think about was how he didn't seem able to succeed in doing anything to help the symbiont—not at Starbase One, not here, not five thousand years ago. The knot of frustrated anger that had settled into his stomach upon reading the first of his old medical logs twisted silently tighter.

"Is there anything else?" T'Kreng asked at last.

Bashir felt Sisko's hand flex briefly on his shoulder, but couldn't tell if the captain meant it as some kind of signal or just an unconscious expression of his own displeasure with the outcome. "I think that's all for now, Professor."

"Very well." T'Kreng reanimated the display behind her with a succinct motion of her hand, but moved to retrieve a data padd from a researcher nearby rather than attending to the newly reactivated panel. "P'sel," she called without looking up at anyone in particular, "please escort Captain Sisko and his officers off the bridge."

The dark male who rose from the station nearest the doors was young by Vulcan standards, but as cool and tight-lipped as the rest. He didn't really make any effort to escort them, Bashir noticed—just stood by the doors to usher them out with a stiff nod, then keyed the bulkhead shut behind them. Bashir watched the light beside the exterior door control, his irrational human emotion knowing that it would blink from green to red even before the Vulcans inside the ship's bridge engaged the lock. Something about the gesture struck him as delightfully human and petty, but did nothing to abate the awful anger he felt at being so helpless.

"I'll have O'Brien prepare a runabout the moment we reach *Deep Space Nine*," Sisko said, very gently. "I'd send you with the *Defiant*, but . . ."

Bashir nodded so he wouldn't have to say the obvious. "I understand."

Dax reached out to place her hand on his arm. "Don't worry, Julian. It shouldn't delay us more than forty-eight hours, and with the symbiont in stasis . . ." She shrugged a little, trying on someone else's smile. "It won't even notice."

"No . . ." Bashir pulled his eyes away from the locked door and his thoughts away from the infuriating, inflexible Vulcan within. "No," he said again, "of course not. Thank you." He gave Jadzia's hand a squeeze before placing it back down at her side. He suspected his smile looked at least as wan and ungenuine as hers. "If you'll excuse me, I should get back to my quarters. I've got five thousand years of medical records to read through before we get home."

CHAPTER
7

"DINNER?"

The utterly blank look on Bashir's face made Dax want to laugh and hit him at the same time. There were times when the human medical officer's obsessive focus on his work exceeded even her vast tolerance of alien behavior. She compromised with an exasperated sigh.

"Dinner, Julian. The meal that comes after you quit working for the day and before you go to sleep at night." She paused, eyeing his haggard face critically. "You do remember what sleep is, don't you?"

Bashir scrubbed a hand across his forehead, looking as if she'd reminded him of an unpleasant chore he'd forgotten. "I know, I know—I'm going to get some rest tonight, I promise. But I still have two hours of work to do before I can be sure I've stabilized the symbiont for the journey." He gave her the boyishly appealing look that had won over many a *Deep Space Nine* heart. "Couldn't you just bring me something back and spare me an hour with the patron saint of singularities? I'll get to bed an hour earlier that way."

This time, Dax did hit him, but she was laughing while she did it. "I'll have you know T'Kreng has won not one but *two* Nobel/Z. Magnees Prizes for her work on quantum chronodynamics and singularity matrices. It's going to be an honor to talk to her."

Bashir winced and rubbed at the shoulder she'd punched.

"It's also going to be as dull as listening to O'Brien explain how he reprogrammed the food replicators. I'll pass, thanks."

"If that's what you want." Dax paused in the doorway of the small passenger's cabin, which was filled almost entirely now with tank, pumps, and tubing. Bashir had already bent back over the ancient control panel, his forehead creased into a frown. "Julian," she said, and waited for his impatient upward glance. "Try not to feel so guilty about keeping me alive all this time. I don't know about Earth customs, but on the Trill homeworld, it's the patient who decides about euthanasia, not the doctor."

"I know." He glanced back into the brine tank, a muscle jerking in his thin cheek. "I just wish I could be sure this patient didn't change its mind after the doctor died."

Unfortunately, there was no way Dax could reassure him about that. Her brine-gleaned memories were only clear about the *Defiant*'s final battle—all the rest was a haze of meaningless thoughts and half-remembered hallucinations. She closed the cabin door quietly behind her and left him alone with her catatonic future self.

She found the *Sreba*'s dining room by the simple procedure of following the sound of conversation down the hall from the sleeping quarters. The Vulcan research ship was built along the same spare lines as one of their diplomatic couriers—a bottom deck for engineering and life-support, a top deck for the bridge and the research labs, and a central deck where the dozen or so crew members lived and ate. There didn't seem to be a recreational area on board anywhere, but knowing Vulcans, that didn't surprise Dax.

Inside the small, undecorated mess hall, a handful of scientists sat along a single long table, many of them scribbling equations on notebook screens while they ate. Captain Sisko sat at one end opposite the elegantly icy figure of T'Kreng. His dark face wore no particular expression, but the stiff set of his shoulders told Dax he'd rather be sitting somewhere else. She suppressed a smile and ordered a bowl of *chfera* stew from the replicator, then went to join him.

"—accept the theory that the wormhole inhabitants play any role in stabilizing the singularity matrix," T'Kreng was saying when she arrived. "In fact, I am not sure the current data even support the existence of these life-forms."

"They exist," Sisko said, his voice brusque enough to make heads around the table turn. "I've seen them."

The Vulcan physicist raised a slender eyebrow at him. "According to the reports I have read, Captain, 'seen' may be too strong a word for what you experienced. Is it not true that these life-forms appeared to you only in the guise of human beings from your own past?"

"Yes."

She made an infinitesimal gesture with her free hand. "Then there is no actual evidence of their existence. What you experienced could have been a sensory by-product of your immersion in the singularity matrix."

Dax cut into the conversation before Sisko could reply. "In that case, Professor T'Kreng, why has no other being— not even Captain Sisko—reported such hallucinations? I believe Sterchak's principle states that any complex phenomenon which occurs only once indicates a high probability of sentient life."

A murmur of agreement drifted along the table toward her, making T'Kreng's opalescent eyes narrow. "That is true," she admitted coldly. "Although I would not have expected a Trill to be so familiar with such a minor branch of Vulcan philosophy."

"I *am* a Starfleet science officer," Dax reminded her gently. "And I also happen to have made the acquaintance of Professor Sterchak when he visited the Trill homeworld three hundred years ago." She gave Sisko a glance full of reminiscent glee. "He got especially philosophical after a few glasses of *ghiachan* brandy, as I recall."

The human captain snorted with laughter, echoed by a quieter voice from halfway down the table. Dax looked that way in surprise, and saw one smiling non-Vulcan face amid the slanted eyebrows and serious expressions. It was a young human female, wearing the practical lab coat of a graduate student rather than a professor's ornate robe. The girl dropped her gaze back to her plate as soon as she noticed Dax looking at her, but a small puckish smile still lingered on her face.

T'Kreng made a soft disapproving sound, more hiss than

sigh. "I do not see that Sterchak's drinking habits are relevant to this discussion, Lieutenant. Furthermore, his principle is merely a guide to logical inference, not a fundamental law of nature." She pointed her eating sticks across the table at Dax. "If indeed there are sentient creatures living in the Bajoran wormhole and keeping it open with some unimaginable technology, would they not represent an evolutionary anomaly? They cannot have evolved from nonsentient precursors in such a hostile environment."

"Perhaps they didn't, Honored Professor." It was a distinctly un-Vulcan voice, full of enthusiasm and excitement despite its attempt to sound logical. Dax wasn't surprised to find that it belonged to the young human graduate student. "Perhaps they evolved in a more hospitable environment first, and only colonized the wormhole later."

"Highly unlikely," T'Kreng decreed.

Sisko's dark eyes gleamed with amusement. "As unlikely as humans first evolving on a temperate planet, and then going to live in deep space?" he inquired. "If another race only knew us from our space stations, perhaps they would consider *us* an evolutionary anomaly."

Judging by the Vulcan physicist's elegant wince, Dax thought she might agree with that. "Comparative cultures are not my specialty, Captain Sisko, quantum singularities are. I cannot conjure up the hypothetical development of a totally unknown form of life as blithely as my young human assistant can. However, I can state with confidence that whether or not these wormhole inhabitants exist, they would not be able to withstand or divert the amount of energy the Bajoran wormhole will absorb when it displaces the *Defiant*. If they could, logic dictates they would have done so during the initial propagation of this timeline." She set her sticks at a precise angle across her lacquered eating tray, and lifted her eyebrows at Sisko. "Have I answered your question?"

"Abundantly, Professor."

T'Kreng inclined her head in a minuscule nod. "Then I will leave you to enjoy the rest of your supper with your colleague. We should arrive at *Deep Space Nine* at 0450 hours tomorrow. Please make sure that your chief medical officer is prepared to off-load his cargo with maximum efficiency at that time. I do not wish to remain docked for more than one standard hour."

Sisko's own nod was barely more noticeable than the Vulcan physicist's. "I'll inform him of that."

Dax frowned, watching T'Kreng leave the room in a dignified rustle of silk robes. "I'm not sure Julian can get the symbiont unloaded that fast," she told Sisko in a quiet voice. "He won't want to disengage the stasis field until we're out of subspace."

Sisko gave her a gleam of teeth that was by no stretch of the imagination a smile. "No matter what the Honored Professor thinks, the authority to dock and undock at *Deep Space Nine* still rests with me. If my chief medical officer needs more time to off-load, he'll get it." He rubbed a hand across his strong-boned face and grimaced. "Talking to Vulcans gives me a headache. You mind if I leave you to finish eating alone, old man?"

Dax glanced down at her empty bowl. "What makes you think I'm not done already?" she demanded quizzically.

Sisko snorted. "Dax, I haven't seen you eat just one bowl of *chfera* stew since we signed the treaty with the Klingons." He rose and clapped a companionable hand on her shoulder. "Enjoy the rest of your supper."

She laughed and followed him as far as the single food replicator, standing in line with her empty bowl while two Vulcans waited for their raktajino cups to stop bubbling in the chamber. Someone else came to stand behind her, clearing her throat in a polite but distinctly human sound. Dax turned and smiled at T'Kreng's young graduate student.

"Doctoral thesis?" she asked companionably, nodding at the note padd the young woman had tucked under one arm.

"Why—why, yes." The human's cheeks turned a more rosy shade of pink. "That's why I wanted to introduce myself, although I guess you sort of know me already. I'm Heather Petersen, the Starfleet Academy student who's been helping you analyze the subspace time-distortion data you collected from the Bajoran wormhole last year. Um—you are Lieutenant Dax from *Deep Space Nine*, aren't you?"

"Of course." Dax's smile widened. "And *you* are the brilliant young physics student who finally explained why the wormhole opens with some inherent rotational energy. Did Professor T'Kreng ever allow you to publish that fourth-dimensional time-transit equation of yours?"

Petersen grinned back at her. "After the editors of *Subspace Physical Reviews* accepted it, she didn't have much choice. Thanks for the advice, Lieutenant."

"Any time." Dax pulled her steaming-hot bowl of *chfera* from the replicator, then waited while Petersen ordered Elasian cloud-apple pie à la mode. She headed back to the end of the table, where Sisko and T'Kreng's absence had left a buffer of space between them and the rest of the *Sreba*'s crew. "So, how did you manage to get aboard a deep-space mission like this, Heather? Isn't Starfleet Academy still in session?"

Petersen nodded. "This is my doctoral internship semester, so I'm not actually in any classes." She lowered her voice to a more discreet murmur. "And I think Starfleet wanted at least one person on board with military security clearance, even if it was just a senior cadet like me."

Dax raised her eyebrows, knowing what a mark of trust that was. There must be more to this quiet young scientist than her gentle face and calm voice implied. "You're the only commissioned officer on board? Who's captaining the ship?"

"T'Kreng," Petersen informed her. "She used to be a Starfleet captain, in command of a small science survey ship, before she resigned to get her second doctorate and teach."

"No wonder Admiral Hayman called her in." Dax scraped up the last of her stew, mulling that over. "How much has T'Kreng told the crew about this mission, Heather?"

The young woman gave her an intent look across their empty plates. "Just that there's a high probability of losing the Bajoran wormhole to an accident in the next few weeks. She says she wants to do a high-precision chronodynamic analysis to pinpoint the time and place where it happens." Petersen paused, a slight frown creasing her forehead. "I think there must be some element of time travel involved in the problem somehow, though, because half the scientists she brought along on this trip are time specialists like me, not just wormhole physicists. Do you know if that's true, Lieutenant?"

Jadzia deliberated with her symbiont for a moment, weighing their previous experience with Petersen's intelligence and good judgment against her youth and the gravity of the situation they faced. "Yes," she said at last, and tugged the science student away from the table before she could ask more. "I almost forgot that I promised to bring dinner to my friend Julian tonight. Can you help me carry it to his cabin?"

"Of course." Petersen looked mildly surprised at the sudden change in subject, but made no protest as Dax ordered up a plate of lamb, lentils, and couscous for Bashir's dinner, then handed her a cup of hot raktajino and two orders of cloud-apple pie. "Your friend must like dessert."

"Actually, he doesn't." Dax balanced the warm plate of couscous in one hand and grabbed two forks in the other. "But I do, and it smelled good when you got it."

Petersen chuckled and followed her out into the hall, not speaking again until the chatter of the dining hall had faded behind the echo of their footsteps. "So, Lieutenant. Just how confidential is what you're about to tell me?"

Dax gave her an amused look. "Was I that obvious? Well, let's just say that you're going to be in the company of admirals once you know it."

That got her a grave look. "Then should you be telling me?"

"I need input," Dax replied just as seriously. "Preferably from a scientist a little more knowledgeable about quantum time paradoxes than I am. I was going to ask your thesis advisor, until I saw how unsympathetic she was to new ideas back there."

Petersen snorted with laughter. "T'Kreng can be very sympathetic to new ideas, Lieutenant Dax. They just have to be her own."

Dax paused in front of Bashir's cabin door, juggling plate and forks to press the access panel. "Which is exactly why I'd rather talk to you about what I've been thinking. As far

L. A. GRAF

as I know, no one's ever tested this hypothesis before." She heard the doctor's muffled acknowledgment through the speaker, and stepped back as the door slid open. "Of course, that may be because no one ever had the kind of test subjects I do."

Bashir looked up from a screen covered with his ancient medical notes. He'd obviously been deeply immersed in them, since he looked only vaguely puzzled by the sight of Heather Petersen and Dax in his doorway. "Did you want something, Jadzia?"

She made an exasperated noise and skirted a pile of spare tubing to wave the plate of couscous under his nose. "I want you to eat supper, that's what I want. And to introduce you to a friend of mine." Dax glanced back at Petersen, who had come just far enough into the room to examine its odd array of equipment with thoughtful eyes. "Heather, this is Julian Bashir, chief medical officer of *Deep Space Nine*. Julian, this is Heather Petersen. It's all right, she's a research colleague of mine from Starfleet Academy."

The doctor raised his eyebrows, ignoring the plate she'd deliberately set down in front of his screen. "Right now, I wouldn't care if she was a member of the Obsidian Order, if that *raktajino* she's holding is for me."

"Of course it's for you. You know I don't like mine flavored with hazelnut." Dax handed him the steaming cup and one of the dessert plates, then snagged the other for herself. The cloud-apple pie tasted even better than it had smelled. "Heather's doing her doctoral thesis on the time-distortion effects of singularities," she said through a mouthful of pie. "I brought her in for a consultation."

Bashir looked puzzled again. "A medical consultation?"

"No, a quantum-chronodynamics consultation. Eat." She left him poking tiredly at a chunk of lamb, and tugged Petersen across to the brine tank, where the ancient symbiont lay wrapped in the complete silence of stasis once again. "You're familiar with the theory of ansible technology, Heather?"

Petersen looked mildly surprised. "The idea that two twinned quantum particles will resonate in eternal synchronicity with each other, no matter how far you separate them in space? Of course. It's the basis for all our

102

interstellar-communications relays. Why?" She glanced down at the unmoving symbiont below them. "And what does it have to do with this other Trill symbiont?"

"I've been thinking," Dax said slowly, "that ansible technology might work in time as well as in space. Has anyone ever suggested that?"

Petersen shrugged. "I've seen some casual discussions of it on the science nets. But in practice, it would be impossible to test. We can establish true synchronicity between two particles separated in space, but once we separate them in time, there's no way to know if their resonance is truly synchronous."

"But if we were dealing with sentient beings instead of quantum particles—" Dax could sense Bashir's sudden focus on her from the silence behind her back. "—we could test for an ansible linkage just from shared thoughts. Couldn't we?"

Petersen frowned. "But that would require two sentient beings that were absolute twins of each other. Even cloning processes would never work precisely enough to—" She broke off, her startled gaze dropping to the brine tank below them. "Unless this is—Lieutenant, are you saying this Trill symbiont is *you?*"

"Yes," Dax said calmly. "My exact internal self, particle for particle, but separated from me by five thousand years of time."

Like racing shadows, quick realization flickered in the human scientist's eyes. "The accident with the Bajoran wormhole—it threw you back that far? And somehow your symbiont managed to survive until now even though your host body couldn't?"

"Yes." She dropped a hand to the lid of the brine tank, feeling the blend of Jadzia's faint horror and Dax's amused affection that was starting to become familiar. "I'm here, and I'm there. The question is, am I now an ansible?"

Petersen chewed on her lower lip, looking intently thoughtful. "There's no theoretical reason why you couldn't be," she replied after a long moment. "Of course, you wouldn't notice any effects of it with—with your twinned self in stasis and unable to resonate. We'd need both of you awake and thinking in order to test for resonance synchronicity."

Dax glanced back at Bashir, and found him watching her with an odd mixture of awe and disbelief in his pale brown eyes. She guessed what he must be thinking and smiled. "I might not like the idea of living in a brine tank for five millennia, Julian, but that's no reason not to take advantage of the fact that I did it. And this is a scientific opportunity no one else in the galaxy has ever had. Can we bring the symbiont out of stasis?"

The doctor shook himself, as if he were throwing off some waking dream. "No, you may not," he declared firmly. "Jadzia, you may be a brilliant scientist, but you're not being realistic. I'm not sure the symbiont's going to survive the stress of this voyage as it is. Putting it through some kind of scientific experiment now would be the worst possible thing we could do."

Dax frowned. "But we won't be able to run the tests once we get to *Deep Space Nine,* Julian. Captain Sisko wants me to stay on the *Sreba* with him. And if we succeed in keeping the wormhole safe—" She broke off, glancing down at the brine tank with a slight frown. "—this one of me will disappear forever."

Bashir sighed and dropped his fork into his half-eaten food. "How long will these tests of yours take?"

Dax exchanged glances with Heather Petersen. "About an hour, minimum?" she asked, and the young physicist nodded. "Does that mean you'll let us run them now?"

"No, but it means I'll let you run them as soon as I get the symbiont out of stasis and stabilized, before you leave *Deep Space Nine* for the wormhole." He frowned at their glum expressions. "What's wrong with that?"

Dax snorted. "According to the patron saint of singularities, we're only going to get an hour of turnaround time once we dock. Of course," she added thoughtfully, "Benjamin did say that he would make sure you got as long as you needed to off-load the symbiont."

A ghost of Bashir's usual mischievous smile lit his tired face. "Then you just leave everything to me. If I can't manage to transfer this equipment slowly enough to give you two time for your experiment, then I'll just ask O'Brien to help me. That will make it take at least twice as long."

Dax chuckled appreciatively, but Heather Petersen gave them both a puzzled look. "Why will it take longer with someone else helping?" she asked.

"Because the person helping will be our chief engineer," Dax explained. "And he won't be able to look at this equipment, much less move it—"

"—without telling me all the ways I could have put it together better," Bashir finished for her.

Ragged metal tongues curled outward along the edges of the breach, yawning open to the stars like teeth in a roaring mouth. Frost dusted the tips, laid there by the lick of escaping gases some unknown number of hours ago. *Less than ten,* Kira reminded herself as she stroked one gloved hand around the curve of the long rip. They hadn't startled up the militia cell ten hours ago, or stumbled onto the first blown-open vessel. Initially pleased with herself for noticing the derelict on Odo's sensors and stopping to offer assistance, Kira had ceased to feel any satisfaction five minutes into their futile search for survivors. By this, the third drifting, lifeless shell, the only thing inside her was a numb, gnawing anger.

A ripple of movement reflected against the curve of her environmental suit's faceplate. Turning, glad to put her back to the unwelcome expanse of vacuum, she trod carefully across the buckled deck to meet the glossy mass that pooled at the base of one doorframe. It was an old ship, not well built even in its younger days; the force of whatever had blasted the long rip across its belly had blown most of the inner bulkheads askew, sucking out the air they should have protected, and the fragile life within. It had been a huge price to pay just for the convenience of cracks wide enough for Odo to slip through.

The constable swirled up to Kira's height, congealing into himself with his face already set into a waxen frown. Kira envied him his ability to move about in vacuum without a suit, but not the unexpected responsibilities that sometimes came along with it. She still felt guilty for sending him alone to check out the lower decks. *You never have a hardsuit around when you need one.* And no matter how much she griped to O'Brien, she did understand what a danger first-stage radiation could be.

She waited for Odo to press his hand against her faceplate, spreading it into a translucent tympanum, before asking, "Anything?"

"Only what we found before." The vibration of his hand against her faceplate translated only the ghost of his voice to her, a thin, blurry echo that seemed to come from everywhere and nowhere at once. "The reaction mass is gone, and the engine room is completely gutted." All three ships had been old, primitive sublight creepers, getting by with the cheapest fusion mass drivers that private shipmasters could legally buy. "Whoever they are, they're in a hurry— this fusion pile was cut out with the same lack of finesse as all the others. I'm amazed the thieves themselves survived."

Kira nodded, winding her hands into frustrated fists. "No sign of the crew?"

Odo shook his head even as his ghost voice whispered, "Not even bodies. I suspect the pirates either ejected the remains, or weren't particularly careful when they breached the ship and blew the crew out into space."

They weren't taking time to loot the ships of their ore, much less run down individual crew members just to pitch them out the locks. Still, scans of the other two wrecks had found no evidence of organic remnants within a hundred thousand kilometers. Could a ship really decompress with enough force to tumble humanoid bodies so very far away? "How can Bajorans do this to each other?"

Odo cocked his head—curious or reproving, Kira couldn't tell which. "Major, we have no proof the militia was even involved." Ah—pragmatic. She should have guessed.

"Who else could it have been?" She resisted an urge to turn away and pace in frustration, realizing at the last moment that it would break her contact with the changeling and leave him unable to hear her voice. "They were the only ones headed out this way—we were following right behind them!"

"Precisely." Even this dim version of his voice managed to catch her attention with its hard certainty. "Why would they take the time to accost these ships, much less steal their fusion drives?"

"To slow us down. They knew we'd have to stop and make sure there were no survivors."

The snort that rattled against her faceplate sounded more like a flat buzzing. "If I were escaping with an illegal plasma device, I wouldn't take that for granted," Odo said. "Besides, they would have made themselves infinitely easier to track. Any ship carrying three fusion reaction masses will be detectable up to half a light-year away."

Kira lifted her head inside the helmet, startled. "Odo, we're not following them."

He answered with a corresponding jerk of his chin. "But, Major—"

"We've got a runabout!" she blurted, grabbing him by the shoulders as though she could shake him into understanding. "They've got a plasma warhead and enough plutonium to ignite a small sun! Have you ever seen what's left after you detonate a thermonuclear bomb?"

The question seemed to strike him as meaningless. "I've seen holofilms," he admitted with just the faintest of frowns.

Kira nodded, and slowly removed her hands from his arms. "Well, I've seen real life." She turned away from him just enough to glimpse the breach around the sweep of her helmet, and felt him step up close behind her to follow her gaze even though she couldn't hear his movement. "Just three years before the Occupation ended." She walked carefully through the tangle of her memories, concentrating hard on keeping the image of the placid stars foremost in her mind. "Three years before it was all over, the Pak Dorren resistance cell raided an ancient plutonium mine in Veska Province. They wanted to smuggle a shielded nuclear bomb up to Terek Nor, because they thought it would cripple the Cardassians to lose their prefect *and* their base of operations all in one glorious starburst." A bitter smile twisted her lips. "And Pak wanted to be the one whose name we sang." She shook away the memory of her first and only meeting of Pak Dorren, as one of Shakaar's attendant bodyguards when the two Resistance legends came together to argue about Pak's crazy plan. Hateful now even more than then of Pak's smug laughter and conceited grin, Kira made the mistake of closing her eyes. "Instead of winning Bajor her freedom, they mishandled the payload before they even finished constructing the bomb. The blast took out twenty kilometers of countryside when it set off the rest of the mine. That whole valley is still just one big sheet of black glass." *And blistered bedrock, and twisted bodies, and burning stone—!* She jerked her eyes open on a silent gasp. The stars, each one its own sea of nuclear fire, provided little comfort.

If Odo recognized her pain, he didn't seem able to share in it. "The runabouts can withstand a direct hit by a photon torpedo. Even three thermonuclear devices couldn't get past our screens."

"If we meet up with them in space," Kira allowed. "If they go to ground on a colony, or even one of their own moonbases, being the last runabout standing wouldn't exactly make me feel like a winner." She reached up to close her hand around his elongated wrist. "No, we're going back to the station and warning Bajor. I'm not going to let what happened at Veska happen anywhere else." And she peeled him off her faceplate before he could argue with her further.

She let Odo thread himself through her equipment belt before stepping through the breach to the outside. He might be able to hold himself to a gravityless deck within the shelter of a ship's hard walls, but Kira despaired to think about how well he could hang on under a barrage of solar wind and micrometeorites. Clamping her booted feet to the ship's fragile outer skin, she gave herself a moment to find a new sense of "down" beneath this topless sky before looking across the bow of the freighter to where *Rio Grande* waited. Kira had wanted to land right on the nose of the derelict once she found out that the residual radiation prevented a direct transport, but both Odo and the ship's computer had convinced her that the runabout could match the freighter's tumble closely enough to make a short, suited jump reasonably safe. That argument seemed particularly hollow now as three points of blue-white light picked themselves out of the confusion of stars by their brightness and their precise triangular spacing.

Tapping Odo with the side of her hand, Kira waited for

him to reach a pseudopod up to her faceplate before remarking, "I suppose it's too much to hope those are Starfleet ships that just happened to be in the area."

He formed a partial face at what seemed an uncomfortable angle to the rest of his mass, and studied the three nonstars with customary blandness. "Not coming from the direction of the Badlands."

"Hang on." Breaches littered the surface of the freighter like fissures. On the way out from the runabout, Kira had taken the time to navigate carefully around each of the jagged splits for fear of tearing her suit or slicing a bootheel on the edges. Now she kept her strides long and steady, and let momentum carry them over the chasms with a graceful slowness that was still faster than the irregular detours. Even so, it seemed to take forever to reach *Rio Grande*'s waiting hatch and swing into the ship's comforting gravity.

She tore off her gloves the instant the airlock gauge blinked green, throwing them to the floor when the hatch slid open and attacking her helmet stays on the run to the console. "Computer! Identification on ships approaching on—" She glanced aside at the sensor display as she threw herself into the pilot's seat. "—heading three one two one mark seven."

"Working." Lights came up around them like campfires on a summer night, and Odo was only just pouring free of Kira's belt when the system announced, "One Kronos-class dogfighter, registry unknown. One Corsair-class cruiser, registry unknown. One Vinca-class tow barge, registry unknown."

Odo settled into his seat and reached immediately for his panels. "That doesn't sound like a very official gathering."

"Fifteen thousand kilometers," the computer reported, "and closing at warp factor seven."

Kira canceled the autopilot and seized back flight control. "Let's not stick around to see who they're representing."

An ore carrier, no matter how large, had little enough gravitational field, even when fully crewed and loaded down with water and oxygen. Still, leaping into warp too close to anything larger than you were always ran the risk of attenuating your mass across distances stretching into the infinite, and while that was not something Kira had ever

seen or even really heard described, it was something she
endeavored to avoid whenever given the opportunity. She
lifted *Rio Grande* up over the subjective "top" of the
freighter—for no reason other than she felt safer, more in
control with the greater mass underneath the runabout's
belly instead of looming over her head.

When she felt the first jolt, she thought with a flush of self-
irritation that she'd misjudged the distances and clipped an
engine nacelle on the freighter's hide. Then the second
impact slammed them. With all settings at full-go, the *Rio
Grande*'s engine readings went redline as she wrenched to a
complete stop.

CHAPTER
8

THE LAST THING Benjamin Sisko remembered before toppling into sleep on board the *Sreba* had been asking his room computer unit to wake him when they reached the outer fringes of the Bajoran system. He'd expected the usual polite computer-generated voice, but what dragged him out of uneasy dreams a few hours later was the repeated chime of a two-toned bell. Sisko rubbed his eyes, wondering why an advanced Vulcan science ship would have such an old-fashioned wake-up system. It didn't even turn off when he sat up.

"I'm awake," he growled at the faint ripple of lights that marked the room computer. "Turn that alarm off."

Instead of the instant response he expected, he got a long pause full of continued ringing. "Passengers do not have the authority to issue that command," the computer said at last, in prim Vulcan accents.

"What?" Sisko scrambled out of bed and the room lights rose in response, letting him see the time on the monitor's small display screen. Zero-three-hundred hours—a full hour and a half before T'Kreng's estimated arrival time at *Deep Space Nine.* His sleep-fogged brain finally woke up enough to notice that the doubled tone he heard was the muffled outside echo of the bell still ringing in his cabin.

"What kind of ship alarm is that?" he demanded, diving into his uniform with more haste than care.

"Captain T'Kreng has called an all-hands science alert," the computer informed him. "Passengers are not required to respond."

Sisko snorted. "Well, this one's going to respond whether she wants him to or not." He stamped on his boots and headed for the door. To his relief, it opened for him. Whatever kind of situation produced a "science alert," it evidently didn't involve keeping the passengers locked in for their own safety.

He met Dax out in the corridor, looking sleepy and curious but not particularly alarmed. Her long hair was still wrapped in a sleeping-braid around her head, exposing more of the freckles on her neck than usually showed above her uniform collar. "What's the science alert for?" she asked him, her words stretched around a yawn.

"Exactly what I'm going to find out." He strode down the hall to the *Sreba*'s single turbolift, with his science officer at his heels. A whistle of motion took them to the bridge and into the silent intensity of a Vulcan crew at alert. A quick glance showed Sisko that the most active stations were those monitoring the multitude of long-range sensors that this science vessel carried instead of weapons. Neither the *Sreba*'s shields nor her navigation panels showed signs of hostile activity. He felt his adrenaline-kicked tension ease a little.

"Captain Sisko." T'Kreng glanced up from the most crowded of the sensor stations, her pale eyes glittering with single-minded intensity. "Have your science officer contact *Deep Space Nine* on a priority channel immediately."

It had been his own first instinct, but the Vulcan's arrogant assumption of command irked him. Sisko fought off an irrational urge to disobey her, reminding himself that he was a passenger aboard her ship, and instead sent Dax over to the empty communications console with a silent nod. "You haven't been able to raise the station on a normal subspace channel?" he demanded.

Only the continuing peal of the science alarm answered him. T'Kreng's attention had been sucked back to the sensor screen in front of her, intent on the fire-blue parabolas intersecting and expanding across the screen. It was left to his own science officer to say quietly from behind him,

"There's too much subspace interference coming from the wormhole, Benjamin. I'm having trouble getting even a Starfleet priority channel punched through it."

"From the wormhole?" Sisko let his exasperation lash out in a question so fierce it lifted heads around the bridge. "What the *hell* is going on here?"

T'Kreng gave him a Vulcan frown as delicate and sharp as a paper cut. "A few minutes ago, we began reading an unusual number of subspace oscillations coming from the Bajoran wormhole. It appears to be opening and closing at a rate of—" She glanced down at the sensor screen. "—once every ten seconds."

Sisko felt something twist inside his gut. In all the time he'd commanded *Deep Space Nine*, he'd never seen the wormhole act that rapidly. He glanced at his science officer and saw the same blend of disbelief and foreboding on her quiet face.

"Dax, can that be right?" he asked bluntly.

She was watching the long-range scanner output with nearly the same intensity as T'Kreng. "It could be an artifact of subspace symmetry and our own warp speed," she said after a moment. "Under certain conditions, that might create a quantum reflection, doubling or even quadrupling the frequency of the real signal. Did you check for that?"

Her question startled Sisko, until he realized it wasn't directed at him but at the solitary human on the *Sreba*'s crew, seated at the science station beside her. The young woman nodded without taking her eyes from her own equation-filled screen.

"Yes, sir. We also tested for sensor-ghost errors and for any signs of artificial generation of the signal. All results came out negative. It's a real-time subspace oscillation, Lieutenant, and it's really coming from the wormhole."

"But what does it mean?" Sisko demanded, hoping the young human physicist would answer him even if T'Kreng chose not to. To his surprise, it was the Vulcan who replied, in the crisp pedantic tones of an academy professor. She could ignore practical questions, Sisko thought wryly, but she couldn't pass up an opportunity to lecture him about her specialty.

"One possible hypothesis, Captain, is that we are seeing the reverberation of a massive disturbance in the singularity matrix. The simplest and most elegant interpretation would suggest that it was the same disturbance which threw your ship back in time, although that cannot be proven without a closer scan."

Sisko scrubbed at his face. "Then the wormhole's already been destroyed, without us being in it? But if that's true, why hasn't—" He snapped his teeth shut on the rest of that sentence, but threw a baffled look at Dax. If the ancient symbiont had disappeared along with its timeline, Julian Bashir would surely have let them know by now.

T'Kreng clicked her teeth in a distinctly Vulcan sound, somewhere between impatience and stoic resignation. "You are thinking about this too linearly, Captain Sisko. Singularities like the Bajoran wormhole deform time just as much as they deform space and gravity. Any change in their internal matrix will ripple through the fabric of space-time in *all* directions." She tapped one slender finger against the parabolas twining across her monitor screen. "This reverberation we are seeing—if it is indeed a reverberation—represents the upstream echo of the disturbance in the wormhole."

"Upstream echo?" Sisko repeated, frowning. Wormhole physics always gave him the same queasy feeling that stepping into microgravity did. "You mean we're seeing an aftereffect from something that hasn't happened yet?"

"A crude description, but essentially correct." The Vulcan physicist steepled her fingers together meditatively. "Of course, that is simply one hypothesis. There is another, also theoretically valid although much less elegant. Unfortunately, until we can make contact with your station, we cannot determine which of the two is correct."

"What's the second possibility?" he demanded.

T'Kreng moved her fingers in a tiny circle, which somehow managed to convey the sense of a shrug. "That these oscillations are merely the result of extremely heavy wormhole usage. A multitude of ships, passing through the singularity at ten-second intervals, would generate an identical subspace oscillation."

"Impossible," Sisko said shortly. "It takes at least fifteen seconds for the subspace ripples of a wormhole passage to dissipate. Sending a second ship through any sooner than that is too dangerous to do."

"Under normal conditions," his science officer reminded him from behind.

T'Kreng raised one slim Vulcan eyebrow. "Then perhaps conditions are no longer normal."

Sisko scowled and took two long strides across the small bridge to join Dax at the communications station. "Still no luck getting through to *Deep Space Nine?*"

She shook her head. "I could punch a contact through if I had the *Defiant*'s comm—or if the station's narrow-band receiver were tuned to our transmission—but *Sreba*'s comm just doesn't have enough power to boost our signal-to-noise ratio. I don't think we'll get through until we're within normal hailing range."

"And by then it may be too late."

"If T'Kreng's second hypothesis is the correct one, you mean?" The Trill's blue-gray eyes reflected back his frown. "I don't think even an emergency evacuation to the Gamma Quadrant would risk running the wormhole every ten seconds, Benjamin."

"I'm not worried about an emergency evacuation," he said. "I'm worried about an invasion."

"They're holding us!"

"Magnitude-four tractor beam." Odo confirmed what Kira had already guessed with a quick look at his sensors. "Originating from the Vinca-class tow barge."

Kira growled under her breath. "Of course . . ." She'd been on a Vinca for a year and a half when the Cardassians still used the clumsy ships to tractor salvaged vessels to the maintenance yards. Then someone had figured out that it was cheaper just to vaporize the wreckage and have a ramscoop sweep through the cloud and strain out the raw materials. They could usually salvage enough gold and rare isotopes to fund the building of a new ship and still have cash left over. It had been the scrap yard for the Vincas themselves then—all the ones that hadn't been sold black-market to anyone wanting enough tow power to yank an ore freighter to a standstill.

"It's used to hauling derelicts," Kira said aloud as she diverted shield power into the drive core. "Let's see how it holds up to a real engine."

She pushed the impulse engines until the overrides kicked in and forced a cutback of power, then added maneuvering thrusters to the mix in the hopes that the little bit of extra would snap them out of the Vinca's grasp. Something at the back of the runabout groaned loudly, and Kira felt the panel start to shiver under her hands.

Odo, watching her struggle with her controls, grunted once. "It holds up fairly well, apparently."

Sarcasm from an ill-tempered changeling was the last thing she needed right now. "Can you get the station on subspace?" Kira asked as she knocked everything back down to idle.

He shook his head, running quickly through several attempts while he answered. "They're jamming us." He paused and glanced aside at Kira. "But I am picking up a hail from the Kronos."

"At least they're willing to talk to us before they blow us up." She nodded for him to put the call on the main viewscreen, and sat back in her seat so that her tension and frustration might not show so plainly to their captors. "This is Major Kira Nerys of *Deep Space Nine.* You'd better have a real good reason for hijacking a station runabout, because Starfleet tends to take exception to losing its equipment."

The older Bajoran woman who appeared on the viewscreen smiled with a bitter dryness that matched her sparse lines and weathered angles. "Then Starfleet should exercise more discretion about what it does to other people's ships."

Kira found herself drawn to the woman's simple earring, and had to force her eyes away from whatever half-memory it awoke to scowl at the owner. "What are you talking about?"

"We discovered this ore transport and three others like it while patrolling on official business," Odo explained. Leave it to the constable to understand a paranoid's ravings. "We had nothing to do with whatever happened here."

The woman snorted, and her almost-familiar earring jangled. "So you say."

Her easy dismissal of the truth burned in Kira's stomach.

"Starfleet's here to help protect Bajor. Why would anyone at the station attack Bajoran vessels?"

"Because you can't protect Bajor without something to protect against. If we're not kept afraid and helpless, we might look up and notice that the Occupation never ended."

"That's not true!" Kira leaned forward over her panel, wishing this woman were more than just a projection so she could grab her and shake her. "If you'd ever worked with Starfleet, and seen how they treat each other, you'd know that it's not true."

The incredible bitterness etched into the woman's face ran deeper than any brief run-ins with the Federation, deeper than anything Kira had personally known, but was still somehow familiar in its flavor. "I know that they may wear prettier uniforms," this older, harder version of herself snarled, "and they may talk with prettier words. But they still lord over us in their Cardassian-built station, too far away to talk to or touch, and they control everything we do." She spat off to one side with a hatred so dry it left only harsh air. "Slavery is slavery, no matter how attractive the masters."

It was the phrase—the phrase, and the gesture. *Slavery is slavery,* a long-ago voice had declared with the same lack of interest other people used to talk about the weather. And Kira remembered being disgusted at the long streams of *chaat* juice Pak Dorren could land with such accuracy even a full meter away.

She'd been younger then, and Pak had been someone she was supposed to respect. And she hadn't. She still didn't. "Does terrorizing your own people with bombs and hijackings make you any better?"

The terrorist's pale eyes glittered, and she smiled a smile still faintly off-color from years of chewing *chaat.* "You know who I am."

Kira nodded somberly. "I thought you were dead."

"I almost was." And the honest grief in Pak's voice startled Kira into feeling a pang of sympathy. "I should have been. I never should have left children to finish something just because I thought it would be easy. I should have known that what came so naturally to me wasn't obvious to everyone." She refocused her eyes with obvious effort, fixing on Kira's face. "I still have nightmares about what I did to Veska Province. It's my greatest regret."

Kira refused to be moved by Pak's contrition. "You don't seem to learn from your mistakes."

The terrorist shrugged with a kind of easy acceptance of herself. "I'm more hands-on now," she explained. As if they were businessfolk, discussing how to maximize their profits. "From start to finish, I supervise every bomb we make. We don't have accidents anymore."

"Now," Odo interjected, "you only kill people on purpose."

Pak smiled again. "Funny you should mention that."

Kira hadn't consciously been waiting for any particular cue from Pak; she just reacted with an instinctive speed that even she didn't fully understand. She launched two torpedoes aft with a single swipe of her hand, then lunged for the helm controls as both missiles impacted against the Vinca's forward shields. *Rio Grande* was just enough below the tow barge's ecliptic that the blast rocked the bigger ship up and back; Kira slammed *Rio Grande* straight downward as powerfully as her engines would fire. If there was one thing she'd learned in a year and a half on a Vinca's crew, it was that tractor beams were damned near unbreakable under direct force, but surprisingly fragile when stressed on the sheer.

The runabout hesitated, a hill rover caught in the mud, then lunged forward so violently that Kira slammed back in her seat hard enough to bruise her neck on the rim of her environmental suit. She flailed for the controls that had been under her hands only a moment ago, caught the edge of the panel, dragged herself forward, and arced the runabout down and behind the ruined freighter without taking the time to verify coordinates. She heard the resounding crash of *Rio Grande*'s tail skipping across the derelict's surface just as one of the ships behind them carved away a section of the ore carrier's hull with a sweep of phaser fire. A roiling cloud of glowing vapor washed across the runabout's path. Kira struggled to level *Rio Grande* as they scraped off the aft side and into clear space, leaping them into full warp. The freighter's massive presence at her back didn't even enter into the equation—this was just one of those times where there were too many odds to play, and she had to pick which one to go for.

They were five seconds into flight before Kira dared to risk a look at her companion to see if they were both still there. She found Odo staring pensively out the front screen, an expression of peevish consideration on his smooth face.

"Still think this is something we can handle on our own?" Kira asked.

"We were following nine fugitives in an overloaded Orion transport when I made that suggestion," Odo pointed out, with more than just a little impatience in his tone. "Given recent developments, I think a return to the station might be in order."

Kira couldn't quite smother her smile. "I'm glad you agree." She laid in a course for the station, then let the runabout steer itself while she watched the cluster of sensor blips behind them recede, and blink, and finally vanish. "We can't let them go on like this," she said. The emptiness where Pak's trio of ships used to be fueled her with an idea she thought she should have had before this. "I don't care what sort of patriot Pak Dorren thinks she is, I'm not going to let her blow apart everything Bajor has worked for." She opened a subspace channel with a definitive flick of her thumb. *"Rio Grande* to DS9. Chief, prep the *Defiant* to leave the station. . . ."

"Captain Sisko?"

Sisko glanced up from drumming impatient fingers on the *Sreba*'s silent communications panel. Even at the top warp speed he'd insisted on, they were still several light-years out of *Deep Space Nine*'s normal hailing range. The wait chafed Sisko's tenuous hold on his temper, each minute dragging with it a different nightmare vision of his station being blasted by waves of invading Furies. Dax had sensed his seething impatience and wisely left him alone, moving over to join her younger human colleague at the adjacent science station. It was the Academy graduate student's voice hailing him now, softly enough not to catch the attention of T'Kreng and the other Vulcan scientists clustered around the main long-range scanner.

"What?" Tension made his voice sharper than he'd intended, and Sisko made an effort to soften it. "I'm sorry, Ensign, I don't remember your name—"

"It's Petersen, sir. I thought you might want to look at this."

"This" was the solitary equation now occupying her screen, full of imaginary numbers and integral signs, but surprisingly short compared with the complex calculations that had been crawling across the screen a few moments before. Sisko glanced at it briefly, then lifted an eyebrow at his science officer.

"Well, what does it mean?"

"No invasion," Dax said succinctly.

He scowled in disbelief. "How can you tell that from here?"

"We applied a moving-detector deconvolution program to get better resolution on the source frequency curve," Petersen said.

Sisko snorted. "Try that again, Ensign. This time in English."

Her apple cheeks turned a rosier shade of pink. "Sorry, sir. Lieutenant Dax and I have been able to find out exactly how fast the wormhole has been opening and closing, by correcting for our own warp speed." She toggled something on her board and the equation rippled off the monitor screen, replaced a moment later by an ice-white curve and a matching scatter of multicolored dots. "There's the actual data and our best-fit curve. It approximates a constant pattern of ten-second intervals, just as T'Kreng said, but the actual pattern is much more complex."

"So?"

Dax leaned forward, tracing the line with one confident finger. "What this shows, Benjamin, is that the wormhole is opening and closing in repeating octets, each event separated by precise inverse-logarithmic intervals of time. Even if an invading fleet tried to maintain a complicated pattern like that for some reason—"

"—the slop of individual ship passage times through the wormhole would destroy it," Sisko finished for her. The cold knot of tension in his gut dissolved a little. "So we really are seeing aftereffects of the wormhole throwing us back in time?"

"We do not yet have sufficient data to reach that conclusion," said T'Kreng's thin-edged voice from behind him. Sisko swung around to meet a crystalline glare, distributed with Vulcan impartiality to all of them. "I would appreciate it, Lieutenant Dax, if you would refrain from making unsupported hypotheses aboard my ship. Ensign Petersen, you know you are not supposed to run full-scale data reductions on the main computer without my direct authorization. And Captain Sisko—" She stepped back with a tiny gesture of two fingers toward the communications panel. "—if you had been carrying out the task for which I believe you volunteered, you would have noticed that someone is trying to hail us."

Sisko cursed and dove for the adjacent communications station. Just once, he thought fiercely, why couldn't this pedantic Vulcan professor give him information in order of its importance rather than its relevance to her own academic concerns?

Two quick focusing scans, and he had the hailing signal locked in, throwing it onto the main screen without bothering to ask permission from T'Kreng. It wasn't until the familiar contours of *Deep Space Nine*'s operations center appeared across the bridge, and he felt the hard knot of ice in his stomach finally melt, that Sisko realized how much he'd feared his station's complete destruction.

Onscreen, Ops seemed unusually noisy, as though many voices were talking just outside the viewing range. Without even looking up from his workstation, a stocky figure in coffee-stained engineering coveralls said, "Approaching Vulcan ship, please be aware that all traffic through the wormhole—"

"Chief O'Brien, it's Sisko."

"Captain!" The engineer swung toward them, a look of quick relief chasing the scowl off his blunt face. "Thank God you're back, sir. I've been trying to get a priority hail through to you by way of Starfleet headquarters, but there's too much quantum interference coming from the wormhole."

"I know." Sisko's internal time clock, calibrated by years

of shipboard service, told him this should be the daylight shift back at the station. "Where's Major Kira?"

O'Brien scrubbed a hand across his face, looking both tired and tense. "She and Odo are out chasing Bajoran paramilitary forces. They've been gone since yesterday night."

Sisko felt his gut clench tight. "Did they take the *Defiant?*"

The engineer shook his head. "No, there wasn't time to get it crewed before they left. The paramilitary cell aboard the station started a firefight when they were discovered, and the major went straight from there to a runabout to follow them. Her latest transmission came from just outside the Bajoran solar system."

The most annoying thing about Bajor's fledgling terrorists, Sisko decided, was their ability to make trouble at exactly the times when you wanted to pay them the least attention. "So you've been in Ops all day? How much traffic has there been through the wormhole?"

"None, sir." The tired lines around O'Brien's eyes creased deeper. "I revoked everyone's departure permits three hours ago, when the wormhole started opening and closing for no reason. Without Lieutenant Dax here, I didn't want to take any chances." He gave Sisko a brief, mirthless smile. "There's a bunch of Ferengi and Orion merchants standing outside Ops right now, screaming about me having exceeded my authority. I expect you can hear them."

Sisko grunted. "Patch me into a stationwide audio loop," he ordered, and waited for O'Brien's confirming nod. "This is Captain Benjamin Sisko, commander of *Deep Space Nine,* declaring a Class Five Sector Emergency. On Starfleet Command authority, all departure permits for the Gamma Quadrant are canceled indefinitely. All visiting crews who have not left the station within three standard hours will be confined to their vessels. Anyone attempting to pass through the wormhole will be stopped or destroyed by station phasers." He nodded at O'Brien to cut the audio echo, then said into the ensuing quiet, "Did that chase them out of Ops, Chief?"

"Like Cardassian voles who just got a whiff of fumigant,"

O'Brien confirmed. "And with any luck, you'll be back here before Quark shows up to complain about his lost profits."

Sisko's mouth twisted wryly. "I expect so. We should be docking in—" He glanced over at Dax, who'd taken over the navigation panel from a disgruntled-looking Vulcan scientist.

"—approximately ten minutes," she finished.

"Good. We've got docking space available on pylon two. O'Brien out." The communications channel closed in a small sizzle of static. When Sisko turned back, it was to find T'Kreng giving him a steely look across her bridge. She had resumed her captain's chair, sweeping her slim fingers back and forth across its small control panel as if to reassure herself she was still in command here.

"I trust you are not including the *Sreba* in your prohibition on travel through the wormhole, Captain," she said flatly.

Sisko met her colorless glare with one he hoped looked just as implacable. "Yes, I am. My chief engineer is right— with the wormhole behaving like this, it's too dangerous to let any ship through. And if I allow you in there, every Orion and Ferengi ship onstation is going to try and go right in after you. Your singularity survey will have to wait, Professor."

Nothing moved on T'Kreng's face, but all its lines and angles took on a severe, glass-sharp look. "If I wait, there will be nothing left of the wormhole to survey. Our only chance of preventing the time avulsion is to locate the exact time and place when it starts."

This time, Sisko didn't have to force a glare. If there was one thing that exasperated him about scientists, it was their single-minded belief that you couldn't solve a crisis without first finding its ultimate cause. "And if you do locate it, then what? We can't risk sending the *Defiant* through the wormhole if the problem's on the other side, and there's no other heavily armed starship within range—even assuming Starfleet would risk sending one into an unstable singularity." He overrode whatever the Vulcan physicist was trying to say by the simple expedient of raising his voice to drown out hers. "And if the problem turns out to be on our side, all we need to do is watch the wormhole and blow up any ship, probe, or object that tries to approach it."

T'Kreng's delicate voice sounded as if it might shatter with the intensity of her restrained Vulcan rage. "That, Captain, is a typical military solution, made in total ignorance of the true scientific complexity of this situation. I find myself forced to remind you that you do not have the authority to revoke my research commission from Starfleet Command."

"But I *do* have the authority to defend the Bajoran wormhole," Sisko retorted. A quick glance behind showed him not only Jadzia Dax's decisive nod of agreement but an unexpected hand gesture from the young physics graduate student sitting beside her. The fingers of Petersen's left hand first curled into a fist and then snapped outward again—a gesture Sisko remembered from his own days at Starfleet Academy. It was the silent hand signal that meant a cadet's assigned ship had been destroyed during a battle simulation.

Sisko scowled and turned back to T'Kreng, who was tapping commands into her control panel as if the argument were over. He dropped his voice to its deepest and most somber note, dragging her reluctant attention back to him. "If the *Sreba* is destroyed during its passage through the wormhole, Professor T'Kreng, isn't it possible that you will trigger the very time avulsion we're trying to prevent?"

The quantum physicist gave him a glacially affronted look. "I believe that to be an extremely remote possibility, Captain."

"But it is—at least theoretically—possible?"

He had her trapped on the unyielding bars of Vulcan logic, and they both knew it. T'Kreng's eyebrows tightened in a look as near frustration as Sisko had ever seen a Vulcan come. "Yes. Theoretically, yes."

"Then until and unless we get a countercommand from Starfleet Headquarters, this ship will be detained as soon as it docks at *Deep Space Nine*," he said crisply. "If you leave station and approach the wormhole, Professor, I'm afraid I will have to apply the same sanctions to you as I have threatened to apply to any other ship at *Deep Space Nine*."

He'd expected a flood of logical Vulcan argument in

response, but T'Kreng surprised him with a minuscule nod. "A strategically defensible move, Captain, even if it is a completely transparent one. You and I are both aware that as long as the Bajoran wormhole continues to be racked by quantum echoes—in fact, quite probably until the very moment of its destruction—we will be unable to contact Starfleet Command on any subspace channels." She lifted one slender shoulder in a shrug so slight it barely stirred the fabric of her platinum robe. "Afterward, of course, it will be too late. The wormhole will be gone."

"Assuming your scientific analysis is the correct one, Professor," Dax pointed out calmly from behind. "We have *Deep Space Nine* and the wormhole in visual range now, Benjamin."

Sisko glanced up at the viewscreen, seeing the familiar crowned silhouette of his station backlit by the disturbing glow of the wormhole as it writhed open and shut. The spiral of singularity-funneled light had lost its pristine symmetry, shredding into tendrils and shreds of bright ionized gas that lingered in phosphorescent shadows even when it closed. Each time it opened, its edges looked more frayed, as if it were eating away at itself from within.

"No one's going through that wormhole again," Sisko said with grim conviction. He swung around to give T'Kreng a hard look. "We've arrived too late for you to do any good here, Professor."

"Do you think so?" T'Kreng asked, a little too politely. "I do not agree."

Compared to the delicate restraint of all the Vulcan's previous gestures, her sudden stab down at her control panel hit Sisko like a blow. He cursed and took a step toward her, guessing what she meant to do, but by then it was too late. In midstride, he heard a familiar hum and felt his muscles freeze inside the paralyzing shimmer of a transporter field. His dissolving senses caught the edge of a surprised cry from Dax, echoed more faintly by one from Heather Petersen, and then nothingness closed in around him.

CHAPTER
9

THEY MATERIALIZED WITH annoying Vulcan precision, directly centered on *Deep Space Nine*'s main transporter pad and so well aligned that Sisko didn't even feel the usual slight drop to the floor. For some reason, the perfection of the maneuver blasted his anger at T'Kreng to an even hotter pitch. He slammed a hand over his comm badge the instant his muscles were released from the beam's tingling paralysis.

"Sisko to Ops," he snarled. "Locate the Vulcan science ship *Sreba*—"

"Medical override!" Bashir snapped out from behind him, and Sisko swung around to see the doctor lunging toward the ancient stasis chamber that had been beamed in with them. Disconnected from the *Sreba*'s power supply, it stood dark and ominously silent on one edge of the transporter pad. "An occupied medical stasis chamber has just been beamed aboard without internal power, repeat *without internal power*. I need immediate onboard transport to medical bay—"

"I'm on it, Julian," said O'Brien's voice from the comm.

"—and technical assistance with the power linkage—"

Bashir disappeared in midword, along with the symbiont's chamber. Dax took one step toward where it had been, then pulled herself up with a visible effort and turned to Sisko. "We have to get to Ops and stop T'Kreng."

He was already heading for the door and the nearest turbolift. "Sisko to Ops," he snapped at his comm badge again. "O'Brien, I want you to stop that Vulcan ship before it enters the wormhole!"

The voice that answered him was Commander Eddington's. "Chief O'Brien had himself beamed down to the infirmary to help Dr. Bashir, sir. And the computer reports no Vulcan ships docked at the station now."

Sisko slammed the turbolift call button with a great deal more force than it required. "It's not docked, Mr. Eddington, it's in transit—"

"Moving at warp five approximately five hundred kilometers out from *Deep Space Nine*," Dax added. "Concentrate your scan toward sectors nineteen, twenty, and twenty-one."

"Yes, sir."

The turbolift doors hummed open at last, slowly enough that Sisko was inside with Dax before they had even finished moving. "Ops, priority one," he snapped at the lift computer. The doors moved with more satisfying speed this time, although they made an ominous screech as they did so. "When was the last time we overhauled the turbolifts?" he demanded irritably of his science officer.

Dax gave him an exasperated glance. "Just last month. Remember, I told you that a lot of them needed to be replaced? *Deep Space Nine* was never designed for the kind of commercial traffic it's getting these days."

He grunted. "That may not be a problem for much longer."

"True."

There was a long, tense pause. Sisko forced himself to concentrate on the numbers that flicked across the lift's location display rather than on the lengthening silence from Ops. He knew all too well where part of his anger was coming from: his illogical but complete conviction that if Kira Nerys had been up in Operations, instead of out chasing a straggle of would-be Bajoran terrorists, the *Sreba* would already be locked tight in the station's tractor beam. She might not be Bajor's best diplomat or even a very comfortable second-in-command, but when it came to anything military, Sisko trusted Kira's instincts and abilities almost as much as he trusted his own.

"Captain, we've located the Vulcan ship," said Eddington's voice from his comm badge.

"Good." The turbolift doors screeched open at Ops and Sisko vaulted through them, feeling the immediate gut-deep reassurance of being in command of his own crew and station again. The main viewscreen showed an infinitesimal *Sreba,* barely visible against the ionization haze of the pulsing wormhole. "Is she out of tractor range?"

"Yes," said Eddington and Dax simultaneously. The Trill had wasted no time reclaiming her usual place at the science station.

Sisko took a deep breath, trying to purge all anger from the decision he was about to make. "Then fire phasers on her immediately, Mr. Eddington."

The Starfleet security commander swung in his chair at the weapons console, staring across at Sisko incredulously. "You want me to fire on a *unarmed* Federation vessel, Captain? Can't we just—"

"Fire your phasers, Mr. Eddington. That's an order."

Eddington's narrow face folded into disapproving lines, but his Starfleet training was far too ingrained to let him make the fierce protest Kira would have in his place. He punched in a firing sequence, with a careful precision that made Sisko's teeth ache with gritted impatience. "Initiating phaser blast now, Captain."

Streaks of fierce white light punctured the space around *Deep Space Nine,* burning a curved path toward the wormhole. Sisko scowled as he watched the increasing deviation of the usually lance-straight phaser beams. He knew, even before Eddington spoke, what he was going to say.

"Phasers off by point-four degrees of arc, Captain. A complete miss." The Starfleet security officer spun around to give him a baffled look. "My weapons system still insists those are the right coordinates, sir. Do you want me to fire again?"

Sisko shook his head irritably. "Dax, what's going on?"

"The wormhole's fluctuations are bending the local curvature of space, Benjamin." Dax looked up, face splashed red and gold by reflections from the computer model now pulsing on her screen in perfect synchronicity with the wormhole. "Either the *Sreba* isn't exactly where our instruments say she is, or our phasers are being deflected away from her by the singularity matrix."

"Can we correct for the curvature?"

The Trill's strong hands were already moving across her control panel. "I'm sending new coordinates over to your weapons console, Commander."

"Too late," Eddington said bluntly. "She's entering the wormhole."

Sisko swung around to stare up at the monitor. The wormhole's once slow and majestic portal, into which ships had skimmed on a sea of calm radiance, now cracked open and shut in a series of irregular bursts, like the grand finale of an old-fashioned fireworks display. The *Sreba* had been a small flake of dark ash silhouetted against that flickering fire, but now it glowed inside an ominous haze of ionized gases, reaching out from the singularity like a tentacle to drag the small Vulcan ship inside. It vanished in a spike of light as bright as any phaser burst.

"Hull breach?" Sisko demanded of Dax, without taking his gaze away from the screen. It seemed to him that the ship's disappearance had been followed by a longer than usual pause in the wormhole's frenetic dance of opening and closing.

"No trace of ship debris or ionic pulses from a warp-core overload," his science officer reported after a moment's intent silence. "I think they made it into the wormhole. There's no way to know if they made it out again."

Sisko slammed one big hand against the nearest non-breakable surface, which happened to be the transparent aluminum panels of his own office doors. His palm stung from the impact just enough to calm his icy rage and let him consider his alternatives.

"Dax, do you remember the *Sreba*'s main communicator frequency?" he demanded after a moment. "Can you bounce a narrow-beam signal to them through the wormhole?"

"It's possible. I'll have to compensate for the space-time curvature effects first, though. Give me a few minutes." She glanced up from the relativistic model on her science monitor, lips tightening in a somber expression that he recognized from his time with Curzon. "I'd appreciate it, Benjamin, if you'd check in with the infirmary in the meantime."

"Of course, old man." Sisko glanced at the mixed crew of Starfleet and Bajoran personnel staffing Ops, then turned and entered the more discreet silence of his own office. He waited for the doors to hiss shut before tapping his comm badge.

"Sisko to Bashir. What's the status of your patient, Doctor?"

The voice that answered after a moment was O'Brien's. "We've got the stasis chamber plugged in and back on-line, Captain." There was another, longer pause. "Julian says the patient survived the transfer better than he expected—no additional physiological trauma and only a little neurological shock. He says it actually seems to have stabilized itself at more normal levels of—um—vital chemicals."

From the engineer's carefully guarded tone, Sisko deduced that O'Brien had been both admitted into the doctor's confidence and given a strict lecture on keeping it. "Tell Dr. Bashir that's the first good news I've gotten since I beamed back aboard." He saw Dax glance up again from her console and gave her a thumbs-up sign through his window. The Trill's face lit with a brief flash of smile before she bent back over the pulsing glow of her monitor. "Has anyone else but you seen our—um—patient?"

"No, Captain. Julian's assistant was off-duty when we got here."

Sisko sat back in his office chair, scrubbing a hand across his beard thoughtfully. If he remembered correctly, the medical assistant was also from Bajor. "Can you rig up some kind of security access panel to isolate that stasis chamber, Chief? I don't want anyone visiting down there unless they've got a Priority One clearance from Starfleet Command."

"I've already designed a portable isolation barrier for the infirmary, Captain." Part of what made O'Brien such a good engineer was his ability to foresee and prepare for the kinds of problems he'd eventually be ordered to solve. "It'll block off this whole wing and give us room to move in a cot and food replicator for Julian. If you don't need me up at Ops, I'll get started on it right now."

"Do that," Sisko agreed. "And tell Dr. Bashir to start thinking up a good cover story for his assistant, to keep any rumors from starting."

"No problem," said the doctor's crisp voice from the comm. "I'll just find a disease I've been exposed to that she hasn't."

"Tartha pox?" O'Brien suggested. "Keiko said they had an outbreak of it in Molly's day-care center on Bajor a few weeks ago. It hit the Bajoran kids pretty hard."

One corner of Sisko's mouth kicked up in brief amusement. "I'd prefer something just a little more deadly than that, Chief. I want to make sure anyone else who might be curious about what we beamed in doesn't decide to drop in and pay poor Julian a visit."

"Garak, for example," Bashir said wryly.

O'Brien snorted. "Or Quark."

"Exactly, gentlemen. Sisko out."

He started to lever himself out of his chair with both hands, his shoulder muscles stiff from too much stress and too little sleep. Before he'd even finished rising, the translucent comm screen on his desk rippled with color, signaling an incoming call. Sisko groaned and fell back into his chair.

"Deep Space Nine, Captain Benjamin Sisko."

"At last." The prim outrage in that voice told him who was calling even before Kai Winn's chilly face had finished coalescing in his screen. "Emissary, I have been trying to reach you for *two hours."*

Sisko scrubbed a hand over his face again, hoping he didn't look as grimy and unwashed as he felt. "I was off-station—on a high-priority Starfleet assignment—until just a few minutes ago."

"Well, perhaps the Prophets know why you had to be gone during such a critical time for Bajor," Kai Winn said, with her usual infuriating blend of dulcet voice and malicious words. "Have you at least begun to address our problem, Emissary?"

For a second time, Sisko found himself silently cursing the absence of his second-in-command. "I believe Major

Kira is currently engaged in tracking the—er—the alleged terrorists—"

"You think that these are *terrorist* attacks?" Winn's pale eyebrows lifted in what almost looked like real amazement. "But why would the Maquis want to attack and destroy ordinary Bajoran freighters?"

"Who said anything about the Maquis?" Sisko demanded absently, his attention shifting past his viewscreen to Dax. She had transferred whatever signal relay she was working on to the main viewscreen of Ops, but so far all she had to show for it was a queasy blur of subspace static. He glanced back at Kai Winn's frowning face, and what she had said finally sank in. "For that matter, who said anything about Bajoran freighters?"

She gave him an irritated look. "I did, Emissary, in my very first message to you. In the last twelve hours, three Bajoran ore-carrying freighters have been attacked and destroyed within our solar system by some unknown force. *Within our solar system.*"

The interior steel that the Kai usually kept hidden under layers of false sweetness gleamed naked and fierce in her final words. Sisko eyed her narrowly. Despite all of Winn's secret maneuverings for power, there was no doubt that her one and only commitment was to her planet's future. Any threat to Bajor that could peel away her hypocritical mask of demure sweetness and expose the tiger beneath had to be real.

"The terrorists I was thinking of were Bajoran—a cell that Major Kira uncovered here on *Deep Space Nine*," he told her. "Could they be the ones responsible for these attacks?"

"No." For once, her reply was as blunt and honest as his question. "I have observers placed in the group on *Deep Space Nine* as well as in the Bajoran militias. Neither has space weapons powerful enough to destroy ore freighters."

Sudden exasperation flared through Sisko. "You mean you knew about the terrorist cell on my station, and didn't bother to inform me about it?"

Kai Winn gave him a sweetly mocking smile. "How could I, Emissary? There was always the chance that some of your own staff might have been involved with it."

And you wouldn't have minded if Deep Space Nine *had been blown up, anyway,* Sisko wanted to snap back, although he knew he couldn't. He gritted his teeth and tried to ignore the frustration that his conversations with the Kai usually devolved into. Unlike the Cardassians, who never much cared if you told them what you thought of them, Winn would stalk off in insulted and uncooperative hauteur if you called her on her manipulative power plays.

"Were there any witnesses rescued from the damaged ore freighters?" he asked instead.

"None." Winn's smile vanished and her elaborately ringed hands tightened in her lap. "Every freighter was found sliced open—completely breached to vacuum, without a trace of crew left aboard alive or dead. We're not even sure what weapons were used to do it." She gave him a glance as cold and hard as latinum. "Our economic recovery depends on our new ore-processing plants, Emissary. Any threat to our freighters is a threat to our entire planet."

"I understand that."

Kai Winn made a graceful gesture, more sweeping than any T'Kreng would have used but somehow exuding the same utter sureness and self-possession. "Then you will have to hunt these raiders down and stop them immediately. As the captain of the only starship permanently stationed in this quadrant, I believe that is your responsibility."

"One of them," he agreed. Out in Ops, he could see a wavering image starting to melt through the static on the monitor. "Unfortunately, right now my main responsibility is to Starfleet and the Priority One operation I'm engaged in. Your raiders will have to wait."

"Emissary." The Kai gave him a hurt and puzzled look, although he could read the shark-swift calculations rippling through her pale eyes. "Surely, you can't mean that."

"I mean it."

"But the only reason we agreed to have a Starfleet presence in this region was to protect us while we recover from the Cardassian occupation. If you can't protect us, we may have to find someone else who can."

Sisko gave her an exasperated glance. "Like the Romulans?"

Winn glanced down at her gently clasped hands, a picture of religious humility. "Perhaps," she agreed softly. "Or the Klingons."

Sisko's lips tightened. "Neither of whom would be very interested in Bajor if it weren't next door to the only stable wormhole in the galaxy," he said bluntly. "Before you start issuing ultimatums to Starfleet, Kai Winn, I suggest you call up some of your university astronomers and find out how stable the Bajoran wormhole is. Or isn't." He paused, savoring the rare gratification of shaking Winn's hypocritical mask completely off. Her face had gone steel-hard with shock, eyes narrowing to suspicious slits. "In the meantime, I'll assign Major Kira the job of protecting your ore freighters, as soon as she's back on board *Deep Space Nine*. Sisko out."

He stabbed the end-transmission button, cutting the Kai off before she could utter the indignant protest he saw gathering on her face. The instant he did, his comm badge beeped, as if Dax had toggled it to wait until the Kai was offline. "Benjamin, get out here," she said urgently. "We're getting a signal from the *Sreba*."

Sisko rounded his desk in two strides, turning his shoulders sideways to slide through his office doors as they opened. On the main viewscreen, a haze-streaked view of the *Sreba's* bridge had coalesced out of the subspace static, peopled with ghostly Vulcan figures at barely visible monitor stations.

Dax looked up at him from the science panel. "From the way their signal's resonating, I think they're still inside the wormhole," she informed him. "I'm compensating for the subspace fluctuations as much as I can."

Sisko grunted and punched a communications channel open. He could just make out a familiar slight, still figure in the center of the screen. "This is *Deep Space Nine* hailing the *Sreba*," he said. "Can you hear me, T'Kreng?"

"You are interfering with our ability to scan the singularity matrix," said the Vulcan physicist's annoyed voice, oddly clear and sharp from that clouded image. "Stop transmitting at once."

After dealing with the Kai, Sisko was in no mood for

another civilian's condescending orders. "Why are you still in the wormhole? Can't you get out?"

"We were in the process of running our fourth and final scan—" The signal wavered and buzzed with static, then reformed. "—have to redo it from the opposite end now."

"No!" From the corner of his eye, Sisko could see heads turn throughout Ops at the force of that shout. He concentrated all his attention on the ivory smudge of T'Kreng's face. "Whatever you do, don't go out the opposite end of the wormhole!"

Whatever gesture T'Kreng made to her navigator was too subtle to carry across the blurred screen, but her voice sounded less annoyed and more serene. "We are in no danger, Captain. We have identified the onset of the time rift to a high degree of confidence, and have a satisfactory buffer within which to operate. We are proceeding to exit the wormhole now—"

Her voice didn't break off—it was swamped beneath a sudden thunder of explosions, ship alarms, and the bone-chilling roar of air escaping into vacuum. The *Sreba*'s visual signal flared into meaningless prismatic colors, and a moment later its audio plummeted into utter silence.

"We've lost contact," Dax reported, breaking the appalled hush that filled Ops.

"Did they get caught in the wormhole as it closed?"

"Maybe." Her freckled forehead creased with frustration as she scrolled through her sensor readouts. "I can't tell from here what destroyed them. I can't even tell if they made it out into the Gamma Quadrant or not."

Sisko felt the muscles along his jaw tighten. It was fear more than intelligence that told him what to do next. "Put the wormhole back on the main viewscreen."

Dax punched in the command, and a familiar tattered glow of ionized gas replaced the subspace static. Sisko waited, watching for the explosive flash-dance of the wormhole to appear in the midst of that afterglow. A moment crawled past, and then another. Nothing happened.

"Captain," Eddington said sharply, as if he was worried that Sisko couldn't see it for himself. "The wormhole's not there anymore!"

Sisko had thought that nothing could be more unnerving

than the irrational tremors of a singularity opening and closing for no reason. He was wrong. The sudden, inexplicable absence of the wormhole's inner radiance made the skin between his shoulders crawl with dread. He swung around toward Dax. "Has it been destroyed?"

Her hands raced across her science station. "No, not according to my instruments. It's not gone, just closed. Back to normal."

"Back to normal," he repeated softly. A chorus of relieved sighs rustled through Ops at those words, but Dax met his gaze with deep foreboding in her eyes. Sisko gestured her toward his office with a silent jerk of his chin. "Mr. Eddington, you have Ops. Keep a channel open to the *Sreba,* in case she reappears."

"Yes, Captain."

Dax followed him up the steps, still frowning. "Do you think T'Kreng was wrong about the time?" she asked, as soon as the doors slid shut behind them.

"Maybe." He turned to watch the viewscreen through his windows in somber silence. The tortured glow of ionized gas was slowly fading around the wormhole, leaving the screen lit only by the tiny diamond sparkles of distant stars. "She was certainly wrong about something. If the wormhole's back to normal, then whatever was going to happen to it must have either happened already, or somehow been averted."

"I agree," Dax said. "Should I check to see if—if Julian still has a patient?"

Sisko nodded grimly. "Yes. But I already suspect that Starfleet Command won't care what the answer is. They're going to want to know what's on the other side of the wormhole now that it's stopped spasming."

His science officer gave him an intent look. "You think the wormhole's new stability means that the Furies have already finished using it as their jump gate?"

"Yes." He took a deep breath, abruptly thankful that Jake was spending his school vacation as Keiko's field assistant down on Bajor. This situation could only get worse. "What happened to the *Sreba* didn't sound like an accident to me. For all we know, the Furies could be in position to invade us from the Gamma Quadrant right now."

"Possibly," Dax agreed. "Maybe we'd better ask Judith to send us some of those ships she's hoarding at Starbase One."

Sisko clenched a fist around his antique baseball, feeling its normally strong sides yield beneath his fingers. "But the *Defiant* is still the only ship in Starfleet that can scout the Fury fleet and bring the information back without being detected." He looked up and met Dax's somber gaze. "Whether we like it or not, old man, we're going to have to go through the wormhole one last time."

After nearly two days in a runabout with no shower and no bed, the only thing Kira really wanted to do was strip out of her sweaty uniform and go to bed. Duty always complicated things, though. First, duty had kept her diligently awake while Odo puddled in the back of the passenger compartment—embarrassed about being there when the constable was forced to revert to liquid, resentful of having no such good excuse herself for taking a much needed time-out. Then duty had trapped her into a decidedly short and sour conversation with Eddington as she brought *Rio Grande* into dock, all because she thought it proper to ask someone what had gone on at the station in her absence. No, Chief O'Brien wasn't available to talk to her, yes, the station was still all in one piece, and would the major mind very much if Mr. Eddington put off answering any further questions until they could talk face-to-face? As if anything that prissy Starfleet dandy had to say would be worth someone's effort to monitor. Still, it was as good an excuse as any to get him off the comm, and she'd finished docking *Rio Grande* in sleepy, aching silence.

Now, duty had brought her to the airlock just outside the *Defiant's* berth before even letting her point herself toward home. She had some silly notion that O'Brien might be down here, preparing the ship for launch like she'd told him. Instead, two of Eddington's boys in gold stepped up to form a solid wall of grimness the moment she came near the airlock doors.

"Good evening, gentlemen." She meant it to come out politely, but couldn't even remember how that was supposed to sound, so she suspected she spoke more irritably than she'd intended. "Is Chief O'Brien still around?"

The taller of the two slipped neatly into her path when she moved to step around him, not even backing down to avoid their brief collision. "I'm sorry, sir, but this area is restricted to official Starfleet personnel."

She couldn't hold back the sharp laugh that huffed out of her. "I'm the first officer on the station, mister. I think that's official enough."

This time when he blocked her, he at least had the grace to look apologetic. "Not anymore, sir. I'm sorry."

You bet you are. But she quashed that feeling quickly—it wasn't his fault that her last two days had been less than ideal. "Who ordered this?" If it was Eddington, she was going to burn his skinny little Starfleet ass.

"Captain Sisko, sir."

"Captain Sisko?" Not at all the answer she'd expected. "He's not even on the station!"

The guards exchanged what Kira assumed was supposed to be a discreet glance; then the younger of the two volunteered, "He is now, sir. He got back last night."

Well, that at least simplified things more than doing the Starfleet shuffle with Eddington. Slapping at her comm badge, Kira kept a stern glower on the two guards as she called, "Kira to Sisko. I'm just outside the *Defiant's* berth in upper pylon three, and two of Eddington's jarheads are try—"

"Hold that thought, Major." Sisko's voice, as smooth and collected as always, still managed to sound brusquely distracted as he cut her off. "I'll join you in a moment."

This was apparently everyone's day for hustling her off the comm. Crossing her arms—and not caring if that made her look unpleasant or aggressive—she paced back and forth in the stubby stretch of hallway in front of the guards. She wasn't even mad at them anymore; she was tired past the point of being angry. All that was left was a sort of grumpy irritation that she'd been stupid enough to come down here in the first place, and an almost childlike longing for the comfort of her own warm quarters, and for sleep.

She had her back to the airlock—staring down the main hall for Sisko's arrival, even though she knew it was far too soon to expect him—when the airlock door rolled aside with a bone-deep rumble. She jerked a look behind her from habit, and was surprised to see the captain sidestep through the hatchway while it was still barely wide enough to admit him. "Major," he greeted in a tone of polished neutrality. "Welcome home. Commander Eddington got down here just a few minutes ahead of you, and told me you were back."

Kira bobbed up on tiptoe to steal a glimpse of whatever was happening beyond the big round door, but Sisko's height and the artfully placed security guards prevented her from seeing much before the lock boomed closed. "What's going on?"

Sisko nodded toward the other end of the hall—away from the ubiquitous security drones—and Kira was just as happy to oblige him. She only made it half the distance, though, before demanding grumpily, "Why didn't Eddington tell me you were back? I didn't even know you were down here."

"Commander Eddington has a tendency to err on the side of caution, I'm afraid. I didn't specifically ask him to tell you, and he didn't want to appear presumptuous." He slowed to a stop with a dry smile, pulling her around in front of him so that his body blocked her view of the security team. Or blocked her from them, it occurred to her, and the thought gave her a chill. "I'm down here with Dax and O'Brien. We're getting the *Defiant* ready for launch."

At least some things were stumbling along in the direction she expected. "When do you think we'll be leaving?"

"*We* aren't going anywhere," he corrected her with gentle emphasis. "*You* are staying on the station to keep an eye on militia activity while Dax and I go to the Gamma Quadrant."

She was too tired to do more than hiss with frustration. "We already know everything we need to about militia activity! Odo and I just spent thirty-six hours chasing them into the Badlands after they hulled four sublight freighters!" She flashed an angry hand back toward the airlock. "I came back to the station for the *Defiant* so we could finish tracking them."

A certain careful stillness settled over his face. "The *Defiant* isn't available."

She'd seen him like this very rarely—his expression

leached of all emotion, the elegant angles of his face smoothed into planes like coffee-colored marble. And then you looked into his eyes, and you could see the awful power of the emotions he was trapping behind that mask, and you realized that what you dealt with was only a fraction of what this man could call upon if he chose. Kira had seen that frightful coldness slip into place for countless Cardassian Guls who still thought their rank gave them power in this sector, for Kai Winn when she presumed to argue her personal goals in the name of the Prophets, for Bajorans who insisted on making him their spiritual Emissary no matter how he rejected that mantle. Kira had even seen Bashir slapped with that look once when the doctor was foolish enough to interrupt an official subspace transmission. But in all her years of working beside him, Sisko had never turned that face on her.

"You're the commander of this station, aren't you?" she asked, doing the only thing she knew to do with her frustration—lash out. "You could make it available."

The captain's face never stirred. "I'm afraid it's not that easy."

"Why not? Because Starfleet's decided the engine's isotopic ratios are more important than a few Bajoran ore transports?" She'd expected the hint that she'd sensed the importance of yesterday's comm call to at least spark a flicker of surprise in his dark eyes. Instead, he only held her gaze with his own as though trying to will his thoughts directly into her. The sheer intensity of his stare finally forced her to turn away under the pretense of pacing. "I can't believe we're having this conversation. You told me once that you were really dedicated to helping Bajor, no matter what Starfleet's motives for being here might be." She stopped on the other side of the corridor, that little distance giving her the bravery to scowl back at him again. "Isn't that true anymore?" Then, because it was really the crux of her fear and anger, "What did they talk to you about back at Starbase One?"

He opened his mouth to answer her, but Kira could see him swallow whatever he'd originally begun to say even before he gusted a frustrated growl and started over. "Believe me, Major, my concern for this system is greater now than ever. And sometimes Starfleet's motives and the good of Bajor really do run hand-in-hand." He glanced aside, as though conferring with himself, then turned back to her with his mask peeled aside and a confusion of emotions roiling in his eyes. "For right now, all I can tell you is that Admiral Hayman has already ordered the starship *Mukaikubo* to DS9. She's not as heavily armed as the *Defiant,* but she should be able to handle any militia hunting you might need."

Kira wasn't sure what unnerved her most—what Sisko wasn't telling her, or what he'd almost said between the lines. "A rear admiral like Hayman can't possibly care about a little militia trouble in Bajoran shipping lanes. Why is she sending the *Mukaikubo* here?"

"If what we're doing in the Gamma Quadrant is successful," he said with a care that was chilling, "it won't matter why the *Mukaikubo* came."

Kira nodded, understanding enough to know that she hated not knowing more. "And if you're not successful?"

She could see the apology in his eyes, and in the way his jaw muscles knotted with the effort of keeping silent.

"Don't do this to me!" she flared. "Don't leave me in the dark like this!"

"I don't have any choice—I don't really know anything more for certain than you do."

"You know enough to be afraid," she countered.

He met her gaze frankly. "Don't you?"

This time, it was Kira who glanced away.

"The *Mukaikubo* should be here within two days," Sisko went on, almost gently. "Captain Regitz knows you're my second-in-command. She'll give you her full cooperation."

She swung about at the sound of his footsteps, stopping him just before he joined the guards at the airlock door. "What about you?" she challenged. "When are you bringing the *Defiant* back?"

An odd, not-quite smile ghosted across his face. "That's a very good question, Major." He keyed open the lock behind him. "I hope I get the chance to tell you the answer."

CHAPTER
10

"JADZIA, YOU CAN'T do this."

Dax looked up from where she knelt beside the *Defiant's* piloting panel, surprised by the flat intensity of that familiar voice. Bashir was nothing more than a rail-thin silhouette against the flare of light from the flash-welder O'Brien was using beside her, but what she could see of the set of his shoulders and jaw radiated worry. Across the bridge, she noticed Sisko pause in his intent reprogramming of the weapons station with Eddington and give the doctor a long, considering look. As far as she knew, this was the first time since they'd beamed aboard that Bashir had left the infirmary.

"I have to, Julian. We're only taking a skeleton crew through the wormhole with us." Dax glanced down at the optical cables she was holding for O'Brien, to make sure she hadn't joggled them. "Don't worry, my reflexes are fast enough to handle engineering and fly the ship at the same time. That's the advantage of having two cerebral cortices."

"That's not what I meant and you know it." Bashir came closer, squatting beside O'Brien as if to inspect the chief engineer's work. The spit and sizzle of optical cables fusing in the heat of the laser-welder shielded his words from the rest of the *Defiant's* small bridge. "How can you even *think* of taking the *Defiant* to the Gamma Quadrant? Didn't you tell me that the isotopic ratios in the old

Defiant's warp core meant it would be thrown back in time on its very next voyage?"

"Assuming we were still trapped in our original timeline, that would be true," Dax agreed. "But the wormhole's been stable for six hours now. That means there's a high probability the original time rift has been averted."

"Then why hasn't the old Dax symbiont disappeared?" he demanded tightly.

She started to shrug, then realized that would joggle the cable in her hands and forced herself to be still. "Starfleet Command thinks that five thousand years of being embedded in our time flow gave the old *Defiant* and her crew so much temporal inertia that even the elimination of their original time shift couldn't destroy them. It has something to do with conservation of space-time energy."

Bashir looked appalled. "That means the other Dax is going to stay in our timeline forever? As—as a relict?"

"I believe the technical term is 'timeline orphan.'" She watched the last microscopically fine crystal strands of optical cable fuse together in a prism of laser-sparked reflections. "Of course, it's just been a theoretical term until now. The *Defiant* will be the first documented case on record."

"Only if the time rift in the wormhole really has been averted." O'Brien toggled off the laser torch, and replaced the circuit-panel cover with a grunt. "And I thought you said the probability of that was sixty-eight percent, Lieutenant."

Dax gave him an exasperated glance. She should have known better than to give Julian a reassuring version of the odds against them with an engineer as meticulous as O'Brien in hearing range. "That was my minimum estimate," she said, seeing frown lines crease back into the doctor's thin face.

"And what was your maximum estimate?" Bashir demanded.

Dax bit her lip, and scrambled to her feet so she wouldn't have to see his expression. "Seventy-two percent," she admitted, then bent over her piloting board to fend off whatever reply he would have made to that. "I'll start running diagnostics to make sure the engineering circuits are completely tied in, Chief. Why don't you go help Captain Sisko and Commander Eddington automate the phaser firing sequences?"

O'Brien shot Bashir a perceptive glance. "I think the captain's got that pretty much under control. Maybe it would be better if I went back to the infirmary and kept an eye on Julian's patient for him."

"Yes." Bashir rubbed a hand wearily across his face. "I would appreciate that very much."

O'Brien rose and dropped a hand on the doctor's shoulder to give him a quick, admonitory shake. "Take a shower and get something to eat before you come back to work," he advised. "If the lieutenant's right, your medical problem's not going anywhere."

"I wish I knew if that was good news or bad." Bashir leaned back against the base of the piloting console from his seat on the floor and closed his eyes with a tired wince. Dax and O'Brien exchanged concerned glances over his head; then the chief engineer shrugged and walked away.

Respecting the troubled silence at her knee, Dax busied herself punching a diagnostic routine into her hybridized piloting/engineering panel. A sprawl of engineering plans began to strobe across her screen while her piloting grid condensed to an inset window in one corner. She played with the color and contrast controls, trying to find the maximum visibility of both displays.

"Which crew members *are* you taking through the wormhole?" Bashir asked after a moment. Although the words sounded almost absentminded, a glance at his tense face told Dax this wasn't idle conversation. "The same ones we saw on the bridge log?"

"No." Dax closed her eyes for a moment, then swept her board with a quick scanning look to see if her helm coordinates were still visible. "Even if the rift hasn't been averted, Benjamin thinks we'll have less chance of getting thrown back in time if we take a different crew. We've whittled it down to three engineers and three bridge officers—me on piloting and engineering, Commander Eddington on weapons, and Ensign Hovan on the cloaking device.

"Who'll handle communications?"

"I will," Sisko said from behind them. Dax swung around

to see the captain checking the miniature comm panel O'Brien had installed beside his command chair. "We won't need to do much hailing, since we'll be running cloaked the entire time. If there really are Furies on the other side of the wormhole, the last thing we want is for them to know we're there. We'll do a quick pass to gauge their strength and numbers, check the status of the *Sreba,* then come back to this quadrant to inform Starfleet Command."

The doubtful look on Bashir's face told Dax he wished he could believe it would be that easy. "What about medical staff?"

"I wanted your opinion about that." Sisko steepled his fingers and gave the doctor an intent look. "How secure is your patient in the infirmary?"

Bashir shrugged. "Chief O'Brien's rigged up an emergency bulkhead to isolate one alcove. But we can't very well ask Odo to provide security guards without telling the whole station there's something more in there than a Vulcan physicist with a case of *mactru* fever."

"I thought as much," said Sisko. "That's why I'm taking your medical assistant on the *Defiant.*"

Bashir's chin jerked up. "Instead of me?"

"How can we take you, Julian?" Dax asked, before the captain could reply. "You have to stay with my—with your patient."

"But if you're wrong about the timeline—"

"Not here," Sisko said abruptly. He rose to his feet, a slight jerk of his chin gathering them up without any further need for words. Eddington gave them a curious look as they left the *Defiant's* bridge, but made no comment.

"Medical bay," Sisko told the turbolift computer, when the doors had closed behind him.

Dax frowned up at him. "There's not much room in there to talk, Benjamin. Wouldn't it be better to use your quarters?"

He shook his head, dark eyes intent. "There's something down here I want the doctor to see." The turbolift doors hissed open on the enlarged hallway that served as the *Defiant's* medical bay. The tiny area, clearly a designer's afterthought on this prototype attack ship, seemed even

more cramped than usual to Dax, but it took her a moment
to realize why.

Beside her, Bashir said something beneath his breath, so
softly she couldn't tell whether it was a curse or a thankful
prayer. Dax followed the direction of his gaze, and finally
saw the familiar translucent tank that had completely
replaced the central diagnostic bed. Its brand-new transparent
aluminum panels were set into a shock-absorbing plasfoam
column, and in place of the original spaghetti-tangle
of emergency fittings, a neat candelabraum of power cables
and brine tubes emerged from a dilithium-powered recirculating
pump at the base.

"O'Brien," Bashir said, with a wondering shake of his
head. "When he insisted on doing a full-scale engineering
scan of the symbiont's tank this morning, I thought it was
just so he could tell me all the things I'd done wrong.
Where did he find that pump?"

"I think he wheedled a couple of them from a liquid-
atmosphere merchant ship that's docked here now," Sisko
said. "He's replicating another version of this for your
patient on *Deep Space Nine,* but I wanted one on board the
Defiant first." His gaze swung back to Dax, who was still
staring at the tank. "Well, old man, what do you think?"

She took a deep breath, trying to sort out the odd swirl of
feelings that the sight of the brine tank had evoked. Usually,
the emotions felt by her host and symbiont overlapped each
other so comfortably that she had stopped noticing whose
brain was generating them. That was one of the things that
made her Trill pairing so successful. But for once, Jadzia's
uneasiness at the thought of deliberately preparing for a
five-thousand-year internment found no echo in her symbiont.
Instead, the emotion resonating out from Dax was a
quiet and ironic amusement. She was reminded again that
the passing of time for symbionts, with their millennial life
spans, held much less fear than it did for shorter-lived
organisms.

"I think," she said calmly, "that I'll have to make sure
you don't get in the way of any quantum-torpedo explosions
for the next few days, Benjamin. I can't very well put myself
to bed in that thing, can I?"

Sisko snorted. "And what makes you think *I'm* going to be able to do it, old man?"

"Well, I've seen how neatly you can filet a trout."

Bashir made an almost strangled noise of protest at their banter, and Dax exchanged contrite looks with Sisko. Whatever happened, she knew the doctor was never going to be completely comfortable with his role in preserving her symbiont. She tried not to think about what a second time rift would do to his sense of mingled responsibility and guilt.

"Don't worry, Julian," she said reassuringly. "Remember, there's a seventy-percent chance we won't need to use this tank at all."

Bashir scowled at her. "That means there's a thirty-percent chance that you will!" He swung around to face Sisko. "My assistant's a medical intern—not a doctor, not a surgeon, and certainly not an expert on Trill physiology. If you want to save Dax's symbiont again, you have to take me with you."

Sisko lifted an eyebrow at him. "Even if that means leaving the symbiont you already saved alone on *Deep Space Nine?*"

"But it doesn't have to." He flung out a hand at the renovated brine tank. "We can bring the old symbiont with us—maybe even manage to wake it up enough to help us avoid getting caught in the time rift this time."

"Hmm. That might work—"

"No!" Dax said fiercely. Both men turned to look at her in surprise. "We're not going to bring the old symbiont with us through the wormhole. I'd rather risk a thirty-percent chance of getting thrown back in time without you, Julian."

"But, Jadzia—"

"Old man, I don't see why—"

She wanted to shake them both. Even at their most sympathetic, humans could never truly fathom the ethics of symbiosis. "Listen to me, you two. As a Trill, there's only one thing that's important to me right now, and that's keeping my symbiont alive. It doesn't matter *which* symbiont that is. If the old Dax can regain its sanity—and with Julian's help, I think it can—then whether I get thrown back in time or get killed going through the wormhole, *one* Dax will still survive to return to Trill and the pools of memory. All of its wisdom and knowledge will still exist." She glanced at Bashir and saw the look of dawning unhappiness in his eyes. "And *I* will still exist, Julian, inside it. You know that."

He nodded, although he didn't look much happier. "But what if Starfleet Command is wrong about this temporal-inertia theory of theirs? If you do get thrown back in time, and if there's no one around to preserve the symbiont for you, *both* versions of it might disappear."

"There are three 'if's in your argument," Dax retorted. "Mine has just one: If we put both symbionts together on the *Defiant,* there's too much chance that neither of them will survive a Fury attack on the far side of the wormhole."

A somber silence descended on the medical bay. After a moment, Sisko cleared his throat to break it. "Dr. Bashir, you'll stay on *Deep Space Nine* and continue to rehabilitate the old Dax symbiont. Your medical assistant will be assigned temporary Starfleet status aboard the *Defiant.*"

The doctor nodded reluctant agreement. "I'll put copies of all my Trill physiology references on board, as well as my notes from the old *Defiant.*" He ran a hand across the gleaming surface of the empty brine tank, his expression unreadable. "If worst comes to worst, she might even have time to make sense of them."

Sisko didn't want to enter the wormhole.

In the eight hours since the *Sreba* had disappeared, the tortured glow of gas at the portal site had drifted away. Now the region of space where the wormhole opened looked like it always did: backlit by light from Bajor's sun, freckled with distant stars, and far too ordinary to house the galaxy's only known stable singularity.

"Any signs of subspace fluctuation?" he asked Dax.

She punched a command into her combined helm/engineering panel and scrutinized the flicker of output carefully. The pause seemed longer to Sisko than it should have. "I think what I'm seeing is just the normal leakage from the wormhole," Dax said at last, but he knew the Trill well enough to read the shade of doubt buried in her voice.

"What's not right about it?" he demanded.

"The frequency," she said. "It seems distorted—as if the gravity well around the singularity still hasn't returned to its normal configuration." She glanced back over her shoulder at him, inquiringly. "Proceed with wormhole approach?"

Sisko drummed his fingers on his jury-rigged communications console, aware of the watchful silence from Eddington at the weapons panel and Hovan at the cloaking controls. He'd chosen this skeleton crew for their high-level security clearances and their lack of immediate families, which meant they were mostly recent transfers to *Deep Space Nine*. In approved Starfleet style, neither offered an unsolicited suggestion to their superior officer. Deprived of Kira's outspoken opinions, Odo's blunt questions, and O'Brien's resourcefulness, Sisko turned his scowl on his oldest and most trusted friend. Fortunately, she knew him well enough to know it meant he was thinking through his answer.

"We need to know if the wormhole functions," he said flatly. "If it doesn't, Starfleet won't need to worry about a possible invasion through it."

"Agreed," Dax said calmly. "I'll pilot us to the usual trigger site."

Sisko grunted agreement, forcing himself to sit back in his chair while she entered the course coordinates. The *Defiant* sliced through Bajoran space with its usual surging kick of sublight acceleration. Its overpowered impulse engines, designed to give it maximum maneuverability in close-range battles, had an unfortunate tendency to outrun its inertia dampers. Sisko suspected that the gut-wrenching result was one of the reasons this prototype had never been made into a standard Starfleet model. He'd grown so used to it, however, that better-behaved ships like the *Enterprise* no longer felt like they were really moving.

"Approaching wormhole now." Dax toggled something on her board, giving Sisko a glimpse of the same kind of space-time contour maps he'd first seen on board the *Sreba*. He could see the *Defiant* on it, a bright blue dot moving toward the place where those glowing white curves converged. It looked unnervingly like a fly diving headlong into the heart of a spiderweb.

"Engage cloaking device, Mr. Hovan," he said quietly. "We don't want anyone to see us come out the other side."

"Aye-aye, sir." Her voice was commendably steady for a recent Academy graduate on her first crucial mission. The

Romulan cloaking icon glowed to life on his command panel and the *Defiant's* viewscreen flickered its usual initial protest while the cloaking field coalesced around them. Then the short-range sensors compensated for the additional electromagnetic radiation and the flicker was damped out.

"Subspace radiation fields increasing," Dax reported. Sisko saw the glowing white lines on her display begin to move in a familiar swirling pattern, and glanced back up at the main viewscreen in time to see the gold-streaked bloom of the wormhole spiral open directly in front of them. It looked as it always did—immense and impossibly bright with its gravity-defying burst of light. "The wormhole appears to be functioning normally, Captain."

He took a deep, soundless breath. "Then take us through to the Gamma Quadrant."

"Aye-aye, sir." She punched the new course into her panel, and Sisko felt the *Defiant's* usual impulse surge take it straight into the maw of the swirling singularity.

Then everything went away.

"Destruction," said T'Kreng's crystalline voice, "is imminent."

Sisko blinked and swung around, unsure of where he was or how he had gotten there. All he knew at first, from the lost tug of acceleration on his body, was that he was no longer aboard the *Defiant.*

"Destruction has already occurred."

His physical movements had a queasy unreal quality which told him, even before he saw the empty bridge of the *Sreba,* that he wasn't truly on board the Vulcan research vessel. His senses felt correspondingly unfocused, so that T'Kreng's platinum-robed figure shimmered insubstantially at its edges and the banks of machinery behind her looked more like sketches of themselves than actual equipment.

"Destruction is to come."

Despite the years that had passed since he'd last experienced it, this alien feeling—something like sleepwalking, something like fever dreams, and yet far more vivid than either—had been etched forever in his memory. For some reason, the wormhole's time-defying inhabitants had dragged him into their dimensional refuge again.

"Whose destruction?" he asked T'Kreng, or the image of her which the wormhole aliens had borrowed from his memories. "Yours or mine?"

The Vulcan physicist's quartz-pale eyes lifted from the screen she was watching, to meet his with a calm tranquillity she had never possessed in real life. "All beings who live and have lived and will live near the time bridge—"

"—must suffer the same fate." Admiral Judith Hayman stepped out of the *Sreba's* turbolift, her graveled voice less calm and her steely gaze more intense. Sisko wondered if it was his own brain that chose the shapes the wormhole dwellers wore, or if they selected images appropriate for their mental states.

"When the strands of the time bridge are unwoven, all energy escapes."

"So the wormhole is going to explode after all." He curled his fingers into tense fists, feeling and yet not feeling the sensation of pressure. "But *why?*"

"There will be and has been and is too much energy," T'Kreng said simply.

Hayman made an oddly human sounding snort. "We accept the energy outputs your vessels give us, Sisko. They feed us and we use them to sustain the bridge. But the ones who send from the side beyond you send too much for us to absorb."

"We have moved, will move, are moving the time bridge to escape." T'Kreng made an infinitesimal gesture of regret. "As soon as cancellation will be, has been, is no longer possible."

Sisko scowled. "Cancellation of what?"

The bridge of the *Sreba* melted into the bridge of the *Defiant,* with misty images of his crew all speaking at once.

"Ripples—" said Hovan.

"Echoes—" said Eddington.

"Shock waves—" said Dax.

Sisko took a deep, comprehending breath, although he never felt the resulting flow of air. "The subspace fluctuations that were tearing the wormhole apart. You're damping them out from inside."

"We can, have, will," agreed Eddington, his vocal rhythms unchanged despite the shift in form.

"But our resources are finite." Dax gave him another version of Hayman's intense gaze. "We cannot sustain the time bridge at all points in the continuum. Rupture is inevitable."

"Destruction is inevitable." Hovan's voice suddenly held a ringing power that the young ensign would not have for years, if ever. "All times and places are one to us, Sisko. We cannot unmake what for us exists. That is the power of those who live inside the river that we bridge."

Dax nodded. "Those that live inside time. They must take away the energy or suffer the destruction."

"They must go, will go, have gone through the time bridge," Eddington said with surreal calm. "They might come, will come, have not come back."

Fear crawled up Sisko's back. The scene around him shifted again, this time to an alien bridge studded with weapons panels and lit by the glow of external phaser fire. A face like a massive horned gargoyle lifted from a bank of firing controls, breath steaming in the cold of its unknown atmosphere and eyes flame-lit under translucent amber lids. He desperately hoped his own fear had called up that half-remembered image of the enemy from Admiral Hayman's totem figure, and not from the wormhole dwellers' actual experience with them.

"We are holding the time bridge open for your passage to the other side." Despite the Fury's growl, so low-pitched it was almost inaudible, Sisko could still hear the ring of command. "We promise nothing about return. Unless you have prevented the energy from entering, you would do well not to enter yourself."

"I understand," Sisko said curtly. "I'll do my best."

The Fury glared at him a moment longer, then disarmingly shimmered into a smiling image of his long-dead wife. "You no longer live in the past, Benjamin Sisko," she said. "That is good. We wish you to continue."

He opened his mouth to reply, but the sudden tug of acceleration in his gut told him he was back on the *Defiant*. Dax looked over her shoulder at him oddly.

"Captain, did you hear me? I said I'm reading damped-down quantum fluctuations inside the singularity matrix—the same pattern we saw on board the *Sreba*."

"I know." He sprang out of his chair, wanting to feel the impact of real decking beneath his feet. Above him, the *Defiant's* viewscreen roiled with the coruscating energy flows of the wormhole's interior. Sisko tried not to watch it too closely, for fear it would transform without warning into the explosion he was supposed to prevent. "The aliens who live inside the wormhole are cancelling the upstream echoes from the time rift."

"How do you know—" Dax broke off, narrowing her eyes at him with an intensity eerily similar to that of the wormhole dweller who'd borrowed her form. "You mean you saw them again? Did they tell you anything else?"

Sisko sorted through his incoherent memories, ticking off what he was sure of. "That the input of energy which destroys the wormhole will come from the Gamma Quadrant side. That they'll move the wormhole—through time, apparently—to escape it. And that we can't come back through until we've managed to avert whatever that input of energy is."

Dax took a deep, audible breath. "Then Julian was right after all. We *are* still on our original timeline." Her freckled face closed in a little tighter, but otherwise she lost none of her usual Trill self-control. That was the advantage of having several centuries of experience under your belt, Sisko reflected. He wished his own composure were as steady, but he could feel adrenaline fizzing more strongly through his blood with every second they stayed inside the singularity.

"The wormhole dwellers couldn't tell you what the source of this disruptive energy was?" Dax asked.

"No." He paced across the bridge to make a superfluous check on Ensign Hovan's cloaking panel, then prowled restlessly back around the curved perimeter toward Eddington. The security officer was absorbed in running computer simulations of all the automated firing sequences they'd programmed into the phaser controls, apparently in an attempt to fine-tune them down to the last millisecond. Sisko thought about ordering him to stop the needless use of computer time, but refrained. Everyone had their own methods of coping with the stress of wormhole passage, and for all he knew, those milliseconds might prove to be crucial.

He returned to drum his fingers restlessly against Dax's

piloting console. "Is it just me, or is this wormhole passage taking longer than usual?"

The science officer glanced at the clock inset into her display. "Passage times vary depending on initial entrance velocity, and we deliberately came in slow. We're only five percent over the median time interval for the trip." She toggled back her singularity matrix model and pointed at the position of the blue dot among the gently pulsing braid of fire-white lines. "According to this, we should be getting close to the exit."

Sisko bent over her board. "These changes in intensity you're showing here—that's the subspace fluctuation?"

Dax nodded again. "It hit a maximum in the heart of the singularity and has been fading since then. I don't think it will—"

Something changed in the *Defiant's* heading, a subliminal shift of vectors that told Sisko the wormhole was getting ready to spit them back into normal space. He threw a look up at the screen, watching the quantum interference patterns of singularity condense back into star-swept darkness. There were no other ships in view.

"Dax, throttle down the impulse engines to the minimum thrust needed to get us out of the wormhole trigger site," he commanded, feeling his helpless tension settle into the calm, driving rhythm of command. The wormhole washed them with a final bluish benediction of light, then spiraled shut. "I want to leave as little ion trail as possible. Mr. Eddington, give me a long-range sensor scan for enemy vessels."

"Aye-aye, sir."

Sisko swung back toward Hovan. "Are you reading any variations in the cloaking field that could indicate somepone's trying to scan us, Ensign?"

Her nervous gaze flashed from the viewscreen down to her controls. "No, Captain. I'm not seeing any fluctuations in field strength at all."

Sisko grunted and glanced across at the weapons panel. "Results of long-range scan?"

"Completely negative, Captain." Eddington scowled down at his station, as if he thought its sensors could somehow have been subverted by the enemy. "No detectable vessels, no leakage from shields, not even any trace of warp-drive ion trails. According to sensors, we're the only ship within parsecs."

Sisko scowled and sank into his command chair, hands clenching in frustration on its padded arms. The one scenario he had not prepared himself for was that they would emerge from the wormhole to find nothing at all on the other side. Something threatening *had* to be out here in the Gamma Quadrant—the destructive energy that would explode the wormhole back in time couldn't have come from nowhere.

"There are no signs of the Vulcan science ship that entered the wormhole before us, Commander?"

Eddington punched in another command, then shook his head. "Not if it still exists as a powered vessel, sir."

"Which it may not," Dax said quietly. "Captain, helm sensors are picking up a microgravity field at nine-thirteen mark three. It's the right size to be the *Sreba.*"

Sisko grunted acknowledgment. "Set course to circle it at ten kilometers."

The *Defiant* kicked its way across deep space, its viewscreen filled with stars whose steady fire was undimmed by planetary atmospheres and nearer suns. Just as they began to slow and angle into their precautionary orbit, Sisko caught a small, drifting flicker of darkness across the starscape of the Gamma Quadrant. Something had momentarily blocked out those stars—something much nearer than they were.

"I think I see our microgravity field," he said softly. "Magnify starfield vector eight-nineteen, Commander Eddington, and put it on the main viewscreen."

"Yes, sir."

The distant stars swung sideways as the *Defiant's* short-range sensors changed their angle of focus. The darkness became more visible, tracing out a spiral of random motion against the starlight. If it was a spaceship, it was a derelict one. Sisko flicked an inquiring glance from Dax to Eddington.

"Analysis, gentlemen?"

"According to our tactical sensors, there's a ninety-eight-percent probability that it's a ship," Eddington said promptly. "And a sixty-percent probability that it's unarmed."

"But the long-range science sensors aren't picking up any trace of a warp core," Dax said.

Sisko scowled. "You mean the *Sreba's* containment field was breached? Or did the warp core actually explode and somehow manage to leave a big chunk of the ship intact?"

"Neither of those can explain this." Dax swung around to give him a baffled look. "I'm not reading any core radiation in that ship at all, Captain, contained or exploded. *None.*"

He scrubbed a hand across his face, feeling as if he'd just emerged from Alice's rabbit hole rather than a singularity. "Well, if they don't have a warp core, they're not going to attack us any time soon. Take us to visual range, Lieutenant."

"Aye-aye, sir." With the *Defiant's* oversized impulse engines, it took longer for the crew to give and acknowledge that kind of command than it did for the ship to carry it out. Sisko watched the dark patch as it seemed to swoop toward them, growing and resolving into a familiar stubby shape. This darkened hulk was definitely the *Sreba*—or what was left of her. Not even a gleam of emergency lights remained alive aboard the Vulcan research vessel.

Eddington whistled softly as the ruined ship enlarged to fill the viewscreen. "It looks like they got *sliced* open, Captain."

"Yes." Sisko eyed the damage with disbelieving eyes. No phaser burns had seared along the *Sreba's* hull, no jagged photon-torpedo eruptions had torn away her flanks. Instead, a myriad of impossibly neat cuts had razored off the roof of her bridge, cut through her warp nacelles, and quarried through her breached decks to leave a gaping hollow where her warp core must have been.

"Dax, have you ever seen weapons damage like this before?"

He could see a distinct shiver run along the Trill's freckled neck. "I don't—no. No, I don't think so." The trace of uncertainty leached out of her voice. "It's certainly not Jem'Hadar work."

"Nor is it Romulan, Klingon, or Cardassian." Sisko leaned back in his chair, glaring at the derelict Vulcan ship as if he could somehow make it yield up its secrets by sheer force of will. "Are there any signs of life on board?"

"Negative, sir," Eddington reported.

"I started a carbon-scan for organic remains," Dax added quietly. "Also negative, Captain."

Sisko frowned. "Can you detect any sign of internal backup power? If any of the computer memory is still online, we might be able to download her instrument records."

The science officer punched another set of commands into her hybrid engineering/helm panel. The resulting readout made her stiffen in her seat. "Captain, I'm detecting a strong internal power source inside the ship. It looks like an emergency stasis generator—and it's coming from the area of their sickbay."

Sisko straightened, feeling his pulse quicken. "An injured survivor?"

"Very possibly." Dax swung around to give him an urgent look. "Permission to beam the stasis chamber aboard?"

"Can you do it without releasing the stasis field?"

"Yes."

He vaulted to his feet. "Then let's beam it right onto the bridge and see what we've got. Commander Eddington, Ensign Hovan, keep your phasers trained on the beam-in site in case of hostile action—and Dax, I want a continuous transporter lock on the power generator, so we can spit it right back into space if it turns out to be a Trojan horse."

"Yes, sir." She programmed a series of commands into her boards, her freckled face creasing with concentration. "Ready on your mark, Captain."

Sisko took a deep breath and drew his own phaser, moving to the empty right side of the bridge so they had the beam-in site covered from all angles. Hovan had braced her phaser on her console and Eddington had his locked in both hands, in approved Starfleet style. He hoped neither of them would get so nervous they fired at the seeming motion of the transporter sparkle.

"Begin transport."

CHAPTER
11

THE ENVIRONMENTAL SUIT helmet banged into the back of the locker, bouncing out onto the floor again as though begging Kira to kick it back inside. She indulged it with passionate force, then followed it up with the chest piece, arms, and trousers of the suit. She had to twist her entire body into the throw to make the pieces crash into the cabinet with satisfying violence; even then, she still pulled out part of the suit just to be able to sling it again and again to re-create that sound. It didn't fit very nicely among the other suits without its proper hooks and hangers, but Kira didn't really give much of a damn. As far as she was concerned, this little color-coded, height-proportioned arrangement was just one more example of Starfleet's anal compulsion for rules and order instead of for what any half-minded gennet-herder could tell you was *right*. Faced with that awareness, the concept of returning *Rio Grande's* environmental suit to its assigned position in the public locker seemed an unendurable act of submission.

The *Defiant* had spiraled down the wormhole's maw while she was dragging the suit out of the runabout one and two pieces at a time. Light, as brilliantly refracted as a Prophet's Orb, winked unexpectedly at her through an observation port, and habit had forced her to pause and watch as space unfolded in a helix of color. The ship slid down the singularity's throat like a dim black bead, dwarfed by the wormhole's size and beauty. For just an instant, her traditional twinge of religious respect was beaten back by a fist of anger. She felt like a helpless native whose world, people, and faith had been swept up and put away for safekeeping by well-meaning outsiders. "Play amongst yourselves for a while," Great Father Starfleet seemed to say. "We'll be back later to tuck you in."

But even as the image exploded in her mind while the wormhole peeled in on itself and disappeared, she knew it wasn't fair. She knew it wasn't fair now, as she kicked and rekicked the last boot into the environmental-suit locker. Somewhere in the rational landscape of her thoughts, she knew that Starfleet's presence in the Bajor system had meant more to their growing independence than anyone could ever have dreamed, and Sisko's arrival as the long-prophesied Emissary was one of the most important events in Bajoran history. She should be relieved and honored to be part of such great accomplishments, to help lay the path toward the future with every passing day.

Instead, she felt like a child who'd been given a miniaturized spaceport set for her birthday, only to have her father play with it without her.

This time when a blossom of light gleamed through the nearest window, she almost didn't turn to look. She didn't want to see the wormhole again, and be forced to think about being trapped on one side of it while the man she was mad at was unreachable on the other. But there was always the chance Sisko and the *Defiant* might return this quickly—she hated open-ended time frames—and the thought of not having to wait for the *Mukaikubo* to head after Pak Dorren was certainly appealing. Shouldering closed the door to the suit locker, she trotted over to the window just to satisfy her curiosity so she could go to bed without having to wonder what she missed.

A single Lethian passenger coupe ghosted slowly in and out of the station's shadow, rhythmically catching and leaving the light from the distant sun. Of course. Nothing so useful as the *Defiant* coming home, or the *Mukaikubo* appearing ahead of schedule. She let out a tired snort and began to turn her back on them when one detail about the ship's stately progress prickled the hair on the back of her neck.

Running lights. The Lethian ship was drifting past the station without its running lights.

She tapped thoughtfully at her comm badge as she turned back to the view outside. "Kira to Ops. Chief, are you in contact with the Lethian transport just passing the station?"

O'Brien's voice when he answered carried just the slightest hint of confusion beneath his normally businesslike tone. "We've got no record of a Lethian transport in the sector."

"About fifty kilometers out from runabout pad F, thirty degrees above the ecliptic."

She waited in silence for him to run a scan of the area. The passenger coupe continued its dreamlike glide toward the edge of the window, its elongated nose just disappearing from Kira's sight when O'Brien came back with a short little *hmph!* of surprise. "Composition and size match Lethian registries," he reported, obviously reading from something in front of him. "But it's too light on mass, and I'm not picking up a drive signature."

"That's because it doesn't have one." Kira didn't realize what she was thinking until that whisper breathlessly escaped her; then disbelief and fury tangled together deep inside her. "Chief, tow the Lethian ship into cargo bay four and have Bashir meet me down there." Not that there would be survivors. She was already certain of that.

Still, there was something uniquely infuriating about trotting up to the cargo-bay airlock and finding no one there to meet her but the shapeshifter with whom she'd already spent the last two fruitless days.

"I happened to overhear your conversation with Chief O'Brien," Odo remarked before she even asked him. "I took the liberty of joining you."

"I'm glad you did." The deck under her feet hummed on a note too deep to be heard as pumps somewhere in the station's structure kicked into life. Kira paced impatiently in front of the airlock, glancing toward first one end of the long corridor, then the other. "Where the hell is Bashir?"

"He isn't coming." Odo met her fierce scowl with a serene lift of one shoulder. "He's sending Ensign Maile, so he can stay in the infirmary with Professor Stel." Then, as though imparting some meaningful tidbit of evidence, "One of the Vulcan physicists has a case of *mactru* fever."

Kira threw her hands up in frustration. "Vulcan physicists? *What* Vulcan physicists?"

"The ones who came back from Starbase One with Captain Sisko." Odo's face took on one of his few unmistakable expressions—the one Kira always associated with teachers who could no longer hide their disappointment in an inattentive pupil. "Really, Major, you must learn to bring yourself up to date on station business when you've been away for an hour or more."

She managed a wry little smile for him, and paced back down the corridor to rejoin him at the lock as the bay finished flooding with air and the ready lights blinked green. "Sorry, Odo. I don't have quite your flair for 'overhearing' other people's conversations."

"Pity. It would save us both time and discussion." And he sounded not the slightest bit embarrassed by the major's implication, even when running footsteps announced the arrival of one of Bashir's human medical assistants close enough on his words to have picked up at least the gist of their conversation. Thinking it best to avoid any further gossip in front of the girl, Kira merely nodded her a terse greeting and activated her comm badge.

"Okay, Chief, we're all here. Open up."

A quick exchange of air puffed cold into the corridor as chill, space-touched gases flowed together with the warmer station atmosphere. Ensign Maile unfolded a medical tricorder into the silence, and its shrill song bounced around the huge bay like a springball in a box. Something about the smallness of that sound against the creaks and hisses of the transport warming to the station air made Kira wish for a phaser as she stepped into the open bay.

It wasn't a big ship, as far as passenger transports went. Enough to hold maybe twenty-five adult Lethians, fifty if they didn't mind being chummy. Squat and irregular like the Lethians themselves, it reflected their fanatical privacy as well—no external markings, no windows, no hint as to where it was going or why. The only thing Kira was fairly certain of was that the curling petals of sliced metal gaping open down the length of its side weren't part of the standard Lethian design.

"I'm picking up faint life signs. . . ."

Kira halted, turning toward Maile's voice when it rang out suddenly above the shush of blooming frost. She'd almost forgotten anybody else was with her.

"Inside the Lethian airlock," Maile continued, never raising her eyes from the tricorder's dance of readings. "Or very close to there."

"Lethian life signs?" Odo asked.

Kira thought the ensign hadn't heard him at first, but then Maile shook her head with a little frown. "I can't tell. The hull's carrying a pretty heavy transperiodic charge. It's reflecting more of the tricorder signal than it's letting through."

A radioactive derelict—just what they needed. Kira backed a few more steps away. "Are we safe out here?"

Maile pulled alongside her, nodding. "For at least a half-hour." A somewhat nervous smile played across her round, golden face as she glanced up from the tricorder. "I wouldn't go leaning against any bulkheads, though."

Ah—humor. Something else Kira might appreciate more if she weren't so tired. Or so scared. "Constable. . . ." She swept a gallant gesture toward the ruined hulk, earning a curious tilt of the head from Odo. "If you'd be so kind."

Whether or not he understood her strange, tired sarcasm, he understood what she wanted of him, at least. Lifting one arm shoulder high, he stretched himself across the remaining distance to trigger the passenger ship's outer airlock door. It seemed a pointless exercise to Kira—there were a hundred places to enter the ship through the gashes torn into its frost-speckled hide. But actually boarding the ruined vessel would have required another stint in one of O'Brien's ISHA approved hardsuits, and Kira had neither the patience nor the stamina for another suit walk right now. Besides, she'd seen enough of these ships in the last two days to write up a convincing report without even going inside. What they were doing here now were technicalities—going through the motions, just in case.

Frost and damage had warped the door in its frame. It bumped something deep inside, grinding helplessly, and

Kira could whiff just the faintest trace of something chemically sharp, and burning.

"Wait a minute!"

Maile again, intent on her tricorder and impossibly close to Kira's elbow, the strain of making sense from the small machine's trilling knotting her face and eyes into a tangle of concentration. "I—it—" She pursed her lips in scholarly frustration. "I lost the reading for a moment. Like it moved, or changed, or—"

A great crash of screaming metal exploded through the bay when the door finally let go and slammed open. Kira whirled toward the Lethian ship, instinctively going for the phaser that wasn't there as Maile shrieked and leapt against her. Movement flashed in the suddenly open airlock—dark, smooth, long, low—and Kira found herself jerking aside to free herself of the ensign's clutch in the same instant that Odo recoiled from the skritch-skitter of claws on decking and the ugly, hairless escapee rocketed between their feet to dash across the bay and disappear into the station's halls.

When it was all over and the strange, brittle silence had returned to the ship and the bay, the only thing Kira could think to say was, "Ah, dammit!"

Maile extricated herself with only as much dignity as Kira expected from someone who'd throw herself into someone else's arms in the first place. "Well," she said, a little shakily, as she stooped to retrieve her tricorder, "whatever it was, it wasn't a Lethian."

Kira snorted at this lovely example of well-trained Starfleet attentiveness. "It was a Cardassian vole." Still, she had to admit she was surprised by how much it calmed her to say that out loud. Proving only the power inherent in one ensign's overreaction. "Just what Chief O'Brien needs," she sighed, striving for a lighter note. "Fresh breeding stock."

Odo didn't turn from where he examined the Lethian airlock doorway. "I'll try to break it to him gently."

Kira was just as glad not to be saddled with that chore on top of everything else this ship represented. Drawn by the tricorder's renewed song, she glanced aside at Maile. "Any other life signs?"

The young medic—composed now, but still flushed with

what Kira assumed was embarrassment as she scanned the ship—shook her head. "Not even voles."

Damn.

Beside the opened airlock, Odo straightened. "Four," he said simply, catching Kira's eye.

"Only this one's not Bajoran." She slammed one fist against her leg, longing instead for something to throw, or kick, or break. There were disadvantages to loosing your temper in the middle of a nearly empty hold. "Seal off the bay until O'Brien can get down here to examine the remains," she told Odo. "And put together teams to meet every ship that docks here from now on. I don't want any more militia sneaking on board until we find out what they've done with those engine cores."

The constable called out as she turned to leave, "And you're going . . . ?"

"To talk to Starfleet." She paused in the cargo bay's entrance, clenching her hand into a fist on the jamb as she looked back at the ruined Lethian ship. "Maybe now that a government with more money than Bajor is involved, they can make a little time for us in their busy schedules."

The hum of the transporter faded, replaced by the hiss and crackle of space-cold metal hitting room-temperature air. Dax swung around to see a haze of contact fog blossom inside the *Defiant's* bridge, turning Sisko and Eddington into vague shadows and obscuring Hovan entirely. Whatever she had beamed aboard was hidden behind that pale gray veil, but it was large enough to trigger an urgent buzz from life-support systems. Dax glanced down at the priority screen that had popped up on her engineering panel, noticing that the temperature had dropped fifteen degrees.

"Dax, can you get rid of this mist?" demanded Sisko's tense voice. "I can't see anything inside it."

"I'm adjusting life-support now." She dialed down bridge humidity levels and tapped in permission for heating rates to temporarily exceed standard safety thresholds. A rush of arid air swept through the bridge in response, making her skin prickle unhappily but clearing most of the fog away. What emerged was a frost-spattered gleam of metal, shaped like an upright coffin. It looked like the medical stasis generator she'd expected, although Dax couldn't see if anyone was actually inside it.

Sisko edged farther toward the back of the bridge, craning his head for a better view. He made a frustrated noise. "The window panel's still frosted on this side—Ensign Hovan, can you see through it?"

"A little bit, sir." She looked both surprised and uncertain. "I think there's a Starfleet cadet inside."

"That's Petersen!" Dax engaged the automatic helm controls and vaulted up without asking Sisko for permission. The captain motioned Eddington to cover her station with a silent jerk of his chin, then moved back to allow her to round the deck in front of him. Dax frowned, seeing that he hadn't yet put away his phaser.

"Benjamin, you can't suspect Heather—"

"Can't I?" He followed her to the front of the stasis chamber, where the last of the contact frost was melting into a faint glitter of mist. His dark eyes held a wary look Dax remembered from past battles—something had triggered his cautious military instincts. "Then why is she in that stasis field, old man? Does she look injured to you?"

Dax scrubbed the last of the mist from the transparent aluminum, finding it still achingly cold to the touch, and eyed Heather Petersen's frozen form. Not a trace of blood or battle grime darkened her Starfleet uniform, and her rounded face still held the rosy bloom of complete health. The only thing that looked out of character was the grimace that twisted her quiet mouth and the fierce downward slant of her eyebrows.

"Maybe she had internal injuries," Hovan suggested.

Dax shook her head. "I don't think so, but I'd need a medical tricorder to be sure." She glanced across at Sisko. "Do you want me to get one from sickbay before we drop the stasis field? If the scan is negative, we'll still have to decide whether or not to release her."

He grunted reluctant agreement to that logic. "All right, drop the stasis field—but don't get between me and her."

Dax didn't dignify that unnecessary command with an answer. She leaned forward to press the release controls on the stasis field's internal power unit, then backed away while the seals on the transparent aluminum cover hissed open. A moment later, the glimmer of stasis beneath it transformed into a blur of arrested motion—not a forward lunge but a backward slam, as if Petersen had been pushed violently into the stasis chamber just as it was being closed.

"—can't do this! This is a Starfleet mission, dammit, T'Kreng! You can't—" Petersen's fierce shout died as soon as her gaze focused on Dax. Her eyes widened and she vaulted out from the stasis chamber with a gasp. "You came back?" she demanded eagerly, her gaze moving from Dax to Sisko. Then she took in the black military curves of the *Defiant*'s bridge, and the color faded abruptly from her cheeks. "This isn't the *Sreba!* What's going on?"

"You're on the Starfleet cruiser *Defiant,* Heather, posted to *Deep Space Nine*. We just beamed you in from the *Sreba.*" Dax paused, trying to find a gentle way to phrase the rest of her explanation. "We found your research ship, floating derelict and abandoned here in the Gamma Quadrant. You were the only survivor we could locate."

"But that's—" Petersen broke off, shaking her head in what looked like utter bafflement. "Lieutenant, that's impossible. If the *Sreba* got caught inside the wormhole, the whole ship would have been torn apart by gravity waves. There's no way my stasis chamber should have survived."

"It wasn't the wormhole that destroyed the *Sreba,*" Sisko said quietly. "Your ship was attacked when it emerged from the wormhole into the Gamma Quadrant. You don't remember any of that?"

"How could I?" Petersen demanded, with unusual bitterness. "Professor T'Kreng ordered her medic to put me into stasis five minutes after she beamed your team away. She said it was so I wouldn't be found guilty of disobeying Starfleet orders, but I think it was because I kept shouting at her that what she was doing was illogical. It was making the crew nervous."

"You should be grateful to her." Dax steered the Starfleet cadet around so she could see the *Defiant*'s main viewscreen. Petersen's eyes widened as she took in the breached ruin of the Vulcan research ship floating against the stars. "Whatever attacked the *Sreba* took her warp core, as well as killing or capturing all of her crew. The fact that you were in the stasis generator was probably the only thing that saved your life."

"But *why?*" It was not a grieving or philosophical question. The cadet's gaze when she looked back at Dax was truly puzzled. "At the Academy, they taught us that when you search for an enemy crew, the first place you look for them to hide is in the stasis chambers of sickbay. Surely the Klingons or the Romulans or the Cardassians—whoever it was that attacked us—knew that, too."

"It wasn't the Klingons or Romulans or Cardassians who attacked you." Sisko sheathed his phaser and crossed the deck to the empty weapons panel. A quick stab at the sensor controls brought the Vulcan research ship into closer focus on their viewscreen. The myriad slices through her hull looked even more alien than before, their edges smooth as polished latinum, their spacing uncannily regular. "Our enemy doesn't know any more about us than we know about it."

Dax tilted her head, hearing the new ring of determination in her old friend's voice. "Have you thought of a way to change that?"

A jerk of Sisko's chin indicated the lightless shadow on the viewscreen. "You can learn a lot about an enemy by seeing what they leave behind on a battlefield," he said grimly. "In this case, that's the *Sreba.*"

Over Dax's objections, Heather Petersen had agreed to Sisko's suggestion that she make up the fourth member of their away team. "The captain's right. I'll know better than you will what's normal on the *Sreba* and what's not," she said through a mouthful of toast and cloud-apple jam. Remembering their predawn departure from the *Sreba,* Dax had insisted on feeding the cadet breakfast before they left. "And besides, I want to see if any of our scientific data is still retrievable. That way, at least we won't have made that wormhole passage for nothing."

The scientist in Dax couldn't argue with that. "That's a good idea," she admitted. "If we have enough time, perhaps we can analyze it and pinpoint the initiation of the time rift."

Petersen frowned, as if something had just occurred to

her. "Are you sure it hasn't happened already?" she demanded, pushing her breakfast away half-finished. "I don't remember seeing any singularity fluctuations near the *Sreba*—and the captain said she was attacked right after she came out of the wormhole."

"The wormhole stabilized when T'Kreng went through it." Dax led her out of the *Defiant*'s spartan mess hall and down to the main turbolifts. "Away-team staging area," she told the turbolift computer, then turned back to Petersen. "We initially thought it meant the time rift had been averted, but when we followed you we found out that the precursor echoes were just being damped down by the creatures that live inside the singularity. They told us that an enormous input of energy from the Gamma Quadrant side is going to force them to wrench the singularity back in time in time to escape."

Petersen's quiet eyes lit up. "You saw them, Lieutenant?"

Dax shook her head wistfully. "No, they only spoke to Captain Sisko." The turbolift doors slid open onto a staging deck scattered with environmental suits and zero-g jet-packs. She raised her voice deliberately. "They seem to like talking to him for some reason. You'd think they'd find a Trill more interesting."

Sisko looked up from where he and one of the security guards were sorting their equipment into order. The quick glint of humor in his eyes told Dax that her teasing comment hadn't been lost on him. "You're welcome to stop and chat with them on the way back, old man," he retorted. "In the meantime, I'd like to check out the *Sreba* before whatever attacked her comes back for us. Ensign Pritz and I have pulled together the equipment we'll need for the away team. Find yourselves an environmental suit that fits, gentlemen, and let's get going."

"Aye-aye, sir." Both Petersen and Pritz answered with the well-drilled promptness of recent training. Dax lifted an eyebrow while the two young women swung away to obey Sisko's crisp command.

"With a crew this fresh from Starfleet Academy, Benjamin, you're going to get spoiled," she said, pitching her voice just low enough to be masked by the clatter of gear.

Sisko snorted and threw her an environmental suit. "I'm

sure you'll keep me from getting too used to being obeyed without question. What do you make of—"

"—ten cc's boromine citrate infused in fifteen percent saline, neurotransmitters now stable—"

"Dax?"

She blinked and looked around. "Did one of you just say something about neurotransmitters?" she demanded of Petersen and Pritz, even though the logical part of her mind already knew the answer. Although she rarely noticed which of her two cerebral cortices processed her sensory input, this time she knew it was Dax who thought that familiar voice had spoken through the clatter of suits being donned. Jadzia's brain had no memory of it.

"No, sir," Pritz said in surprise. Petersen shook her head as well, eyeing her worriedly.

Jadzia summoned up a smile for them. "I guess I imagined it, then," she said lightly, while, inside, Dax insisted that it *had* heard Bashir's voice, right here, right now. She turned back to Sisko, now suited up except for his helmet, and saw from his scowl that he wasn't buying her explanation.

"All right, old man, what just happened?" he demanded.

She took a deep breath and began climbing into her own environmental suit. "Sensory separation," she said without looking at him. "Dax heard something Jadzia didn't."

Sisko snorted again. "Then why were you *gone* for a moment while I was talking to you?"

"I'm not sure, Benjamin." She sealed up the suit's single chest seam and bent to scoop up its helmet. The emotion she was trying to hide from Sisko wasn't fear—it was an embarrassingly unscientific excitement at what she hoped this meant. *You can't extrapolate from a single data point,* Dax told herself firmly. *It's premature to think this was anything more than a stray neural cascade, bringing an old memory inappropriately to life.*

With her excitement reined in to hopeful caution, she straightened to meet Sisko's intent gaze. "It might have been some kind of aftereffect from my merger with the other symbiont back at Starbase One." That had the advantage of being close enough to the truth that Dax could say it without faltering. "I don't think it will compromise my performance on the away team."

He gave her a long, unwavering stare. "See that it doesn't."

With a quick snap, Sisko sealed his own helmet down and picked up one of the flashlights and a heavy-duty laser torch. Pritz was already carrying a phaser rifle strapped across her back in addition to her flashlight and hand phaser, while Petersen had hefted the emergency medical kit. That left a flashlight and a tricorder for Dax. She found room for both in her suit's bulky pockets, then slid her hand phaser into its loop on her utility belt.

"Away team prepared for zero-g vacuum transport, Captain?" Eddington's voice asked inside her helmet.

"Affirmative, Commander." Sisko gathered them together with a jerk of his chin. "You're in command of the *Defiant* while we're gone, Mr. Eddington. Whatever happens, do *not* take her back through the wormhole. Not under any conditions."

"Understood, Captain. Four to beam out?"

Sisko gave Dax one last speculative look. She gave him back a nod as confident as she could make it. "Four to beam out," Sisko agreed. "Energize."

Just before the chilly shiver of dissociation swept through her, Dax could have sworn she heard Bashir saying in frustration, "—still not enough isoboromine—"

CHAPTER
12

IT DIDN'T EVEN look like the same ship.

Dax splashed her flashlight around, trying to identify the dark emptiness Eddington had beamed them into on the *Sreba*. In the half-day she'd spent aboard the small Vulcan research vessel, she could have sworn she'd seen every public area bigger than a broom closet, but this towering two-story atrium was unfamiliar. She began to ask Heather Petersen where they were, then stopped. The right shoulder pocket of her environmental suit was vibrating—the only evidence in this hard vacuum that her tricorder was emitting an alarm. Dax tugged it out and cursed in Klingon when she saw the radiation readings flashing on it.

"This is where the warp core used to be!" She and Petersen said it in unison across their suit communicators, but Dax's urgent voice overrode over the cadet's simple amazement. "I'm reading high levels of subspace radiation and ionic particle flux in here, Captain. We have to get behind some shielding fast."

Sisko made no reply, but in the braided glow of their flashlight beams, Dax could see his broad-shouldered form trace out an efficient sweep of the chamber. "Looks like a Jeffries tube opening over there," he said, using his flashlight beam as a pointer. "Pritz goes first, phaser drawn. I'll go last."

The security guard acknowledged the command by unslinging her phaser rifle and pulsing her jetpack in one smooth motion. Before the burst of compressed air had faded to glittering ice motes in their flashlight beams, Pritz had disappeared into the dark promise of safety.

"All clear," her terse voice said inside their helmets after a moment. Dax motioned Petersen after her, waiting while the cadet took a slow moment to orient herself to the tunnel's long axis before she pushed into it. Dax angled her belt jets to follow, keeping her flashlight tucked under one arm to illuminate the display panel of her tricorder. The steady glow of Sisko's flashlight from behind provided more than enough light to guide her through the Jeffries tube.

"Radiation levels?" Sisko demanded after a moment.

"Dropping." Dax changed her jet angle to maneuver through a tight coil in the tube, almost bumping into the magnetized soles of Petersen's boots as she did. The tricorder's silent shiver of alarm went still a moment later. "We're shielded now."

Sisko grunted. "Pritz, any sign of an exit up there?"

"Yes, sir. I don't know if it's the kind of exit you want, though."

Dax bumped into Petersen's boots again, this time hard enough to make the insulation of her environmental suit crunch. "Right now, I'll take any kind of exit I can get, Ensign," she said dryly, then became aware that the boots overhead weren't moving. "Heather, are you all right?"

"Um—yes, sir." She sounded a little shaky. "It's just going to take me a minute—"

Dax craned her head to look past the cadet, noticing a patch of darkness ahead that Sisko's flashlight beam couldn't seem to penetrate. She turned her own flashlight up to join his, but it didn't make a dent in the overhead gloom. It wasn't until Petersen wriggled herself around some obstacle and disappeared that Dax finally saw the distant glitter of stars and realized she was looking out at open space.

"We're going out through a hull breach," she warned Sisko.

"With the level of damage this ship's sustained, walking the hull might be the fastest way to get anywhere." He thumped at one of her own boot soles. "I can't get out until you do, old man."

Dax fired her belt jets, undulating gracefully around the ragged lip of metal that partially blocked the Jeffries tube, then floated out into clear space. Petersen and Pritz were already standing upright on the hull, their magnetized boots anchoring them against the *Sreba*'s slight angular momentum. Dax used her jets to brake herself before inertia took her drifting away from the Vulcan ship, and felt the slight tug of renewed spin as the magnetic plates on her boots made contact with the hull.

Sisko emerged from the breached tube more slowly, easing his broad shoulders through the ragged opening to avoid tearing his environmental suit. Dax felt the unsupported hull shudder beneath her when he finally vaulted up to join them.

"Bridge first," he said curtly. "Petersen, can you find it?"

"Yes, sir." The cadet might be awkward and inexperienced at jetting through microgravity, but walking on the outside of a spaceship seemed to hold no fears for her. She turned and headed across the curving horizon of the hull, easily matching Sisko's long strides. They must have added holoexercises in contact walking to the academy since she had graduated, Dax reflected wryly.

She began to follow them, watching her feet to be sure she was making enough contact with each step, then stopped. A long grooved scratch marred the duranium metal cladding beneath her, although the hull hadn't actually been breached here. Pritz paused beside her without being ordered to, phaser rifle still cradled in one arm.

"Something wrong, sir?"

"Something interesting." Dax squatted, keeping her bootheels pressed flat to maintain her position, and ran her tricorder over the gouge. Its small display screen spit back the expected analysis of the *Sreba*'s hull: layered duranium-titanium-steel alloy, approximately ten centimeters thick. Dax frowned and tapped in a request for trace compounds with one gloved finger, then scanned the long scratch again. There was an anomalously long pause before the tricorder display flashed up a single word: difluorine.

Dax let out an involuntary yelp, more of amazement than alarm. Pritz made a reflexive turn on the hull beside her, scanning the field of view with her phaser rifle armed and ready. From out of sight, Sisko's voice said sharply, "What is it, old man?"

"Something I wasn't expecting." She stood and took a careful step back from the scratch she had squatted so casually over, feeling a shiver reverberate up the twin freckle trails of her shoulders. "Try to avoid touching any of the gashes in the hull, or even stepping on them. Whoever attacked the *Sreba* was using chemical weapons."

"*Chemical* weapons?" Sisko's deep voice couldn't rise in astonishment the way hers had, but she heard the sheer disbelief in it. "What kind of chemical can slice through duranium in hard vacuum at two degrees Kelvin?"

"One that's not supposed to exist outside of Starfleet laboratories." Dax climbed over the *Sreba*'s ragged starboard nacelle, and altered course to join the two suited figures standing near the crater that had once been the bridge. Up close, it looked as if a vast section of hull had simply dissolved away here, with no signs of damage even a meter from thē edge. She now understood how that had happened. "They used difluorine, Benjamin. The most reactive and the most unstable of the transperiodic elements."

Beneath Sisko's soft whistle, Dax could hear someone—she couldn't tell if it was Petersen or Pritz—draw in a startled breath. "And some of it may still be around?" the captain demanded.

"That depends on what material the difluorine encountered," Dax replied. "A metal alloy like duranium should have simply disintegrated and floated away. I'm picking up only a few parts per trillion here, not enough to breach suit integrity. But with all the carbon-rich fibers and resin alloys down there—" She pointed one bulky glove at the tangle of exploded instrument panels and collapsed plasma displays that was all that remained of the *Sreba*'s former bridge. "—it's a different story. If reaction crusts of difluoric carbide formed on any of those instrument panels, it could be protecting pockets of unspent difluorine." She turned so she could meet Sisko's dark eyes steadily through the clear window of their helmets. "I think it would be best if I ran this solo, Benjamin."

Sisko grimaced, but she could already see the grudging

agreement in his face. "Very well, but I want you to scan every step you take. Petersen, can you guide her from up here?"

"Yes, sir."

"Good. Sisko to *Defiant*."

"Eddington here, sir."

"I want you to use a tractor beam to reduce our angular momentum and keep the bridge area in constant view. Be prepared to transport Lieutenant Dax back to the *Defiant* if her internal suit monitor shows any sign of decompression."

"Aye-aye, sir." The nearly ultraviolet sparkle of a tractor beam shot out from what looked like totally empty space above the *Sreba*. Dax felt the tug and sway of deceleration as the *Sreba*'s chaotic spinning drift was stabilized.

"All right, old man." Sisko gave Dax a shoulder clap she could barely feel through her suit insulation. "Try to download normal ship's sensors first, then the helm, then the scientific data stations."

"Yes, Captain." Dax resisted the impulse to take a deep breath, knowing the sudden flux of carbon dioxide would only confuse her suit's life-support controls. She flexed her feet to break the magnetic seal her boots were making with the hull, then fired her jetpack. The quick burst of compressed air launched her straight down into the heart of the destruction.

"Ship's sensors are to your left, Lieutenant, just past that exposed optical cabling channel," Petersen's quiet voice said in her ear. "No, not that panel, the one next to it."

"I see it." Still hovering, Dax scanned the exploded sensor array with her tricorder. The display showed a strong spike of difluoric carbide, but only trace amounts of the oxidant itself. "It should be safe to touch. I'm going to try downloading—"

"Captain!" Eddington's voice sliced across hers urgently. "I'm picking up warp signatures from two incoming vessels. Tactical computer says there's a high probability that both are Jem'Hadar fighters. Even if they can't see the *Defiant*, sir, they're going to see our tractor beam."

Sisko made a frustrated noise. "Not to mention us

standing out here. Estimated time of arrival, Mr. Eddington?"

"Seven minutes, sir."

"Dax?"

She had already powered up her jets and was maneuvering away from the sensor panel. "Difluorine leaching has wiped the main sensor memory board. Give me a minute to check the helm controls." This time, her tricorder scan showed a jagged spike of pure difluorine. Even though she hadn't actually made contact with the panel, Dax jetted back reflexively. "Helm's contaminated, sir. Do I have time to check the science sensors?"

"Only if you can do it in less than five minutes," Sisko said grimly.

"Try a straight data dump through the optical port," Petersen suggested. "If the memory board is still intact, that will go faster than a scan. We'll just have to sort it all out later."

"Which science station should I use?" Dax demanded.

"The main analytical display in the center of the bridge looks like the least damaged."

She glanced around, spotting one upright plasma display in the midst of the wreckage. Her quick tricorder scan reported much less difluoric carbide here, and almost no difluorine. Dax hoped that wasn't because she'd started the scan while she was still two meters away. She made tentative contact with the decking and felt no immediate outrush of air from her suit. With a sigh of relief she couldn't suppress, Dax reached down to align her tricorder's receptor with the panel's knee-level optical port.

"Jem'Hadar warp signature confirmed, Captain," Eddington's nervous voice said over the communicator channel. "Fighters three minutes away and closing."

Sisko grunted. "Lock on to all away-team comm signals. Prepare to release tractor beam and transport us back onto the bridge of the *Defiant* at my mark. Dax, are you getting data?"

Even though her awkwardly bent posture made it impossible to see the display, the slight vibration of the tricorder in her gloved hand—the vacuum equivalent of steady beeping—gave her the answer she'd hoped for. "Affirmative, Captain. Download in progress."

"Jem'Hadar fighters two minute away and closing."

"Let me know the *instant* that download is finished, old man."

"Don't worry, I will." Dax tightened her grip on the tricorder, waiting for its small vibration to cease. How much data could T'Kreng have collected in one short passage through the wormhole?

"Fighters one minute away and closing."

The tricorder rippled one last vibration into her tense fingers and fell still. "Download complete, Captain." Dax scrambled up from her stooped position, cradling the tricorder in both hands to make sure she didn't drop it.

"Begin transport!" Sisko snapped. "Disengage tractor—"

A shiver of molecular paralysis interrupted him. When Dax could hear again, the background noise of red alert ringing muffled through her helmet told her she was on the *Defiant's* bridge.

"—beam," Sisko finished, tearing off his helmet and striding to the empty captain's chair. Dax tossed her tricorder to Heather Petersen and went to take her own station at the helm.

"Tractor beam disengaged, sir." Hovan vacated the engineering and helm panel gratefully, and returned to her own cloaking control station. Dax glanced down at the board and saw nothing amiss, then stripped off her own gloves and helmet. At her left, Eddington turned at the weapons panel and said, "Jem'Hadar fighters are just entering visual range now, sir. I don't think they saw us."

"Good work, gentlemen," Sisko said crisply. "Put the Jem'Hadar on the main viewscreen, Eddington. Dax, get us out to a safer distance, but pulse our engines while you do it. I don't want our friends out there to see a continuous thermal signature."

"Beginning pulsed thrust, vector two-nine-zero mark zero-nine-seven." Dax glanced up at the viewscreen, seeing the distinctive silhouettes of two Jem'Hadar attack ships swoop toward them. She glanced back at Sisko. "It looks like they're heading for the *Sreba,* sir."

His intent gaze never wavered from the screen. "Let's

wait until we see them go past us before we start celebrating. Hovan, be prepared to drop cloaking at my mark. Eddington, I want you to target photon torpedoes on both Jem'Hadar ships."

"Torpedoes locked and ready, sir." The security officer's hands hovered over his board, but after a moment he sighed in what sounded like mixed disappointment and relief. "Fighters overshot us by six kilometers, sir. They're falling into orbit around the *Sreba.*"

"Told you," Dax said softly, eyes fixed discreetly on her helm panel. The snort from behind told her that Sisko had heard the comment, just as she'd meant him to. "Maintain position, Captain?"

"Yes. I want to see what they're going to do."

For a long moment, the answer to that seemed to be nothing. The Jem'Hadar fighters circled the ruined Vulcan research ship like two oversize moons, apparently inspecting it. Then, without warning, a double set of phaser beams licked out from each ship, precisely cross-trained on the *Sreba.* It took only a few seconds for that doubled attack to explode the small ship into a cloud of glowing, vaporized metal.

"Why did they *do* that?" Petersen's voice was raw, as if the sight of that final destruction had triggered all the emotion she hadn't had time to assimilate yet. Pritz had reported to her battle station for the red alert, leaving the cadet standing alone and uncertain beside the disengaged engineering console. "All they had to do was scan to see that the *Sreba* was a derelict!"

"I think they did scan—and something they found bothered them." Sisko came to stand beside the helm, watching the Jem'Hadar fighters circle the now empty space where the *Sreba* had been. "I think they're scanning for it again now." He looked down at Dax, his face tightening with swift decision. "Set a course to follow those fighters back to their base. They appear to know something, and I'm starting to think we should know about it, too."

"Aye-aye, sir." She punched in a series of commands to link their flight controls with tracking scans of the Jem'Hadar ships. "Ships are moving off at vector eight-nine-four mark five-one-four."

"Power scans indicate Jem'Hadar ships are engaging warp drive now," Eddington reported. "Warp five."

"Follow at warp five. Stand down red alert and photon torpedoes, but remain cloaked." Sisko glanced back to where Heather Petersen lingered uncertainly at the back of the bridge with Dax's tricorder still in her gloved hands. "Cadet, I'd appreciate it if you went down to our science lab and started examining the data we downloaded. Report anything you find to Lieutenant Dax."

"Aye-aye, sir." She ducked into the turbolift with decisive strides, the trouble in her face eased with the medicine of an important assignment. Dax gave Sisko an approving nod.

"Thank you, Benjamin. She needed to feel like she survived the destruction of that ship for some reason."

"I know the feeling." Sisko laced his fingers together reflectively, watching the stars flash by in their computer-corrected streamlines. "Are the Jem'Hadar fighters keeping to their original vector, Dax?"

She nodded. "We don't have a good survey of this part of the Gamma Quadrant yet. Some preliminary Ferengi records indicate that the Jem'Hadar have laid claim to several of the star systems in it, although they don't seem to use any of them."

"Strategic buffer zones," Eddington suggested.

"No doubt, Commander." Sisko unsealed the chest seam on his environmental suit and shrugged it off, then motioned Dax to do the same while he watched the helm for her. "In which case, we could be heading straight for a major Jem'Hadar stronghold."

Dax paused in the midst of shedding her own suit to give him a glance of restrained amusement. "I got the impression a few minutes ago that that was exactly what you wanted."

Sisko shrugged. "I'd like to keep watch on what the Jem'Hadar are doing, to see if the Dominion has initiated any dealings with the Furies. I'd just rather not try to do it in the midst of constant starship traffic. Our cloaking device can't protect us from a direct collision."

"No, but your pilot can." After a long, tense hour in an insulated environmental suit, the kiss of cool air on Dax's sweaty skin felt like a dip in the Trill baths. She reclaimed her seat, and Sisko sprawled back in his commander's chair. "It does seem odd that the Jem'Hadar would dispatch two fighters from a major stronghold to deal with the *Sreba,* then go straight back again." She turned to meet her old friend's somber frown. "You don't think—"

"—that they know we're back here and are leading us into a trap? It's certainly one possible explanation. Any trace of other warp signatures in the region, Mr. Eddington?"

The security officer shook his head. "No other ship signatures, although I'm picking up a lot of phaser discharge trails and ionic interference. It looks like the aftermath from some kind of battle." Something beeped for his attention on his tactical panel. "Jem'Hadar ships are slowing back to sublight, sir."

"Match vectors," Sisko commanded, sitting up straight again. "Any sign of their destination?"

Dax adjusted velocities, then scanned her boards and saw the telltale peak on one of them. "We're approaching a moderate-size gravity well on heading six-nine-one mark seven-eight-zero. It looks like a small Jem'Hadar base."

"Establish a perimeter orbit around it as soon as we go sublight. Keep us just inside visual range." He steepled his fingers, staring watchfully through them at the *Defiant*'s main viewscreen. A tiny patch of darkness slowly enlarged as the *Defiant* slowed and swung into orbit. Dax upped the magnification factor, and the darkness resolved into a small military starbase. It had the stark, asymmetrical look typical of Jem'Hadar outposts—built for efficiency and ruggedness in battle, with absolutely no sense of aesthetics—but something about it seemed wrong. Dax frowned up at the screen, trying to figure out what it was. Then she glanced down at her helm control and saw the answer in its still-changing distance displays.

"The base is moving!" she said in surprise. "Eddington, can you confirm?"

"Yes, sir." The security officer glanced over his shoulder at the viewscreen, as if he couldn't believe what his own readouts said. "Tactical sensors indicate a sublight speed of point-seven C."

"That's a lot of velocity for a station that size, even one

built by the Jem'Hadar." Sisko sprang to his feet and began pacing, as if some fuse had finally burned down to an internal explosion. "I'm getting a very bad feeling about this. Are their shields up, Commander?"

"No, sir. I'm not reading any weapons systems active at all." Eddington paused, watching his panel again. "The two Jem'Hadar fighters we followed here aren't docking, sir. They've fallen into orbit around the station."

"The same kind of orbit they maintained around the *Sreba?*" Sisko demanded.

"Yes, sir. Sensors indicate they're scanning it the same way."

Sisko paused, bracing both hands against the helm to scowl up at the viewscreen. "Dax, pulse the impulse engines to bring us in a little closer so we can see what's going on down there."

"Aye-aye, sir." She fed in the course change, and felt the *Defiant's* instant, headstrong response. The Jem'Hadar military base loomed into closer view, occasionally shadowed by the dark silhouettes of the two encircling fighters. Only a few emergency lights blinked along its dark station gantries and bristling weapons towers.

Dax could hear the quick intake of Sisko's breath beside her. "Maximum magnification on the station perimeter," he ordered. She adjusted the sensor controls, and the viewscreen shifted to a close-up rotating view of the Jem'Hadar's thick hull cladding. It looked normal—until a sector pierced with a hundred razor-sharp gashes rolled into sight, trailing escaping shreds of atmosphere and frozen water vapor behind it like white flags.

Eddington whistled softly from behind them. "Looks like this place got hit by the same force that took out the *Sreba.*"

"But not for the same reason," Dax said, scanning the base as best she could through the interference of the cloaking device. "Engineering sensors indicate the internal power source on the Jem'Hadar base is still active. In fact—" It was her turn to frown at her panel displays in disbelief. "—it looks like there are actually *several* power sources inside that station. And at least one of them is emitting the exact subspace frequencies you'd expect from a Federation Mariah-class warp core."

"The type of warp-core the *Sreba* carried?" Sisko demanded. When Dax nodded confirmation, he took a quick stride back to his command console and hit the ship's internal comm. "All hands to battle stations," he said curtly. "Red alert."

Crystalline shimmers a breath of exploding brilliance— steel-gray black spraying metal on metal in the cold dark empty of nowhere, of night—oh, the longness! The heat! The awful heat from every empty spill abandoned to the strangling closeness, to the entrails, to the burst of expulsion as the heat opens up into vacuum, into—

"Julian?"

Bashir jerked upright with a gasp so sharp he thought for a moment that he hadn't been breathing. For a brief, heartbeat instant, fading sparks of memory flicked nonpictures at the back of his eyes—movement swarming black-on-black against a terrible brightness, everything smothered by a fear borne past the point of thought.

Then, just as quickly, whatever he'd almost been dreaming was gone. He was left with his hands dripping where he rested his elbows on the lip of the symbiont's tank, blinking across the contraption at the stocky figure hovering just inside the isolation unit's door. "Chief!" He sounded groggy, even to himself, and he wondered blearily if he was expected to say something more even though his brain didn't offer him anything.

O'Brien shook his head, crossing the small chamber to peer down into the milky brine. "How long have you been sleeping like that?" he asked Bashir, sounding disapproving and concerned all at once, the way only a parent can.

"Like this?" Was he sleeping? Glancing down at the tank, his bare hands, and the symbiont floating placidly in the midst of the medium, Bashir felt the last tattered cobwebs in his brain brushed aside by coherent thought. He'd dropped the stasis field on the symbiont, feeling safe with it for the first time since Hayman showed it to them on Starbase 1. He remembered interrupting its biochemical seizure, then trying to elevate its neurotransmitter levels with a boromine-citrate solution. After that . . .

Bending forward to sink one hand back into the tank, he

grinned sheepishly up at O'Brien as he fished about for the tricorder he'd been holding when he fell asleep with his hands in the water. "Not long." At least he didn't think it had been long. He didn't feel as though he'd slept at all. "Just the last few days catching up to me, I guess. I can't pull all-nighters like I used to." Finally pulling the tricorder up out of the brine, he shook it off as best he could, then searched for somewhere on the front of his uniform dry enough to wipe off the display. "Thanks for waking me."

O'Brien produced an already-stained hand rag from somewhere within his uniform, and offered it across the top of the tank. "Don't thank me yet. Quark's been looking for you."

Bashir paused in accepting the rag to raise his eyebrows. "Quark?"

"Something about a sick customer," O'Brien shrugged. "He wants to see you right away. And he's got *Odo* helping him look for you. That's how we knew you weren't answering your comm badge."

Bashir fingered the insignia on the breast of his uniform, not sure what to say. He couldn't remember the last time he slept so soundly that a comm call couldn't wake him.

"I figured the last thing you needed was the constable snooping around while you were taking care of Professor Stel here," O'Brien continued, gesturing wryly at the very non-Vulcan patient in its equally nonregulation abode. "So I took the liberty of dropping by. Just as well, too, since it seems like I saved you from drowning." He added that last with a puckish grin, but Bashir was too busy closing up the symbiont's tank and gathering his scattered medical gear to do more than flash a tired smile in return.

"What's wrong with this customer of Quark's?" he asked, stuffing tricorder, a hypo kit, and a portable diagnostic scanner into the bag he'd been keeping near the symbiont since leaving Starbase 1.

O'Brien watched him pack with idle interest, shrugging. "Don't know. He's Andorian, and worth a lot of money, that's all Quark would say."

It was something, at least. Andorians had tricky metabolisms—they tended to go into shock with frightening abruptness, no matter how minor their injuries, and

Bashir didn't look forward to explaining to the Andorian embassy why he'd taken so long to answer a sick-call from a bar not twenty meters down the hall from his infirmary. Pausing by the drug cabinet to snatch up an Andorian-specific antigen kit, he'd just slipped the medical bag over one shoulder and turned for the door when his eyes caught on the stasis tank in the middle of the room, and his heart fell into his stomach.

Things were so much easier when there were only two parts of Dax to keep track of. At least they were always both in the same place. While he couldn't very well ignore the rest of his duties and leave other patients untreated, the thought of running out on the symbiont whenever a comm call came in left him feeling nervous and surprisingly guilty. Maybe it was just as well he was falling asleep in the middle of things; he couldn't imagine when he'd next be able to simply lie down and let himself relax.

"I'll stay with it 'til you get back."

Bashir jerked a startled look at O'Brien, still standing with his hand unconsciously feeling out the contours of the jury-rigged coffin. "Can't be that different from watching a three-month-old while she's sleeping, now, can it?" the chief went on with a nonchalance Bashir suspected he didn't really feel. "Besides, when else am I going to have time to rewire some of this mess you call a suspension tank?"

The restless knot of tension in Bashir's chest relaxed by just a little. "Call me if any of its readings change."

"And you keep a couple of hours free the next time Keiko visits the station." O'Brien fixed him with a serious glare that didn't quite match the mischief in his eyes. "There's a Billy the Brontosaur holoplay Molly's been dying to see at the multiplex."

Bashir nodded, smiling gallantly. "I would be honored, Mr. O'Brien. I promise to have your daughter home before dawn."

The faintly horrified expression that washed across O'Brien's face was more than worth the price of the holoplay. "You dating any daughter of mine," the chief grunted as he turned his back on Bashir and started fiddling grumpily with the stasis tank's workings. "That'll be over my dead body!"

Bashir ducked out while the engineer was still grumbling and sorting through the tools he always seemed to carry with him.

The crowded brightness of the Promenade swelled to engulf his senses the moment he stepped out the infirmary door. Noise as palpable as a strong wind buffeted the place, ricocheting off every storefront, every kiosk, every pillar. Bashir had heard of places that claimed to "never sleep," but *Deep Space Nine*'s Promenade was one of the few he'd ever lived in such close proximity with, much less tolerated practically right outside his hospital door. If there wasn't a pocket being picked beside the credit-exchange machines, there was a fight outside the Klingon diner, or an after-hours tongo game whooping it up in the back of Quark's bar. And God forbid that any crisis or accident could ensue without what seemed like half the station's occupants collecting around the scene like platelets around a wound.

That's what first cued Bashir that Quark's dire emergency might not be all that dire—no chaos, no clogging of the station's arteries, no crowding and shoving beyond the normal push and bother of daily Promenade traffic. Aiming for the strident harangue of Quark's voice where it rose above the general hubbub, Bashir wondered if he ought to break into a trot to seem more medically concerned even though the utter lack of gawkers had already told him Quark's patient couldn't be as close to death's door as the barkeep seemed to think. Still, he made a sincere effort to look professionally attentive as he wended his way through the shoppers and the afternoon lunchtime crowd.

Quark bounced up on his toes with a triumphant yelp when he caught sight of Bashir. "There he is!" He stabbed a finger past Odo's shoulder as though pointing out a fleeing felon.

Bashir tried very hard not to sigh as he paused beside them.

"Doctor," Odo greeted him smoothly, sarcasm rampant in his tone. "How nice of you to join us. Is there some reason you weren't answering your comm badge?"

Quark pushed Odo impatiently aside. "What are you

doing down here?" he wailed, grabbing at the front of Bashir's uniform.

The dual questions caught him off guard. "Uh—I was busy," he answered Odo shortly, hoping to stave off further interrogation as he turned an irritated scowl on the Ferengi. "What do you mean 'what am I doing down here'? I thought you had a sick Andorian!"

"No!" Quark bared a serrated grimace of frustration. "I sent *you* a sick Andorian. This morning, just after breakfast." He clasped his hands to the breast of his overembroidered jacket in a show of horror Bashir didn't think was entirely feigned. "Don't tell me you haven't seen him!"

"No one's come to the infirmary all day."

Odo blew a coarse snort. "What a surprise! A wanted smuggler happens to fall deathly ill only moments after finding out the captain is back on the station, then disappears on his way to the infirmary." He angled a skeptical peer down at Quark. "I can't possibly imagine where he got to."

The Ferengi's returning scowl flushed his lobes with what might have been either anger or worry. "Go ahead and laugh! It's not your bar on the line if he lives long enough to sue! Argelian mocha sorbet is very popular with my Rigel-sector customers right now," he explained to Bashir in a voice of almost pleading reasonability. "How was I supposed to know Andorians couldn't tolerate chocolate?"

"Ask them before you serve them?" Odo suggested.

Quark squeaked something indignant in protest to that suggestion, but Bashir lost track of the words under a wire-thin thread of tinnitus that he felt more than really heard. He half-turned to scan the Promenade, his stomach churning with dread. "A transporter . . ."

Odo broke off Quark's ranting with the palm of his hand. "Doctor?"

Blue-white glimmers sprinkled the air near the center of the atrium, and pedestrians scattered in all directions with cries of alarm in an effort to avoid the incoming transporter wave. Bashir gripped the medical bag more tightly under his arm, but stopped himself just short of running out to meet the coalescing figures. It wasn't just common sense that kept him clear of the area of effect—it was the sick anticipation that had been chewing at his stomach ever since Starbase 1, the almost superstitious certainty that something horrible was poised to happen just a tightrope's width away from any moment. So as the transporter's whine rose to a warbling wail and the light and sound braided together into a clutch of humanoid figures wrapped in ragged, soot-stained clothes, Bashir was perhaps the only one not entirely surprised by the scattered, dusty remains that fell to the floor around the group as they solidified—the molecular remnants of whoever had stood near the edges of the beam, too far from the coherent center to make it through.

Whether she responded to the pungent explosion of stench from her less fortunate traveling companions or the shrill chorus of shrieks that suddenly reverberated through the Promenade, Bashir couldn't tell, but the weathered Bajoran woman at the center of the pitiful group had her weapon thrust out at no one, at everyone, before the song of the transporter had completely died. Her wild, pain-shocked eyes found Bashir's on the other side of the atrium, and his heart stopped with a painful lurch as she whipped her phaser around to train it full on him.

"You've got one minute to fetch me your station commander," she called to him in a hoarse, almost tearful voice. "Otherwise, every single one of us is going to die!"

CHAPTER
13

A BLAST OF phaser fire exploded across the viewscreen, disintegrating part of the unshielded Jem'Hadar base. Sisko swung around to confront his replacement security officer, struggling to keep his fierce irritation confined just to the ominous deepening of his voice. He wasn't stupid enough to think that Major Kira would never have fired the *Defiant*'s phasers on her own, but he knew damn well she would never have made the tactical mistake of doing it while they were supposed to remain cloaked.

"I ordered battle stations, Commander, not an all-out attack," he snapped. "Why was our cloak dropped to fire those phasers?"

The Starfleet officer gave him back an almost-affronted look. "Those weren't *our* phasers, Captain. We never lost cloak integrity."

Sisko cursed and swung around to see Dax already adjusting the sensor focus, pulling the viewscreen back for a bigger picture. Stabs of light crisscrossed the darkness as the two encircling Jem'Hadar fighters aimed an unrelenting barrage of phaser fire down at their own base.

"They started firing as soon as their scan was finished," Dax said quietly. "Just like they did at the *Sreba.*"

"Then they know it's been taken by the same enemy." Sisko watched the one-sided battle with narrowed eyes, not sure whether he felt more frustrated or relieved at the

Jem'Hadar action. "And we'll never know who it was. Without its shields up, that base won't last five minutes."

"I wouldn't be so sure of that, Benjamin." Dax changed the angle of the viewscreen again, this time focusing on one of the Jem'Hadar fighters. "I think whoever took that base is starting to fight back."

"I'm not reading any signs of weapons discharge from the station," Eddington protested.

"No." The viewscreen was darkening with an odd refractive haze around one of the Jem'Hadar fighters, as if a flurry of small meteorites had taken it into their heads to converge on that exact spot. Sisko felt his gut tighten in grim premonition. "That's because they're not using weapons. Increase sensor magnification, Dax. I want to see exactly what's going on out there."

"Sensors are already extended to their resolution threshold, Captain," she warned. "We'll lose focus if we go in closer."

"Do it anyway."

Dax shrugged and obeyed him. The crisp lines of the Jem'Hadar ship blurred and melted as it grew to fill the viewscreen, but that softening couldn't disguise the crawling organic shapes that now surrounded it. It looked as if a swarm of large metallic wasps had coalesced around the ship, scrabbling across its external shields with jointed claws and blunt segmented bodies that seemed impervious to vacuum.

"Dax, what *are* those things?"

His science officer took a deep breath, dragging her eyes away from the screen just long enough to scan her readouts. "All our sensors can pick up is that they're made of duranium-carbide alloy, powered by small internal dilithium drives." She glanced back up at the viewscreen. "They could be battle robots, Benjamin. They don't seem to notice any pain when they hit the Jem'Hadar's shields."

"No." Sparks of ionic discharge geysered up every time one of the attackers pierced the small ship's defensive forcefields, but those shocks only seemed to slow the metallic creatures down, not stop them. Sisko noticed that despite the seeming randomness of their swarming, they carefully avoided those areas where they could be caught by the rake of the Jem'Hadar's futilely firing phasers. Gradually, the sparks of light kicking up from each contact were getting dimmer and dimmer. Sisko felt an uneasy premonition wash through him. "Is it my imagination, or are the shields on that fighter getting drained?"

"Tactical sensors show his shields at fifteen percent and falling," Eddington confirmed. "His shield generators appear to be getting overloaded by the impacts faster than they can recharge. They'll fall below integrity threshold in approximately two minutes."

"Allowing access to the hull itself." Sisko squinted through the blur of too-close focus to watch as two of the wasplike attackers coordinated a stab at the fighter's sensor array. The failing shields almost let them reach it. "Dax, can you tell if those things are internally piloted?"

"Scanning for internal life signs." Dax paused, then uttered what sounded like a Klingon curse. "That can't be right! The cloaking device must be interfering with our sensor readings."

"What did the scan show?" Sisko demanded. His premonition was crystallizing into bleak reality, born of the combination of sentient purpose and living grace he was witnessing in this blurred confrontation. No spacefaring robot he'd ever seen, not even the ones constructed by the Borg, moved through microgravity with the sleek coordination of a dolphin pod in deep water. These things looked born, not made.

Dax tapped another series of commands into her jury-rigged engineering panel, then glanced back at him with grave eyes. "According to our sensors, there are DNA-based neural networks inside each of those things out there, extending right into their duranium-carbide shells."

"Bioneural computer circuits?"

Dax shook her head fiercely. "I don't think so. I'm not detecting any evidence of internal engineering circuits, not even around the dilithium power cells." She paused, watching the battle on the viewscreen. For a few minutes, the small fighter blurred with the speed of the pilot's evasive maneuvers, but although the dark swarm of attackers rippled and swayed in response, they remained stubbornly attached. "Benjamin, I think those things out there are *alive.*"

"So do I," he said grimly.

The Jem'Hadar's shields flickered with a final pulse of ionic discharge, then failed before the draining mass of metallic bodies that had piled up on them. A shining lacework of vaporous chemicals shot out from each wasp-like body, and an instant later ship and swarm disappeared together in the glittering white blast of explosive decompression. When the veils of frozen atmosphere drifted apart at last, the viewscreen showed the shredded hulk of the Jem'Hadar fighter being towed back to its former base by a shadowy host of attackers.

There was a long, reverberating silence on the bridge of the *Defiant*. "Well," Dax said at last, with the sardonic black humor that Sisko remembered Curzon saving for times like these. "At least they're not Furies."

"No," he agreed grimly. "They're not Furies. But they might very well be what the Furies were running from."

"Running from?" Dax snapped a startled look back at him. "You mean the three alien ships we saw on the other side—I mean, in the log record Admiral Hayman showed us?"

"The ones that blew up after firing their phasers randomly in all directions. Sound familiar?" Sisko glanced back at Eddington, wishing now that he hadn't snapped at the Starfleet officer. Unfortunately, the middle of a red alert wasn't the time or place to apologize. "Any signs of the second Jem'Hadar fighter, Commander?"

"It's broken off its attack and is departing the system at warp six." Eddington swung around to face him, scowling. For a brief moment, Sisko thought the other man's anger was directed at him, but the frustrated smack of Eddington's hand on his weapons panel said otherwise. "Tactical sensors can't get any kind of fix on the aliens who attacked the Jem'Hadar fighter, Captain! They don't seem to be putting out any EM emission at all. I have no idea where they are—or where they're going."

"I'll see if we can track them by some kind of targeted sensor reflection." Dax paused to throw a warning glance back at Sisko. "In the meantime, Captain, I'd advise keeping our own EM emissions to a minimum. The creatures seemed to home in on the Jem'Haddar fighter by tracking its phaser fire."

"Meaning if we don't use our impulse engines or fire any weapons, there's a good chance they can't see us?" Sisko nodded curtly. "Acknowledged, Lieutenant. Keep us on our present heading." He swung around to face the wide-eyed ensign at the back of the bridge. "Mr. Hovan, I want you to keep an eye out for any voltage fluctuations in the cloaking device. If those things converge on the *Defiant,* I want to know about it before they start draining our shields."

"Yes, sir." Her voice squeaked a little, then steadied. "I can program an internal alarm to sound if voltage fluctuations exceed normal micrometeorite impact levels, sir, but it'll take me a few minutes."

Sisko gave her a wry smile. "No time to begin like the present, Ensign. Dax, have you managed to get a fix on what our new neighbors are doing out there?"

"Yes, sir." As usual, the Trill's voice held no fear, just the quiet satisfaction of meeting a new scientific challenge. "I'm plotting critical resolution of sensor reflections in the duranium-carbide band on the screen now."

The viewscreen pulled back to show the abandoned Jem'Hadar station, now overlaid by a computer-generated swirl of contoured colors. After a moment's scrutiny, Sisko could see that the brightest peak of white and yellow lay deep inside the station itself, with smaller, moving bumps of green ranged across its surface. Only a few bluish specks glowed in the empty space around the weapons towers and gantries.

"Interpretation, Lieutenant?"

"Approximately four hundred of the aliens appear to be huddled in close proximity to each other inside the Jem'Hadar station," Dax answered. "An additional hundred or so are attached to the station's exterior."

"Perimeter guards," Sisko guessed, and saw Eddington's silent nod of agreement. "What about those reflections you're getting outside the station, Dax?"

"They appear to be fragments of creatures blown up by phaser fire or photon torpedoes. Their DNA signatures are degraded and I'm reading no dilithium power sources."

"Then they *can* be killed." Sisko narrowed his eyes,

regarding the pulsing mass of alien life before him. Despite the fact that it filled only a third of the military base, it didn't seem to be moving. "Have you scanned the station for areas of remaining atmosphere? Or for Jem'Hadar life signs?"

Dax threw him a startled look. "You think some of the Jem'Hadar may still be alive in there?"

"There's got to be a reason the creatures are isolated in one part of the station," Sisko pointed out. "If we can find out why, we might have something we can use against them."

Instead of getting him the sensor scan he wanted, however, that reasonable statement brought Jadzia Dax swinging around to glare at him. "Benjamin, why are you assuming we need to fight these creatures? We can't even talk to them yet! There's no way we can assume they're sentient, much less hostile."

Sisko scowled back at her. "What they did to the *Sreba* and the Jem'Hadar—"

"—might have been an instinctive defense reaction, like wasps swarming to protect their nests!"

"That doesn't make it any less a threat to the Alpha Quadrant!"

They exchanged fierce looks for a moment, until Eddington cleared his throat and intervened. "Lieutenant Dax, correct me if I'm wrong. Didn't we come here to find out what kind of accident was going to throw the wormhole back in time?"

"Yes," she and Sisko said in unison.

"Then before you make any arguments about protecting these creatures—" The security officer tapped a command into his tactical station. "—I suggest you look at where they're moving the Jem'Hadar station to."

The Trill took a deep breath, swinging back to examine the data he'd transferred to her helm display. When she glanced over her shoulder at him again, Sisko saw surprise and a trace of unease flicker through her blue-gray eyes.

"Commander Eddington's right—the vector's too exact to be an accident. They're heading straight for the wormhole."

It was Sisko's turn to take a deep breath, but in his case it was one of grim resolve. "Then we *have* to find out why," he said. "And we have to stop them. How much time do we have before they arrive at the wormhole entrance?"

"With them moving at point-seven light speed? At least fifty hours," Dax said promptly.

"Good." He lifted his gaze to the screen again. "I can't believe every Jem'Hadar on that station is dead—they're not stupid, and they were genetically engineered to defend the Founders against threats exactly like this. Find me some Jem'Hadar life signs down there, Dax. And see if they correlate with areas where life-support is still intact."

She nodded and programmed the search into her sensor controls. "And then?"

"And then," said Sisko, "we're going to find out if these creatures can track transporter beams the way they track phasers."

Even though Bashir had warned her, Kira still couldn't hold back a little sound of disgust as she rounded the corner to the Promenade. It really wasn't any worse than half of what she'd seen in the concentration camps—Cardassian corpse-disposal methods smelled almost as strongly. No, Kira had to admit as she slowed to a controlled, professional walk, it was the hollow, almost mindless expressions on their faces as they trembled, back-to-back, in their little circle that somehow made what had happened here so much more horrible than just what the eye could see.

That, and the knowledge that the two Bajorans who lay screaming were really no different than the molecular dust they writhed in—both were victims of standing on the fringe of a long-range transport when the distance transmitted was too long, and the signal began to decay. It made Kira glad that Odo had been able to clear the Promenade of civilians before any real panic could begin.

One of the still standing militia members said something softly into Pak's ear as Kira neared, and Kira saw the older woman twist around to look at her while she was still too far away to really converse. Still, that didn't stop the terrorist from smiling darkly and waving her phaser toward where Bashir knelt in the once living dust to tend to her injured people.

"Useful as well as decorative," she called, voice as pale of life as her face despite her obvious effort. "Do you share?"

Bashir lifted his head at the question, but didn't turn to look at Kira or interrupt his work. It wasn't hard to read the discomfort in the set of his lean shoulders, though. Kira wondered if he was embarrassed. "Dr. Bashir's services are available to anyone on the station who needs them. Even you." She altered her approach just enough to catch the doctor's eye and order gently, "Get these people down to the infirmary."

He nodded, looking oddly grateful as he tapped awake his comm badge. Kira stepped around him to draw Pak's eyes away so he could finish his work without the threat of either her phaser or her sarcasm.

"First Veska Province," she said, shaking her head at Pak as she came to a stop beside Odo and his own brown-clad security, "now this. You certainly know how to make an impression."

The smile that spasmed across Pak's face was too twisted to really be amused. "Desperate times call for desperate actions." She jerked her chin at Kira, phaser gesturing aimlessly. "Where's your commander?"

"You're talking to her." Kira crossed her arms, trying not to scowl in response to Pak's impatient grimace.

"Good try, but I've seen pictures. The guy who runs this place is a human—not to mention much taller and much browner than you."

"Captain Sisko is off the station just now." *I wish I knew why, and I wish I knew where.* "As his second-in-command, I'm what you get until he returns." She waited until the tingle of Bashir's emergency transport to the infirmary had faded, then gave Pak another few seconds to recover from watching her people vanish into that quick, unforgiving shimmer. "Do we talk?" she asked at last, pulling the terrorist's attention back to her.

Pak looked up sharply, as though surprised that she was still alive to partake in it. "What can I say to make you believe me?"

Kira frowned, studying the older woman's face. "You haven't told me anything yet."

"But when I do," Pak persisted. "When I do, you've got

to believe me, or we're all going to wish this was us." She stomped one foot in the dust that surrounded her.

This wasn't a band of human tourists who'd just survived their first clash with the Cardassians. These were children of the Cardassian Occupation, and veterans of both Veska Province and the Kotar Killing Fields. And Pak Dorren . . .

You didn't see her, Kira thought at Odo, afraid to break her stare from Pak long enough to whisper to him. *She's not afraid of anything—not of the Cardassians, not of Shakaar, not even of her own damned bombs!* Yet she'd risked a long-distance transport with who knew how many people, and had said nothing, done nothing, to indicate she regretted the results. Just the thought of what could force a woman like Pak to do that made Kira's muscles ache with cold.

"All right, I believe you."

Odo growled softly in frustration, but the strong relief that moved in Pak's dark eyes frightened Kira far more than the constable's disapproval. "What happened?"

Pak took a deep breath and let her phaser drift down to her side. "I think I found out who did in those ore freighters."

"It really wasn't you." Kira said it aloud without meaning to, too surprised by her belief to censor herself.

Pak threw her head back with a short, harsh laugh. "You didn't listen to a damn thing I told you out there, did you? We're in this to *free* Bajor, little bit, not screw up its economy any worse than it already is. We were looking to stop whoever did this just as much as you."

"And you found?" Odo prompted.

The terrorist's face collapsed into a look of bleak honesty. "I don't know." She snapped her gaze to Kira at the sound of the major's frustrated sigh. "I've never seen or heard of anything like this before," she insisted. "We had a dozen ships patrolling freighter routes when they closed in on us. . . ." Her eyes lost focus, clouding on whatever memories stole the animation from her voice and made her gaze drift to one side as she remembered. "Sensors picked up a dispersed mass of duranium-titanium alloy." Her tone was reflective, almost gentle. It occurred to Kira that she would have had a pretty voice if it hadn't been worn raw by drinking and *chaat.* "I thought it must be ship debris from another freighter wreck, and I dropped us out of warp so we could scan for survivors. By the time they hit our shields, I knew we should never have gone sublight, but by then it was too late. . . ."

Kira waited for her to continue. She didn't. "Too late for what?" Kira asked at last. *"Who* attacked you?"

As if the questions yanked her back into real time, Pak shook off her dim distraction and brought her eyes back to Kira's. "Animals. Aliens of some kind. Big, vacuum-adapted *things* that ate up phaser fire and crawled right through our screens." She shrugged at her inability to describe them with an impatient, angry sound. "I watched them peel open three of our fighters like jil-birds on a redfruit; then did my best to call a strategic retreat. They homed in on our engine exhausts, backtracked along our phaser beams, followed the paths of our torpedoes . . ." Her voice began to fade; then she shook her head with a bitter grimace. "I didn't think this transport would work. It just seemed better to die in a scatter of atoms than to let these things blow me out into space."

Strong words, coming from a woman who had once turned an entire valley into glass. Kira cleared her throat, her mind already racing. "We should contact the Bajoran military," she said to Odo, "see if they can get ships up to deal with this before any other freighters disappear."

"You don't get it, little bit, do you?"

She jerked a scowl at Pak, and the terrorist pushed between the three who circled her to cross the empty Promenade. "I'm not talking about calling out the Temple guard. We ran into these things doing point-eight C while on our way to *here!* If they keep going just the way they were when we first found them, they're going to be here in under four hours." She spread her arms wide, as though laying out the implications for any fool to see. "So—do you want to start panicking now, or shall I?"

CHAPTER
14

A BITTER CHILL burned Sisko's skin as soon as the transporter beam released him. He cursed the confidence in Starfleet sensors that let them beam over with open faceplates to what was supposed to be a pressurized section of the Jem'Hadar station. His hand was halfway to his visor before he realized he couldn't feel the relentless suck of vacuum against his exposed cheeks, only cold. He left his visor up and took a cautious breath. Although his nose and throat protested at the bite of frigid air, his lungs assured him it held a reasonable amount of oxygen.

Sisko glanced around and saw his away team ranged around him, still in the defensive back-to-back circle they'd assumed on board the *Defiant*. They'd beamed into a room lit only by the dim phosphorescent glow of emergency lamps. "Nobody move!" he snapped, seeing the tentative turn of one gold-and-black form in the darkness. "Dax, scan for difluorine."

She tapped an order into her tricorder, scanned the sector of the room she was facing, then handed the instrument on to Sisko. He repeated the motion and passed it to the quiet young security guard beside him. While he waited for the tricorder to complete its circle, Sisko surveyed the area they'd beamed into. His dark-adjusted eyes told him the huge room was full of identical waist-high consoles arranged in precise rows. Something about their shape tugged vaguely at his memory.

Dax took the tricorder back from Pritz on her other side, and scanned its readout. Her relieved breath steamed in the frigid air. "No difluorine readings here at all. The aliens must not have used it after they breached the hull and got inside."

"Probably because they didn't want the station to break apart before they got it to the wormhole." Sisko stepped out of the circle and turned to face the three security guards. They waited silently for his orders, phaser rifles cradled and ready in their hands. His own rifle bumped gently against the insulated back of his environmental suit, leaving Dax the only unarmed member of the party. "Goldman and Fernandez, locate and secure the nearest doors. Pritz, you'll guard the lieutenant."

The two young men turned to leave, one of them stumbling over something on the floor before he swung his flashlight down to light his way. Sisko swung his own light in a wide arc and whistled when he saw the random scatter of Jem'Hadar weapons across the floor, fallen like dead branches after a windstorm. Here and there among them, the steel floor plates were splotched and streaked by ugly dark stains.

"It looks like the Jem'Hadar made a last stand here," Dax commented. "Funny that there aren't any bodies. Do you think the survivors took their dead away with them?"

Sisko's flashlight caught on an odd, curving fragment of what looked like metal torpedo casing, except for a clinging inner rind of fleshy strands oozing something too clear and viscous to be called blood. "Not unless they took the alien dead away too," he said grimly. "Dax, what is this place?"

She scanned one of the waist-high consoles with her tricorder. "These appear to be stasis-field generators, but they're much too small for emergency medical use. I think it's a Jem'Hadar creche, Benjamin."

Sisko sucked an incautious breath of frigid air and coughed it out again painfully. He'd just remembered the similar-looking device in which Quark had once found a Jem'Hadar child. "We're in a nursery full of babies?" he demanded, scanning the cold rows of consoles that stretched into the dim distance of the room.

"A warehouse full of neonatal reinforcements," Dax corrected gently. "Waiting to be grown into fighters at need."

Sisko grunted acknowledgment of that. "You said you'd spotted very weak Jem'Hadar life signs from the ship, old man. Could it have been these children you were reading?"

"No." Dax took one tricorder bearing, then moved down the long aisle of stasis generators to take another. Pritz followed a wary step behind her. "Sensors can't pick up biologic activity from a Jem'Hadar in stasis any more than they could pick up Heather Petersen's life signs on board the *Sreba*. And in any case, the original biologic activity I spotted didn't come from here. This was just the closest site where we could beam an away team into the battle wreckage."

Sisko grunted. "It's interesting that the Jem'Hadar children were left untouched by the aliens, the same way Petersen was."

Pritz cleared her throat. "It means they can't know much about the Jem'Hadar, sir. If they did, they would have eliminated these neonatal reinforcements as a potential threat."

"It may be even simpler than that, Ensign." Dax paused to take a third bearing with her tricorder. "Maybe they just can't recognize anything in a stasis field as a living organism." The tricorder whistled to notify her of its completion of some task, but whatever it told her knotted her smooth brow into a frown. "I've got a triangulated fix on the Jem'Hadar life signs, Captain, but—"

"Which way?" Sisko demanded.

"Outside, a hundred meters to our right, but Benjamin— with readings like this, I don't see how this Jem'Hadar can be alive!"

Sisko swung around, spotting the doors by the stationary glow of flashlights on either side. He motioned Dax and Pritz toward the other two security guards. "But he *is* alive?"

"According to his neural patterns, yes. According to his heartbeat and respiratory activity, no."

Sisko paused at the doorway, running his light over the tangle of broken roof beams and fallen ceiling plates that filled the outside corridor. "Can you tell if he'll stay alive for a while yet? It's going to take us some time to get through this mess."

The taller of the two male security guards lifted his phaser rifle inquiringly. "Captain, we could clear out some of this wreckage with controlled phaser blasts."

"Too much danger of attracting attention that way, Ensign Fernandez. Whatever they are, these aliens seem able to track energy discharge. We'll have to open a path by hand." Sisko perched his flashlight on a broken wall panel to light their path, then squatted to slide his gloved hands under the beam blocking the door. Fernandez slung his rifle across his shoulder and did the same. "One, two, three—"

One heave sent the beam crashing down on the far side of the corridor, rolling a wall of cold dust up toward them as it did. Sisko coughed and scrubbed at his stinging eyes. Maybe he should have put his visor down, after all.

"All right, Dax, which way do we go from here?"

Only silence answered him. With a frown, Sisko turned back to face the green glow of the creche. He got a worried look from Pritz, but no response at all from his science officer. The Trill was staring down at her tricorder, but the blankness of her expression told Sisko she wasn't seeing it. He stepped forward to shake at her shoulder, hard.

"Dax? Old man, where the hell are you?"

There was still no reply. Sisko let out a deep breath of exasperation that steamed in the cold, dusty air. This was what he'd been afraid of when they'd first beamed over to the *Sreba*—a relapse into the odd stillness that had come over Dax once before. Her breath and color seemed perfectly normal, but not even a measured slap against her cheek could rouse her.

"Pritz, Fernandez—stay here and guard the lieutenant until she wakes up." Sisko slid the tricorder from Dax's unresisting hands and squinted at the radial coordinates it displayed. "Goldman, you're with me. Let's go."

It took them fifteen arduous minutes to work their way down the debris-choked hallway, following its sinuous curve to a completely unexpected dead end. Goldman glanced across at Sisko, his blue eyes dubious in the mask of dust that now covered his face.

"Where do we go from here, sir?"

"I'm not sure," Sisko admitted, scowling down at the unresponsive tricorder. "I can't triangulate on the Jem'Hadar's biologic activity the way Dax—"

A fierce hiss and screech of metal from the pool of darkness to their left interrupted him. Sisko swung around, stabbing his flashlight into the gloom like a weapon. He caught the quick leveling of Goldman's rifle from the corner of one eye and threw a hand out to stop the young security guard.

"No! Don't shoot—it may be the Jem'Hadar."

Goldman took in a shaky breath as the flashlight beam found a ripple of movement in the dark. "That's no Jem'Hadar, sir," he protested.

"Yes, it is." Sisko had already recognized the serrated bony edge of the genetically engineered fighter's face. He took a cautious step forward to shine the light more directly on his target. Metallic noise squealed through the room again, and this time Sisko could see that it came from the rippling motion of something behind the Jem'Hadar's limply sprawled body.

He lifted the flashlight to reveal a black, segmented form as tall as a man and as flexibly scaled as an insect. It turned more fully to face them, as if the light had attracted its attention, and Sisko heard Goldman curse in a strained voice. From this angle, they could see that the Jem'Hadar was half-engulfed by a wide central orifice on the creature's belly, with two rows of segmented, claw-tipped appendages closed so tight around him that only his legs and shoulders protruded. The Jem'Hadar's head rolled and lifted, eyes staring out at them unseeingly. Blood-crusted lips moved as if they barely remembered how to form speech.

"Kill me . . ." the Jem'Hadar whispered.

Goldman raised his phaser rifle in unthinking response, but Sisko caught the barrel in one gloved hand and shoved the weapon away again.

"Wait," he ordered, despite the revulsion roiling in his own gut. "We might be able to save him."

"How?" the security guard demanded.

Sisko sent the flashlight skimming around the alcove the alien had dragged its prey into, and saw the shadow of fallen roof panels along one side. "Work your way around to the left and find cover. Be prepared to give the alien a glancing shot when I give you the word. If I can pull the Jem'Hadar out while it's distracted—"

"What if it starts throwing out difluorine?"

"You'll be under cover, and I'll be off to one side," Sisko said grimly.

"No use—" The Jem'Hadar braced his elbows against the metallic carapace of his captor and pushed himself upward in one convulsive jerk so they could see the dangle of raw nerves and blood vessels that was left of his spine. "Not enough left to save. Only kept alive—to bring you here. Kill quick—"

Goldman took a deep breath. "Captain Sisko, it's a trap!" A crash of rubble from farther down the corridor triggered the security guard into a whirl of motion. He aimed a phaser blast into the darkness before Sisko could stop him.

"Don't shoot!" Dax's urgent voice rang echoes off the corridor walls. "It's us!"

Sisko cursed and caught Goldman's arm, swinging him around to face the stationary alien in the alcove. "Cover *that!*" he snapped, then turned to light the way for the rest of the away team. Dax ducked under a slanted roof beam and came toward him, followed closely by Pritz. Fernandez took up a defensive position a few meters down the hall.

"Old man, are you all right?" Sisko demanded.

"Yes, of course." Dax came to a halt a stride away from him, her voice resonating with excitement beneath its professional calm. "Captain, I've just been in touch with *Deep Space Nine!* The ansible effect works!"

"The *what?*"

She grinned up at him, gray eyes bright in her dusty face. "It's long physics derivation, but here's the short version: The two Dax symbionts can communicate with each other across space, instantaneously, because they're composed of identical quantum particles. I've become a living ansible, Benjamin."

Sisko scowled across at her. "You're telling me you

were actually in contact with the other Dax back at *Deep Space Nine?*"

The Trill nodded emphatically. "The old Dax still wasn't very clear, but he warned me about aliens who take over—"

Sisko's glance shot involuntarily toward the shadows now hiding the Jem'Hadar and his captor. Dax followed his gaze and froze. It took Sisko a moment to remember that a Trill's night sight was much better than a human's.

"That's it." Even in the dead stillness of the deserted station, her voice sounded unnaturally quiet. Sisko brought his flashlight snapping back to light the intertwined pair in the alcove. More of the Jem'Hadar had been digested, caving his chest in like a rotten melon. "That's the alien old Dax told me we had to—"

She broke off in horror as the Jem'Hadar lifted his head, dark blood spilling down his chin and his unfocused eyes rolling in involuntary response to the motion. "Kill now, use all phasers," he said urgently. "They will track you by your DNA. They will take you back and divide you—"

It was Sisko's turn to freeze, his skin prickling with the rush of implications. "Jadzia, are you saying old Dax already *knew* about these aliens?"

"Yes." Dax took a deep breath to steady her voice. "It told me over and over to find one of them and talk to what it had eaten. I thought it was still confused."

"Then these *were* the aliens we met when the *Defiant* went back in time."

"But how could they be here now?" Dax demanded. "The wormhole still hasn't shifted—"

"No, but this station is about to shift it."

Their eyes met in swift understanding. Before either of them could speak, however, a proximity alarm went off on one of the security guards' belts and a shout echoed off the wreckage.

"Captain, motion detected out in the corridor, two hundred meters and closing!" Fernandez warned, scrabbling close to them. "Multiple sources."

Sisko cursed and slammed a palm down on his combadge. "Eddington, stand by to transport us back to the *Defiant!*"

"Want your DNA," the Jem'Hadar whispered. For some

reason, the alien was now ejecting him in spasmodic, blood-drenched jerks, but his mouth still managed to form a ghost of words. "No human DNA, not yet. *Kill me now!*"

The last command was a shout, spat out even as what was left of the half-digested Jem'Hadar fell twitching out of the alien's central orifice. Freed of its burden, the segmented form promptly lunged at Goldman, who sprayed it with a reflexive blast of phaser fire. The Jem'Hadar's corpse vanished in that barrage, but the phaser energy simply soaked into the dark metallic carapace of its former captor.

"Damn!" Sisko reached back to yank his own rifle down into firing position, aware that Pritz and Fernandez were scouring the corridor behind them with phaser blasts. Goldman had fallen beneath the alien's sinuous scuttling rush and was screaming as it grabbed at him with jointed claws. Sisko aimed a long, sustained shot from his phaser rifle at it, but despite the dance of hot sparks across its metallic back, the alien refused to move.

"Hand weapons aren't working, Captain!" Pritz shouted over the roar of phasers and the background screech of metallic advance. "Aliens fifty meters and closing *fast.*"

"*Defiant!*" Sisko yelled into his combadge, still firing at the alien. "Prepare for close-quarters transport with possible enemy involvement. Beam us back *now!*"

The raw ends of the data conduits met imperfectly, but there wasn't time to trim them. Kira wriggled onto her side inside the cramped Jeffries tube and reached behind her to grope the back of the equipment belt she'd borrowed from O'Brien, wishing again that she'd been able to fit everything into the front pockets so she could work by sight instead of feel. Oh, well. Added difficulty only heightened the sense of urgency. It was something she'd grown used to during her years with the Resistance—the brisk, zinging excitement that came from knowing what you did was vital, and you only had a short time to get it done. Not a contented feeling, really, she reflected as she finally found the tape to flash-wrap her splice, but so familiar from her early life that it felt oddly comforting, even with the life of a station and all its inhabitants depending upon her.

She bit off the tape and scooted back from her handiwork,

just in case it didn't hold. "Okay, Chief—take her off-line."

"Aye-aye, sir." He sounded tense and focused, even over her comm badge, and Kira suddenly felt foolish for finding any sort of solace in their hurried work. If an action did no good, was it the end result which judged the work, or the fact that you took action at all? As the light and life inside the Jeffries tube flickered and died, she decided not to do too much philosophizing until they were finished rerouting the systems.

"That's the last data path on your deck, Major," O'Brien reported after another long moment of checking and re-checking whatever warning lights Kira was sure they'd set off in Ops. "If you want to take deck five off the loop, too, you're gonna have to find me another power grid to run it through—we're eighteen percent over capacity as is."

"Then we'll work with what we've got." She scrambled backward until her feet dangled out into air, then pushed herself free of the narrow tube with a grateful sigh. She could only stand to belly-crawl for so long. "You did good, Chief. I didn't think we could cut back this far."

"I'm not so sure we can," O'Brien grumbled morosely. "Ask me again in three hours."

Kira smiled, glancing up to look down the corridor toward the sound of approaching footsteps as she stooped to retrieve the Jeffries tube's cover. "I'll make sure I do that. Kira out."

Odo squatted to take half the door as Kira tapped off her comm badge. "If Pak Dorren is to be believed, we may not be here to worry about power consumption in another three hours."

Kira let him help her wrestle it back into place, casting him a sidelong glance. "You don't think I should have listened to her."

He stepped back as Kira secured the bolts, and she realized that he was truly considering his answer when he still hadn't said anything by the time she turned to start for the turbolift. "She wasn't lying," the constable allowed at last. Neither agreement nor argument—simply a straight-forward statement of fact. "Whatever—or whoever—they fought with was frightening enough to drive them onto that transporter. I just don't know that I would evacuate all of the station's outer decks on the strength of one eyewitness report."

She nodded, chewing at her lower lip as a host of conflicting impulses swarmed her for what must have been the hundredth time since she'd met Pak's tortured stare in the Promenade. No matter how many times she swam through her own reasoning, though, she kept coming back to the same simple truth. "You saw those ore freighters." She stopped to pop a circuit box and shut down power to all but one of the deck's turbolift bays. "If Pak's 'vacuum-breathers' really are at fault, then we can't risk sending a runabout just to check up on her story. What have we learned if it just never comes back?" She closed the box with a disgusted shake of her head. "That leaves either waiting for Sisko to get back from whatever field trip Starfleet has him out on, or waiting for the *Mukaikubo* to get here."

"And you can't stand to just do nothing until help arrives."

She wondered sometimes if Odo's stark perceptions were good for tuning her sense of reality, or merely blunt and annoying. "Think of it as a practice drill," she told him, neatly avoiding any real comment on his remark. "If nothing happens, we still get to find out how quickly we can compress station functions without overloading the power grid. If somebody *does* show up, then we've got four decks of buffer for our vacuum-breathers to crawl around in and breach before cutting into vital systems." Distracted by another open Jeffries tube cover, she grimaced in silent criticism of her own sloppiness and squatted to lift it back into place. "All in all, a pretty reasonable trade-off, considering."

At first, she didn't know what made her jerk back from the Jeffries tube opening, only that her breath froze in the back of her throat and a sudden dump of adrenaline into her blood made her feel as though her heart would explode. But it came right on top of the subconscious observation that she'd never been inside this Jeffries tube, and the thought and the movement seemed somehow related until the traveling weight of something hard and heavy slammed the cover plate from behind and threw her backward.

She didn't see it clearly—a flash of dark movement, too

small and amorphous to be humanoid—but she felt its tiny hands scrabbling at the toes of her shoes, and the bright, acidic smell of its sweat burned her nasal passages like fire. Barking a curse she hadn't used since the concentration camps, she heaved against the cover plate to try and rise up to her knees, and the attacker responded by lashing around the edges of the metal until it found a purchase in the meat of her upper arm. The cover plate crashed to the deck between them with a *bang!*

Pain exploded across her senses like a lightning flash; then she twisted sideways so that she'd smash shoulder-first into the wall instead of being yanked deeper into the tube, and the pain leapt back to a more respectful distance. This was the way it should be—pain was a fact of life, not a thing that could destroy you, not a demon to be feared just for itself. Animals gave in to pain—Bajorans used it. Gritting her teeth, she hitched up her legs to make a wedge against the outside of the opening and let her anger eat the pain and feed it to her strength.

A cool, slick rope of pressure snaked across her chest, over her shoulder, around her waist, and yanked her back toward the corridor. She screamed, kicking and jabbing, furious at being ganged up on by some other creature she didn't know and couldn't even see. Whatever had her in its teeth responded with an angry jerk, its tiny metallic fingers feeling out her shape like a swarm of blinded men. The cord around her chest cinched crushingly tight, and cut off her breathing in midscream. Pain, tube, and corridor all splintered into a dull gray cloud, and Kira felt herself yanked back into the tunnel opening so hard that her arm wrenched straight out over her head. A warm pulse of wetness against her cheek smelled sharply familiar; she wondered if she was bleeding, or if some other Bajoran had somehow managed to smear blood all over the decking when she wasn't around.

The edge of the tunnel smacked into her knees, and she clenched herself death-rigid trying to halt her advance. She felt like rag between two warring barsas, pulled inward by the fierce grip above her elbow, outward by the gelatinous hug about her waist. Clawing across her middle for the phaser that should be on her right hip, she closed cold fingers around the pommel and spared only a wisp of thought for what she would do if this were some engineering tool and not her weapon. Then she craned her head back to look into the monster's face, raised her gun, and fired.

An instant's vision of dusty Andorian blue before the phaser's actinic white filled the dark passage and blinded her. The grinding pain of bone on bone washed to nearly nothing as a greater splash of anguish gushed over her arm, her hand, her shoulder. She thought she must have recoiled—she was sure she heard her own scream under the phaser's shrill report—but it wasn't her strength that tumbled her into the corridor, or her voice that whispered urgently, desperately, "Major, get up! Get up and move away from the Jeffries tube!"

I can't . . . ! Even when she felt Odo pushing at her, urging her to her knees, she couldn't seem to find the right nerve pathways to make her tortured muscles answer. It wasn't just the ever-expanding pain that ate away at her thinking—it was the strangely thick distance that had inexplicably spread itself between her and the world. Dulling, muffling, softening all the sharp edges. When a queerly jointed waldo felt its way outside the Jeffries tube to tap and tick at the flooring, no rational awareness pushed its way through that viscous membrane, but the sheer force of her fear slammed her back against the opposite wall. She froze with her feet collected under her, ready to run and too shocky to move as the pain burned into her with a smell like rotten medicine.

"Major . . . " Odo's voice buzzed in her ear from very nearby, sounding eerily wrong and thin. "Please don't fire your phaser while I'm covering you."

At first, she couldn't take her eyes off the creature in front of her. Smooth as brushed metal, almost light-absorbing, but contoured so strangely that she couldn't tell if she was staring at its head or its tail. She could tell that she'd hurt it, though—the eyeless expanse of Andorian blue that had seemed to cover its face now looked like part of its abdomen, and was burned to brilliant sapphire. The only thing Kira recognized for sure was her own blood streaking hieroglyphs on the decking as the not-quite-waldo felt about in patient blindness.

"Major?"

She jerked aside, trying to find him. "Where are you?" But even as she asked, she felt the skin-thin caul across her mouth, and shivered in unreasonable discomfort. "I . . . Odo . . . !" Remembering his request as though from a great distance, she made herself slowly, carefully lower her phaser until it thumped against the floor. Encased in a sheet of softened changeling, it didn't make a sound.

"It doesn't seem able to sense me," Odo remarked with quiet calmness. She realized that he must be vibrating a small tympanum just outside her ear, the way he'd talked with her through the spacesuit helmet in vacuum. "Or perhaps I'm just not to its liking. Either way, this seemed the most efficient option." He fell silent a moment as the thing withdrew into the tunnel, and Kira could hear the fearfully light skitter of its movements as it hurried away. "That's more like it." His mass pushed against her chest— just a gentle pressure, like a quick, chaste hug—and the comm badge on her right shoulder beeped. "Emergency medical transport on this comm badge signal."

"No!" She surged to her feet, stumbling back against the bulkhead as the movement blurred her vision and the pain nearly took her breath away. "Odo, don't do it! That's an order!"

He peeled away from her with almost gentlemanly care, not even slowing as he slipped through the fingers of her grasping hand. "I'm sorry, Major, but I can flow through a Jeffries tube faster without you." He paused at the mouth of the tunnel to form a confident face and look back at her. "Don't worry—I'll file a full report when I get back."

"Odo!" She wanted to grab him, to throw herself on top of him and force him to be transported out along with her so this thing couldn't shred him, or eat him, or find some other way to destroy him. Instead, she managed only one lurching step forward before the itching tingle of the transporter beam folded around her. Her muscles went rigid, the corridor fading away, and the transporter whisked her to nothing even as she drew in the breath to shout her anger.

CHAPTER
15

IT CAME THROUGH the paralysis of the transporter beam like pounding surf with an occasional mutter of distant thunder.

"—talk to them, the only way we can stop them is from inside—"

"—much better stability on these neurotransmitter levels today—"

"—talk to what they've eaten, bring one back and talk to what's inside—"

For the first time, Jadzia tried to turn the quantum-deep resonance between symbionts into a true conversation. "I've met them," she replied, forming the words clearly in her mind. "The aliens you warned me about are here."

It felt as if a spark had jumped through immeasurable time and space. *"—talked to what they've eaten?"* demanded a fainter, distant echo of her symbiont's familiar voice.

"Yes, a Jem'Hadar. He said they would kill us for our DNA."

"Not kill, divide. Divide and share the DNA, divide and share the cerebral cortex."

"Then they retain the knowledge and memories of the organisms they engulf?" She wasn't sure whether that was Jadzia or Dax asking, but the answer was vehement.

"Yes! You must try to find one who will help you—"

"—Chief, will you hand me that thermal diffuser—"

211

"—while I try to make Julian understand."

Jadzia felt a shiver of sadness run through her, so deep and inexplicable that she knew it must have jumped across time and space along with that transmitted thought. "Understand what?"

"That you should have brought me with you."

"You with us, old man?"

Dax opened her eyes, suddenly aware that the rigid freeze of the transporter had worn completely off. She shook away the pervasive sense of déjà vu that lingered after each ansible trance.

"I'm all right, Benjamin. I just got some more information about the aliens from old Dax." She glanced around, seeing that only four forms in dust-stained environmental suits had returned to the *Defiant*'s ready room. The two remaining security guards were disarming their phaser rifles in grim silence. "What happened to the alien who was attacking us when we beamed out?"

"I don't know." Sisko stripped off his gloves and slapped them against his thigh, raising a violent cloud of dust. "I don't know what happened to Ensign Goldman either. Eddington must have left them both back on the station."

"No, we didn't, Captain." The doors hissed open to admit Heather Petersen, flushed and breathless. She must have run straight from the transporter control room. "I beamed them both into stasis chambers in the medical bay."

"Alive?" Sisko demanded, taking her elbow and steering her back around toward the open doors. Dax dropped her own gloves and helmet on the floor, and followed them down the hall to the nearest turbolift.

"Goldman was alive when we beamed him out, but his vital signs indicated massive internal trauma. I haven't talked to the medic yet, but I don't think we'll be able to take him out of stasis until we reach *Deep Space Nine.*"

"Bridge," Sisko snapped at the turbolift computer, then turned his narrow-eyed gaze back on Petersen. "What about the alien that was attacking him?"

"It was picked up, too, but I separated out the transport wave and put it into a different stasis field." Dax lifted an eyebrow at Petersen's matter-of-fact statement, knowing that even Chief O'Brien wouldn't have found that calculation easy to do on the fly. "I'm not sure if it's alive, though. I think only part of it got beamed in."

"That might work to our advantage," Dax said. "If we could selectively activate some of the cerebral matter the alien has incorporated, we might be able to—"

The turbolift doors hissed open on the bridge, its viewscreen still lit by the glowing indicator colors of Dax's targeted sensor scan. Sisko's face hardened in that reflected light. "Let's not run any scientific experiments just yet, Dax. I want to make sure we're safe first." He strode over to drop a hand on Eddington's shoulder, making the Starfleet security officer look up with a startled snort. "Any sign of movement from the Jem'Hadar station, Commander?"

"Not according to Lieutenant Dax's sensor scan, sir." Eddington gestured up at the swirls of whitish green crawling across the surface of the Jem'Hadar station. "The aliens seem to be searching the area near your beam-in site, but they haven't gone out into space from there. I don't think they were able to track the transporter beam back to the ship."

"Good." Sisko threw himself into his command chair, raising a small cloud of dust as he did. "I'd call a senior officer's conference, gentlemen, but I think we already constitute one. Don't just stand there, Dax, sit down."

She threw him an exasperated glance but took her usual seat at the helm. "I'm not going to collapse, Benjamin. I haven't become an epileptic, just an ansible."

"I don't care what you've become, old man. I still can't see through you to the viewscreen." Sisko's gaze lifted to the ominous glow of green and white that mapped out their enemy's occupation of the Jem'Hadar base. "Eddington, what's the latest update on the station's vector of travel?"

Eddington cleared his throat, as if he'd been waiting for exactly that question. "I've refined tactical sensor analysis to plus or minus one-sixteenth of arc, Captain. Bearing of the Jem'Hadar station remains dead-on for the wormhole. Estimated time of arrival is just under seventeen hours."

Sisko grunted acknowledgment of that. The security officer gave him a frustrated look, making Dax duck her head to hide a smile. Anyone who'd served under Benjamin

Sisko for more than a single voyage knew he didn't waste time handing out compliments, but Eddington never stopped trying for them.

"All right, Petersen, it's your turn." Sisko swung his chair to face the cadet. "What have you learned so far from the *Sreba* data?"

Petersen's throat-clearing was much more hesitant. "Um—Lieutenant Dax managed to download nearly all the scientific data T'Kreng recorded on her way through the wormhole. I ran a numerical model of the upstream subspace echoes and was able to pinpoint the precise time and location of the time rift. The singularity matrix will avulse at the Gamma Quadrant entrance in approximately eighteen hours. Plus or minus forty minutes, sir," she added apologetically.

Sisko's mouth twitched. "An acceptable margin of error, Mr. Petersen. That gives the aliens about an hour to detonate the station's augmented power core once they arrive."

"But what reason would these creatures have for doing that?" Eddington demanded. "They barely seem sentient."

"I'm not sure they *are* sentient as we define it," Dax said somberly. "But they appear to have evolved the ability to capture and utilize both DNA and cerebral material from other sentient species. As for why they're doing this—" She paused, feeling the deep swash and pull of the twinned symbionts inside her, like a tidal current running below the bridge that was Jadzia. "—the ancient Dax encountered others of their kind in the time and space the wormhole will be diverted to. The aliens in the station may be planning to travel into the past to join them, or they may be trying to bring their ancient counterparts into our present."

"Either way, we can't let them divert the wormhole to do it," Sisko said flatly. "We'll have to destroy the Jem'Hadar station before it comes close enough to do any damage to the singularity matrix. Ideas, gentlemen?"

"Not an idea," Dax said soberly. "A limitation. Since these aliens home in on energy discharges, we'll have to plan an attack that can destroy the station quickly. Otherwise they'll overwhelm our shields and breach us to vacuum, just as they did the Jem'Hadar fighter."

Sisko scowled. "Won't our ablative armor hold up under difluorine attack?"

"It will resist breaching at first," Dax agreed. "But the protective effect will only last for about a minute."

Sisko swung toward his security officer. "And how long can our shields hold out before they're drained by alien contact?"

Eddington keyed the question into his tactical panel, looking annoyed that he hadn't already thought to do it. "About four minutes, sir."

"Giving us an attack interval of five or six minutes." Sisko drummed his fingers on the arm of his chair. "Estimate of time needed to destroy the Jem'Hadar station, Mr. Eddington?"

This time, the security officer had his answer ready. "It would take a sustained phaser barrage of eight minutes at close range to destroy the station. If we remained at our present distance, the attack time would be doubled."

"Not good enough," Sisko said crisply. "What if we launched all our quantum torpedoes?"

"That would increase our attack range, and reduce attack time to under four minutes. The trouble is, we'd need a complete structural analysis to find and target the station's major stress points first. Otherwise, we can't be sure of total destruction."

"How long will that take?" Dax inquired.

"About an hour."

Sisko scowled up at the slow-moving station on their viewscreen. "This is one battle where we seem to have the luxury of time, Commander. Proceed with your structural analysis and targeting plan. In the meantime—" He vaulted out of his chair and came down to the helm station. "—why don't you see what you can find out about our captured alien, Dax?"

"Exactly what I was about to suggest. Can I take Ensign Petersen along to help me release the stasis field?"

"As long as you take a security guard, too." Sisko reached out a long arm to catch her as she turned away. "And Dax— after you're done examining this thing, see if you can find out how to kill it. I think we're going to need to know."

* * *

"Odo, god*dammit!*"

Bashir whirled without lifting his hands from his patient, as startled by the fury in that shout as he was by hearing it in the first place. This had been a day filled with the unexpected, however—he was getting to where he almost dreaded the sound of the transporter.

"Take him," he ordered his nurse brusquely. She nodded, stepping in front of him to slip the regenerating wand from his hand without interrupting its steady back-and-forth strokes. They were past the point where anything could be done for either patient without a cloning tank and a full rehab unit. Even Pak Dorren couldn't fault him for abandoning her people to an RN's capable hands.

Still, he had to ignore Dorren's shouted "Hey! Where the hell are you going?" as he dashed out of the ICU, and he somehow knew she wouldn't be able to keep from following. She'd been hovering just outside intensive care for the last two hours, volunteering her own medical expertise despite his requests that she stay silent. The image of her haranguing at his elbow during a second emergency was enough to make him want to send her down to Odo on some trumped-up civil charge, or lock her in a supply cabinet, at least, until he was finished.

Then he ducked through the door and into the main infirmary, and all thought of Pak Dorren evaporated on the stench of blood and acid.

His brain cataloged a list of snapshot images as he rushed across the infirmary: the pain-filled hitch in Kira's breathing as she staggered in a clumsy circle toward the exit; the scattered flecks of blood shattering on the deck beneath her; the breathless, devouring sizzle of flesh giving way to some solvent. Ducking to catch her as she crumpled, he grabbed her around the waist, and carefully avoided her mangled arm as he pulled her backward toward an examining table. "Easy does it, Major . . ."

"Let me go!"

She probably would have hit him if she'd had the strength—she certainly tried hard enough despite his efforts to keep her moving. "I don't think so. Not until I've had a look at that arm." A hard, flat surface caught him in the small of his back, and he maneuvered neatly from behind the major to steer her back toward the table he'd bumped into. He spared Pak only the briefest glower as she pushed in beside him to lend her own hands to the effort. "What happened?" he asked Kira, motioning Pak away to fetch a medical kit from the other side of the room.

Kira blinked at him as though only just realizing he was there, then glanced down at the blood and burns smearing her right arm in dull disinterest. "I don't know." She looked like she wanted to lie down, but couldn't quite remember how to do it.

"You don't know?" Pak recrossed the room with a skeptical snort, and thrust the requested medical kit at Bashir without paying much attention to his darkly reproving scowl. "What?" she sneered. "Wasn't your arm with you all day?"

Kira glared at her with an anger so bright, it seemed likely to burn up the last of her reserves. "I'm not sure how to explain it!"

"Well, that's not the same thing, is it?"

Bashir reached out a restraining hand, opening his mouth to banish Pak from the infirmary entirely, as his eyes skipped across the diagnostic scanner's readings by unconscious habit. A single chemical symbol leapt out at him from the morass, and alarm ripped through him like a gunshot. *Maile!*

The nurse skidded into the doorway before his voice had even died. He heard her running footsteps, but didn't turn away from lifting Kira's arm clear of the rest of her body. "Bring me the burn kit and basin we were using in the ICU," he commanded, casting frantically about for some nearby something to use in touching Kira's arm instead of his bare hands. "And a full osteodermal regenerator! And a set of polyteflon body drapes. Stat!"

She was already gone by the time he shouted that last, but they'd done this often enough today that he was confident she'd come back with what he needed. Slipping a hypo out of the medical kit, he set the dosage one-handed and injected Kira neatly in the artery thumping at the side of her neck. If she thought she was in pain now, she wouldn't even want to be in her own body in another five minutes—a heavy dose of painkiller was the least he could do until they managed to contain the acid damage. Leaving Kira to keep her own arm suspended out in front of her, he gingerly slipped a forceps inside her cuff and used a laser scalpel to slit the sleeve from wrist to elbow.

"What's the matter?" Kira's eyes, wide and unnaturally dark due to pupillary dilation, followed every careful little movement as he sliced free each bit of fabric and peeled it back to expose the bubbling skin beneath. "What did that thing do to me?"

Bashir glanced into her face with what he hoped was a reassuring smile, then dropped another strip of blood-soaked uniform into the disposal chute beside the bed. The scrap disintegrated with a hiss and a blue-white flash. "Nothing that can't be fixed." *I hope.* "We'll have you back in Ops in no time, Major." *Amazing the strain that transperiodic chemical contamination could put on your bedside manner.*

As Maile returned with the drapes and equipment, Bashir quickly scanned his own hands for traces of the acid while he let the nurse drape the bed and carefully lay Kira across it. "You've got diflouric acid burns on top of some nasty lacerations," he explained as the readings scrolled across the tiny screen, first one hand, then the other. Beside him, Maile continued to flash bits of Kira's uniform in the disposal chute, one blood-soaked strip at a time. "There's also some blood loss, obviously, and a compression fracture of your upper arm. I've given you something for the pain, but it's going to take a little while to neutralize the acid. We'll work on putting everything else back in order once that's taken care of." The last scan came up clear, and his heart gave a painful throb of relief.

"Difluoric acid?" Kira repeated blankly.

"Yes." Bashir set aside the scanner as casually as he had taken it up, and picked up the subspace reverter in its place. "Major, diflourine is such a rare transperiodic element, I don't even know of any stores of it on the station. It would help to know how you were exposed to this."

She looked up at him very seriously. "I was bitten by an Andorian."

Bashir shot her a startled glance, and Pak snorted derisively.

"All right, it wasn't an Andorian," the major growled

before Pak said anything more. "But it looked like an Andorian—I *thought* it was an Andorian. Only . . ." She shook her head, and Bashir recognized the dull distraction in her eyes when the pain medication finally took hold. "Odo went after it . . ." she went on, more drowsily. ". . . he said it couldn't see him . . ."

Her eyes fluttered closed, and Bashir did nothing to prevent it. It would do her good to sleep, especially once they started on the osteoregenerator—the itch of knitting bone could be maddening. Bashir made a final pass with the subspace reverter, then carefully scanned the length of Kira's arm for any sign of diflourine not forced back into the transperiodic realm.

"If your constable's got any silicate in his structure," Pak remarked in a calmly conversational tone, "he'd better damn well hope that 'Andorian' can't see him."

Somehow, Bashir never expected anyone who spent all her time terrorizing populations to even know how to spell words like "silicate." He gave her a sidelong glance, reaching for his tissue regenerator to close off the worst of Kira's wounds. "Exactly what do *you* know about diflourine?"

Pak shrugged, looking just a little surprised. "You can use it with a carbon plug to make a no-fuss timer for bombs." As though everyone should be born knowing what you could use illegally obtained transperiodic elements for. Maybe in her circle of friends that was true.

"Did you have any on board your ship?"

She burst into what sounded like honest laughter. "Are you nuts? Too big a breach risk to just carry around. We keep that stuff in planetary stores until we need to use it." Then she seemed to read something in his face, and cocked her head suspiciously to peer at him. "Why do you want to know?"

"I suspect it's because your crewmen show evidence of diflourine burns similar to Major Kira's," said a dry voice from the door. "Isn't that right, Doctor?"

"Yes." Bashir glanced up, not entirely reassured by the steadiness of Odo's voice. Except for his tightly clenched hands, however, the changeling showed no evidence of having encountered anything out of the ordinary that afternoon. "Did you find the Andorian who attacked Kira?"

"That's what I want you to tell me." Odo lifted his cupped hands in what seemed to be both explanation and apology. Inside the conjoined blob, a thick, segmented worm coiled whitely around itself, stubby legs twitching sluggishly. "I think it might be best to place this in stasis before you study it, Doctor. I've tried everything I could think of on my way down here, but there doesn't seem to be any way to kill it."

CHAPTER
16

THE ALIEN WAS, in fact, still alive.

"I don't see how it *can* be," said Yevlin Meris, the Bajoran medic who had shipped out on the *Defiant* in Bashir's place. "It looks like there's only about half of it here."

Dax eyed the severed section of metallic shell and trailing filaments of flesh that occupied one of the *Defiant's* emergency stasis chambers. "Less than that," she said. "It was over two meters long back on the station. Are you sure you got life signs when you did the partial stasis release?"

"Watch." Yevlin handed Dax her medical tricorder, then dialed down the stasis control knob. The bluish glimmer of the field faded to an almost invisible sheen, and the tricorder immediately shot up peaks for metabolic processes, cell division and synapse activity. The two jointed appendages that splayed out from the shell began to move, very slowly, as if they were trying to explore the boundaries of their prison. The medic hurriedly swung the knob back to full stasis. "You see?"

"Yes." Dax readjusted the tricorder to map out neural pathways and scanned it over the alien fragment. "I think it's because the creature has a widely distributed cerebral system rather than a single central brain. Even small fragments of it should be able to think and function separately—they just won't be as intelligent as the whole organism." She redid the scan, this time tuning the tricorder's sensors for dilithium and difluorine. "It looks like the alien generates and stores transperiodic elements in the carapace material around its legs." She glanced back at Ensign Pritz, standing just inside the cramped medical bay. "If we keep those areas in full stasis, we shouldn't be in too much danger."

"All right." The security guard hefted her phaser rifle. "But just in case, Lieutenant, I'd like to have a clear shot at the soft tissue. That's the only place phasers seemed to have any effect."

Dax nodded agreement to that. "Yevlin, can you give us a ventral exposure?"

The physician's assistant punched a command into the stasis chamber, and the stilled alien slowly rotated to expose its underbelly. The flesh there was a tangle of thick muscle fibers twined around steel-wire ligaments, with very few sensory organs or other organized structures visible. Crenellated intergrowths of gray cerebral cortex in gel-like pouches were strung throughout the fleshy interior, like loose, moist strings of pearls. Dax looked them over critically, then glanced across the stasis field at Heather Petersen.

"Ensign, can you program the stasis generator to selectively release each of these cortical masses in turn?"

The Starfleet cadet flipped open the control panel and squatted down to eye the transparent array of computer circuits inside. "Probably not each mass, but I think I can release one string at a time. I'll need a phase modulator."

"Here." Yevlin handed her a small, medical version of the standard engineering tool. "What do you want me to do, Lieutenant?"

"Basic genetic analysis on the neural matter." Dax handed her the medical tricorder and picked up her own Universal Translator. "These aliens apparently steal their cerebral cortices from other organisms they engulf and digest. We need to know who those others are before we can talk to them."

"*Talk* to them?" The Bajoran cast a doubtful glance across the stasis chamber at Pritz, who shrugged with one shoulder so as not to disturb the aim of her phaser rifle.

"You think you can actually communicate with bits and pieces of digested brain?"

Dax gave her a wry look. "It does sound insane, doesn't it? But I have it on very good authority that it can be done." She held up the Universal Translator. "I've programmed this to scan for microelectrical synapse activity rather than sound waves as input. We should be able to pick up any conscious or subconscious speech patterns from directly inside the brains."

"How will you talk back to them, Lieutenant?" Pritz asked.

"I won't," Dax admitted. "We'll just have to listen and hope they say something interesting."

This time it was Petersen's turn to look dubious. "But how will the incorporated beings know we're listening to them? Isn't there something we can do to alert them to that?"

Dax exchanged long, thoughtful looks with Yevlin Meris. "Adrenal injection? Microelectrical shocks?"

The physician's assistant shook her head. "An external magnetic pulse would be better. We can send that right through the stasis field, and it will stimulate the neural material to create its own internal electrical stimulation. Given the size of these cortex fragments, I can probably generate enough field strength just by using my tricorder's magnetic resonance sensor at close range."

The young Bajoran medic's quick intuitive leap made Dax smile. Evidently, Julian Bashir was as good a mentor as he was a doctor. "That sounds like our best alternative," she agreed. "Let's start with the cortical string nearest my side of the stasis chamber."

"Releasing stasis on first string." Petersen's phase modulator hummed, and a long stripe of the stasis field vanished. "You might have to align the alien with the field generators to get complete release."

Yevlin adjusted the antigravs, maneuvering the alien until the long, moist strand of gel-encased cortices lay completely within the nullified portion of the field. "Release complete—I'm getting synapse activity along the whole string." She focused her tricorder on the first knotted cortex, then frowned at the result and repeated the action.

"Problem?" Dax inquired.

"The tricorder's database has no record of this DNA pattern, Lieutenant. It's not remotely similar to any known races in the Alpha or Gamma quadrants."

"That makes sense," Pritz said quietly. "Whoever these aliens are, they haven't been in our region of space for a very long time."

"Agreed." Dax glanced ruefully at her translator, then toggled it on and held it over the cortex. "With no language database to draw on, we'll probably only get gibberish out of this, but it won't hurt to try. Magnetic pulse, please."

Yevlin reprogrammed her tricorder and aimed it at the cortical fragment. The Universal Translator promptly squawked and spat out a string of fast-paced whistles and clicks, almost dolphinlike in its vocal range. It was clearly a language, but not one the translator was able to convert to English without extensive exposure. Dax sighed and stepped back.

"Next cortex?"

This time, Yevlin's scan made her tricorder beep decisively. "This one's definitely Jem'Hadar—there's not another race in the universe that has DNA without a single junk genome in it. Ready for a pulse, Lieutenant?"

"Ready." She positioned the Universal Translator over the second, ragged-looking fragment, but this time when Yevlin aimed her magnetic pulse at the alien, the translator stayed stubbornly silent. Dax gave the medic a puzzled look. "You did stimulate it?"

"Positive."

A low grumbling emerged from the translator, and Dax hurriedly dialed its resolution up to maximum. "—Will not obey, will not obey, will not—" said a fiercely determined voice.

"Subsidiary brains resisting takeover." Even filtered through microelectrical impulses and the logic circuits of the Universal Translator, the crystal-sharp arrogance of that second voice was unmistakable. Dax glanced down at Heather Petersen and saw stunned recognition on the cadet's face. "I'm no longer in contact with the other brain strands—"

"That's T'Kreng!" Petersen jumped up and leaned over

the alien, as if she could somehow spot her former advisor among the tangle of muscle fibers and gelatinous sacks of cerebral cortex. "There must be some of her along this neural string—she's communicating with the Jem'Hadar through it somehow!"

"Scan the entire string for Vulcan DNA," Dax ordered Yevlin. The medic punched the request into her tricorder, then swept it along the series of cortices. She paused at the fifth one in the string.

"This one's Vulcan, and female. Should I pulse it?"

"Yes." Dax moved farther down the edge of the stasis chamber to position her Universal Translator over the fifth cortex. It immediately began emitting a stream of precise, Vulcan observations.

"—obvious from nonresponse of ambulatory systems that we're in stasis, and therefore on a Federation vessel. I have lost all contact with Solvik and the Ferengi trader. The strands they dominated either remain in stasis or were detached by edge effects during transport. We knew when we decided—"

"Pulsing now," said Yevlin.

"What?" T'Kreng's crystalline voice sharpened to something approaching irritation. "I assume there is someone out there listening to me. If you cannot communicate more effectively than that, please allow me to talk without inducing unnecessary visual hallucinations."

"That's T'Kreng, all right," Dax muttered.

"I shall start from the beginning. This is Professor T'Kreng of the Vulcan Science Academy. I have been killed and eaten by an alien of unknown affinity, one of a swarm which engulfed my research vessel upon its emergence from the Bajoran wormhole. My cerebral cortex was divided among several of the aliens, but enough remains intact in this individual to allow me almost complete control of its activities."

Dax lifted her eyebrows at Pritz. "I wonder if that's why we found this alien separate from the rest?"

The security guard shook her head in bewilderment. "But if there was a Vulcan in control of it, why did it attack Goldman?"

Petersen looked across at them, her eyes wry. "You have

225

no idea how ruthless Professor T'Kreng can be. I suspect she attacked that man in order to make us do exactly what we have done—beam her back to the ship and examine her."

"In fact," Dax said quietly, "she may even have kept that Jem'Hadar she was eating alive to draw us to her."

"If you are a member of the Federation, as I suspect," continued the crystal-calm voice from the translator, "I must warn you of the immense danger we all face. These aliens have the ability to keep intact cortical matter from any species they ingest. They string it into the organic equivalent of parallel processors, and use it until each piece ultimately degrades into noncognition. When they congregate into a core mass, they connect their individual neural strings to form immense living supercomputers. These core masses are capable of astonishing theoretical calculations. I speak from direct knowledge. I was part of the one gathered in the Jem'Hadar station, until I managed to take control of this individual and send it away."

Dax shook her head in silent wonder. Only a brain with the Vulcan genius—and driving arrogance—of T'Kreng could have summoned the mental resilience to overcome this most complete of alien captivities. It was hard to remember that the Vulcan physicist was really dead, and that just a fragment of her powerful brain was speaking to them from an organic prison.

"I regret to say that these aliens had no intention of destroying the Bajoran wormhole before they attacked my ship," T'Kreng's silken voice resumed. "They were merely following their species' established way of life. They must have evolved as parasites within a thickly populated sector—they drift randomly through space, attacking any spacefaring life they encounter. They feed off its genetic matter, its sentience, and the power cores of its space vessels. They would have continued doing this forever, but the influx of Vulcan intelligence and astrophysics knowledge into their race has given them both a new goal, and the means to accomplish it.

"I have been able to absorb a little of their history from the oldest fragments of cortex present along these neural strands. As abundant as they seem to be, this species

226

evidently has dwindled to a mere shadow of former hordes which once swept across vast portions of the galaxy and demolished every spacefaring civilization they encountered. They have always desired to return to their former glory. Now, after long hunger and deprivation, they have found a quick way to do it. They will use the Bajoran wormhole to bridge space and time to their last great battle, when they were at the peak of their strength and numbers."

"The battle the *Defiant* got caught in when it was thrown back in time," Dax murmured. She saw the chorus of baffled looks thrown at her by Petersen, Yevlin, and Pritz, and shook her head. "It sounds insane, I know, but things are actually starting to fall together."

"Detonating the wormhole with precisely enough energy to make it connect to the proper place and time is a complex and difficult task," T'Kreng said, in typical Vulcan understatement. "However, the aliens have fifteen Vulcan brains at their disposal—including those portions of my own brain which contain my understanding of singularity matrices. What fifteen Vulcans could barely comprehend individually will almost certainly yield to their combined intelligence, linked together as it is in the alien core mass."

The disembodied voice hardened to a knife-sharp edge. "Whoever is listening, you must believe me when I say that the Federation is in grave peril. If these aliens bring all of their kind forward to our time and our quadrant, the combined forces of the Federation, the Klingons, the Cardassians, and the Romulans will not be able to withstand the invasion. Just as the ancient race known as the Furies could not withstand it millennia ago. These alien parasites are the 'unclean,' the very ones who drove the Furies from the portion of Federation space they are now trying to reclaim. It is perhaps the most ironic part of this affair," T'Kreng added acidly, "that we who grew up on this abandoned battlefield now must fight off both the victors and the vanquished."

"It's only a portion of the creature, obviously."

Bashir nodded absently at Odo when the constable crouched on the other side of the open stasis drawer and peered through the field at what he was doing. The tight weave of subspace fabric rippled as Bashir pushed a needle probe through the meniscus, distorting Odo's already misproportioned face and making the little curl of "worm" at the center appear to be floating in transparent liquid.

"I decided against trying to apprehend the entire intruder when it pushed through a level-two containment field on deck six," the constable went on. His eyes seemed to lift involuntarily to something over Bashir's right shoulder, and the doctor suspected he knew what had captured the changeling's attention. Kira was no doubt still visible through the morgue's open doorway, sleeping deeply if not peacefully while Maile finished tending to her wounds. "And it didn't seem wise to expose anyone else until we knew what we were dealing with."

"Well, I certainly can't argue with that." Especially if Kira was any indication what this thing was capable of in only a few seconds' exposure. Piercing the worm as near to its middle as he'd been able to aim through twenty centimeters of stasis, Bashir made sure the probe was well seated in the field before gently releasing it and turning to activate the scan.

A few meters away, Pak Dorren drummed her fingers on the back of the stool she was straddling, her feet tapping an uneven counterrhythm on the rungs. Bashir would have guessed it was close proximity to the alien fragment that made her twitchy and nervous if he hadn't already spent half the afternoon with her ceaseless fidgeting. Now he just suspected she needed medication. "You think this thingamajigger beamed over with us?" she asked, never interrupting her drumming.

Odo straightened with a judgmental sniff, but Bashir looked up from his equipment to announce definitively, "No," before the constable could do more than cross his arms. He answered Odo's scowl of skepticism by gesturing at the soft white body on the other end of his probe. "This is—sort of—an Andorian antenna." He tried to trace out the gentle arc of its endoskeleton, the disklike flare of its tip, without actually touching the stasis screen. "And Quark reported his Andorian customer missing before Pak Dorren's people even came on board." He shook his head down at the bizarre fragment as the first of the medical readings blinked into existence on the probe's output screen. "If this is part of whatever attacked Major Kira, then your intruder either is that missing Andorian, or *used* to be him."

Odo tilted his head to a decidedly skeptical angle. "He seems to have had a particularly bad reaction to Quark's Rigellian chocolate."

"I'll say." Leaning over the back of her stool, Pak squinted across the room as though intrigued with the worm in the morgue drawer but perfectly willing to keep her distance. "Andorian antennas don't usually have legs, do they?"

"No, not usually." Bashir swiveled the probe screen around in front of him and started scrolling through the complex of readings, searching for something—anything—familiar. He paused the screen and frowned at the broken code of amino acids filling one-half of the display. Sliding the probe clear of the alien body, he backed it out of the stasis field and carefully chose another entry point several millimeters from the first. The probe didn't want to push through the leg joint as neatly as it had through what passed as this sample's thorax, but a little patient twisting finally slipped it into place with a click Bashir almost swore he could hear. Pleased with his handiwork, he rocked back in his seat to watch the sensors cycle through their business and throw the answers up onto the screen.

"Oh, now this is odd. . . ."

"What?" Odo appeared suddenly at his shoulder, and he heard Pak's feet thump to the deck as she climbed off her stool to join them. "What do you see?"

A lot of things, and he wasn't sure how to explain any of them. "Well, this—" He split the screen, quickly sorting through the probe's first set of readings until he found the spiral helix he was searching for. "The chromosomal structure in the body of the sample is almost entirely Andorian. In fact, this particular linkage—" He traced an amino-acid chain with one finger when they both crowded closer to look. "—is characteristic of Haslev-Rahn disease, a congenital disorder endemic to Shesh-caste Andorians. But here . . ." This time he bracketed a length of helix with both hands, and wondered if Pak and Odo could see the differences in it as clearly as he did. "None of these even uses the same amino-acid sets as Andorian chromosomes, yet they're spliced into the very same genes."

"Could the Andorian be infected with something?" Pak asked. She studied the readings with a seriousness Bashir wasn't sure how to interpret. "Viruses can copy and replace parts of chromosomes, can't they?"

The fact that she even knew to ask the question startled him. "There does seem to be a certain viruslike behavior at work here," he admitted, "although not in the way you're thinking." He swung his chair to face them, trying very hard to keep his words slow and his sentences coherent, even though his mind had already raced well past his explanation and on to what it implied. "As a general rule, viruses work to alter their *own* genetic structure, not yours. They take over individual cells in a host body, and coopt those cells' reproductive mechanisms to generate copies of the virus. While it's in there, a virus will sometimes steal bits and pieces of the host's genetic code for insertion into its own. That way it can avoid some of the host's natural attempts to identify and destroy it, and pick up new characteristics which might make it easier to transmit, or harder to kill once it's established an infection." He glanced aside at the morgue drawer and its bizarre occupant. "A remarkably elegant organism, considering it's little more than a string of coded proteins."

"Doctor," Odo broke in. "How is this relevant to what happened to Quark's Andorian?"

He shook off a blur of speculation with some effort. "Well, this isn't a simplified organism with one or two Andorian codons on its chain. This is essentially an Andorian organism with entirely alien functions added to its structure." Drawing their attention to the screen again, he pointed out whatever random codons passed across the display as he moved through the readings. "This codes for digestive enzymes, so this bit of antenna could conceivably 'eat' by absorbing organic material directly into itself. These are for sensing organs—light, heat. This is the crux of a Tholian's electromagnetic organelle. *These*—" He tapped the right-hand side of the monitor, where the convoluted findings from the leg probe scrawled around the sensor scan like a mad man's ravings. "These aren't even something I recognize. My guess is there are at least three separate genetic families represented here, all of them no less than ten millennia old, judging from the extent of genetic decay." He looked back at them over his shoulder. "What we have here isn't an Andorian who's been infected by some alien virus's DNA—we have a viroid life-form that's absorbed an Andorian's genetic code for its own selective usage."

Pak stared at the alien readings as though the force of her attention could make them understandable. "So you're saying my ships were attacked by an Andorian who was chewed up by Tholians?"

"I doubt the Andorian genotype had been added to the mix when you were attacked," Bashir said, "but the duranium-titanium traces you detected might well have been caused by a Tholian carapace, yes."

"Then how did it get on board the station?" Odo asked. "Traffic has been at a standstill since before Captain Sisko returned from Starbase One." He cast Pak a dry look that could have been either disdain or derision for all Bashir could tell. "And sensors haven't exactly been brimming with reports of free-floating Tholians lately."

"The Lethian transport."

Bashir jumped to his feet to intercept Kira as she made her way slowly, stiffly into the morgue to join them. Maile must have disposed of her jacket while cleaning out her wounds, because the major was left with only her trousers and a white cotton shell for a uniform. The dark maroon patches that might have passed for spilled coolant against her rust colored trouser legs, though, stood out in brilliant scarlet on the white undertunic. The contrast only served to make her look more pale and fragile.

"This is what took out Pak's armada?" she asked, jerking her chin toward their innocuous prisoner as Bashir came to take her elbow.

He thought about scolding her for being up and about, for climbing out of bed when the new skin on her arm was still delicate and shiny, and they hadn't had the chance to fully replace her blood volume yet. Then he remembered the flare of organic sludge around Pak's escape party when they beamed in, and the evidence of what they'd run from etched into the broken bodies of her cohorts. If that threat was really aboard the station, walking about a few pints low on bodily fluids would be the least of his patients' problems. "I think it must be," he said quietly.

She seemed to sense how his thoughts must have run, because she didn't shake off his helping hand or resist when he guided her toward the chair he'd abandoned beside the drawer. "Then it's what destroyed those freighters we found." She looked at the alien fragment with open hatred. "And it's what hulled that Lethian transport."

Odo nodded slowly. "The missing crew."

"Of course!" Bashir didn't realize he'd blurted the exclamation until everyone looked to him as though expecting something more. He tried not to sound too professionally excited as he explained, "It must have taken them for their genetic raw material."

Kira clenched her teeth so hard that he could see the muscles bunch in her jaw. "And it came on board with that Cardassian vole."

It wasn't something Bashir had thought of, even having heard Maile's horrified account of scaring up some monstrous rodent from the bowels of the Lethian ship. "I can't tell you specifically if it's from a vole," he admitted, thinking back over the scans he'd examined only a few minutes before, "but it does have Cardassian DNA."

Kira sat back in the chair with a wince Bashir didn't think she'd meant to reveal, and propped one elbow on the edge of the morgue drawer. "All right, then—how can we kill it?"

A simple question, really. For some reason, though, he hadn't expected everyone to turn to him as though he were expected to just produce the answer. Not for the first time since the *Defiant* left this quadrant, he desperately wished Jadzia were here. "I don't know."

Pak spun away with a disgusted curse, but it was Kira rubbing wearily at her eyes with the heels of both hands that stabbed him most keenly with regret for letting them down. "This thing has no circulatory blood supply," he told the major, feeling almost like he ought to apologize. "No real nervous system, and no digestive tract. Yet it's capable of developing all of them even as we speak! We're talking about an organism that conceivably has access to any physical characteristic it might need. If it needs to photosynthesize, it will photosynthesize. If it needs to regenerate limbs or nerves or organs, it will do that. Short of disassembling it on a molecular level, I don't know that we *can* kill it."

Kira tipped her head back to sigh up at him, a look that wasn't quite disappointment but wasn't quite resignation, either, in her tired eyes. The chirp of her comm badge saved Bashir from whatever she'd meant to say.

"Major . . ." O'Brien's voice sounded grim, as though he'd been listening in on their conversation and didn't like the answers any more than the rest of them did. "I think you'd better get up to Ops right away."

Kira pushed the side of her fist against the stasis field, watching the weak corona flare to blot out the frozen alien. "I'm a little busy right now, Chief."

"All the same, ma'am," he persisted, "I really think you'd better come. The *Mukaikubo* just arrived—"

"You can patch Captain Regitz through to me down here."

"That's just it, Major. I can't get Captain Regitz on the comm. In fact, I can't get anybody. As far as I can tell, there's not a single soul left on board."

CHAPTER
17

SOMETIME IN THE last three hours, the wormhole had gone insane.

Lurid ultraviolet lashes curled and whipped across the fabric of Bajoran space, invisibly shattering the starscape like cracks across a darkened mirror. The filters on the Ops viewscreen painted each wave in intricate detail. Kira hugged her arms across her chest, watching the *Mukaikubo* drift sleepily through the swirl and throb of radioactive night, and wondering if she ought to order O'Brien to drop the UV filters, so they couldn't see how bad the outside world was getting.

"I wonder how they got them to drop out of warp." She didn't mean to murmur it out loud, but once it was spoken she couldn't take it back.

Beside her, Odo studied the lifeless starship with a clinical stoicism Kira envied. "Probably the same way they trapped Pak Dorren's people—by reading like ship debris."

It just seemed like it shouldn't be that easy. Nothing should be able to lure a Galaxy-class starship into sublight, then overwhelm it like ants on a peach before it could think of some way to defend itself. Yet here it was, its secondary hull stripped open in a dozen different places, the great flat disk of its primary hull divested of its bridge assembly entirely, as though the whole ship had rotted away from within. Only the busy skitter of alien bodies—the size and

234

shape of ticks from this distance—gave the ship's outer skin any movement, any life. Its running lights were as black as a Vegan's eyes; the darkened husk looked incredibly small, impossibly fragile hung against the wormhole's silent roars.

O'Brien cleared his throat from the upper tier. Kira didn't look up at him, but he must have sensed her shift of attention. "Should I catch her with a tractor beam and bring her to a standstill?" he asked.

She thought about Pak's armada, about the aliens following the paths of their phasers and their engine exhausts. "No." Then, because an officer as good as O'Brien always deserved a straight explanation, "I don't want to draw their attention."

"Well, we've got to do something," he countered. It was what Kira liked about O'Brien—he was never disrespectful, but he always spoke his mind. "She'll drift into the wormhole's gravity well in another thirty minutes or so, and that hoard of engine cores she's carrying will never make the passage without exploding."

"I know that, Chief." They'd been through all this when Kira first noticed the eerie glow in the hull plates along the *Mukaikubo*'s belly, and O'Brien identified its cargo as four separate, unshielded reaction masses. At least now they knew where the stolen engine cores from the ore freighters and the Lethian transport had gone.

"We could try to destroy the ship from here," Odo suggested. "Detonate the payload with torpedoes or phaser fire."

O'Brien made a blunt, unhappy noise that earned an impatient scowl from the constable. "With the wormhole oscillating like it is right now," the chief explained, "an explosion of that magnitude even at this range would collapse it for good."

"And letting the *Mukaikubo* drift into its event horizon won't?"

It would, and all of them knew it, so Kira wasn't surprised when O'Brien answered Odo's question with little more than a growl of frustration.

"We're not going to let the *Mukaikubo* destroy the wormhole." Kira pulled her eyes away from the viewscreen with painful effort, and turned to limp a few steps closer to

235

O'Brien so she could crane a look up at him from below. "Can we get a transporter signal into the ship?"

He lifted his eyebrows in thought, and looked over her head at the viewscreen. "Her shields are down, and she's well within range, but I wouldn't want to trust that we could maintain a coherent pattern with all the leakage from the wormhole."

"That's all right," Kira told him. "I don't want a coherent pattern."

She held tight to the rail as she hauled herself up the steps to join O'Brien. No matter what Bashir claimed, there didn't seem to be a painkiller in existence that could touch the bone-deep ache in her muscles, much less the pounding tension that had crawled up the back of her neck to burrow in at the base of her skull. She felt like she'd hiked forty kilometers with a field pack and bad boots, never mind the hand-span bruise across the outside of her thigh. The acid burns on her arm were just about the only place on her body that didn't hurt right now.

Odo trotted up the steps close behind her, smart enough not to try and help her move now that she was back on duty and in front of the crew. "What are you thinking?" he asked, his voice dryly suspicious.

Kira eased herself onto the seat O'Brien never used, swallowing a grimace. "Disassemble them on a molecular level, Bashir said. That's the only way to be sure." She stared past O'Brien at the drifting starship on the screen. "I want to transport those things off the *Mukaikubo* and into space on a wide-dispersal setting."

O'Brien nodded, reaching for his panel. "The cargo transporter would work best for that. We could pick them up in loads up to ten cubic meters—still only a handful at a time, given the size of those things out there, but better than the one or two we could get with the personnel transporter." His hands flew across the engineering console without waiting for Kira's reply.

"Pak Dorren said these aliens could backtrack a phaser beam to find an attacking ship." Odo took up a position behind them and peered over O'Brien's shoulder. "What's to stop them from doing the same thing with a transporter beam?"

"Because they didn't," Kira said. "When Pak brought her people here, the aliens didn't follow. That means for some reason they can't, or they don't, and we're going to make use of that."

"It's a higher-energy beam," O'Brien volunteered in the distracted, almost expressionless voice of a man deeply immersed in his work, "but it's got a much shorter duration than the sustained phasers the militia's been using. The aliens probably don't have time to get a fix on the transporter signal." Looking up from his computations, he nodded once to Kira. "Ready when you are, Major."

"Give 'em hell, Chief."

Kira half-expected to hear the whine of the powerful transporter engaging several decks below—she remembered it cycling almost continuously, day and night, when the need to quickly restaff and restock the great station had kept her awake with all its noises and demands. But that had been when DS9 still orbited Bajor, and a cargo transporter was still an acceptable alternative to sending up a freighter. In the years since they'd moved the station three light-hours away from its previous home, she couldn't recall hearing the cargo transporter fired up even once.

So it wasn't the distant hum of the awakening transporter or the rumbling throb of its compensators coming on-line that made her grip the sides of her seat and shoot a nervous glance toward the ceiling—it was the flicker in the Ops main lighting, and the little shudder of brownouts that swept through half the surrounding panels.

"You're going to overstress the capacitors," Odo warned, and O'Brien pressed his lips into a grim line.

"No, we're not."

Even so, the lights took another alarming dip as O'Brien swiftly reversed the beam to bounce back whatever ugly cargo he'd picked up. Kira just barely glimpsed the silvery shimmer of a transporter materialization on the viewscreen somewhere between the *Mukaikubo* and the station, then a thin white line of expanding crystal as the tiny motes of matter wisped away in their silent dance of annihilation and scatter. Ops broke into a ragged cheer of relief.

"There's your first shipment," O'Brien announced over the shouting.

Kira clenched one fist in her lap in grim triumph. "Keep at it," she commanded. It was a little frightening how in control of a situation you could feel once you knew your opponent was killable. "I want that ship empty, no matter how long it takes."

The second pulse and fade of the lights didn't seem nearly so dramatic as the first, and, if anything, the glowing cloud of gassed matter deposited outside the *Mukaikubo*'s walls looked even larger and more luminous than before. A series of urgent chirps from the comm station reminded Kira that the entire station must be feeling the punishment for Ops to be so hard hit by the power drains. Waving for a noncom to handle the calls from the other decks, she looked expectantly toward O'Brien for the third transporter cycle to begin. "Chief . . ."

O'Brien acknowledged her with a quick, frustrated nod, never looking up from his controls. "It's being a little slow about cycling the matter converters. We'll be all right. . . ."

Even as he spoke, Ops sank into near darkness, and a third spray of deconstructed matter dusted the radiation-torn space outside. It seemed to take forever before the power rebounded, though. Kira gave O'Brien fully twice as long to make the fourth transport before prodding, "Isn't there some way we can cut that delay?"

"Not without dumping half those rerouted systems off the grid." He chewed on his lip, swearing almost subvocally as he fought with the controls. "Cargo transporters were designed for pattern capacity, Major, not for speed."

"Then I'd suggest we quit while we're ahead." Odo touched Kira's shoulder and pointed up at the viewscreen. "Our friends seem to have noticed their missing comrades."

Dark floes of what appeared to be oil dribbled from the wounds in *Mukaikubo*'s sides. Kira wondered if this was the acid these aliens seemed to use for breaching starship hulls—and how quickly it could eat through the structure of her station; then the rivulets broke apart into individual motes, and the dozens of mitelike passengers on the surface of the ship scuttled down to meet the outgoing rush.

Kira pushed anxiously to her feet. "Chief . . . ?"

He didn't answer, even when the first wave of aliens leapt out into space toward them on little puffs of steaming gas.

The cargo transporter rang out with a great rumble and disintegrated most of the nearest ones just as half the lights across Ops crackled brilliantly and died.

By the time her eyes adjusted to the almost-dark, Kira couldn't even tell where in the onrushing force O'Brien's blow had been struck. They swarmed as aimlessly as puff-weed spore, driven on by their own expulsions instead of the wind.

"Major . . ."

She ignored Odo, concentrating instead on O'Brien's muttering. "Just one more, you damned thing—one more!" You could tell a lot about your timing just by listening to your engineer swear, she thought absently.

"Major," Odo repeated, more firmly, "this is not going to work."

Of course not. Nothing was working. That didn't mean they had to stop trying. That didn't mean they could run away.

Something deep and urgent moved through the skeleton of the station, and O'Brien crowed "She's coming up! Here we go!" just as the transporter's distinctive whine rose to a wail and Odo shouted her name in honest alarm.

And the first of the oncoming aliens passed the point of no return.

"Raise shields!"

Deflectors flashed into being before the echo of her shout had died. Sparking like steel against steel, two, then three, then dozens of the duranium-shelled creatures bounced against the screens to skitter sideways, and the transporter beam smashed a psychotic explosion of misplaced energy against the inside of the shield as it reached out for a target that was no longer within its reach.

The backlash boomed through the station like an asteroid strike. Kira knew without asking that the jolt and thunder she felt through the decking was the cargo transporter blowing most of its workings out into space, and the shadows that gyrated on the Ops ceiling and floors after the last working light went dead told her there were fires at the stations even before the hoarse roar of extinguishers drowned out the frantic shouts. Somehow, the back of her brain took note of every detail of the mechanical carnage as she leaned over the upper bridge railing and glared her hatred at the distant *Mukaikubo*.

Until the spark and shimmer of alien bodies impacting the deflectors grew too bright to see beyond.

Something was happening down on the Jem'Hadar station. Under ordinary circumstances, Sisko might not even have noticed it, but he'd been concentrating so hard on keeping his gnawing tension under control that he'd forced himself to focus all his attention on the central portion of the Jem'Hadar station. The color contours there were changing, slowly dimming from arctic white in the center to a pale greenish ivory.

"Dax, do your sensors show any changes in alien distribution down on the station?" he demanded.

The science officer tapped a command into her panel and frowned at the answer she got. "There seems to be an overall decrease in alien concentration, but I can't find out where the missing mass has gone. I've scanned the whole system and I'm not picking up concentrations of duranium anywhere but the station."

Sisko felt a chill of distrust crawl down his spine. "Set up a motion-sensing scan around the ship, with the smallest resolution you can manage. I want to make sure we don't get surprised by those things. Eddington, what's the progress on your structural analysis of the station?"

"Eighty-three-percent complete, Captain. Estimated time to targeting is ten minutes."

Sisko grunted. Some instinct was hammering at him, telling him that the luxury of time was no longer on their side in this battle. The logical part of his brain knew he was probably wrong, but his gut refused to be convinced. "If we fired on the basis of our present data, how much chance would we have of destroying the station?"

Eddington gave him a baffled look. "Sixty-three percent. But why would we need to fire now, sir?"

"I don't know. Just be prepared to do it." Sisko vaulted out of his command chair and went to lean over Dax's shoulder. "Have you got that motion detector in place, old man?"

"I'm bringing it on-line now. It's set to trigger a proximity alarm for anything bigger than a micrometeorite."

"Good." He straightened and scowled up at the Jem'Hadar station on the viewscreen. Its color change was more obvious now, with the entire interior painted in shades of green rather than the concentrated whites it had once glowed with. Sisko ran down a mental list of further precautions he could take. "Lay in a course back for the wormhole, Dax, and program the piloting computer to engage at warp five at the first sign of shield penetration. I don't want to risk a diflourine breach."

Unlike Eddington, Dax obeyed him without question. Afterward, though, she swung around in her chair to give him a grave upward look. "You've figured something out about these aliens, haven't you, Benjamin?"

Sisko opened his mouth to deny it, then realized she was right. His subconscious had put together the pieces during the past hour while he had been simply concentrating on staying calm. "You told me these creatures take both DNA and cerebral cortices from the species they attack. Why take the DNA unless they're going to use it?" He paused, glancing down at his science officer to gauge her reaction. She nodded agreement. "Well, what the hell are they using it for?"

"They obviously don't use it to reconstruct the cerebral cortices they take," Dax said thoughtfully. "T'Kreng said they simply keep them intact until they decay into noncognition."

Sisko nodded. "So they either use the DNA to reconstruct other parts of their bodies—or to make themselves completely different bodies for use in different environments."

"Bodies that might still be vacuum-resistant, but wouldn't show up on our duranium scans?" Dax frowned. "But without their duranium carapaces, they couldn't store diflourine safely. How much damage could they do us?"

Eddington looked over his shoulder at them. "They could still overwhelm our shields by sheer mass."

Sisko nodded at him. "And they could also make atmosphere-tolerant bodies, ones that could use the Jem'Hadar defenses on the station—"

Dax frowned. "But they can't shoot at us as long as we're cloaked."

From the back of the bridge, Ensign Hovan cleared her throat apologetically. "Sir, I've been meaning to tell you . . . You asked me to watch out for voltage fluctuations on our cloaking screen? Well, for the last fifteen minutes, I've been reading a consistent loss of fifteen millivolts. It's well within our operating tolerance, and much too small to be due to an alien of the mass we'd seen before—"

Sisko gave her a narrow-eyed look. "But not too small if they can change shape or size? Where is it located, Ensign?"

"Near the aft thermal diffuser panels, sir."

Dax looked disgusted with herself. "Where our waste heat from the warp core is vented to space," she said. "I should have known that any space-dwelling species who preys off spaceships would have developed sensory organs able to detect thermal trails."

Sisko's vague swirl of unease crystallized into decision. "Eddington, target our quantum torpedoes now. Dax, I want immediate departure as soon as—"

The blare of a proximity alarm sliced through his orders and made them meaningless. Sisko's fierce curse was lost beneath its banshee echo.

"Motion detector scan has picked up incoming aliens in all sectors." Dax's fingers flew across her panel. "Initial estimates are over two hundred individual entities."

"I'm reading voltage drops across our entire cloaking screen," Hovan added. "They've penetrated the cloak and are approaching shields, Captain."

"Captain, our weapons sensors are picking up activity in the Jem'Hadar phaser banks," Eddington warned. "Someone down there is preparing to fire on us."

Sisko scowled. "Can we track the aliens with sensors for close-range phaser attack?"

Dax shook her head. "I'm getting no response on scans for duranium or other metallic alloys. This version of the aliens must be constructed entirely of light carbon polymers. They're nearly invisible to our sensors." She gave Sisko a quick, sidelong glance. "I'm also reading negative on scans for diflourine."

"That's because these are just the shock troops, designed

to take down our shields so the station's weapons can destroy us." Sisko stared up at the uninformative viewscreen, feeling the muscles along his jaw clench and quiver with frustration. This was an impossible battle, fought against an unseen enemy whose strengths and weaknesses fluctuated too quickly to counter. He began to understand why the Furies had fled before their onslaught. A gentle quiver of contact rolled through the ship as the first of the aliens made contact with their shields.

"How long before we can fire torpedoes, Mr. Eddington?" Sisko demanded.

"Two minutes, sir."

"Status of shields?"

"Holding," Dax said. The *Defiant's* quiet occasional shivers became a constant growl of vibration as more and more aliens descended on her shields. "But the power drain is increasing so fast that even if the shields hold out for two more minutes, we'll have lost our ability to engage the engines."

"*Damn.*" Sisko took in a deep, decisive breath. "All right, Dax. Get us out of here at maximum impulse, *now.*"

The *Defiant* surged into motion with its usual kick of unbalanced acceleration. Sisko watched in grim silence as the Jem'Hadar station dwindled to a greenish speck in the distance. "Do we still have our passengers, Dax?"

"We've lost some of them, but not all," she replied. "Shield drains are now constant at half of previous levels."

Sisko grunted. "Drop us back to one-quarter impulse." He caught the worried look Dax cast him, and responded with a grim sliver of smile. "Don't worry, old man. I know what I'm going to do will work. Eddington, release one quantum torpedo and detonate it just outside our shield containment radius. Without their duranium shells, those things should be vulnerable to EM radiation."

"Releasing torpedo now, sir." A prism of hyperpowered light exploded just off the port nacelle, rocking the *Defiant* through her shields as it engulfed her in its shock wave. "Torpedo exploded," the security officer added unnecessarily.

"Shield drains have dropped to zero," Dax added a moment later. "The aliens have been destroyed." She glanced over her shoulder at Sisko, one eyebrow lifting quizzically. "How did you know that would work?"

"Because it's how we saved the *Defiant* from these aliens, five thousand years ago," Sisko said bluntly. "The only difference is, this time we had intact shields to protect us."

His science officer winced. "Should I plot a return course to the Jem'Hadar station, Captain?"

Sisko rubbed a hand across his face, feeling the grit of incipient beard under his callused fingers. For the first time in hours, he became aware of the aching tiredness in his bones that came from too much stress and too little sleep. A glance around the bridge told him that his skeleton crew wasn't in much better shape. He shook his head. "Let's head back to the wormhole first," he said. "We've got sixteen hours left before the Jem'Hadar station gets there. And now that we know what we're up against, I think we could use some reinforcements."

CHAPTER
18

WHEN THE BLAST and rumble of faraway damage shuddered through the station infirmary, Julian Bashir glanced toward the ceiling as though that might help tell him what had happened. He'd always thought that an interesting reflex— even if he'd been working in a planetbound facility, it wasn't like looking skyward could tell him anything except the color of the ceiling. Yet it was the first thing humans the galaxy over did when surprised by unexpected sounds and movements. And it probably didn't tell them anything more than it told him now; just as he lifted his gaze from the symbiont's quietly bubbling tank, the lights overhead shivered, flickered, and died. Black rushed in from all sides to erase every contour of the room, and the growling tremor of distant danger passed away into silence.

Which left him in the darkened room with a life-support tank that was no longer bubbling.

He drew his hands carefully out of the clammy brine. Not because he was worried about startling the symbiont, really, but just because it felt wrong to shock the dark with any unnecessary noise now that even the stasis tank had fallen silent. *I should have had O'Brien hook up a stand-alone generator for the symbiont,* he thought, patting about for a rag on which to dry his hands. It wasn't like it couldn't be done—he'd nagged O'Brien into fitting the ICU with an uninterruptable power supply the first month he was on the station—and God knew he had little other use for the three stand-alones currently taking up space in the back room storage locker. But he hadn't wanted to bother the chief when there seemed to be so little likelihood of a power failure, and—deep down inside—he'd also known T'Kreng was right, and there was a very good chance he wouldn't be caring for the symbiont much longer. It had seemed an unnecessary bit of effort for something that might not exist in another twenty-four hours.

Shows what I know. Folding the rag as neatly as he could in the dark, Bashir dropped it onto the chair he'd just vacated and sighed down at the symbiont. "You know," he remarked aloud, "when I said I'd give anything to be locked in dark room with Dax, I rather assumed Jadzia would be there, too."

The symbiont, not surprisingly, didn't answer.

Bashir wasn't sure how much of his vocalizing the symbiont was aware of, but his ancient medical records at least indicated that he'd spent a lot of the last five thousand years talking to it. "Today, taught Dax how to make b'stella," was his favorite of the old entries. Perhaps it was because there was no way he could have kept silent for nearly a hundred years. Or perhaps it was because even a hundred years with the displaced symbiont never erased his gut-deep certainty that it somehow knew and cared when it was being inter-acted with, even when that interaction was only a heartsick human who could offer it nothing more than one-sided conversation. Whatever the reason, the precedent had clearly been set long ago, so he still talked to it now whenever they were alone.

"I don't know if you've noticed, but we've just lost all power in the infirmary. Which means I'm standing here in the dark, and you're floating in your medium without any of your support equipment running." He found the edge of the tank through the blackness, and curled his hand over it to tickle the surface of the water with his fingers. "I'm going to get a generator from the back room—it ought to be able to run you and a couple of small trouble lights with no problem, so we'll be back in business in no time. I won't be gone long. I promise."

He thought he felt the symbiont's cool, soft mass brush

against his fingertips, but the feeling was gone again before he could be sure.

As impenetrable as the darkness inside the infirmary seemed, Bashir was surprised to discover gradations in its relative depths as he turned slowly toward the examining-room door. The main infirmary glowed an icy gray beyond the adjoining doorway, lit from within by the isolation field at the mouth of the ICU, and from without by whatever illumination leaked through the open front entrance from emergency lanterns on the Promenade. While both those light sources would have been completely inadequate under most conditions, they proved marvelously helpful when compared to the absolute dark in the other parts of the infirmary. Bashir passed from the examining room into the open with a sense of little more than dark against darker, but it was enough to steer him toward the morgue at the rearmost of the infirmary without bumping into anything or tumbling himself head over heels.

He didn't particularly like keeping equipment in the same room where they occasionally kept cadavers. It felt oddly callous to tell a nurse, "Go fetch the dual-organ bypass cart from the morgue," as though all you had was one oversized coat closet that you also stuffed dead bodies into because you hadn't anywhere else to put them. In reality, it was more the other way around. The Cardassians had been quite particular about preserving their comrades' remains while they were occupying Bajor, but either hadn't the finances or the compassion to invest in the large lifesaving equipment that came standard with any Starfleet sickbay. With no interrogations, no lethal disciplinary actions, and at least a good deal fewer liberation operatives romping about the station nowadays, Starfleet's tenure at *Deep Space Nine* had seen a gratifying decline in the number of dead bodies coming through the infirmary. Bashir had been able to remove more than half of the stasis drawers to create some much-needed autopsy and storage space. (Cardassians, apparently, didn't see much use in postmortem exams, either.) Trying to explain that you really *did* have a morgue and you were using it as a coat closet sounded even *more* callous and bizarre, though, so Bashir had a tendency to avoid mentioning precisely where the large equipment was kept. "Nurse

Gerjuoy, could you please go get the bypass cart? I believe you know where it is." It didn't seem to hinder efficiency, but it did keep incidents of anxiety-induced hypertension among the patients at a minimum.

As he slowed at the doorway to the morgue, Bashir pointedly refused to let himself think that the small chamber was now dark as a tomb. He felt as if the walls rushed in to blind him on both sides as he stepped into that darkness, then rebounded to an impossible distance filled with echoes, bigness, and distracting not-quite sounds. He found himself picking his way gingerly across the smooth decking, tiny steps, feet barely leaving the floor, as though the slightest miscalculation would send him plunging into the abyss. That thought alone spiraled a brief moment of vertigo through his head. He was just about to stop to let the dizziness wind down when his hip barked against something jutting out of what should have been empty air, and all sense of place, orientation, and balance evaporated like flash-burned nitrogen. He flailed wildly for a grip on the obstacle, half doubling over it, half tumbling to his knees, and just managed to catch himself before he did more than stumble in an indelicate circle around the end of the barrier. Feeling the hot flush of embarrassment in his face, he was glad for the dark and the privacy as he carefully got his feet back under him and slowly straightened. He bumped something—light and angular—with his knee while still getting his bearings, and it scooted with a dry coughing sound before banging into something bigger and heavier, then fell silent.

Bashir took a deep, steadying breath, and splayed his hands on the cool, flat surface in front of him. *You're in your own infirmary,* he told himself sternly. *You know where everything is—where you are—if you just relax and think about it.* Trouble was, he'd never tried navigating the infirmary's Cardassian-designed rooms in the dark before, and right now the only thing he could think of that should be this tall and smooth and long was the autopsy bench. But he hadn't turned in that direction, or at least hadn't walked that far, and if this was the bench then the door with its view of the brighter main infirmary should be directly in front of him and there should have been no chair where he could kick it—

Steady ... steady ... Another deep breath, this one consciously aimed at relaxing the tension across his back, slowing the rapid trip-hammering of his heart. Finding his balance firmly, with both hands on the surface at his waist, he made one more slow inhalation, and closed his eyes.

The character of the darkness didn't really change—no blacker, no less total and pervasive. But instead of being trapped and confused in a room with no lights, now he'd simply closed his eyes. It removed the disorientation somewhat, and left him feeling focused and in control. He carefully imagined the layout of the morgue without trying to place himself anywhere within it. Then he felt out the edges of his mystery obstacle—smooth, wide, only about a table's thickness but without legs or other supports. When his elbow thumped against what felt suspiciously like a wall, he trailed his hand to where his "table" ought to be butted up against the bulkhead—only to have his arm slide past the plane of the wall into more nothingness.

"Oh, this is ridiculous!"

His voice echoed queerly, flat and immediate against the bulkhead right in front of his face, with a hint more resonance from somewhere farther down. This time when he reached in front of him, he found the wall immediately, and instead followed it downward toward the table. His hand found the opening with an abruptness that nearly made him dizzy again, but he was rewarded with a crystalline image of the wall of morgue stasis drawers and realized with an almost physical snap of recognition where he was. Each of the individual drawers could pull out to form an examining table of sorts, creating both a room-crossing hazard and an empty space in the wall that normally housed it. But why in hell had somebody left an open morgue drawer—

Memory washed over him with a knife-sharp gasp: the alien.

Bashir jerked his hands away from the open drawer as though they'd caught fire. He hadn't forgotten about the lethal fragment, precisely. He'd just gotten so tied up in trying to stabilize the symbiont's readings, and it had never occurred to him that the stasis fields in the morgue drawers were dependent on the main station power. Now it had been—how many minutes had it been? Too many, surely. And if you were a motile alien fragment, where would you go?

Whirling, he caught sight of the brighter dark of the main infirmary, with its untended patients and its open outside door.

Any anxiety about dashing through the big room in the dark was burned away by memories of Kira's burned, bubbling flesh and the smell of outgassing carbon and oxygen. He nearly always kept the door to the infirmary open when he was there, so that everyone would know they were welcome even if they weren't human or even Starfleet. Now, as he slammed shoulder-first into the jamb and groped madly for a handhold on the inside face of the door, he cursed himself for his egalitarianism, and wished he were enough of a paranoid to keep every door closed and locked behind him. Then, at least, there'd be less chance that this creature had escaped into the station proper while he was bumbling about.

The doors moved slowly and thickly with nothing to push them but one young man's admittedly meager weight. It occurred to Bashir, as he braced his back against one narrow ledge and pushed with every micron of his strength, that each of the two main doors no doubt massed in at twice his own measure, with Cardassian hydraulics designed to withstand everything short of direct phaser fire. Thank God they didn't have adrenaline, as well, or he might never have gotten them closed all by himself. As it was, when the second door bumped the first and cut the light in the room by nearly half, the sound of their seals mating was as solid and final as a closing coffin. That image pulled a little moan of anxiety from him, and he turned to face the room with his back pressed against the door, his hands flat against its surface and the light from the small, high windows spilling weakly over his shoulders.

Somewhere near the floor and unlocatable, something scuttled through the darkness.

Bashir slapped his combadge without taking his eyes off the shadows. "Bashir to Security!"

The badge hadn't even beeped. His mind registered that only a moment before realizing no one in Security was going to answer him, but he hit it again, harder, because he didn't want to believe he was completely alone. "Bashir to Ops!"

Nothing.

Lightly, like the occasional tapping of sand at a beach house's window, what sounded like the *click-tick*ing of tiny arthropod footsteps punctuated the silence. Bashir tried to follow their progress through the infirmary, but kept losing the delicate clatter to distance, and objects, and the pounding of his own blood in his ears. At the hindmost part of his brain, a tiny, terrified voice screamed at him to *run!*, to put himself outside and leave this thing inside, to let people trained in handling dangerous life-forms take responsibility for what happened in this room. But when he looked across the puzzlework of shadows toward the glowing mouth of the ICU and the absolute black of the symbiont's chamber, the clearest thought in his mind was the 1st Rule of Hippocrates: Do no harm.

"I can't leave the patients." Saying it out loud drove away all fears for himself or his own safety. The patients came first—the patients *always* came first. That had been true when he first set his heart on medical school, when he took up his first scalpel to cut into his first living patient, and when he denied himself a quick, peaceful death for nearly a hundred years to insure that a damaged Trill symbiont could survive. Leaving now when there were patients still needing his protection and help was simply not an option.

The room where he'd been hiding the symbiont didn't seem as dark as it had when they'd first lost the lighting. Bashir could just make out the blurry lines of the jury-rigged stasis tank, and while he couldn't see anything inside the tank itself, he knew the symbiont was aware and waiting for him when it greeted his hurried approach with a soft electric *snap!* and a whiff of ozone.

"I don't want you to panic," Bashir whispered, shoving his chair and work cart aside on his way to the rear of the tank, "but we've got a little bigger problem than just the lights at the moment." He bent to brace his shoulder against the tank's narrow end. "I'm going to move you into the ICU with the rest of Pak Dorren's people. It's got a level-nine quarantine field, which ought to keep out damn near anything, and if it doesn't . . ."

Well, they'd have to fudge those results when they got to them.

Regulation Starfleet boots slipping on the polished decking, he could barely get the purchase to keep from sliding off his feet, much less wrestle the brine tank into motion. He scooted it twice, sloshing medium all over the floor and the back of his uniform, both times accomplishing little more than inscribing an ugly arc in the infirmary's deckplates. He remembered his joke about the tank weighing nearly as much as the Brin Planetarium, and feverishly wished he hadn't been quite so accurate.

"I'll be right back!"

Almost two years ago now, Bashir had requisitioned a pair of light-cargo antigravs after he, Odo, O'Brien, Kira, Maile, Yevlin, Gerjuoy, and Sisko spent the better part of an afternoon serving as lift-and-carry team for a narcoleptic Morn while Bashir muddled his way through inventing an appropriate Vegan choriomeningitis treatment regimen for Morn's species. According to the medical texts, Morn shouldn't have been able to contract the disease at all; Bashir had gotten an excellent paper out of the experience. He'd also gotten the antigravs. Since then, he'd used them a total of once—to move the confocal microscope during one of his late-night "rearrange the infirmary" binges—but he remembered distinctly pushing them to the back of a floor-level cabinet when he was finished, briskly reminding himself not to forget where he'd put them in case he ever needed them again.

Julian Bashir, bless your anal compulsive little soul!

He half-ran, half-stumbled to the bank of cabinets, finding his way more by the feel of the furniture and equipment beneath his hands than by anything he could clearly see. As he thumped to his knees in front of the featureless doors, a sudden certainty of just how dark, and close, and crowded the inside of the cabinet would be clenched his lungs with dread, and he hesitated.

This was not a good time to be crawling about in places where you couldn't see.

He caught the counter above him and pulled himself to his feet. The drawer just above the storage cabinet jerked open with a great metallic jangle, announcing itself as exactly the random-junk collector it was. Lock screws and sleeves that seemed to go with nothing, but looked too useful to just throw away; laser scalpels with one or two damaged focal elements that weren't quite fine enough to use on flesh anymore but would cut most anything else you wanted; O-rings looking for a joint to seal, and scores of broken forceps, probes, and once-hermetic vials. Bashir pawed through the clutter as best he could, seizing on anything of about the right shape and length and circumference, then lifting it up into the paltry light from the Promenade to better determine its dimensions.

He had half the drawer emptied, scattered around the top of the counter, when his hand closed on something cold and hard-shelled that squirmed spastically in his grip. Taking a breath to scream but uttering little more than a strangled cry of disgust, he flung it away from him, toward the morgue, toward the dark. It struck what must have been the top of an examination table, skated across the smooth surface with a wisp of friction, then smacked to the floor with a distinctive rattle and crash that Bashir had learned to identify by the end of his first term as a surgical resident: a jointed *k'fken* probe for xenobiological biopsies, probably a number-four aluminum by the sound of it. Useless and potentially awkward in the wrong hands, but hardly what one would consider dangerous. He sighed shakily, and reached into the drawer more carefully this time to test what was left with the tips of his fingers.

He found the flashlight snugged into the back corner, trying to hide itself against the side of the drawer. O'Brien had forced it on him several months ago when an epidemic of tonsillitis had every parent on the station accosting Bashir in the Replimat, on the turbolifts, at his quarters, demanding that he peer down the throat of their child before he did another thing with his day. "Don't haul 'em down to the infirmary!" O'Brien had snorted. "You know what strep looks like, don't you? Use this, give 'em a peek, and send 'em home. That's all they want."

He'd been right, as usual, and Bashir had carried the small light as though it were Excalibur for almost two months. Now, all he cared about was that it lit when he depressed the end with his thumb, and that it seemed bright enough to drive back space itself after all this darkness.

He climbed back to his knees with the penlight clutched in one fist. Easing open the first of the two cabinet doors, he knelt for what seemed an eternity with only his light reaching into that inner darkness. All manner of useful paraphernalia littered the cabinet's landscape; lots of crannies and hollows for something the size of an Andorian's antenna to hide in. He crouched forward slowly, leading the way with the penlight, carefully examining every contour on every device, supply, or container before shoving it aside.

The farther into the cabinet he worked, the easier it became to steady his breathing and still his shaking hands. It was a closed cabinet, after all—the likelihood of the fragment finding its way inside was astronomically small, and surely the noise and light of his presence would have flushed it out or scared it off by now. If it were here. Which it clearly wasn't.

All the same, his heart throbbed painfully with relief when the penlight's beam danced across the antigravs' storage case all the way at the back of the cabinet. He took the light between his teeth, and went down on his elbows to squirm deep enough to pull on the antigravs with both hands.

Soft, ghostlike scuffling, then the faintest prick of tiny fingers through the fabric of his pants. He jerked back with a startled yelp, banging his head on the top of the cabinet, tangling himself with the doors, the supplies, the equipment as he thrashed to pull out of the enclosure. Halfway up his leg, its thousand limbs digging in like needle stings, a thick worm of movement pressed against the outside of his knee, and started to burn.

Fear more than pain dragged a wild cry from him, and he slammed back against the wall of cabinets rather than clutch at the squirming intruder for lack of anything better to do with his hands. *It's not difluorine!* his rational mind screamed at him. *Whatever it's doing, it's not difluorine!* And in a very real sense, that was all that mattered. Twisting sideways, he struggled to keep his burning leg as still as possible as he pushed himself high enough to slap awkwardly at the top of the counter.

Probes, forceps, and O-rings scattered, going wherever the flashlight had gone when he'd shouted with it still in his mouth. When his hand came down forcefully on a pile of clutter painfully on the edge of his reach, touch sorted what he wanted from the confusion with a speed and certainty that bypassed conscious thought. The scalpel was already humming when he flashed his arm down and slit the pant leg from ankle to knee.

The Andorian-pale fragment smelled like burning walnuts where the laser scalpel cut sizzling across it. For some reason, he half-expected it to squeal or shriek at the touch of pain—instead, it twitched loose in a writhe of silent anguish and scrabbled off into the dark.

It was looking for new DNA. That had to have been what attracted it to him, through the dark clutter of the morgue. And now Bashir knew where it was headed without even having to track its skittering progress. The only other DNA it could sense and want lay across the infirmary in an unguarded brine tank.

"Dax!"

Biting his lip in an effort to pretend his leg wasn't still on fire with pain, he wrenched himself to his knees and took only a moment to lunge after the flashlight in the bottom of the cabinet before surging to his feet. The cold spray of the penlight's beam danced crazily about the darkness as he ran for the symbiont's chamber.

The gentle splash of a body into brine crashed across the small room like a thunderclap. Bashir wailed in despair, the tiny light illuminating the shadowy struggles of a worm that was once a sensory organ now turned voracious attacker. Plunging his hands into the tank, he clapped the wriggling fragment between both palms, interlocking all his fingers, and swept it clear of the brine in a long rooster tail of fluid. He had almost reached the independently powered disposal unit when whatever passed for awareness within the fragment registered that it was in danger. The gush of difluorine across his hands hissed like hot oil over ice.

When he pushed the disposal chute open with his elbow,

he couldn't tell whether or not he was screaming. He only knew that disintegration was his only hope, and that the blinding flash of all its atoms bursting free to seek a new existence was the most beautiful fire he had ever seen.

Nausea crashed over him, nearly buckling his knees. *No!* he thought desperately, catching himself with one elbow as he slewed against the wall. Thrashing, thumping from the symbiont's tank pulled him back across the room when every neuron in his body wanted to slump down into shock. In the dilute glow of the penlight from the bottom of the brine, he could just glimpse Dax writhing and bucking as if to escape, as if—

Oh, God! Difluorine mixed with water produced the most corrosive acid known to science, powerful enough to chew through a starship's hull, not to mention the flesh of a frail, ancient symbiont. *Oh, no please no! Not after five thousand years—I didn't keep you five thousand years just for this!* It didn't matter that his own hands were already seared raw, or that submerging any part of himself in the brine put him as much at risk as the symbiont. He could rush them both to the subspace reverter, banish the acid into subspace, repair whatever tissues melted under the acid's sting. Murmuring over and over, "I'm sorry! . . . Dax, I'm so sorry . . . !" Bashir slid both aching hands underneath the thrashing symbiont—

—and the infirmary around him corroded into starlight and blood, scouring his thoughts off the face of the world.

"Oh, no. Not again."

Sisko glanced up from the entry he was jotting silently into his captain's log, alerted by the half-wry, half-serious tone of Dax's voice. A glance at the viewscreen showed him only the normal computer blur of star trails streaming past them. "What's the matter?"

She glanced over her shoulder from the piloting console. "Engineering sensors are picking up a quantum resonance in subspace, and it's getting stronger as we approach the wormhole."

Sisko exhaled sharply, jamming his note padd back into its slot in his command chair with more force than it needed. "Upstream echoes?" he demanded.

"It looks like it, but I'll need Heather's input to be sure. She's still down with T'Kreng."

Sisko palmed the comm button on his chair. "Ensign Petersen, report to the bridge immediately." He sat back, trying to spot visual evidence of the wormhole pulses the sensors had detected, but all of the stars he could see burned bright and steady, slowing in graceful arcs across the viewscreen as the *Defiant* slowed from warp speed to sublight. "How far are we from the wormhole?"

"We're coming up on it now." Dax cast a puzzled look up at the screen as the *Defiant* braked to a swift, stomach-tugging stop. "That's odd."

Sisko lifted an eyebrow at her. All that showed on their viewscreen was the familiar stretch of empty space that their visual sensors were programmed to lock on to in this region. "It looks normal to me—the wormhole's not even opening and closing."

His science officer shook her head, looking baffled. "But according to our sensors, it *is*. I don't understand—" She glanced up as the turbolift doors slid open to admit an again-breathless Petersen. "Heather, have you been watching our subspace readings lately?"

The cadet's cheeks turned a rosier shade of apple-pink. "No, Lieutenant, I'm sorry. T'Kreng and I were setting up a magnetic communications relay in the medical bay."

Sisko blinked, a little taken aback by this casual mention of the dead Vulcan physicist, but Dax seemed to take it in stride. Of course, to a Trill, the idea of communicating with the preserved sentience of a long-dead person was perfectly normal.

"Well, take a look at these readings." Dax punched them up on her panel, and the two scientists bent to study them together. "Doesn't that look like the wormhole has destabilized again?"

"Worse than before." Petersen tilted her head to study the unremarkable expanse of deep space on the screen before them, speckled with the dim bluish glows of distant stars. "If it's emitting this much energy leakage, it may have shifted below visual frequencies. Have you tried scanning this area with sensors tuned to ultraviolet and microwave frequencies?"

"Not yet." Dax swung around and tapped the command into her jury-rigged engineering controls. The viewscreen broke up into visual static for a moment, then settled into a solid black display. Sisko watched it with a frown. "Dax, I don't see—"

"Subspace pulse arriving now," the Trill said tersely, and the blackness abruptly blossomed into a shriek of swirling white shadows across the screen, like a ghostly negative of the wormhole he was used to. Sprays like snowy avalanches tore across the jet-black emptiness, then fell back into their fiery white center and were gone. "You're right, Heather. The wormhole's downshifted entirely into short-wave ultraviolet display."

Sisko felt the pressure of his frown dig deeper into his tense face. "Does that mean we can't travel through it?"

His science officer exchanged thoughtful looks with the Starfleet Academy cadet. "The ultraviolet by itself isn't a problem," Dax said absently. "Our shields can handle a lot worse in the way of EM radiation. But the instability levels are almost back to what they were before the wormhole-dwellers neutralized them. I don't think anything bigger than a photon torpedo would get through the singularity matrix safely now."

Sisko rasped a hand across his chin, thinking hard. "So even with your ansible connection, old man, we're not going to be able to get any reinforcements from *Deep Space Nine.*"

"No, Benjamin. I'm afraid not."

"That's not our only problem, Captain." Petersen glanced up from the display of subspace data, the expression on her face making it look far older than its actual years. "The wormhole's releasing more energy than our original models can account for. If I didn't know better, I'd say it meant the subspace rift is so close to happening that the wormhole-dwellers can't control the quantum resonance fluctuations anymore."

Sisko scowled. "But since we know the Jem'Hadar station will take sixteen hours to get here—"

"—then it means the time rift will be a lot larger and more destructive than we'd expected," Dax finished. She swung around to face Sisko, her eyes grave. "It's not just the wormhole and *Deep Space Nine* that we'll save by preventing this time rift, Benjamin. It's the entire planet of Bajor."

He shot to his feet, the coiled-spring tension in his gut winching even tighter than before. Jake was on Bajor. Two hundred million other people were on Bajor—and he could only think of one or two who deserved to be swallowed by an exploding singularity. *"How* do we save it?" he demanded, pacing the length of the *Defiant's* empty bridge in a vain attempt to burn off his angry frustration. "These aliens can track us through our cloak by our waste heat, they can overwhelm our shields, they can pierce our ablative armor, they can apparently even use the Jem'Hadar's defenses against us! What can we do to *them?"*

"Infiltrate them," Petersen said unexpectedly. Sisko shot her an incredulous look, but although her cheeks reddened a little under it, she didn't back down. "It's not my idea, it's T'Kreng's. And seeing this—" She jerked her chin at the fierce white-shifted splash of ultraviolet radiation painted on the viewscreen behind them as the wormhole opened and closed. "I think you better come down and talk to her about it, Captain."

CHAPTER
19

THE ALIEN LOOKED like something from a Tellerite antivivi-sectionist tract, lying belly-up with its gelatinous strings of crenellated cortical fragments nestled inside loops and strings of gently pulsing flesh. Sisko paused in the door of the medical bay, startled by the absence of any blue glimmer around the creature.

"Dax, I thought you were going to keep that thing in stasis," he snapped. "It almost killed Ensign Goldman."

"A minor miscalculation, Captain." The words were spoken by an electronically generated voice routed through the medical bay's comm speakers, but their silken serenity was unmistakably T'Kreng's. "I intended only to entangle myself with a member of your away team, to ensure you brought me back with you." The two remaining appendages on the alien flexed and went limp again. "Unfortunately, my control of my newly acquired Jem'Hadar sub-brain was not completely established at the time."

Sisko slanted a disbelieving glance across the examining table at Yevlin Meris. "She can hear me?"

The Bajoran physician's assistant nodded. "The medical computer is digitizing all our speech and sending it to her via microelectrical impulses. It was Professor T'Kreng's idea." She pointed at the tiny remote electrodes embedded in one of the larger brain fragments. "She's receiving our words in binary computer code and converting them back to speech almost instantaneously."

"That's remarkable—even for a Vulcan." Dax leaned over the stasis chamber, seemingly oblivious of the diflourine-laced claws waving a few centimeters below her freckled face. Sisko gritted his teeth and resisted the urge to pull her back. "Professor, are you engaging your sub-brains as parallel processing units, the same way the aliens link their separate strings of cortices into a massive processing network?"

"Precisely, Lieutenant Dax." T'Kreng's artificially generated voice still managed to sound unbearably superior. "That is why I had Petersen release stasis on the other strings. I need them to process your voice input correctly."

Sisko cleared his throat. "And you are in complete control of this organism, Professor? It has no volition—no inherent personality—of its own?"

"Only a set of very basic survival instincts and drives, Captain, encoded within its cellular genetic material— which I suspect is not DNA. All higher logic and emotional input is determined by a process of internal competition, cooperation, and dominance among the incorporated cortical fragments. This portion of my cortex had very little trouble taking over the neural strings of the original organism, although I did have assistance from one of my Vulcan associates and a rather irate Ferengi trader."

Sisko scrubbed a hand across his face, trying to assimilate the concept of a clearly sentient species whose individual members had no sentience of their own. "If all the thinking and feeling is provided by the organisms they digest, how can these aliens carry out any consistent actions and goals? How can they even have the desire to bring the rest of their species through the wormhole to join them?"

T'Kreng was silent for a moment, as if that was a question that had not occurred to her. "I suspect that immersion in this alien matrix creates a generic identification with the host for those cortical fragments lacking will and memory. Even parts of my own brain seem to have been affected in this way. On the other hand, cortical fragments which were deeply involved in self-consciousness and personality also appear to retain their anger at being engulfed, even after many hundreds of years of immersion. It is those fragments that I believe will unite to help us."

Dax nodded. "Then all we need to do—"

"*Dax,*" Sisko said sharply, seeing the blankness of an ansible trance start to creep over her face and steal away its expression. The Trill opened her eyes again with a fierce shudder. "You all right, old man?"

Shock leached her face of all color but its freckles. "I am—but the other Dax isn't. Benjamin, some kind of genetically altered creature is in the infirmary, attacking Julian and the symbiont right now! Some of the aliens have already traveled through the wormhole!"

"*What?*"

"The core sent an advance party of two hundred and fifty individuals through the singularity matrix, long before they attacked my ship," T'Kreng agreed. "Whatever communication method they use between themselves apparently transcends space and time. The alien core here has given their Alpha Quadrant counterparts instructions to rift the wormhole on their side, if they can't accomplish it from ours."

"*Damn.*" Sisko thudded his clenched fists together, hard enough to make his knuckles ache. He saw both Yevlin Meris and Heather Petersen wince, and channeled his roiling temper into the fierce restrained fury of his voice. "Then we can't save the wormhole, even if we destroy the Jem'Hadar station?"

T'Kreng made a sound of crystalline disapproval. "An inability to control all aspects of a problem is no excuse for neglecting the aspects you *can* control, Captain. We must trust that your station crew will be able to deal with the aliens on their side of the wormhole. Our task now is to deal with ours."

Sisko paused, then pushed out a breath of renewed determination. "All right. How many of them are we facing?"

"There were over five hundred individuals inside the Jem'Hadar station when I left it."

"And you think we can infiltrate them? How?"

"By putting an intact cerebral cortex directly into their neural processing core." For once, T'Kreng's reply was as blunt and concise as Sisko's question had been.

Dax looked down dubiously at the string of disembodied brains that was talking to them. "You think a single individual can dominate the thousands of cortical fragments in there?"

"Unlikely," T'Kreng agreed. "But a highly motivated and intelligent cortex could find sufficient allies to dominate a small part of the core—and that part could be used to initiate the station's self-destruct sequence while it is still a safe distance away from the wormhole."

"Could you do it?" Sisko demanded.

This time, he could almost feel T'Kreng's ice-cold irritation echoing through the pause in her speech. "Of course I could, Captain—if I could somehow be reassembled into my original cortical pattern. But you are speaking to less than sixty percent of T'Kreng's consciousness, and I have no idea where the rest of me is. You will have to locate another, more intact cortex to carry out this plan—or you will have to create one."

Dax's eyes narrowed, and she looked across the alien fragment to meet Sisko's equally grim gaze. He put their unwelcome conclusion into harsh words. "You mean, deliberately deliver someone to be attacked and digested by one of the core aliens?"

"And to be killed moments later when the station explodes. Not an appealing strategy, perhaps, but one I know will work." The Vulcan's voice turned crystal-sharp with the force of her conviction. "I can assure you, Captain Sisko, nothing else will. The linked core mind will manage to out maneuver any other attack you make on them."

"We'll see." Sisko straightened to his full height, suddenly wanting to get away from this mangled alien and the impossibly preserved and implacable Vulcan inside it. "We've got sixteen hours and one of the best fighting ships in Starfleet. I'm not ready to send out any kamikaze missions just yet."

"Of course not." T'Kreng's disembodied voice was a cold shiver of silk in the silence of the medical bay. "But in fifteen hours or less, when you will be ready to do it, you can come to me for your final instructions. After that, I suggest that you terminate this entire alien fragment by wide-angle transporter dispersion."

Sisko scowled, caught on the verge of leaving the medical bay by a strange note in the Vulcan physicist's voice. "Is that a strategic suggestion, Honored Professor?"

"No," said what remained of T'Kreng. "It is a plea for mercy."

"We've got to get Dax to the Gamma Quadrant."

Wedged inside the guts of the external sensor panel, her torso weighted down by what felt like the Prophets' own collection of tools and burned components, Kira snorted wearily in response to Bashir's bleak announcement. "Dax is *already* in the Gamma Quadrant, Doctor. If you left the infirmary once in a while, you might know that." She pulled another brace of cracked, cloudy isolinears, and threw them out to join all the others in an ever-growing pile. "Now, do me a favor and—"

"Oh, my God! Julian, what happened?"

The startled alarm in O'Brien's usually calm voice registered on Kira's raw nerves like a breach alarm, but it was Odo's dry observation, "The power loss must have deactivated the stasis field on our little guest," that flooded her stomach with sick dread. She shivered violently under a roil of remembered terror and anguish, overlaying Bashir's slight frame on that horrific memory, and slid herself out from under the panel with a single frantic pull. *Don't let us lose our medical officer!* she prayed. *Don't let me have to explain to Sisko how I didn't even take care of our doctor!*

He stood near the Ops ladder access, his hands held out in front of him as though he wasn't sure what to do with them and his uniform smelling strongly of sour blood and brine. O'Brien reached him first, and had him pushed into a chair with his wrists firmly pinned by the time Kira rolled to her feet and bounded up the steps to join them. She could see the dark sheen of blood on Bashir's palms, and found herself wondering wildly how he could have possibly climbed all the way from the lower decks in such a state.

O'Brien caught the doctor's chin in one hand and glared sternly into his eyes the way only a parent could do. "Don't move!"

Bashir obeyed only marginally after O'Brien released him, leaning forward to keep sight of the chief as O'Brien trotted across Ops to fetch an emergency kit from under a panel.

"What happened to the alien?" Kira asked him, grabbing at his shoulder in an attempt to catch his attention.

"Chief, I'm all right—it's neutralized. . . ." He was shaking so hard, the words stuttered out of him in fits and starts. "We're both neutralized . . . it's fine . . ."

"Julian!" She shook him until he blinked up at her, dark eyes almost without focus in his thin, sallow face. "Julian, what happened to the alien? Where is it now?"

He shook his head faintly. "Gone—I flashed it in the disposal bin."

She remembered the sound and smell of her diflourine-soaked jacket disappearing into that maw, and her guts uncoiled with relief. A small victory, maybe, but better than they'd managed up here so far. Resting one hand on the top of his head in silent approval, she stepped around behind his chair to give O'Brien access to his hands.

To her surprise, the doctor drew back and away from the chief, his face folding into an impatient scowl as he lifted his hands out of O'Brien's reach. "Look, we don't have time to worry about this! We've got to find a way to get Dax into the Gamma Quadrant."

O'Brien dropped the opened medkit across Bashir's lap to snatch at his hands. "Julian . . ." His voice carried a warning that seemed all out of proportion with Bashir's resistance.

"You don't have to worry, Doctor," Kira told him, thinking it would calm his fidgeting. "Dax is already in the Gamma Quadrant."

He twisted a desperate look at her over his shoulder. "Not Jadzia," he said plaintively. "*Dax!*"

"Julian." O'Brien's voice snapped the doctor's head around as though he'd been slapped. "Starfleet's orders—"

"I don't give a damn about Starfleet's orders!" The violence of his outburst startled Kira. "You've got a shipload of viroid life-forms outside draining our power systems, and I've got a Trill symbiont in the infirmary who says it can help us." This time when he looked up at Kira, his face was flushed to an almost normal color for all that his eyes were still cloudy with shock. "But we don't have much time. Whatever's going to happen to the wormhole, it's going to happen soon, and . . ." His gaze drifted to one side, focus fading to somewhere dark and internal. ". . . they're part of it somehow," he murmured, frowning. "I . . . I'm not sure . . . I don't entirely understand . . ."

Odo snorted and folded his arms. "Well, at least we're all in the same position."

Kira silenced him with a sharp glare, then gave Bashir's shoulder a bracing shake. "Why don't you start with explaining what the hell you're talking about?" she suggested tartly. "If you've got Dax, who's with Jadzia?"

Bashir pulled himself straighter with obvious effort, but didn't seem able to look away from O'Brien's inexpert but meticulous inspection of his hands. "When we were called to Starbase One, it was because Starfleet had . . . evidence that Captain Sisko, Jadzia, and I would be . . ." He used the side of his hand to tap one of the regenerators in his lap, and O'Brien plucked it dutifully from the kit to switch it on. "They knew we would be lost in some sort of temporal rift caused by the wormhole," he went on softly as O'Brien played the regenerator back and forth across his palm. "Part of their evidence was Dax—the Dax that *would* be lost, that *was* lost, that . . ." He squeezed his eyes shut and shook his head as though trying to jar his thoughts back into order. "It outsurvived us all, and it's the only one who knows what happened. if we don't get it into the Gamma Quadrant, it's all going to happen again!"

"And this symbiont . . ." Odo leaned back against a panel, his voice fairly dripping with skepticism. "It *talks* to you?"

A thoroughly arrogant clarity flashed into the doctor's eyes. "Of course not. Symbionts communicate electrochemically, both with their hosts and with each other. I . . . this other me . . . I lived with the symbiont for a long time after the others died. I think it must have learned to . . . match my bioelectric patterns, to link with me somehow so that we wouldn't feel so all alone. And now with the tissues in the my hands exposed . . ." His voice trailed away, caught again in the riptide of whatever memories still churned too close to the surface. "I don't hear words, or even thoughts, I just . . . I just *know!* I *feel* things that aren't mine, and see . . ." Another bout of stumbling silence, then he craned desperate eyes up toward Kira and stated with fearful lucidness,

"You've got to let me take a runabout to the Gamma Quadrant. We have to get Dax to the *Defiant* before it's too late."

The thought of letting him pilot anything in his current state was nearly laughable, but O'Brien saved her from having to tell him that by blurting, "Julian, that's impossible! Even if we could get anything bigger than a torpedo through the wormhole right now—which we can't!—those things would home in on your engine exhaust and tear your ship apart before you were a thousand klicks out."

"And if we don't try," Bashir countered quietly, "those things are going to destroy the wormhole and possibly change the course of history."

A foreboding she didn't want to acknowledge shivered through Kira's aching muscles. "How can these things destroy the wormhole?"

"I don't know!" The thin edge of panic crept back into his voice as easily as it had vanished a moment before. "All I know is that if we don't get Dax through the wormhole, it will have spent five thousand years in a brine tank for nothing!" He raked his one healed hand through his hair, knotting it at the back of his neck in frustration. "I can't do that to it . . . I won't."

"Which leaves us with what options?" Odo paced to stand at Kira's side, his crossed arms and downturned mouth radiating a dissatisfaction she suspected related more to having no clear-cut answer than to their impending demise. "We can't send this symbiont outside the station in anything containing a power source, and it certainly isn't going to swim through the wormhole on its own. What else is there?"

When Bashir jerked his head up to whirl a startled frown toward the constable, Kira thought he meant to rail at Odo for his insensitive doom-crying. Then an expression of almost beatific revelation spread across the young doctor's face, and he settled back in his chair to look Odo carefully up and down. "Actually," he said, very slowly, "I do have one idea. . . ."

If there was one bad habit Jadzia Dax knew she had as a science officer, it was her tendency to fidget with the color scales of her sensor displays whenever she was nervous or bored. Right now, she was both. As a result, the color index she had created to display the wormhole's bursts of high-energy radiation on the main viewscreen kept shifting from an angry bruiselike red-violet to an icy borealis shimmer of translucent blue to a deep electric indigo sparked with hot white highlights. No matter how she changed the colors, the wormhole's frantic spasms of opening and closing kept looking more and more ominous.

"I still think we should use the quantum torpedoes," she said, more to distract herself from the silent convulsions on the viewscreen than because she had any hope of being listened to. "They're our most powerful weapons."

"Too much thermal signature, old man." From somewhere under the weapons panel, she heard Sisko grunt as he wrestled off the cover panel from the phaser controls. "A cluster of shelled aliens could intercept them and kick off a premature detonation. Hand me the phase modulator, Eddington, and read me off the wavelength we want."

Dax swung around to watch them work, still frowning. "We could link all the torpedoes into one stationary spacemine, and rig it to go off as soon as it entered the Jem'Hadar station's gravity well. There wouldn't be any thermal signature emitted that way."

"With an untargeted blast like that," Eddington said, "we couldn't be completely sure the reaction core would be destroyed. And we need core destruction—"

"Wavelength," Sisko reminded him curtly.

"Three hundred and ninety-three nanometers. We need core destruction because just breaching hull integrity on that Jem'Hadar station isn't going to stop it from exploding in the wormhole."

"I *know* that," Dax said. There were times when the Starfleet security officer's tendency to restate the obvious became really annoying. "But I'm not sure that tuning the phasers to the resonance frequency of the Jem'Hadar reaction mass is going to ensure core destruction either. There are still four hundred duranium-shelled aliens wrapped around the station's reaction core. They might absorb a lot of our phaser blast."

"Not if we can provide them with a distraction somewhere else." Sisko rolled out from under the weapons panel, his face dusted with feathery flakes of insulating cable. "*That's* where the quantum torpedoes come in."

Dax shifted the viewscreen color scale to a purple so deep it was almost black. The wormhole faded to nearly invisible lacework explosions against the darkness of space. "I suppose I could modify the torpedoes to emit the same power signature as a large ship's warp core," she said thoughtfully. "That might lure a significant fraction of the aliens out to attack them."

"Especially if we send them out on two different headings," Sisko agreed. "How long will it take you to make the modifications?"

A shrill warning buzz yanked Dax's attention back to her engineering sensors before she could answer. She felt the freckles on her neck and back tighten with sudden tension. "That depends on whether we have any torpedoes left to modify, Captain. Long-range sensors show five warships approaching us. Eddington, can you confirm their identify?"

The security officer punched his rewired weapons console back to life and scanned it intently. "They're definitely Jem'Hadar ships, but there's something odd about their warp signature. Oh, my *god!*"

Dax threw him a startled look. Eddington might be annoyingly supercilious at times, but she'd rarely seen him display anything other than the most professional demeanor at his station. Sisko's eyebrows lifted nearly to his hairline. "What is it?" he demanded.

Eddington swung around, his narrow face stiff with shock. "The Jem'Hadar ships—they've all got their tractor beams locked on a joint target, sir. I think it's the station the aliens took over."

"*What?*" Sisko crossed to inspect the weapons sensor output for himself, his dark eyes narrowing with intensity. "Dax, put us on an intercept course *now,* at maximum warp."

"Coming about," she warned, punching the commands into her helm computer. At steep accelerations, the *Defiant's* undercompensated warp drive tended to throw people across the bridge if they weren't braced. "Intercept in five minutes, visual contact in four."

"Put it on screen as soon as you get it," Sisko ordered.

"All right, people. Why the *hell* would the Jem'Hadar be bringing that station to the wormhole?"

Hovan cleared her throat nervously from her station at the cloaking device. "Maybe the shapeshifting aliens have taken over some Jem'Hadar ships," she suggested.

"It's more likely the Jem'Hadar have just picked the most convenient way to dispose of a problem they want out of their quadrant," Dax said wryly. "If they yanked the station into warp without warning, the aliens couldn't travel out to attack them. Even duranium bodies couldn't sustain warp-level accelerations without tearing apart."

"Too bad we didn't think of doing that, in the opposite direction," Sisko said grimly.

"We'd have had to destroy the station the instant we dropped out of warp," Dax reminded him. "I think the Jem'Hadar will find the aliens coming at them like a swarm of wasps as soon as they recover from warp exposure."

Sisko grunted acknowledgment, then glanced up as the turbolift doors slid open.

"What just happened?" Heather Petersen demanded urgently. "I was running a relativistic analysis to tighten up my estimate for the onset of the time rift—" Her face lifted to the main viewscreen and paled visibly. Dax turned to see five sleek Jem'Hadar warships, blurry with maximum magnification, enter visual sensor range. Their crossed glitter of tractor beams backlit the unmistakable half-ruptured silhouette of the alien-captured station. "Oh, my god. They've brought it here!"

Sisko turned away from the disturbing image on the screen to regard the cadet intently. "What happened to your estimate for the time rift, Ensign?"

Even from across the room, Dax could see that Petersen had to swallow before she could answer. "It suddenly jumped from fifteen hours to forty-five minutes."

An ice-cold shock of fear tore through Dax, although she couldn't be sure if it was coming from her symbiont or from its ancient twin. She closed her eyes and took a deep breath, fighting off the tidal pull of ansible trance.

"The Jem'Hadar squadron has just entered attack range, Captain," Eddington said. "Should I target phasers on the station or on the warships?"

Sisko threw a furious look at the console he'd just retuned. "At that low frequency, the phasers will bounce right off the ships' shields, and we'll have given away our location for nothing. Aim quantum torpedoes at the ships, Commander. We'll try to take out as many of them as we can, then blow up the station."

"Aye, sir." Eddington punched the commands into his station. "Torpedoes ready."

Dax wasn't sure what warned her—a premonition of numbness in her fingers, a dance of odd lights at the edges of her vision. The deepening tidal pull she felt inside confirmed that she was falling into another ansible trance, one too strong to fight off.

"Benjamin!" she called out urgently. "Get someone to cover my station—"

She was barely aware of his shadow falling over her before the *Defiant*'s bridge rippled and went away. Instead of the wet, dark quiet that usually settled over her when she joined with old Dax, she found herself engulfed in a roar of impossibly vivid colors and a glare of shrieking noise. With a jolt of terror, Dax wondered if she was sharing the old symbiont's death throes. There was no way an unjoined symbiont could perceive actual visual stimuli—

"—sensory illusions created by alternation of intense magnetic fields—" The words were very faint, but Jadzia still recognized the voice that spoke them. That unquenchable interest in new experiences, no matter how life-threatening, could only belong to her symbiont. "—insufficient shielding for these conditions, survival uncertain—"

A glowing burst like a tracer torpedo ripped through the slow fade of colors, splashing another bright aurora across her mind. The noise had become a thunderous howl of static, so deep now that she felt more than heard it. Had some catastrophe hit *Deep Space Nine*? She couldn't hear Bashir's or O'Brien's voice in the background—maybe the station was being attacked by the same aliens they were fighting here. If the warp core had been breached, the explosion of subspace energy would send an immense magnetic flux surging through the station.

"—at midpoint, magnetic fields still increasing—"

A fiercer, more chemical jolt shrieked through Dax's

body, and the colors and noise promptly vanished. She tensed, reaching out with all the strength of her joined minds to find the ansible connection again.

"*Lieutenant*!" Fingers dug into the muscles of her shoulders, hard enough to make Dax wince. Suddenly aware that she was back in her real body, she dragged open her eyes and stared up disbelievingly at Yevlin Meris.

"What did you do?"

"Lowered your isoboromine levels." The physician's assistant held onto her tightly as an evasive maneuver sent the *Defiant* skating sideways hard enough to make even Dax's space-hardened stomach lurch. "They were twice normal. Whatever this ansible effect is that Heather keeps trying to explain to me, I don't think it's good for you."

Dax winced and scrambled to her feet. "What's going on?" she demanded, seeing only a spiral of fast-moving stars on the viewscreen. "Where are the Jem'Hadar?"

Sisko never took his eyes off the helm panel he was manning. "We got one of them with our first torpedo blast, but two more split from the convoy and came after us. They're firing at extrapolated positions of our ion trail. Do you have a fix on the lead ship yet, Eddington?"

"If you could give me just a few more seconds on this heading, Captain—"

The *Defiant* slewed into an abrupt downward corkscrew and Dax grabbed at the edge of the empty command chair to steady herself. The viewscreen blazed with the fierce white light of the phaser beam that had just missed them. "Sorry," Sisko said between gritted teeth. "That's as long a targeting interval as they're going to give us before they fire."

Dax frowned and skidded across the bridge to join Eddington at the weapons station. "Have you tried programming the torpedoes to home in on the Jem'Hadar shield signature?"

"Of course. But as soon as they realized that we weren't firing our phasers at them, they dropped their shields."

"Then we should be able to program the torpedoes to recognize the activated metallic spectrum of their hull armor. Running unshielded at these speeds means they're getting blasted with cosmic radiation." Dax took the seat next to Eddington and began to input a series of quick commands into the torpedo-control panel. "If we convert the energy-dispersive scanning system on the torpedoes to an X-ray fluorescence detector tuned to the indium emission peak of duranium alloy—"

The security officer gave her a baffled look. "And that won't make the torpedoes home in on us?"

"Not unless we lose our own shields." Dax finished her reprogramming, and readied two of their last five torpedoes. "I'd suggest firing both launchers together, Commander, so the Jem'Hadar don't have time to put up their shields."

"Whatever you do, do it fast." Sisko swung the *Defiant* into another impossibly tight curve, nearly sliding Dax off her seat. This time, the phaser blast they avoided was close enough to make the ship shudder and the viewscreen flash completely to white. "They're getting better at tracking our ion trail."

"Torpedoes armed and ready," Eddington said. He took a deep breath, then slapped at both launch controls. "Torpedoes launched on homing mission, Captain."

"Good." Sisko yanked the ship into a fierce upward zigzag as two sets of phaser beams crisscrossed the place they would have been in another second. "Estimated time to impact?"

"Five seconds," Dax said, before Eddington could reply. "Four, three—"

The fiery explosion of a ruptured warp core across the viewscreen stopped her. The bridge crew waited in tense silence until a ghostly white gas cloud bloomed in another sector of the screen. "I think that one raised his shields at the last minute," Dax said thoughtfully. "But the torpedo still came close enough to clip him."

"Close only counts in horseshoes and hull breaches." Sisko pushed himself away from the helm station. "Thanks, old man. Now, can you plot us a course back to the wormhole? We still need to intercept that damned station before the other Jem'Hadar dump it into the wormhole."

"They can't have kept up the same acceleration with only two warships tractoring it." At the back of the bridge, Petersen let go of the back of Hovan's chair and took two steps forward. Dax skirted around Yevlin Meris, who was cautiously rising from her braced position against the disconnected engineering panel. "If we can convince them to alter course away from the wormhole and release it at warp speed—"

Sisko gave the cadet a wry look. "I don't know what they teach you about the Jem'Hadar at the Academy, Ensign, but in all my interactions with them, I don't think I've ever convinced them of anything but their own superiority."

Dax typed in the course changes and sent the *Defiant* surging back toward the wormhole, now several thousand kilometers away. "I'd suggest hitting them with our last quantum torpedoes before they even know we're there."

Sisko gave her a curt nod. "Provided they're not so close to the wormhole that the torpedo impact will accomplish the very thing we're trying to prevent."

"Heather should be able to tell us that." Dax sent the cadet an inquiring look and got a confident nod in return.

"Good." Sisko sat back in his command chair, looking far too calm for a captain who'd just piloted his ship through the fiercest dogfight of its life. Only the occasional jerk of his fingers into an impatient fist betrayed that this was anything other than a routine cruise of the Gamma Quadrant. "Any sign of the Jem'Hadar station on long-range sensors?"

Dax swung back to her engineering panel. "I don't—no, it just entered visual range." She frowned, eying the readout on her panel. "That's odd."

"What?" Sisko demanded.

"According to this, the Jem'Hadar ships and the station have all come to a halt, just outside the wormhole's gravitational field."

Sisko's forehead creased. "They're not moving any closer?"

"No. They're just—stationary."

The captain scrubbed a hand across his face. "You think the aliens are already attacking them?"

"Perhaps." She glanced over her shoulder at him. "We'll rendezvous with them in two minutes. Orders, Captain?"

"We'll come in cloaked and establish a minimum-thrust orbit around the station, just like we did before," Sisko decided. "If the aliens have swarmed out to attack the Jem'Hadar ships, we won't have to worry about using our quantum torpedoes to divert them. We'll fire phasers immediately at maximum sustained power directly into the station's warp core."

"*No!*" Heather Petersen's voice sounded more like a startled squeak than an articulate protest, but the panic in it was sharp enough to jerk all their heads around. "Captain Sisko, that would set off a subspace explosion big enough to trigger the time rift, even at that distance!"

Sisko blew out a distinctly frustrated breath. "Well, what do you suggest we do, Ensign?"

Petersen dug her teeth into her lip, looking as stymied as Dax felt. "I don't know, sir," she said at last. "All I know is that we can't do *that.*"

"Jem'Hadar ships are now in attack range," Eddington reported. "Revised orders, Captain?"

Sisko paused, watching the two fighters and the towed alien station congeal out of darkness on the viewscreen. Dax toggled her color display to overprint the screen, and the purple-black explosion of the wormhole appeared just behind the stationary ships. "Remain cloaked and establish minimum-thrust orbit," he said again. Dax punched the course into her helm, and the *Defiant* rolled into a soft, energy-conserving ellipsoid around the Jem'Hadar station. "I want to see what's going on here before I decide what to do. Dax, scan for alien distribution."

"Scanning." She diverted one of the sensors from its focus on the wormhole, dimming the dark purple display to near invisibility. A flare of white-and-green alien concentrations bloomed inside the station when she reprogrammed it to scan for duranium, but not even the isolated blue specks of individual shelled aliens appeared in the surrounding space. "It doesn't look like they're doing anything to the Jem'Hadar ships, Benjamin. The aliens may need a while to recover from the unprotected warp exposure they just got."

Sisko smacked a fist into his palm with a frustrated slap. "Then why the hell did the Jem'Hadar stop short of the wormhole?"

From behind them, Ensign Hovan cleared her throat. "I might be wrong, sir—but I think that left-hand Jem'Hadar ship has switched its tractor beam to something else beside the station."

Dax frowned up at the viewscreen, seeing the slight

switch in angle and extension that meant Hovan was right. "I'm increasing magnification to see if I can detect what they're pulling in." The Jem'Hadar ships and station enlarged to fill the entire screen, and Dax focused in on the altered tractor beam, tracking it past the alien station to where it now terminated: at the tiny silhouette of a single floating figure in a radiation-shielded hardsuit. In the glittering phosphorescence of the tractor beam, the suit's markings were easy to read.

Sisko cursed, in a raw, startled voice Dax couldn't remember ever hearing from him before. She wasn't sure how he managed—the image on the viewscreen had left her completely speechless.

"What's the matter?" Heather Petersen glanced around the bridge, the puzzled look on her face deepening as she took in their stunned expressions. "All I see is someone in a hardsuit, getting hauled in from EV work. Maybe the Jem'Hadar had to stop for emergency hull repairs."

"I don't think so, Ensign." Although the shock had faded from Sisko's voice, he still sounded as amazed as Dax felt. "They wouldn't be using a hardsuit marked with *Deep Space Nine* insignia—and with no life-support attachments on its back."

"No life support?" Petersen repeated blankly. The distant suited figure was deliberately turning, as if it wanted to be sure the Jem'Hadar could see its tankless exterior. "How can someone be alive inside a hardsuit without life-support?"

"As far as I know, there's only one possible way." Sisko slammed a palm against the control on his makeshift communicator panel that opened all Starfleet frequencies. "Sisko to Odo. What the hell are you doing here, Constable?"

CHAPTER
20

"WE'VE GOT A hull breach!"

Dammit! Kira whirled away from the observation port near *Deep Space Nine*'s smallest airlock, turning her back on the spasming wormhole, the lingering image of Odo's tiny figure spiraling down that flaming abyss, and the bleak sadness on Bashir's face as he stared after Odo and the symbiont in uncharacteristic silence. She was almost glad for the interruption, relieved to drive off the melancholy with some form of productive action. "Where, Chief?"

"Habitat ring," his voice answered promptly, "section three."

A hollow, ringing bang echoed through the station's bones before Kira could even place the coordinates in relation to her and Bashir's position, then the brief, chilling roar of air blasting out into vacuum with such explosive force that it barely left a sound behind.

"And another in section twenty!" The sheer urgency of O'Brien's shout would have told Kira how nearby that was even if she hadn't felt the bulkhead's fracture. "Damn, but I was afraid of this!" he reported grimly. "I'm getting multiple duranium readings from all over the outside hull. Major, we're compromised."

But they'd had to drop the screens in order to send Odo through, and not sending him had ceased to be an option the moment Kira had knelt in front of the cloudy brine tank to speak to its ancient occupant. Any discussion about the wisdom of their actions was pointless now.

"Chief—" Bashir pulled himself away from the window with what Kira thought a very definitive resolve, drawing her with him down the hall as though he hadn't been the one holding them back. "Isolate those hull breaches as much as you can. If I'm right about what draws them, the viroids will be trying to reach the Promenade safe zones, and I don't think they'll let a little thing like bulkheads stand in their way."

The very thought of ripping the atmosphere from halls still lined with people made Kira's head ache. Grabbing Bashir's arm, she urged stiff muscles into a limping run.

"What about the shields?" she asked O'Brien, dragging the doctor down a side corridor to take them deeper into the station.

"Are they back up?"

"For now. I've still got fifty or sixty buggers skating around the screens on the side of the station we left shielded, and another hundred or so on the ship." He sounded as tightly stretched as a Vedek's drum. "I don't know how long we'll last."

"Pick off as many as you can inside our defenses," Kira ordered. "And use the personnel transporter in Ops, not the cargo unit!" Even if the delicately repaired power systems could survive the big transporter's draw—which Kira thought less likely by the minute—she didn't want to risk beaming entire sections of the station out into space until they ran out of other options.

O'Brien made a grumbling little sound of unhappiness. "That'll be slow going."

"It's only for starters." The deckplates shivered with another surge of brittle creaking, and Kira felt the heavy *thud-thud-thud* of emergency bulkheads slamming into place in corridors too empty of air to transmit sound along with the sensation. She tried to ignore the thin chill threading the metal of the turbolift controls when she punched at the call button with the heel of her hand. "I'll see if we can't initiate something faster from down here. Just buy me a little time."

"Not exactly something we're swimming in at the moment," the chief said morosely. Kira found herself smiling at the accuracy of his complaint as she pushed Bashir into the arriving lift. "I'll do what I can, Major. O'Brien out."

Bashir moved back against the wall of the lift, giving Kira room she didn't feel she needed as he crossed his hands behind him to grasp the inner rail. A few minutes with the tissue regenerator and a hypo full of stimulants had worked wonders—although dark smudges of exhaustion made his eyes seem even bigger and more attentive than usual, his complexion had rebounded to a dusky cinnamon that left him looking weary but reasonably functional. "What are you thinking?" he asked, his voice as calmly polite as if he'd been inquiring what she'd ordered for lunch.

Kira sighed and leaned back against the wall opposite him. "That we can't just wait for Sisko to solve his problems and come back here to save us," she said, meeting his earnest face with what she hoped was equal sincerity. "We've got to get rid of these things on our own."

The floor heaved powerfully, spastically beneath her, and Kira crashed to her knees with a horrible certainty that everything was finished, the station had died. Then her eyes locked with Bashir's where he'd fallen to all fours on the other side of the lift, and the unnatural stillness registered on her nerves like an electric shock: they were no longer moving.

A thump like the landing of a hundred booted feet thundered on the top of the lift. Craning a look skyward, Bashir suggested dryly, "Whatever your plan is, it had better be a doozy."

She was across the car before the last word left his lips, jerking one arm out from under him to knock him to the floor and clap her hand across his mouth. His eyes narrowed into an impatient scowl, and Kira felt his mouth twist with annoyance as he peeled her fingers away. "They're vacuum-adapted, Major," he told her while the busy clattering on the roof of the lift grew louder. "I doubt they've much in the way of ears."

Kira leaned half her weight into gagging him this time, and bent to put her lips almost against his ear. "Maybe not," she whispered fiercely, the words little more than angry breath, "but they just ate an entire Starfleet crew with

279

perfectly good hearing, and I don't want to find out how quickly they can use that DNA!"

His eyes above the clench of her hand widened in silent horror, but he made no effort to comment. *Wonders never cease.*

The clamor overhead collected into a single knot of intense thunder, and Kira pushed away from Bashir to scrabble for the turbolift doors. They were the same ornate, clumsy slabs of metal the Cardassians had installed a dozen years ago, with only enough strength to keep the passengers from falling out and a lip almost as wide as Kira's hand to curl your fingers around. Her back complained with a waspish twinge as she struggled to haul one door aside, but Bashir scrambled to his feet to join her before she'd done more than grit her teeth against the discomfort, and their combined force wrenched the door open with deceptive ease.

Exposing a blank stretch of dull gray wall. *Between decks.*

Kira slammed a fist against her thigh, cursing silently, and Bashir mouthed a wide-eyed *What now?* as the entire lift trembled at a blow from above.

Good question. She put her back to the exposed shaft wall and swept the inside of the car with eyes that had once been well-practiced at seeing the weaknesses in machines. Without even knowing what she reacted to at first, her attention zeroed in on an access panel only as wide and as tall as the length of her arm. Access panels led to compartments. Compartments led to outside walls.

Outside walls could be broken.

She had the panel yanked off and resting awkwardly across her knees before Bashir had left the door to squat beside her. He took the door, settling it flat on the floor some meters away with amazing delicacy, then squeaked in inarticulate protest when Kira used both hands to tear a huge tangle of workings from the hole.

"Major—!" He managed to sound remarkably shocked, considering the circumstances.

She pushed the wad of circuits and cables at him, motioning for him to get rid of them as he had the access door. "It doesn't work anyway," she hissed, ripping out another load. "Do you want to get out of here, or don't you?"

He frowned, but disposed of the torn-out workings with the same swift efficiency he'd applied to the door. Kira was tempted to point out that they could requisition new components for the turbolifts—only the aliens had a similar option available for their bodies. She suspected he'd come to the same conclusion, though, when he leaned past her to tear out the next clot of workings on his own.

The outer skin of the turbolift trembled faintly from the pounding overhead when Kira found it with her hands. Feeling frantically along the edges, she bumped the ridged heads of permanent bolts instead of the inner hatch seal she'd expected to find. No access panel, then. Just standard Cardassian plating. Acid chewed at her stomach, and she squirmed back out of the hole with her mind racing in a ratlike whirl.

Sometimes, it was best not to think too hard before plunging down a path you'd been forced into following. Pulling her knees up to her chin, she grasped the rail above her head and blasted a two-footed kick at the outside panel without bothering to warn Bashir. Bootheels against metal rang through the lift like a warp-core explosion, jarring her teeth together with a painful *clack!*, and popping the sheet off its rivets with a scream of stripping threads. Reaching back to grab Bashir by the collar, she yanked him toward the opening as the plate tumbled away down the shaft below.

The scrabbling on the roof of the lift fell silent.

Bashir cocked a leery peek over his shoulder. "So much for subtlety."

"Go! Go!" She pushed him through the opening with both her hands and feet, trying not to beat him in her own panic to clear out of the lift and be gone. Time paced itself to the pounding of her heart instead of seconds, and the few moments she was sure it must have taken Bashir to crawl through the access seemed an anguished eternity. Halfway through, he squirmed onto his back, scraping for purchase on the floor of the lift with one foot, then slid cleanly out of sight. She hoped desperately that he'd pulled himself through somehow, and hadn't had unwanted help from above.

Beside her, something struck the deck with a fragile little

tick, and a ragged circle of metal next to Kira's hand began to bubble.

A great, curving scythe pierced the roof of the lift. There must have been some sound, some scraping of monster on metal, but Kira heard nothing as they split the car open as though it were soft butter. Fluid the color of plasma drizzled from a huge claw tip, cutting a sizzling line across the floor, and Kira grabbed the edges of the hole to shoot herself through without waiting to see what intended to follow the acid inside.

Her legs hit open air beyond the outside edge of the access, and hands gripped her ankles in almost that same instant, guiding her toward a narrow bar that she could hook with her feet even as an arm looped strongly about her middle and pulled. For some reason, she hadn't expected Bashir to be so athletic; he clung to the emergency ladder by the virtue of one hand and one leg locked around an upright, pulling her across to join him by bracing his other leg against the side of the car for leverage. Kira grabbed at the rungs with a breathless nod of startled gratitude. "Keep moving!" Then she hooked her feet around the outside of the ladder, took the uprights lightly in her hands, and let artificial gravity take her on a quick slide straight down.

She didn't pay attention to decks, or distances, or anything besides the damnably unchanging contours of the wall beside her. Only when it swelled open into a lift-sized tunnel of black did she tighten her grip on the ladder and jerk herself to a stop. Discomforting warmth itched across the surface of her palms, and she suspected she'd left more than just a few layers of skin behind on the slick metal. A small price to pay. Swinging sideways into the tunnel, she jigged on adrenaline overload, blowing on her hands, and waited for Bashir to climb in behind her.

And waited.

There was no doubt in Sisko's mind that the person in the hardsuit had heard him—even at this distance, he could see the involuntary turn of the head that followed his inquiry, although he knew there would be nothing to see with the *Defiant* cloaked. A moment later, a familiar dry voice emerged from howling static to say, "—moment, Captain, I am attempting to convince the Jem'Hadar—"

Sisko scowled. "Dax, can we boost Odo's signal?"

The Trill shook her head without taking her eyes from her sensor controls. "Hardsuit transmitters aren't designed for ship-to-ship distances, Benjamin. All you can do is reduce the static from the wormhole by attenuating all frequencies except the central band."

Sisko grunted, toggling switches on his makeshift communications board. The banshee howl faded to a more bearable hiss. "Odo, repeat transmission."

With the static reduced, the exasperation in Odo's voice was plain to hear. "I said, at the moment, I am attempting to convince the Jem'Hadar that they shouldn't dump their garbage into other people's wormholes. Do you have an objection?"

"Not in the slightest." Sisko scrubbed a hand across his face, blessing his security chief's adamant sense of right and wrong. Without even knowing what was going on, the one being whom the Jem'Hadar would obey without question had managed to avert catastrophe, at least for now. "Can you order them to—"

Dax swung around before Odo could reply. "It's too late for the Jem'Hadar to do anything, Benjamin. Look at the station."

Sisko cursed. Fountains of white-green fire were exploding from the ruptured Jem'Hadar station as the aliens inside boiled out with the wasplike fury Dax had predicted. "Odo, tell the Jem'Hadar to release their tractor beam so we can transport you to safety!" He didn't wait for a reply, leaping down to join Dax at the helm. "Prepare to beam Odo over as soon as he's free. Any sign that the aliens are heading for us?"

She shook her head. "The cloaking device and our low-energy orbit aren't attracting their attention—and I've routed our waste heat to the internal heat exchangers this time. They should be able to soak it up for at least an hour."

"According to Petersen, that's all the time we'll have anyway." Sisko glanced up at the viewscreen. The onslaught of alien attackers had begun to crash down on the two Jem'Hadar warships, making their shields glow and spark with contact. Both ships began to fire their phasers in return, in random sprays of short-range energy. The translucent glitter of the tractor beam was still pulling Odo's suited figure closer to the maelstrom. Sisko scowled and stabbed at his communicator controls.

"Odo, have you told the Jem'Hadar to release the tractor beam?"

"They don't appear to be paying much attention to me right now, Captain," his security officer said dryly. "I recommend you come up with an alternative strategy."

Dax glanced up at Sisko. "If we drop our cloak for a moment, we can send out a tractor beam programmed to neutralize theirs," she suggested.

He nodded. "We'll have to decloak to transport Odo aboard anyway." A quick glance over his shoulder caught Heather Petersen's expectant gaze. "Ensign, get down to the transporter room and prepare to lock on to Odo as soon as we drop our cloak. Hovan, I want minimum decloaking exposure. Synchronize your controls and make sure you get us cloaked again as soon as Odo's on board."

"Aye-aye, sir," they said in unison; then Petersen shot toward the turbolift, leaving Hovan to reprogram her cloaking controls. Sisko swung back to the viewscreen. The shields of the right-hand Jem'Hadar ship were dimming beneath the piled mass of alien bodies, and its random phaser bursts were slowing, a sure indication of power drain. "Status of battle, Mr. Eddington?"

"Starboard warship has shields at twenty percent and phaser controls at fifty percent," the weapons officer reported. "Destruction expected in two minutes or less. Port warship is less heavily engaged and may survive another four minutes before destruction."

Sisko made a swift decision, and opened all hailing frequencies on his communicator. "This is the U.S.S. Defiant, hailing the Jem'Hadar," he said curtly. "You are in imminent danger of destruction. If you drop your shields on my mark, we will beam you to safety."

A Jem'Hadar face appeared on screen, its serrated chin plates dripping with condensation in a ship's atmosphere overheated by failing shields. Sisko couldn't be sure which of the two pilots he was seeing. "Why should I believe you?" the warrior demanded. "You attacked us first!"

"Only to prevent the destruction—" Sisko broke off as the viewscreen flashed with the vapor-white explosion of a hull breach washing over them at close range. He shot a fierce scowl at Dax. "Is that tractor beam still on?"

"I'm afraid so." Her slim fingers flew across her panel faster than any human's could have, powered by the ferocious intellect of two cerebral cortices working in unison. "Our neutralizing tractor beam is ready to engage. We can drop cloak on your command."

Sisko stabbed at his communicator controls again. "Jem'Hadar warship, this is your final chance," he said to the last warship, glowing fiercely now under its swarm of alien attackers. "Drop shields when you see us decloak and we'll transport you aboard along with the Founder."

There was no reply. Sisko cast an assessing look at the shortening distance between Odo and the flare of battle, and felt the muscles of his jaw tighten with decision.

"Hovan, drop cloak *now*," he commanded. "Dax, engage tractor beam. Petersen, prepare to transport."

As sometimes happened in high-precision starship battles, the actual maneuver took less time to perform than his orders.

"Cloaking device disengaged—" said Hovan.

"Tractor beam locked and nullified," said Dax, in overlapping echo. The fierce glitter of their own tractor beam, dark gray to the Jem'Hadar's pale silver, slapped out like a snake striking through the darkness. "Petersen, begin—"

"Transporter beam locked and activated," said Petersen's voice, before Dax had even finished speaking. "Transport complete, Captain."

"Cloaking device reengaged," Hovan reported promptly. "We're cloaked again, Captain."

Sisko took a deep breath, cut off abruptly when the screen frosted with another ghost-white hull breach. He waited until the outward burst of gas and vapor had cleared around them, leaving the *Defiant* alone with the alien-occupied station. The bright sprays of white and green that marked high concentrations of aliens were swirling like angry wasps around the shattered remnants of the Jem'Hadar fighters. "Any sign of aliens heading in our direction?"

Dax shook her head. "I'm not picking up anything, on either the duranium-keyed scan or the close-range motion sensor. They may not be sensitive to short energy discharges like that tractor-beam pulse."

Sisko grunted and turned toward Eddington. "How fast is the station heading toward the wormhole now, Commander?"

Eddington answered in the slightly-too-fast voice of a man still running on battle adrenaline. "One of the Jem'Hadar's tractor beams was still attached when it was breached. The residual momentum from that is actually pushing the station farther away from the wormhole right now. I don't know how long it will take the aliens to realize that and make course corrections, but it's in no immediate danger of falling into the wormhole."

"Good." Sisko stretched with a sudden bone-cracking release of tension. "That gives me time to find out why Constable Odo decided to take a slalom ride through an unstable wormhole. Dax, you have the comm. Notify me the instant that station reverses direction."

His science officer swung around to give him a severely meaningful look. "With your permission, Captain, I think I should come with you down to the transporter room."

Sisko lifted an eyebrow, recognizing the fierce Joran tone that meant he disagreed with the Trill at his peril. "You want to talk to Odo, too, old man?"

"No," she said bluntly. "I want to talk to myself."

Kira knew Bashir was dead.

She knew it with a certainty that made her stomach burn as she leaned out into the shaft and looked back up the ladder. If the aliens hadn't caught him and torn him into pieces smaller than the fragment Odo had found, Kira would do it for them, just to pay him back for fraying her nerves to such a splintered jangle.

"Doctor!" No sense trying to be quiet anymore—it wasn't like the aliens didn't know they were there. She watched Bashir's brisk hand-over-hand progress down the ladder with her fingernails dug into her palms, knowing it

was dangerously fast for someone not accustomed to working on ladders every day, fearing that it wasn't fast enough.
"*Hurry,* goddammit! We're supposed to be fleeing!"

He glared down at her without slowing. "I'd rather not
break both my legs in the process, if it's all the same to
you."

Kira growled, wishing he were close enough to hit. "I'll
break both your legs . . ." she grumbled. But she didn't pull
back into the tunnel, afraid he'd vanish for real if she let
him out of her sight.

The stench of corroded metal blossomed through the
open shaft. What seemed only an arm's length from her
face, acid twisted in a sparkling ribbon, and Kira jerked a
horrified look toward the stopped car above them just as it
shuddered, tilted, and dropped a dozen rapid meters.

"*Julian!*"

Fear stiffened him so sharply, Kira was afraid he'd freeze
while still within the aliens' reach. Instead, he didn't even
waste a glance at the crash and scrabble overhead. Straddling the ladder, he tucked his chin to his chest and
surrendered to the controlled fall. Kira stepped out onto the
rungs, into his path, and braced herself to stop him before
he could slide past. He hit her with less force than she
expected, but still enough to jar her feet off the rungs and
send her heart leaping into her throat as she flailed to
recover her hold. She lost track of which of them clambered
into the side passage first—all she knew was that the light in
the turbolift shaft seemed to constrict abruptly, roaring like
a summer storm, and she felt the weight of the Prophets
rushing down toward her head just as she tackled Bashir
and dragged him away from the tunnel's opening.

The turbolift crashed past in an angry blur. Flat, segmented forms clung like ticks to its roof and sides, looking
too much like machines themselves to be easily separated
from the metal. Kira recoiled instinctively, blind to any
thought but her inborn compulsion to protect anything
more helpless than herself. Locking her arms around the
doctor despite his indignant yelp, she whirled him away
from the entrance and beyond the snaking grasp of one of
the viroid creatures.

It slapped the deck with a thick, three-fingered paw,

curling its digits to grip at the decking as its black-mantled body hurtled past. *It'll slip!* Kira thought, a desperate wish as much as a realization. *Its weight'll pull it down the shaft!* But the bang of its carapace striking the wall outside only dislodged its grip by a millimeter, and three glossy talons the color of polished hematite halted even that tiny movement by shooting down into the decking as though it were cork. She couldn't see muscles flex through the translucent sheen of its carapace, but she heard the crack and grind of its power along every joint and seam. A second, more insectoid appendage joined the first, tapping daintily at the walls, and the creature hauled itself above the lip of the passageway to peel open the long vertical slash of its mouth—

—only to vanish in an ear-shattering blast. Three deep, sharp grooves torn into the floor of the shaft were all that marked where it had gone. High overhead, a shrill whoop of triumph clapped off the turboshaft walls.

"For some jobs, nothing beats explosive percussion!"

Kira wondered if she was supposed to feel lucky, or if they'd just traded one problem for another.

When they crawled to the mouth of the tunnel, Pak grinned down at them from a distinctly nonregulation rift in the wall high above where the turbolift had been. Switching the heavy, wide-bore shotgun over to her left hand, she snapped Kira a manic salute, and loosed another exultant howl.

"Well?" she hollered, waving them up with such exuberance Kira was sure she'd overbalance and fall. "Close your mouths and get up here—we've got bugs to kill!"

"All right, whose idea was this?" Sisko growled.

Fortunately, Odo was as impervious to human fury as he was to Ferengi whining. "According to Dr. Bashir, my passenger was the one who insisted on coming." His stern dignity wasn't even hindered by the enormously pregnant bulge in his abdomen, at which Dax was looking with a mixture of disbelief and dismay. Inside, according to Odo, was a volume of hyperoxygenated and isoboromine-spiked brine sufficient to maintain the ancient symbiont on their passage through the wormhole. That hadn't seemed to reassure Dax much—after a momentary ansible trance, she'd sent Heather Petersen running for the spare brine tank Bashir had sent with them. "He said you would need it to save the wormhole."

Sisko exchanged a long, assessing look with Dax. "That has to be true," the Trill said at last. "Julian would never have agreed to send the symbiont into danger otherwise—"

"Which means the ancient symbiont knows something about this mess that we don't." Sisko stepped back as the transporter room doors hissed apart to admit Petersen and Dr. Bashir's assistant, rolling a cartful of tank and tubing before them.

"Considering all of this is déjà vu for it, I'd say that's understandable." Odo's bulging midsection abruptly flowed up and out to engulf the cart in streaming liquid changeling, making the Bajoran medic gasp and step back. The tank abruptly filled with a glittering wash of brine and squirming symbiont. Dax had both hands immersed and wrapped around the symbiont before Odo had even finished recongealing into his humanoid form. Sisko watched the worried lines on the Trill's face smooth into the now-familiar blankness of trance.

"All right, Constable," he said softly, so as not to break Jadzia's concentration. "How bad are things aboard *Deep Space Nine?*"

His security officer made a gruff noise that was not quite a snort and not quite a laugh. "Bad enough that sending me in a hardsuit through the wormhole seemed like our best alternative. Need I say more?"

Sisko scowled. There were times when he wished Odo had a little more Starfleet training and a little less of his own peculiar sense of humor. "Is the station being attacked by the aliens on the other side of the wormhole?"

Odo cocked his head, his equivalent of a lifted eyebrow. "If by aliens, you're referring to viroidal vacuum-adapted organisms who appear to steal DNA and ship reaction masses with equal facility," he said with careful precision, "the answer is yes."

"Are they on board *Deep Space Nine?*" Sisko speared the changeling with a fierce glare. *"How many?"*

"When I left, only one," his security officer replied.

"Outside, there were enough to take out three Bajoran ore freighters, one Lethian transport, and the starship *Mukaikubo*, not to mention an entire wing of the Bajoran militia. My guess is about two hundred. We managed to disassemble some of them with the cargo transporter, and Major Kira has closed down all the station's outer decks as a hull-breach buffer. I think she hopes to lure them in there and kill them."

"Luring them's not the difficult part," Sisko said grimly. "It's killing them afterward that's hard."

"So we've noticed," Odo agreed.

A soft splash from the brine tank yanked Sisko's attention back to his science officer. Dax was still staring down at her immersed hands, oblivious of the wetness soaking up her uniform sleeves, but a horrified expression had replaced her previous blankness. The wetness glistening on her cheeks could have just been splashed brine, but something about the rigid way she was breathing told Sisko differently. He went to stand behind her, his hands dropping to her shoulders and squeezing hard.

"What's the matter, old man?" he demanded.

The Trill dragged in a spasmodic breath. "The old symbiont—it heard us talking about T'Kreng's plan to infiltrate the aliens, Benjamin. It's coherent now and it thinks it should be the one to go—" She took in another heaving breath. "And *Dax* agrees with it!"

Ah—so this was Jadzia talking. Sisko bit back the acid comment he would have made to Curzon and replaced it with a carefully neutral question. "You don't?"

"No!" She swung around to scowl up at him. "A Trill's first responsibility is to keep her symbiont alive, you know that! I can't sentence any version of Dax to certain death—"

"Even if it means saving another version from five thousand years of solitary confinement?" He shook her gently. "Jadzia, stop thinking of the old Dax symbiont as a thing you have to protect! It's an extension of you—and don't tell me you wouldn't sacrifice yourself *and* your symbiont if that was the only way to save the entire quadrant from this alien invasion."

"Of course I would," she said without hesitation. Then

her blue-gray eyes darkened. "But it's too late now, Benjamin. Even if we infiltrate the alien core in the Jem'Hadar station, we can't blow it up. It's too close to the wormhole."

"We can tow it—" he began.

Dax shook her head. "Not from a dead stop. I did the calculations just before we came down here. The *Defiant* is powerful, but it can't match the acceleration of five Jem'Hadar warships. That's the minimum thrust we'd need to get the station into warp fast enough to keep from being attacked."

Sisko vented his frustration in a snarl. "Don't tell me there's nothing we can do now, Dax, because I *don't* want to hear it. After everything we've gone through—and everything Odo's done to help us—I refuse to stand here and just watch the wormhole be destroyed!"

From across the transporter room, Heather Petersen cleared her throat hesitantly. "Um—Captain? Remember you asked me if I could think of some other way to destroy the Jem'Hadar station, beside firing our phasers at their reaction core?"

"Have you?" he demanded intently.

"I think so, sir." The cadet glanced at Dax. "Isn't it true that most self-destruct sequences are designed to release the containment fields around the reaction mass before they explode it, so it scatters harmlessly into space? Just in case other vessels are nearby?"

"Yes, of course."

"Do you think the self-destruct sequence programmed into the Jem'Hadar station would work the same way?"

Sisko frowned. "Probably," he said before Dax could answer. "But that doesn't do us any good, Ensign. We can't initiate the Jem'Hadar's self-destruct sequence without the proper code."

"I know," she said. "But I thought maybe you could convince him to give it to us."

Sisko's frown became a scowl. "Convince *who?*"

"The Jem'Hadar pilot I beamed out of the second warship when it dropped its shields." Petersen turned toward Dr. Bashir's assistant, oblivious of Sisko's astounded expression. "He wasn't hurt too badly to talk, was he, Meris?"

The Bajoran medic shook her head. "No. In fact, he

called me so many names while I was treating him that I finally had to put him in stasis just to shut him up. He certainly didn't seem very happy to be rescued."

"Probably because he didn't drop his shields on purpose," Sisko guessed. "They must have failed at exactly the moment you were trying to beam him out, Ensign."

Petersen winced. "Then I suppose he wouldn't agree to give the self-destruct sequence to us." She glanced back at Sisko apologetically. "Do you think we can drug or hypnotize him into doing it, sir?"

"I don't believe that will be necessary, Ensign," Odo said with dark amusement. "Just take him out of stasis and leave him to me."

CHAPTER
21

THEY BROUGHT THE old Dax back to the medical bay with them. There was really no good reason to, since the self-contained brine tank O'Brien had made would have functioned perfectly well wherever they left it, but Dax couldn't bring herself to leave the ancient symbiont alone with the transporter that would soon be sending it into a suicidal battle.

"—not a millennium too soon—" Even standing in the turbolift, Jadzia could hear the echo of her other self in her mind, although it wasn't possible to reply without sliding into the concentration of ansible trance. The pleasure she heard in the ancient symbiont's voice confirmed what her physical contact with it had already told her—it was not only coherent again, it was totally committed to carrying out T'Kreng's battle plan. "—I've been waiting for this ever since Julian died—"

Dax shivered at that matter-of-fact statement, then caught the concerned glance Sisko threw at her. "You okay, old man?"

"Jadzia's a little shaky, but both Daxes seem to be fine," she admitted ruefully. "Between the three of us, I think we'll manage."

Odo snorted, flattening himself back against the turbolift wall so Yevlin Meris could wheel the occupied brine tank out into the passageway. "I hope so, Lieutenant. Otherwise, we'll all be collecting our pensions by the time we make it back to *Deep Space Nine*. Assuming these viroids don't destroy civilization as we know it in the meantime," he added acidly.

Sisko paused in front of the medical bay to give his security officer an exasperated look. "Constable, have you ever heard of the power of positive thinking?"

"I was taught about it on Bajor," Odo admitted, following him inside. "As I recall, they considered it one of the defining myths of the human psyche."

"Well, it was a myth that Curzon shared," Dax retorted. She paused beside the brine tank, which Yevlin had tucked into a back corner of the medical bay, and pressed a hand against its reassuring warmth. An ivory glimmer emerged from the gray-green brine and pressed itself urgently against the glass on the other side.

"—talk to the entrapped Vulcan—" said the ancient symbiont's voice in her mind. "—things I must know—"

Dax nodded and glanced over at the stasis tables. The alien fragment still lay belly-up under the nearest pale-blue shimmer, unmoving. The other stasis field guarded the surviving Jem'Hadar pilot. He'd lost one leg and half his facial crest to whatever explosion had destroyed his shields, and most of his chest glowed pale-pink with regenerated flesh, but his expression was still one of frozen fury, not pain. Dax wondered if the genetically engineered warriors *could* feel pain.

"Captain, the other Dax wants to ask T'Kreng some questions," she said quietly. "Can Petersen and I release her from stasis while you talk to the Jem'Hadar?"

Sisko lifted an eyebrow at her. "How will you ask her questions if you're entranced at the time, old man?"

Dax gave Yevlin Meris an inquiring look. "You said my isoboromine levels rose when I went into trance. It may be that losing consciousness is due to that side effect, not to the ansible connection itself. If you could monitor my isoboromine and keep it stable—"

"It might work," Yevlin agreed, and went to get a hypospray from a supply cabinet.

"If it does," Dax said even more quietly, for Sisko's ears

alone, "I'll be able to tell you as soon as Dax succeeds in taking over the alien core—or as soon as it fails."

Sisko nodded grim agreement. "In which case, we'll try the tuned phasers as a last resort." He gave Odo an ironic look. "Ready to play Founder, Constable?"

Odo nodded. "I'll restrain him as soon as you drop the stasis field. That should keep his—er—irritation with us in check."

"And if not, I've got a phaser." The blue glimmer rolled into invisibility as Sisko released the control, and Odo's hands closed around the Jem'Hadar's wrists with a steely snap. The warrior spit out a long curse that sounded like a hyena's bark.

"Are you ready to try talking to T'Kreng, Lieutenant?" Petersen asked. Yevlin Meris stood at her shoulder, hypospray ready in one hand.

Dax spread her fingers across the front of the brine tank, catching a faint hint of the symbiont's electric sizzle through the transparent aluminum. For some reason, she didn't want to move away from that tingling connection. "Can your microphone pick me up from here, Heather?"

"No problem." The cadet squatted beside the stasis table, fitting her phase modulator over the controls. "Dropping stasis now."

The second blue glimmer of stasis faded. "Well?" demanded T'Kreng's silk-cold voice. "Have you failed yet in your attempt to destroy the aliens with your ship's weapons?"

Dax saw Sisko cast an irritated look over his shoulder at the second stasis table. "Yes," she said, before he could start to argue with what was left of the Vulcan physicist. "And we plan to infiltrate the core as you suggested—"

"Tell me the self-destruct sequence of the station you were towing here," said Odo.

"I have heard of you. You are not a true Founder. And I will not cooperate with Federation scum!" the Jem'Hadar pilot snarled. "These vermin probably came from their side of the wormhole—" He nodded at Sisko and the others.

"—but we have some questions to ask you first," Dax finished, hoping the Vulcan's partial brain could sort out the several conversations going on around her. She took a deep breath and nodded at Yevlin Meris, then reached down into herself for the tidal swash and pull of the ansible connection, ocean-deep now that the second symbiont was only a few centimeters away. She barely felt the cool hiss when Yevlin injected the isoboromine suppressor, but the white haze that had begun to thicken around her senses boiled away again, leaving her feeling vaguely disconnected but quite aware of what was going on around her.

"I need to know how to establish connections with like-minded subsidiary cortical masses," she said, and although it was Jadzia's lips making the words, it was the mind of ancient Dax that thought them, "in order to establish a network which can dominate all preexisting networks inside the core."

"That is indeed the crux of the infiltration problem," T'Kreng's crystalline voice agreed, sounding a little surprised by her perceptiveness. "The neural connections are not a problem. The aliens' messenger RNA will establish those on a cellular level as soon as you come in contact with them."

"And they can be used as communications networks immediately?" Dax asked.

"Yes," said T'Kreng. "My strategy was simply to broadcast my identity through the neural network in as many languages as I could, and listen to the replies I got. In my immediate alien environment, I found one of my shipmates that way, as well as one like-minded Ferengi. While I was still connected to the larger core, I also got echoes from others of my crew, as well as several other engulfed minds, old and new, who appeared to understand Standard English. Including several Jem'Hadar."

"Who speaks of Jem'Hadar?" The warship pilot's eyes rolled sideways and widened at the sound of T'Kreng's voice emanating from the fragment of bloody flesh next to him. "I knew it! The vermin are members of the Federation!"

"No, the vermin have *eaten* members of the Federation." Odo thumped the Jem'Hadar soundly against the table when he tried to lunge at the alien fragment. "The same way they've eaten Jem'Hadar. And they'll eat a lot more of you, if you don't tell us the self-destruct sequence for your station!"

"I'll tell you *nothing*," the warrior shouted fiercely. "You're lying!"

"No," said a new and deeply graveled voice. "He's not."

The Jem'Hadar jerked against Odo's hold, his dark eyes rolling sideways again. A wash of almost supernatural awe swept the fury from his face at last. "Commander Kaddo'Borawn?" he demanded. "Where—where are you?"

"Dead," the Jem'Hadar voice said bluntly. "And eaten by the alien vermin, just as this Federation Founder told you. But I survive as a mind inside it, as do many of our brothers. They must be freed to real death, Manan'Agar. The station must be destroyed."

The Jem'Hadar warrior made a frustrated movement of his hands, as if he would have slammed his fists into something if Odo hadn't been holding them in his steely grip. "Exactly what we planned to do, Commander!" he said hotly. "We would have cast the station with its vermin horde into the wormhole to be crushed, if these awards had not stopped us."

This time, the hyena-bark cursing sound came from Dax's jury-rigged Universal Translator. "The alien vermin would have abandoned the station before the wormhole destroyed it, as they always planned to do once they arrived there. And our brothers would have lived forever inside that vile imprisonment—as I would have, if not for the Federation female who controls this vermin fragment. We must destroy them outside the wormhole, Manan'Agar, and we must destroy them utterly." The gravelly Jem'Hadar voice paused. "I would tell them how to do it, myself, if this part of my brain remembered. It does not. You must tell them how to blow the station up. And then you must make sure they do it. Will you honor this command from a dead man?"

The Jem'Hadar warrior swallowed convulsively, then jerked his head sideways in what Dax hoped was a Jem'Hadar nod. Sisko made an ominous growling noise, and Odo shot him a reassuring look. "I believe Manan'Agar has just agreed to cooperate with us," the security chief said. "Hasn't he?"

"Yes." The warship pilot's voice sounded almost sulky. "But you must promise to kill me afterward."

Sisko let out an exasperated breath. "I'll add you to my list," he said. "Provided there *is* an afterward. Now, what's the self-destruct sequence for that station?"

The Jem'Hadar took a deep breath. "Self-destruct."

Dax saw Odo and Sisko exchange skeptical looks. "That's it?" the security officer demanded. "All you have to do is say 'self-destruct' and the entire station blows up?"

"Of course." Manan'Agar drew himself up on his elbows, looking baffled. "What else would you need?"

Sisko cleared his throat. "How about a voiceprint security identification? Or a seconded command from another officer?"

The injured pilot made an impatient coughing sound that seemed to signify irritation. "Starfleet bureaucrats may need such things, but the Jem'Hadar do not. Any one of us must be able to destroy our stations alone, because after a lost battle, one may be all that is left. And if that one is injured or dying, why make it more difficult than it needs to be?"

Odo shook his head, looking baffled himself. "But if an enemy came on board, how would you prevent *them* from giving a self-destruct order?"

"Simple." Manan'Agar's dark lips pulled back to bare his scaled teeth in a grimace that might have been meant to convey anything from amusement to disgust. "None of our enemies knows our language. We are careful never to speak it around them."

The information reached Jadzia through a serene detachment that seemed to settle on her like snow the longer she stayed linked with the ancient symbiont. It might be coherent now, she thought in sudden realization, but millennia of solitary confinement had still left their mark on its psyche. She took a deep breath, and threw off the numbing tranquillity with an effort. "So that's why the Jem'Hadar always speak the language of their adversaries?" she demanded.

Odo grunted. "They do it because they are genetically programmed to learn languages within moments of first hearing them, Lieutenant. It gives them a distinct tactical advantage over races that depend on Universal Translators." He frowned down at the Jem'Hadar. "All right, then. How *do* you say 'self-destruct' in your language?"

Manan'Agar's dark eyes flashed with scorn. "I will not tell *you* that. I will tell only the one who goes to destroy the station."

Sisko cast an exasperated glance at the brine tank beside Dax. "That may be a little difficult. Right now, the—er—organism we're sending to destroy the station can only see and hear through its mental link with my science officer."

The Jem'Hadar's puzzled gaze traveled from the tank to Dax, still standing with her palm pressed to its window. "Then your science officer will be going with it to the station?"

"No," Sisko said flatly. "We'll be transporting it straight into the aliens' central core—straight into their brain."

Manan'Agar spat out another untranslatable curse. "Impossible. When we tried to transport a photon torpedo into that mass of vermin, the output of subspace energy from their stolen power cores disrupted the beam and made it totally incoherent. And that was not even a living organism!"

"Damn!" Sisko swung around to scowl at Dax and Heather Petersen. "Are we going to have the same problem?"

Dax threw a questioning look at the younger scientist, knowing she had more expertise in transport physics. Petersen chewed at her lower lip for a moment, looking increasingly worried. "I'm afraid so," she admitted at last. "We could try to compensate by increasing the confinement field on the transporter beam, or we could just try to get a coherent beam in as close to the core as we can—"

The cadet broke off abruptly, but Odo finished her thought with his own relentless logic. "—and send the symbiont in with someone who can carry it the rest of the way."

"Unacceptable, Constable," Sisko said flatly. "We'll have to find another way to get the symbiont into the core."

Dax frowned at him, feeling a tidal wave of urgency crash through the ansible link. Before she could find the words to express it, however, T'Kreng's crystalline voice had already broken the somber silence. "That may be an ethically responsible goal, Captain Sisko, but it is one that will be impossible to achieve. The singularity matrix will undergo irreversible chronologic displacement approximately thrity-five minutes from now."

"Well, that gives us enough time to—"

"No!" The Vulcan's voice rose to an unexpected shout, buoyed by a sudden infusion of Jem'Hadar ferocity. "The Trill symbiont you're sending will need *at least* that much time to form a neural network strong enough to dominate the rest of the core. Every minute—every second!—you delay now could cost it the time it needs to save the wormhole."

Dax exchanged troubled glances with Sisko and Odo, seeing the same bleak acceptance creep into both their faces. She took a deep breath, flexing her hand against the chill of the brine-tank window. "Then it's settled," she said at last. "One of us has to take the symbiont into the alien core."

"Yes." The steel-hard set of Sisko's jaw told Dax he had finally accepted the necessity of what they had to do. "How do we decide who goes?"

"That's the easy part, Captain." Odo's pale eyes glittered with sardonic humor, although Dax had no idea what he could find amusing about this situation. "All you need to do is ask for a volunteer."

"What the hell are you doing down here?"

They'd had to wait for what felt like an hour while Pak and her cronies hunted up a length of purloined bulkhead to lay a makeshift bridge. It wasn't hanging on the ladder that had eaten away at Kira's patience as much as the awareness that very little prevented the aliens from scuttling across them again. She didn't want to count on being so lucky the next time.

"What do you think I'm doing down here?" Pak tossed a crooked grin back at Kira as she caught Bashir by one elbow and pulled him off the ersatz platform to relative safety. "I've still got another twenty-three of those things to kill before I start to break even for what they did to us."

Bashir flicked a disdainful wave at the gun balanced across Pak's shoulder, and Kira noticed that his hands were shaking, ever so slightly. He was running on nothing but the stimulants and adrenaline by now, she realized. It wouldn't be long before they lost him to exhaustion completely. "If that's what you've been using," Bashir told Pak in a voice already hoarse from too much excitement, "you haven't killed any of them. At best, you've inconvenienced them a little."

Pak shrugged and nodded her people off down the corridor ahead of them. "I'll settle for inconvenienced until somebody thinks of a better idea."

"I'm working on that. But first—" Kira flashed her hand up behind Pak's neck, snatching the still-warm barrel of her antique weapon and sweeping it out of her grasp. The old-fashioned weapons had been popular among the resistance when Kira was young—easier to stockpile than phasers, since the Cardassians' weapon scans only looked for more modern energy weapons. The militia had probably managed to hide this one on the station in much the same way. Pak grumbled with an adolescent pout, but didn't resist when Kira slipped back the gun's chamber and pulled out all six of its remaining slugs as they walked. "The last thing we need is you putting a 100-caliber hole through the bulkhead."

"I didn't hear you complaining a few minutes ago." She stretched out her hand to reclaim the gun, then grimaced again when Kira switched it to her other arm to keep it out of reach.

"What about the rest of your crew?" Kira demanded. "Are there more of these?"

"Maybe," Pak shrugged. "Probably. My people had weapon components stowed all over this station. It took me a while to find all the pieces for this one, but I've got enough spare parts to say there's probably at least two more of 'em scattered around. Why?" She grinned wickedly and bumped Kira with her elbow. "You want some more?"

For just an instant, Kira was sorry she'd emptied the gun. "I want to know that I can trust you! I want to know that while I'm trying to haul our butts out of the fire, you're not running around behind my back screwing everything up!"

"Since when does saving you and pretty boy from the lunch rush count as a screwup?"

"You know damn—!"

"All right, both of you, *stop it!*" Bashir pushed between

them with a force that startled Kira, shoving her back against one wall of the corridor and Pak against the other. "I don't know if either of you has noticed," he whispered fiercely, "but we're not exactly in the best position to indulge this little androgen display right now." An angry sweep of his arm encompassed their whole section of station. "There are aliens crawling all over these decks! Instead of butting heads to decide which of you is really queen of the hill, you should be getting us to the Promenade ahead of the viroids!"

Kira wasn't sure which was worse—being in debt for her life to the dictionary definition of "militant radical," or being lectured on duty by a Starfleet doctor whose idea of a rough childhood was having to pay for your own tennis lessons. Fighting back a scowl of embarrassment, she clapped an arm around Bashir's shoulders and pulled him alongside as she pushed through the little knot of militia.

"That's the second time you've mentioned the aliens heading for the safe zones," she said. "What do you know that I don't?"

Bashir tipped his head in uncharacteristic reluctance. "It's only a theory. . . ."

Pak jabbed at him from behind. "Spit it out!"

Kira tossed the militia leader a warning scowl, but if anything, Pak's rough insistence seemed to wake up some of the doctor's usual enthusiasm.

"Well, we already know that they coopt DNA." He ducked out from under Kira's arm, turning sideways so he could face the small group and still keep them walking at the brisk pace Kira had set. "It's obviously vital to the structure of their own genetics, vital to what their bodies do and how, probably vital to whatever passes among them as reproductive success. It only makes sense, then, that they must have some way to analyze the genetic makeup of their potential victims. If they didn't have some built-in drive to seek out genetic material not already assimilated into their structure, the behavior itself wouldn't persist. They'd make do with a finite set of traits, and pass those on to future generations the way every other life-form does."

Catching sight of a cross-corridor that led deeper into the station, Kira turned them without warning and had to lean out to snag Bashir and guarantee he made the turn with them. "So what you're saying," she prompted as he jogged to catch up, "is that if they've never 'assimilated' a Bajoran before, that makes them *want* to eat Bajorans?"

"In a manner of speaking, yes."

Pak snorted loudly, spitting dryly toward the wall. "These things have eaten plenty of Bajorans."

Bashir shook his head, lean face youthfully earnest. "We don't know that." He held up his hands to silence her before she could do more than open her mouth to disagree. "We know they raided four ore carriers," he elaborated hastily, "and that you lost twenty-four of your people. That's perhaps fifty Bajorans, all total. There are *hundreds* of those things out there—they can't *all* have assimilated Bajoran DNA. Even if they have, they most likely *haven't* encountered Ferengi, or Vulcans, or Tellerites, or Klingons." He turned plaintive eyes on Kira, as though to make sure she was listening. "We've got all of those and more gathered down in the safe zones."

She'd been more than listening. She'd been thinking two steps ahead. "No wonder you thought they'd make their way to the Promenade."

Bashir nodded bleakly. "They shouldn't be able to resist it."

"So what are we waiting for?" Pak skipped eagerly forward, drumming her palms on Kira's back as though they were wartime comrades and soul-tight friends. "If we know where they're going, let's meet them there and do some damage!"

"Because people might get hurt!" Frustrated anger flushed Bashir's face with color, flashing brightly in his exhausted eyes. "The point is to *stop* the aliens from reaching the station inhabitants, not to use the safe zones as bait!"

A shocking kick of realization brought Kira to a standstill. "Not the safe zones, maybe . . ." Heart racing with something she didn't dare yet call hope, she grabbed at Bashir's arm. "You examined one of them. Do you think you could make a good guess as to what sorts of DNA they *haven't* already absorbed?"

He frowned down at her, clearly torn between answering

her question and railing at her for wasting time with unimportant details. "Remnant DNA traces from various species place the viroids along the eastern spiral arm for at least the last five millennia," he said at last. "If nothing else, species from the galactic core and western edge should be completely new to them." The faintest flicker of understanding seemed to skip through his eyes, and he answered Kira's grip on his arm with one of his own. "Why? Major, what are you planning to do?"

It made too much sense. The idea exploded to fill her mind with intricate detail, and she couldn't avoid following it to its inevitable conclusion. "Draw them away from the station. Put together a meal ticket their instincts can't say no to, and launch it into space."

Bashir tried to pull away from her, horrified. "You can't do that! That's tantamount to condemning whatever spacefaring race they next come in contact with to death!"

"Send 'em to the Cardassians!"

"No!" She spun an angry glare on Pak, shaking the empty shotgun at her in a silent warning not to challenge her on this of all points. "I'm not going to dump my problems at anybody else's door." She tried to gentle her voice as she turned back to Bashir, knowing how much she hated what she was about to say, knowing he would never really see that. "We lure them out away from the station, all to a single place, and blast them down to molecules, just like you suggested. A couple torpedoes to the *Mukaikubo's* warp core ought to do it."

Silence swept around them like a cold wind, and Kira almost couldn't look at Bashir as understanding settled tragically across his face.

"You heard what O'Brien said." He sounded younger than she'd ever heard him before, his voice nearly a whisper, as though he didn't want Pak and the others to hear. "If you destroy the *Mukaikubo* while the wormhole's still in flux, the subspace surge will collapse the singularity. You'll be trapping everyone in the *Defiant* on the other side."

But that was the nature of command—to know, to feel, to hate the hard decisions you were forced to make, and then to make them anyway so that innocents like Bashir would never have to.

"You can't have it both ways." The calmness of her words lied shamelessly about the sick despair tearing her up inside. "We either save the Alpha Quadrant, or we save the *Defiant*. Which will it be?"

His eyes burned into her with stark misery, but he didn't voice an answer. She hadn't expected him to.

"You know what you guys really need?" Pak laced her hands behind her head and tipped herself back against the bulkhead with a maddeningly contented grin. "You need some piece of low-tech wizardry powerful enough to waste alien butt without throwing any subspace crap to interfere with your wormhole." She sighed like a woman remembering a favorite lover. "You need a good ol'-fashioned fusion bomb."

Kira resisted an urge to kick the terrorist's legs out from under her. "And you know where we can get one on short notice?" she snarled, too mad at herself and the terrible constraints of necessity to suffer sarcasm gladly.

Pak Dorren only smiled even wider, and winked at her in broad delight. "Why, little bit, as a matter of fact, I do."

CHAPTER
22

THE BRIGHT GLEAM of the transporter effect flashed over two shapes on the *Defiant's* bridge, making their silhouettes glow like wind-gusted candles just before they vanished. The high-pitched drone of the matter-to-energy converter faded a moment later, leaving a somber silence behind it. Dax closed her eyes, feeling the ansible link vanish for the few seconds the ancient symbiont was in transport, then rematerialize much farther away.

She heard Petersen's relieved voice from the auxiliary transporter control panel to her right. "We got coherent beam arrival, sir, six hundred meters away from the reaction core. They're in."

"Good work." Sisko's command chair hissed as he swung it around. "What's the station's current vector, Mr. Eddington?"

"It's completing the turning maneuver they started five minutes ago, sir." Dax opened her eyes to see the ruptured Jem'Hadar station stabilize itself with synchronized bursts from its impulse engines. Behind it, the wormhole's ultraviolet corona was strobing from indigo-black to wine-dark red on her color scale as its energy output intensified. "It's now headed directly for the wormhole entrance, at point-zero-three of light speed."

"Estimated time of arrival?" Sisko demanded.

"Twenty minutes, assuming they don't accelerate."

"That doesn't give us much time to infiltrate the core." Sisko slapped at the communicator controls beside his command chair. "*Defiant* to away team. Report." A long silence filled with the tense crackling static of the wormhole was all that answered him. After a moment spent listening to it, the captain finally exploded. "Dammit, I *knew* this was a bad idea! Dax, give me the Jem'Hadar translation of that self-destruct code. I'm going over there."

"Oh, no, you're not." Dax swung around to face him, recognizing the outburst of fierce frustration that could overwhelm Sisko's common sense when he wasn't the one carrying out a crucial maneuver. "Give them time to get their bearings."

"And keep in mind that the Jem'Hadar are programmed for maximum self-reliance," Odo added dryly. "The first report you get from Manan'Agar may be when the station blows itself up."

"That's *exactly* what I'm worried about, Constable." Sisko vaulted out of his chair and began prowling the bridge, as if he could no longer stand to sit and wait. "I'm afraid he'll try so hard to destroy the station himself he'll forget that the main point of his mission is to deliver the symbiont to the alien core."

Dax shook her head. Faint but steady through the ansible connection, she could feel the vibration of water sloshing around her other self. "No, Benjamin—the symbiont can feel that it's moving. Wherever Manan'Agar is trying to go, he's taking the brine tank with him."

"Not surprising, since he's using its antigravs to support himself," Odo reminded her. "If I had to guess what he's doing, I'd say he's trying to find a part of the station that still has power, so he can deliver the self-destruct command himself."

Sisko paused in front of Dax's jury-rigged engineering panel. "Can we see where the aliens are still running power through the station?"

Dax recalibrated one sensor to scan the Jem'Hadar station for live power circuits, then scrutinized the results. "Aside from the engineering sector they're occupying, the aliens are only supplying power to the station's impulse engines and navigational thrusters." She pointed at the strands of light that ran like faint spiderwebs through the station's darkened outline. "And those areas are all breached to space."

Sisko grunted, a little of the tension fading from his face. "So if Manan'Agar's heading for a live power circuit—"

"—he's going in the direction we want him to." Odo slanted Dax an inquiring look from his seat beside Eddington at the weapons console. "Can you pinpoint exactly where your counterpart is on the station, Lieutenant?"

"No." Dax closed her eyes again, trying to glean whatever sensations she could from a naked Trill symbiont enclosed in brine. What she got back was a fierce sense of impatience and determination, accompanied by the prickle of a hallucinatory aurora. "They must be getting closer to the stolen reaction masses, though. The symbiont is feeling some kind of unshielded magnetic flux—"

She gasped and broke off as a violent lurch of motion slapped the ancient symbiont against one cold aluminum wall of its tank. The ansible connection between them skated into screaming white haze. Through it, she was vaguely aware of Sisko swinging around, then coming to join her at the helm. *"Yevlin!"*

Dax couldn't hear what the physician's assistant said or did in reply, but a moment later a shock of cold rippled through her, and her senses returned. The first thing she saw was Yevlin Meris's intense Bajoran frown, a few inches away. "I can't keep depressing your isoboromine levels forever, Lieutenant," she said grimly. "If the ansible connection gets cut off, your internal suppressors may rebound and send you into systemic shock."

Dax took in another gasping breath and tightened her grip on whatever was supporting her. "I don't think—this will take forever—"

"What's going on, old man?" Sisko demanded. *"Talk to me!"*

Both symbionts responded to that familiar whip-crack of command. "We think Manan'Agar's been attacked—" Dax said. "Something heavy hit the brine tank a moment ago. And now—"

She broke off again, feeling another lurch of motion in the brine, along with the fierce vibration of ripping metal. Then came the worst nightmare a Trill symbiont could have: an uncontrolled splashing fall through released water, followed by the horrid thud of unprotected neural matter against a bitterly cold surface. Dax gasped in shared shock and pain.

"—tank's ruptured—I've been thrown out!" She reached out to grab at the nearest hard surface, her fingers scrabbling blindly over her helm panel until they reached and clutched around the strength of Sisko's wrist. Something lifted the symbiont in a harsh metallic grip, something turned and twisted it, nearly breaking its fragile cortical envelope. "An alien has picked me up—" Dax screamed and convulsed against the surge of transmitted agony, barely feeling Sisko catch at her shoulders to keep her from falling. "Oh, god, I'm being *eaten*. . . ."

"And it's a winner! They're takin' the bait!"

Kira sighed with such explosive relief that she fogged the inside of her helmet. For a moment, the immediacy of their danger seemed almost lost behind that cloudy sheen, but her memory held fast to the image of a lone runabout lifting away from the station on a preprogrammed course, its onboard transporter sprinkling a chum line of exotic DNA behind it. Then the hardsuit's internal environment controls compensated for the rise in humidity, and her vision cleared just as O'Brien announced, "You're on, Major."

She nodded, even though several meters of station separated her from the chief up in Ops. "I read you." There was something bizarrely comforting about watching alien carapaces slough off the station like scales, drifting and swirling like windblown leaves in the runabout's wake. Even from here, she could see that one of those wriggling bodies wore a shape different from the rest, with a streak of Andorian blue staining its hematite-colored carapace. Some fierce inner part of her wished suddenly that she hadn't left her phaser rifle behind to lighten her trip. *It wouldn't have worked anyway,* a more rational part of her brain reminded her. With an effort that felt almost physical, Kira dragged her gaze away from the alien that had attacked her.

"We're on our way," she told O'Brien, unnecessarily, then stepped out of the airlock. The transition from the station's artificial gravity to the free-floating world outside the hull

washed Kira's muscles with a wave of weary relief. She'd
almost forgotten how much she still ached until that ever-
present pull was gone; the release from it now almost made
her want to go back inside. In the great scheme of things,
pain was fairly easy to ignore—comfort had a way of
sneaking up on you and making you complacent.

"I hope you're planning on making this quick," Pak
Dorren complained, shuffling her own suit over the threshold between Starfleet's regulation Earth-normal and space's
zero-g. "I hate this EV stuff. I don't want to be out here any
longer than we have to."

Kira waited for the terrorist to creep up beside her, but
didn't offer a hand to help. "It was your idea to hide the
bomb outside."

"My idea," Pak snorted, "but not my job." She turned
her head to show Kira a wan smile, then flailed her arms as
though that tiny motion had stolen away her balance.
"That's the point of being the boss, little bit," she gasped,
throwing herself at Kira's arm and wrapping it in a bear hug
with no consideration for whether Kira was interested in
helping. "You don't have to crawl around on the outsides of
ships unless you really, really want to."

Or someone has a weapon to your head. Peeling herself
free from the other woman, Kira shifted her grip to the
storage hook on the back of Pak's torso, thinking that might
reassure Pak without slowing them too badly. "In the
Shakaar resistance cell, we were taught that the point of
being in charge was that you did your own dirty work."

Pak gave a rough grunt, but let Kira push her gently
forward. "Yeah, well, Shakaar was an idiot."

Kira would have been disappointed if a woman like Pak
felt otherwise.

Dark, silent, the station's exterior looked deceptively
placid compared with the turmoil inside. They'd stepped
onto the hull opposite most of the gaping breaches, and the
abrupt lack of aliens crawling about the screens left the
starscape to all sides as clear and still as a summer night.
Even the wormhole seemed to have quieted to its usual
darkling simmer. Only the clumsy bulk of their hardsuits
and the radiation gauge on the edge of Kira's display
betrayed how much the wormhole was vomiting outside the

visual spectrum. That, and the lacy-fine whispers of ultraviolet fluorescence that frosted bits and pieces of the station like morning dew. Kira wondered if they'd have been able to pick up the radiation signature of Pak's hydrogen bomb through all this noise even if Pak hadn't thought to hide it within the blind spot of the station's own sensor array. Considering the range and volume of the wormhole's output when compared with even the most poorly shielded bomb, it seemed rather unlikely.

"Step it up, Pak." Kira resisted an urge to poke her in the small of her back, aware that there was always the chance it would send Pak tumbling out into space, and they actually needed her now if they were going to make sure the bomb was functional. "You're the one who said you wanted to hurry."

Pak wheezed a hoarse little sound that might have been a laugh. "Little bit, for me this *is* hurrying." She came to a sudden clumsy standstill before breaking her foot's contact with the hull to lift it over a conduit box. "I told you I didn't like EV."

It wasn't until that moment that Kira realized Pak hadn't actually pulled her feet loose from the hull plates since they stepped outside the airlock doors. She been shuffling, sliding the magnetized soles of her hardsuit's shoes across the station's surface like some ridiculous ice skater. Irritation and amazement overcame Kira in equal measure. "You're not afraid of hydrogen bombs, but you're afraid of spending fifteen minutes EV."

On the other side of the conduit, Pak planted her second foot carefully beside her first, and took up her snail-like shuffling again. "Hey, honey—that's why they call it a phobia."

But at this rate, the runabout would be at Organia before they could get to the bomb.

"O'Brien to Kira. Major, we've got a problem."

She lifted her head, startled by the river of static roaring underneath the chief's transmission. Constant but distant, as if someone had left the faucet on. "What's the matter, Chief?"

"The buggers," he reported urgently. "They're all over

the runabout like voles on a cat. Julian's got the onboard replicators producing his DNA concoction at top capacity, but once they destroy the stand-alone generator and the replicators shut down, they'll do away with the whole load in under a minute."

She was suddenly viciously resentful of having to remove the bait runabout's engine core. Glancing keenly in the direction she knew the little ship had taken, she was only slightly surprised to find she couldn't pick it out from the other flecks of brightness that were the surrounding stars. "Start pulling the aliens off with the transporter," she told O'Brien, stepping intimately close to Pak and wrapping her arms around the older woman's middle. "We've got to decrease the load on the runabout or it won't last long enough to receive the bomb."

"That'll mean dropping the shields, Major, and with you right out there in the open—"

"We'll just have to hope Bashir's concoction smells more appetizing than we do. Kira out." She cut off their comm channel without waiting for his acknowledgment, then tightened her grip around Pak with a warning bump from her helmet. "We're going to jump."

She could feel Pak's body stiffen even through both heavy suits. "No, we're not!"

"Yes, we are. Hold on!" It wasn't like she'd meant for Pak to have a choice.

As far as double-time suit jumps were concerned, the surface of DS9 was one of the more convenient locations to navigate. An irregular moon, where gravity's bothersome pull could interfere with your trajectory, was far harder to sail across, and the spinning outer hull of a centrifugal cylinder ranked among the worst suit walks of Kira's life. *Deep Space Nine*—a steady, immobile behemoth wider in girth than some of Bajor's colonies—released her into her leap with no jealous efforts to pull her down, no spiteful rotational movement to spoil her aim. She caught herself neatly against an upthrust communications antenna, pausing a few seconds longer than perhaps absolutely necessary to make sure Pak's added mass had equalized alongside hers before stepping into the last short hop as though she were stepping through an open door.

To her credit, Pak made not a sound during their rapid flight. She didn't struggle, or curse, or do anything that might have jeopardized their safe arrival at the station's upper tier. *She may be phobic,* Kira thought as her feet clanged and locked on the sensor array's outer housing, *but she's not stupid.* Using one foot to stomp on Pak's boots and ensure they were firmly mated with the hull, Kira carefully released her passenger and squirmed around in front.

"Okay, Pak, what do we—"

Catching one glimpse of the terrorist's face, Kira cut herself off with a sigh. Pak stood rigid as a statue, her face the color of frozen cream, her eyes and mouth clamped so resolutely shut that Kira almost wondered if she was breathing. *My fault,* the major chastised herself. She should have known that anything Pak Dorren was afraid of frightened her through-and-through.

"Dorren . . ." Rapping her knuckles on the other woman's faceplate, Kira did her best to keep the worst of the irritation out of her voice. "We're at the sensor array. You've got to open your eyes and look—you said the bomb was here, but I don't know what we're looking for."

Pak slitted her eyes as though afraid of the light, but nothing else about her stance or expression dared to change. Kira stepped aside, giving her a clear view of the crowded array, and waited as patiently as she could for Pak to scan the workings for what they needed. Thinking of the overwhelmed runabout and its load of priceless genetics, she felt a tickle of sweat trace its way down the middle of her back. "Pak, you've got to tell me. Where is it? Where's the bomb?"

Her eyes as wide and sightless as dabo wheels, Pak lifted her shoulders in only the most tiny of helpless shrugs. "I don't know," she whispered. "I just know it's not where it should be. It's not here."

Rehk'resen.

The alien word glowed like a spangle of light in the darkness, warmed Dax like a shivering flush of color melting its way through coils of translucent gel. In this floating state of barely liminal consciousness, it was all Dax knew, without even knowing what it meant. But remembering it was crucial. *Rehk'resen. Rehk'resen.*

Something tugged at Dax's awareness, in the vague nerveless way things happened in fever dreams. *Maybe I'm sleeping,* Dax thought. *Maybe I'm sick.* With an effort, Dax tried to crawl free of the floating numbness, and only succeeded in making the surrounding nothingness feel more like a tight, strangling shroud than the warm blanket it had been a moment before. *Maybe I've been drugged.*

The mental tugging came again, this time sharper and more electric, as if tiny circuits were plugging themselves directly in. Dax tried to focus on that feeling, tried to pin down what was happening. There was a familiar funneling rush, eerily similar to the rush that happened when a symbiont first connected to a brand-new host and began pouring itself in to share their brain. Except this time, what Dax's blind, encapsulated consciousness poured itself into wasn't a Trill brain trained and disciplined to receive it. It was utter chaos.

Mental links stretched out in all directions, linking to five thousand moving appendages, five hundred digestive systems, a thousand light-sensing organs all transmitting shared images like the faceted eyes of a bee, except that each of them saw something different. A warp exhaust, a portion of breached hull, a curve of duranium carapace . . . too many disparate images to make sense of. And hearing was no better. From every direction came the roar of hundreds of overlapping mental voices, some speaking, some screaming, some making only mindless animal grunts. Dax reeled under the cascade of random sensory input, choked on the wild schizophrenic explosion of voices. This was insane! What kind of host was this?

Rehk'resen, said an urgent internal voice, closer to Dax than all the rest. The alien word stirred a ghost of memory, like ashes floated by a vagrant breath of air. This was no host. This was an alien life-form, and Dax was here to do something to it, with it—but could not remember what!

". . . can't lower her isoboromine any more than that . . ."

". . . have to know whether the infiltration is working . . ."

Now, there was something different about *those* voices. Unlike the surrounding crash and babble of sound, those came from a more distant place, through the soothing swash and ripple of familiar Trill host-mind. Dax pulled back from the chaos of sight and sound that was the newly formed neural connections, and concentrated instead on the internal channel that seemed to link with someplace else.

". . . old man, can you hear me? Do you know where the symbiont is now?"

"Benjamin?"

With enormous effort, Dax opened what seemed to be someone else's eyes, and had a dizzying moment of seeing the clean lines of the *Defiant*'s bridge overlaid on jigsaw-puzzle insanity. The sight of the breached Jem'Hadar station on the viewscreen above her brought memory crashing back, cold and heavy as an avalanche. Her twinned symbiont had just been linked into the alien neural core on that station. Now it had to learn how to bend that group mind to her will and use the Jem'Hadar self-destruct code before it was too late.

"Rehk'resen," she murmured, only vaguely aware of her own real voice above the fitful clamor around the symbiont. "That's the Jem'Hadar code for self-destruction."

"You with us again, old man?" A strong hand slid behind her head and turned it so she could blink muzzily up at Sisko's face. "What's happening on the station?"

"Symbiont is linked in . . ." She swallowed past an odd dryness in her throat, hoping it was just a side effect of all the medication Yevlin had been injecting her with and not a precursor of systemic host-symbiont shock. "How much time . . . ?"

Sisko's voice turned bleak. "Twelve minutes, maximum. The station's accelerated to point-oh-five of light."

"Can't tell time in there," Dax warned him. "You'd better keep us posted. . . ."

"Us?" Sisko demanded.

She nodded and closed her eyes. "The symbiont can't do this all by itself. I'm going back to help. . . ."

It was easier sliding back into the chaos of the alien group mind, now that she knew her own name and self and purpose. Dax felt herself merge into the familiar Trill symbiont-mind that was her ancient counterpart, feeling again its fierce millennia-old determination to stop the wormhole from rifting. She grounded herself in that shared emotion, then stretched her mind—their minds—out along the newly grown nerve pathways that bound her to the other mental entities trapped in this strangest of alien prisons.

"I am Dax of Starfleet! Who will join with me?" She launched the demand in Standard English like a quantum torpedo, using the mental force of three joined brains to power it through the babble of voices. It made a surprisingly loud explosion in the chaos, followed by a short, startled silence. Just as the random chatter began to rise again, she repeated the words in her own native language. The musical rise and fall of the Trill speak/song echoed down the neural network, and this time the silence lasted a little longer. Dax identified herself over and over again, first in Vulcan, then in Ferengi, then in Klingon—

"Dax of Starfleet!" It was a Ferengi voice, not far away, sounding half insane with frustration. Dax felt an electric crackle of power rush through her as another mind added its control of the network to hers. "I'll join with you, I'll do anything you want. Just get me out of here!"

"Dax of Starfleet!" A half-familiar Vulcan voice, echoed by others a little farther away. This time, the power surge was enormous but far more controlled, connecting to her through what felt like miles of precisely calibrated computer circuits. "If you're here to rescue the wormhole, the crew of the *Sreba* will join with you. We have already formed a network around the navigations controls. Tell us what we can do!"

"Dax of Starfleet!" It was a distant thunder of Klingon voices, their accent the archaic growl of a previous millennium but their lust for battle undiminished by their time inside the group mind. Dax felt the power of their joining roll through her like the shock wave of an earthquake. "Dax of Starfleet, wherever that kingdom is, you speak our language. We hold the territory near where the fires of hell burn brightest. Share with us your battle plans."

"Dax." The faint, tired whisper barely reached her, from somewhere very deep inside the alien core. A jolt of recognition and disbelief shivered through Dax as the familiar mind-pattern overlapped hers. "This is . . . Jadzia. I've been waiting for you, for so long . . . tell me what we have to do to save the ship."

CHAPTER
23

"NOT HERE?" KIRA GRABBED AT Pak's gloved hands, martialing every ounce of her control not to shake the terrified woman senseless. "What do you mean the bomb's not here? You said it was hidden on the sensor array!"

"It's supposed to be!" Pak screwed her face into a pale semblance of her normal vinegar, and Kira was afraid for a moment that she was going to spit inside her helmet. "Those lazy little sons of raskers—I should've known they'd cut corners somewhere." Tipping her head back, she shouted in the general direction of the alien-covered runabout, "I'd kick your sorry asses clear to the Prophets' Temple if you hadn't already been eaten!"

An understandable sentiment, considering their circumstances, but not immediately useful. "Kira to O'Brien." She released Pak and turned away to survey the station's wheel laid out below her. "Run a sensor sweep on the outside of the station. Can you find any evidence of stray radiation *anywhere?*"

The few seconds it took to run the scan seemed to stretch on forever. When O'Brien's voice came back to her through the wall of static, Kira could barely hear the words past the growl of his frustration. "The wormhole's got everything in the vicinity so excited, the only things I can pick out of the background are the engine cores on the *Mukaikubo* and that leaky weapons sail we were working on the other day."

The other day . . . Time flies when you're having fun,
stretches days into eons when your life is on the line. Kira
shook her head at the tall weapons sail, and tried to
remember what it felt like to have your biggest problem be
explaining the word "no" to an obsequious Ferengi toad.

The radiation gauge on her helmet display blinked as
something in the wormhole rearranged itself beyond the
threshold of sight, and she paused, caught by the spiraling
numbers. Caught by a fragment of memory that hadn't
quite been there before. "Chief . . . do self-diagnostics still
show everything as normal in weapons sail two?"

"For what it's worth," he answered slowly, "yes, sir, they
do. And it did all right as far as bug zapping before. But,
Major—" She could tell he was striving hard to retain a
tone of respectful objectivity. "—figuring out what's wrong
with that weapons sail isn't exactly our first priority anymore."

Kira twitched a little smile and smacked one fisted glove
into the other. "Maybe it is." She turned awkwardly in her
suit, only to find Pak squatting with her hands folded over
her head and her eyes screwed tightly shut on the world.
"You're right, Pak." She knew the terrorist could hear her,
whether or not she would look. "Your cronies were lazy. It's
a shorter jaunt from the closest airlock to the sail housing,
and they wouldn't have to try and sneak the bomb through
as much of the station." She threw a defiant gesture toward
the arcing sail, her heart starting to race with a fierce and
angry thrill. "It's the bomb, Chief," she announced trium-
phantly. "The radiation leak in the weapons sail is Pak
Dorren's bomb."

"Jadzia—" A surge of horrified pity swept through the
Dax aboard the *Defiant,* and she reached out with all the
power of her three linked minds to pull that long-lost fourth
into the joining. Another, deeper jolt of completion echoed
down the ansible link, as ancient host and ancient symbiont
reunited after milennia apart. Dax used the resulting sense
of doubled power to project her mental voice down every
neural pathway she could find, speaking first in Standard
English, then in Klingon.

"My plan is to make this station self-destruct. I know the

code, but we need a mouth to speak it and a powered computer junction to hear and implement it. Where can we get them?"

"We could fashion a vocal apparatus from the DNA these creatures hoard," one of the Vulcans suggested.

"Too slow," said the ancient Jadzia fragment, with a certainty that came from centuries of gleaned knowledge about these aliens. "My other selves tell me we have only a few minutes before we enter the wormhole and our group mind scatters again. We must find an existing mouth to use."

Flickers of searching thought sparked through the alien core like heat-lightning. "I've got one!" crowed the Ferengi voice after a moment. "The shell right next to mine is digesting a dead Jem'Hadar—"

"Manan'Agar." Dax suppressed an unexpected swell of remorse, reminding herself that the warship pilot had known he was going to certain death when he volunteered to take the ancient symbiont to the aliens. "Can you see if his mouth and throat have been destroyed?"

From out of the kaleidoscope of a thousand visual images that crowded in on her, Dax got a stronger flash of Manan'Agar's bony-plated face, disappearing into an alien that had apparently already swallowed the rest of him. She winced, but the ancient Jadzia merely made a thoughtful noise as she sampled the image with her. "Looks like they've already extracted most of his cerebral matter," she commented. "We'll have to incorporate that neural strand into our network." Then she added, in perfect archaic Klingon, "Lords and officers of Qu'onos, you are best suited to wage this battle. Can you conquer the territory that's being added to the enemy's kingdom?"

"The assault has already begun," a Klingon voice growled in reply. Dax got another flashing image of Manan'Agar's face, jerking to a stop just before it was swallowed. "We have wrested the main roads from the enemy's control, and stopped their advance," reported a distant member of the Klingon network. "Where shall we link the newly acquired land? It does not seem to speak our language."

"Let me have it." Dax felt a smooth scuttle of motion as the Ferengi-controlled shell maneuvered around the outside of the alien core until it could burrow beneath its neighbor. She felt the electric jolts of connection as the newest neural strands were woven into the Ferengi's network, but no sense of Manan'Agar's furious personality came with them. "Hmm—looks like this joker shot himself in the back of the head when the shells caught him. Smart guy."

"Is there enough neuromuscular tissue left to issue commands to his voluntary muscles?" Dax demanded.

"Just barely." Another flash of compound vision showed her Manan'Agar's head at close range, his lips moving in a convulsive jerk. "Now, where's the closest powered section of the station?"

Another bright explosion of mental searching flickered through the group mind, and this time it was a Vulcan voice which spoke first. "I have found the main power switches." This time, the flash of vision Dax got was in a lighted corridor, where a duranium-shelled alien had plastered itself up against what looked like a cracked-open engineering panel. "If we can take control of this entity, we can simply reroute power to the Ferengi's location. But it is one of the enemy—its captured minds have no will of their own to join us."

"Then let all of us combined bend this one quickly to *our* will," a Klingon voice growled.

"Heads up, old man," said Sisko's unexpected voice, sounding light-years distant now. "You've only got five more minutes. . . ."

"Time is running out," Dax warned her allies, then reached out through the neural network to her ancient counterpart and felt her determination redouble. "Send all your excess power to me—*now!*"

Mental energy cracked like lightning across the chaos of the group mind, joining and growing like a river in flood as it channeled into Dax. For a moment, she struggled to contain it, but the strength of four Trill minds in complete ansible contact rose to the challenge and hammered the energy into a single flaming bolt, then flung it onward to its mark. She saw the targeted alien jerk as the attack reached it. One by one, the cerebral nodes inside the duranium shell tried to ward off their joint assault. One by one, each of them failed.

As the last one shattered beneath her assault, Dax grabbed control of the neural strands that ended in slender, claw-tipped digits and the ones that fed in vision from a pair of thick-stalked eyes. She swiveled those eyes to regard the power grid beneath her, seeing a dim glow in only one of its hundred circuits. The aliens were releasing only a trickle of power from their hoarded reaction masses, just enough to run the navigational thrusters.

". . . three minutes, old man . . ."

"Tell me the instant you have power," she ordered the Ferengi, then began tapping each circuit in turn, diverting the power trickle to other parts of the station. She was slow at first, but as her new neural connections solidified, she gained the ability to move her alien fingers faster and faster until she could make the dim glow of connected power race across each row of the circuit board. She heard the Ferengi's anguished mental yelp two lights past the correct one, but it only took a few seconds to backtrack power to his sector.

". . . two minutes left, Dax . . ."

She left the ancient Jadzia holding the enemy network in check, and reached the rest of her mental presence back through the network of her allies to join the Ferengi-dominated shell. *"Rehk'resen,"* she told him urgently. "That's what we've got to get the Jem'Hadar to say. *Now!"*

"I'm working on it." A flurry of energy sparked out from the Ferengi's local network, and in a fragment of her compound vision, Dax saw Manan'Agar's slack jaw clench and quiver. A faint hint of sound trickled back into their neural network, gleaned from the Jem'Hadar's own ears.

"Reeh—" It came out sounding more like a groan than a word. "Reehek—"

". . . one more minute. Old man, whatever you've got to do, do it now!"

With one last desperate effort, Dax shoved her consciousness past the Ferengi's startled mind and down into the inert dead nerves of what was left of Manan'Agar, forcing air through his stiffening throat muscles and vocal cords. "Rehk!" he shouted abruptly. "Resen. *Rehk'resen!"*

And with the blinding speed that the Jem'Hadar built into all their military equipment, every containment field on the station's reaction mass exploded outward. The last

321

thing Dax remembered was a violent swell of joy from the trapped minds in contact with hers, just before the pure white fire of superheated plasma seared them into nothingness.

"Okay—" Kira took a deep, steadying breath, and fixed her gaze on the towering weapons sail in front of her until the pit of her stomach ceased its twisting. *It was just a simple leap—no tethers, no controls, but still a simple leap.* The stalwartly rational chant in her head had started to sound decidedly hysterical about halfway across the long, empty expanse between the sensor arrays and here. Faster than walking, perhaps, but not conducive to an intact stomach lining. Kira hoped she'd bought enough time to make the future health of her insides a legitimate worry. "I'm at the weapons sail."

"That fast?" Pak Dorren's voice scratched across the wormhole static as relentlessly as ever, no matter that she still crouched with her eyes presumably shut in the shadow of the sensor array. "I don't even want to know how you got there."

Kira played clumsy gloves across the sail's exterior door controls. "Don't worry—I wasn't going to tell you." As the hatch slid aside in vacuum silence, she stepped forward into her past from just a few days before.

The sail stretched up into what seemed an impossible distance, pinching in to a dark point somewhere far above the crowded floor. Kira moved carefully among the confusion of torpedo handling equipment and targeting brains, leery of touching anything now that she knew O'Brien's radiation threat was more than just some minor capacitor leak. "I'm in the final delivery chamber," she reported to Pak as she worked her way toward the center. "This is where the phaser capacitors charge and where the photon torpedoes are armed before launching."

Pak grunted. "The idiots probably thought that would hide the radiation signatures from the plutonium and tritium."

"Good thing they were wrong." All unbidden, a vivid, glowing image of Veska Province blasted into Kira's mind, and she forced herself to crush the panic in her clenched fist as she instructed, "Tell me what I'm looking for."

Suit joints cracked and clattered across the open channel, and Kira heard Pak make an odd little grunt. She hoped the terrorist wasn't trying to move herself. They couldn't afford to have their only bomb expert go catatonic just now. "It's gonna be a two-part contraption." Her voice sounded a margin more steady, and the sounds of her suit movements had ceased. "The first part is the plutonium detonator, which should already be inside a delivery shell. Look for something about as big around as a disposal bin, maybe half a meter long. If there's someplace where your torpedoes stockpile—like waiting for arming, or something—that's probably where the morons put it."

She'd moved herself to where she couldn't see, Kira realized. Of course. If you couldn't see a danger, it wasn't really there—if you stared at the welds surrounding a brace of deck rivets, you couldn't notice that a gentle flexing of your feet would send you sailing off into infinity. With only a plutonium detonator and nightmare images of Veska Province to keep her company, Kira wished her own fears could be so easily avoided.

She remembered studying the diagrams—years ago, when she'd been sent to the station as a teenager on some idiot mission to incapacitate the weapons systems. Torpedoes were stored deep inside the station, away from the habitation areas, shielded to protect them from detonating every time a rival force managed a direct hit to the station's hide. For that very reason, the Cardassians never stockpiled torpedoes in the weapons sails. Better to lose the sail and all its associated phaser batteries than to suffer the damage of forty photon torpedoes all going up in concert. Instead, the torpedoes stayed in stasis until needed, then were conveyed to the sails and armed for launching. It was an elegant design that the Bajoran Resistance had bitterly resented— what they could have accomplished with a single suicidal operative "if only the Cardassians weren't so anal with their weapons" had been everyone's favorite pointless debate.

Now that Starfleet ran the station, protecting against constant bombardment and sabotage were no longer primary concerns. Still, the torpedo system was already there and well designed; the only difference in Starfleet's procedures was what became of the weapons after they were loaded into the sail and armed for launch. Any duds among the Cardassian supplies were summarily launched into space—after all, just because a torpedo couldn't arm didn't mean it couldn't still explode, and keeping it inside the sail still posed a significant danger. Starfleet took a dimmer view of such wanton technological pollution; Starfleet had built a special storage rack along the arching spine of the sail, and this is where her duds went to rest until engineers with nothing better to do could come outside and repair them.

There were two sleek black casings waiting in the rack now—far fewer than the Cardassians threw out in a single day, Kira noted, and this was no doubt the dregs from the last time Sisko had ordered torpedoes armed more than a month ago. No wonder Starfleet could be so gracious about cleaning up its own messes. It was probably a lot easier when you didn't make much mess to begin with.

She couldn't see the higher of the two torpedoes from where she stood at the foot of the rack, but a dim, roseate glow against the empty sling above it caught her attention as it silently came and went and came again. Planting one foot on the wall of the sail, she gave herself a moment to reorient to the new position, then walked up what now felt like a gently sloping floor to stand beside the blinking casing. Just above the beautifully embossed Starfleet emblem and neatly printed PROPERTY OF DEEP SPACE STATION #9, the message ribbon embedded in the torpedo's nose shouted redly, ERR 3453 'RADIATION CONTAMINATION HAZARD.' REBOOT AND RELOAD.

Kira thought at first that it must mean that something inside its own structure had malfunctioned and flooded it with a fatal load of subspace radiation. Then she noticed the first-stage indicator in her rad meter as it sailed steadily redline, and she realized just whose radiation this forgotten torpedo was reporting. It slid easily into another holding bracket when she pushed it, exposing the slim silver casing of someone else's bomb tucked underneath.

Kira read the elaborate scrawl winding its way around the narrow casing's nose. "'The Hand of the Prophets.' Very subtle."

On the other side of the station, Pak chuckled dryly. "Do yourself a favor, little bit. Don't even try to pick that up and move it. Just unscrew the nose and slide out the workings until you see the cup where the tritium goes."

Kira touched her suit fingers to the casing as lightly as possible, wishing she could somehow unscrew it without having to actually make contact. The instant the nose cone swung open, she jerked her hand away to let the workings slide out by themselves. "It's open." She wished her voice didn't sound so stretched tight and breathless. "Now what?"

"Now you slip the tritium inside. It's plasma, inside a magnetic bottle, about as long as your forearm. I'd suggest checking among your phaser batteries for that one."

But it wasn't hidden somewhere within the batteries, or underneath the second torpedo, and there was nothing to open or move among the targeting equipment that was big enough to hide anything larger than the palm of her hand. Swearing, feeling tears of frustration burning at the backs of her eyes, Kira aimed a useless kick at the bottom of the phaser optic tower.

"Little bit?"

The force of her kick shivered through the body of her hardsuit, breaking her contact with the deck and setting her spinning lazily several meters above the floor. It didn't matter—nothing mattered. They were one step away from assembling a functional bomb, and unless she could locate the tritium, they might just as well have played tongo until their whole world rolled to an end. Putting out one arm to catch herself against the optic tower, she took angry satisfaction in the jolt of discomfort that sent shooting up her arm. *Serves me right. I can't even put together a hydrogen bomb! What have I got to be careful about now?*

A brilliant glitter high overhead danced its reflection across her faceplate, then swept out of her sight as she rotated.

Her breath catching in her throat, Kira grabbed the tower in both hands and pulled herself toward the ceiling so hard her helmet cracked against the upper optical mount before she could slow her ascent.

"What are you doing in there?" That panic was the most honest thing Kira had heard come out of Pak since she'd met her. "Little bit, what happened? What'd you drop?"

"Nothing. I just hit my helmet on the ceiling." The magnetic bottle was more delicate than she'd expected, thin and sparkling, like a cylinder of summer sun. "I've got the tritium."

"Good! Now put it in the detonator. Make sure it clicks into place. You'll know it's seated right when the lights in the control display come on."

She was already on the floor and halfway across to the weapons rack. Walking carefully, calmly up the curving wall, Kira eased the magnetic bottle into its cradle as though it were a sleeping baby. It fit more perfectly than anything she'd ever seen, and even the sudden brightness of the lights jumping to life around it did little to take away from its luminance.

"That's it!" O'Brien's cry was so obscured by static, Kira was barely certain that she heard him. "I've lost all power readings from the runabout, Major. You've got one minute!"

One minute's all I need! "Get a lock on the transponder, Chief!" She dug the little clip out of its carry pocket on the leg of her hardsuit and placed it with exaggerated care on the bomb's sleek outer shell. Then, as her hoarse breathing slowly obscured the inside of her faceplate, she used the smallest finger on her glove to punch the seconds into the blinking timer. She could just make out a blurry number ten when she slipped the tray of workings back inside and gave the nose cone a two-handed spin.

"Energize!"

The transporter's telltale sparkle danced across the silver metal housing just as Kira shoved off from the weapons rack and headed for the floor. She wasn't sure what she expected. Some impossible shock wave, maybe, or some searing blast of heat such as once wiped Veska Province from the face of Bajor and laid a platter of glowing silicate in its place. Instead, she stepped out of the weapons sail in time to see only the reflection of brilliance as it dashed itself against the station's parts. Like the striking of a match in the middle of darkness. Or fireworks underneath a cloudy sky. A shriek of cheering voices swelled to fill her hardsuit helmet, and Pak Dorren sighed with a murmur of quiet contentment. "Now, that's what I call beautiful."

Kira climbed to the top of the nearest docking light, turning away from the contaminated weapons sail and toward the secretive wormhole. Her suit comm rang with a clarity that seemed almost unnatural, and the station all around her lay undisturbed and dark. "Chief . . ."

"We're doing some last mopping up with the transporters, Major." He sounded giddy and restless, and ready to drop on his feet. "Not that there are many left to worry about. That was one hell of a bomb."

Instead of the smug response Kira expected from Pak, all she heard was silence. "Pak?" she demanded.

Still no answer. Worried that the terrorist had finally gone catatonic with fear, she slid over the far edge of the docking light's gantry to bring her into view. All she saw below her was an empty curve of gunmetal hull. Exasperation and suspicion burned through the last of Kira's mindless relief. *"Pak!"*

A gravelly chuckle, devoid of the slightest traces of fear, greeted her across the comm. Behind it, Kira could hear the rush of air whirling into an activated airlock. "Hey, you did good, little bit. And don't worry—no one's going to blame you for being so busy saving the wormhole that you let one sneaky old Resistance fighter slip through your fingers."

She'd been faking it! Kira should have known that any woman who could stare a nuclear bomb in the face without flinching couldn't possibly be afraid of something as simple as open space. She couldn't believe she'd fallen for a ploy that any first-year Resistance fighter should have seen through.

Kira growled and swung herself out to follow Pak into the station. Before she could do more than reach for her next handhold, however, an outward blast of released air from a shuttlebay nearly knocked her off her precarious perch. She cursed and clung to it with scrabbling fingers. "Chief! What just happened?"

O'Brien sounded even more irritated than she felt. "The

Platte just took off from docking bay three with your friend Pak inside, that's what happened. We didn't have enough controls on-line to stop her."

"Not the *new* runabout?" Kira felt like banging her head against the station's hull in frustration. "I'm going to *kill* her."

"Good luck, little bit," said Pak's mocking voice, this time with a chitter of Starfleet machinery behind her. "But you have to catch me first, you know. Boy, I can't wait to see how much tritium this baby ship will trade for on the black market. . . ."

Kira lifted her head abruptly, her attention caught, not by Pak's taunt, but by the lack of static behind it. "Chief," she said again, this time in wonder, "am I hallucinating, or is that a stable wormhole I'm not hearing?"

O'Brien didn't answer for a long moment, and the stark clarity of the silence on the comm made Kira scrabble around on the docking light to view the velvet dark space behind her with a weary laugh.

"Well, what d'you know," O'Brien said in an awkward attempt at levity. "I guess fusion bombs fix wormholes."

She tipped her head sideways to prop her helmet against one hand, and watched the first azure streamers swirl stationward as the wormhole blossomed into life. "I don't think so, Chief."

It exploded across the sky with a blinding radiance that made her heart swell almost to bursting with its beauty. This is what the Prophets' Temple was supposed to be, a thing of life and mystery—the future of Bajor, not its destruction. As the fleck of black that was an arriving ship flowed out of that giving mouth and into reality, Kira dared to send the smallest prayer toward the gods who had watched over her people for so long. *Thank you.*

"*Defiant* to *Deep Space Nine*. Request permission to dock and off-load this weary crew."

She sat up straighter, her hands on her knees, and smiled as the Temple twined its doors tight shut behind the stars. "*Defiant*, this is DS9. Permission most happily granted, Captain. Welcome home."

CHAPTER
24

THERE WAS SOMETHING wrong with the silence.

Awareness drifted back into Dax, slow and cool as the water that trickled through layers of salt travertine to feed the brine pools of Trill. Even after she felt mostly awake, she kept her eyes closed for a long, puzzled moment, trying to decide what she wasn't hearing in the silence. She knew she must be in the *Defiant*'s medical bay—she could hear the discreet chirps and clicks of sickbay diagnostics overhead counting off her pulse, her breathing rate, and all her other metabolic functions. Beyond that quiet machine noise, there was only a slow whisper of life-support fans circulating refiltered air, and the gentle, occasional rustle of someone else in the room. It all seemed normal, but something *was* missing, Dax knew. There was a sound she should be hearing, a sound she had grown so used to she couldn't even remember what it was now that it had gone.

Then liquid splashed very softly in the distance, and memories of the tidal swash and pull of her ansible link with the ancient Dax symbiont flooded into her mind. Dax gasped and sat up, reaching out with all the force of both her joined minds. She met nothing but silence. The ancient symbiont was gone.

"Jadzia." Something clattered against a table nearby, and a moment later a gentle hand brushed across her forehead. "Are you really awake?"

L. A. GRAF

Dax's eyes flew open. The thin, dark face bending over her in concern was the last one she'd expected to see. "What are *you* doing here?" she demanded.

One corner of Julian Bashir's mouth kicked upward in a wry smile. "Well, at least that was more original than 'Where am I?'" He glanced up at the diagnostic panels above her head and made a satisfied noise. "Isoboromine levels back to normal, and all your other neurotransmitters steady as a rock. Looks like you're fit to go back on duty, Lieutenant."

"But, Julian, if you're here—" Dax broke off, seeing the wider contours of *Deep Space Nine*'s infirmary behind him instead of the *Defiant*'s cramped sickbay. She took a deep, disbelieving breath. "I'm on board the station? We saved the wormhole?"

"You saved the wormhole," Bashir confirmed. His brown face hardened into more finely drawn lines, as if he'd remembered something that made him unhappy. He turned away from her gaze, picking up the steaming mug of raktajino he'd left across the room. "You and the old Dax symbiont."

It wasn't the sadness in Bashir's voice that worried Dax—it was the underlying wash of bitterness that told her he blamed himself for the symbiont's long-overdue death. She took a deep breath, choosing her next words with care.

"We had some help," she told him quietly. "The Vulcan scientists from the *Sreba,* a lost Ferengi, a phalanx of Klingon warriors . . . and another Jadzia host."

"What?" Bashir slewed around to face her so abruptly that hot liquid slopped out of his cup and ran down across his hand. He cursed and set the cup down again. "Jadzia was *there?* Inside one of the viroids?"

She nodded. "Enough of her to help us. She told us the best way to use the alien core to destroy the Jem'Hadar station."

"Oh, my god." The doctor sat down on the bed across from her, horrified realization darkening his eyes. "When the *Defiant* was attacked on the other end of the timerift, it must have been by the viroids, not the Furies!"

"Yes," Dax agreed. "Benjamin used one of our own photon torpedoes to blow most of them off the ship—"

"—but with shields down, Kira and O'Brien got killed doing it," Bashir finished for her. "While the captain only

330

survived long enough to find us a hiding place in that cometary fragment."

"And Jadzia got so much radiation damage that she separated from Dax and sacrificed herself to lead the rest of the viroid aliens away. That's when she was attacked and digested by the viroids."

"We must have known by then what they were," Bashir said softly. "We must have captured one and seen the living brains it contained."

Dax nodded, clasping her hands around her upraised knees thoughtfully. "That's why the ancient Dax was so insistent that we talk to what the aliens had eaten. It wanted us to find the ancient Jadzia."

"Yes." Bashir suddenly seemed to notice the wet stickiness on his hands and cursed again in a more normal voice. He jumped up and went to fetch a cleaning swipe from one of his dispensers. "That must have been what kept it alive all those centuries. It knew it had to save her."

"See, it wasn't just your selfishness after all."

He gave her a startled and oddly guilty look. "How did you know—"

"That you were afraid you'd only kept Dax alive to keep you company on the *Defiant?*" Dax shook her head, sighing. "Julian, you've always been a medical ethics debate looking for a place to happen. It makes you a wonderful doctor—"

"—but an inconvenient friend," he finished, smiling wryly. "Yes, I know. Garak tells me that all the time." His comm badge beeped for attention, and he tapped it reluctantly. "Bashir."

"Doctor, is Lieutenant Dax awake yet?" The breathless voice on the other end was definitely Heather Petersen's, but Dax couldn't imagine what had put so much excitement into it. "I really need to talk to her."

Bashir grimaced. "She's only just woken, Ensign. I really don't think she's up to critiquing the rough draft of your new subspace-physics article—"

"It's not that—it's the wormhole! It's doing something wonderful. Something that she *has* to see."

Bashir's voice had settled back into doctorly steadiness. "I'd really like to keep her under observation for another hour or so—hey!" He lifted his hand from his comm badge and scowled at Dax. "What are you doing?"

"Discharging myself." She sat up straighter in the bed, patting about beneath her for the drawer that should hold her uniform and comm badge. "You said I was fit to go back to duty. Now get out of here, so I can get dressed and see the wormhole."

"For a Trill who's just recovered from systemic shock, I really can't recommend—"

"Julian, scram!"

Dax found Heather Petersen standing together with Kira and Sisko at the large observation port on the Promenade. Outside, the usual darkness of space had been blasted into luminescent brilliance. A waterfall of light poured from the wormhole: fierce volcanic crimson melting into iris bronze, soft apple green shading to translucent glacial blue. Kira watched it with almost supernatural awe, but Sisko only looked tense and tired. He glanced up at Dax as she joined them, his worried look easing into a smile of welcome.

"Well, old man, it's good to see you on your feet again." He clasped Dax's shoulder warmly and drew her closer to the thick transparent aluminum of the observation port. "What do you make of the fireworks out there?"

Dax watched the steady outpouring of light for another moment, then glanced over at Petersen. The cadet was engrossed in whatever readouts she had linked to her portable data padd, but there was no fear or tension in her face. Dax relaxed, her own suspicions confirmed by the excited smile the younger scientist turned on her.

"Energy equalization?" she asked, before Petersen could say anything.

The cadet's smile widened. "Yes, exactly! How did you guess without seeing the subspace matrix scans, Lieutenant?"

"I've been living with this particular subspace matrix for a long time, Heather." Dax watched a vivid purple corona sink into ultraviolet invisibility for a moment, then flash back to dark dragon's-blood red to start the cycle all over again. "And there's clearly no destructive patterning to this—it's just pure energy release through the visible spectrum. That's the part of the EM spectrum," she added for

Sisko and Kira's benefit, "that poses the least threat to living organisms."

Kira made a sound of vague comprehension. "So the Prophets are doing this on purpose? It's some kind of release—"

"—of the excess chronodynamic energy they've absorbed over the last fifty hours," Dax finished, nodding. "It would be a lot more thermodynamically efficient for them to release it in a few high-intensity bursts, but they appear to know that would be hazardous to our health. So they're sending most of it five thousand years into the past. What we're seeing is the visible-specturm backwash."

"Which proves beyond any scientific doubt that there really are sentient organisms in the singularity!" Petersen was flushed and breathless again. "I can't wait to write *this* up for the *Journal of Subspace Reviews!*"

"Five thousand years in the past?" Sisko's face went blank. "Tell me, Dax, what will happen—what did happen—when those bursts hit the Fury fleet?"

Dax thought for a minute. "That much energy shooting out of the wormhole would cause major subspace tunneling. The Furies could have been thrown anywhere in the galaxy. Anywhere at all."

"An energy blast we caused," Sisko said, his voice heavy. "So they were right. We did it. We banished them. Threw them out of 'heaven.'"

"Or saved their lives," Dax, said, a little too lightly. "It's all in how you look at it." The two of them turned back to the circular rainbow of shifting colors outside the viewport, which now seemed much more than a pretty light show.

"How long will this backwash last, old man?" Sisko asked, his eyes still fixed on the expanding rainbow colors.

Dax consulted Petersen's data padd, tapping in a quick energy-decay curve and plotting the wormhole's current emissions against it. "Oh, I'd say it'll last for at least another day or so. After that, the wormhole should be safe to travel through again."

Kira's quick glow of smile chased the lines of strain from her face. "That's wonderful! That will give us time to fly the Kai and all the Vedeks up from Bajor to observe the Prophets in action."

Sisko gave her a considering glance. "And mend some of the bridges we burned by misplacing Pak Dorren? That's not a bad thought, Major. Why don't I issue those invitations personally—"

"Oh, no!" Kira brought both hands up to shoulder height, as if to ward off a threat instead of an offer of help. "No, Captain, you're going to be *much* too busy explaining to all the Ferengi and Orion traders on board why they're going to have to wait here another day before they can travel into the Gamma Quadrant. I wouldn't dream of taking up more of your time."

"Actually, I was hoping that you—"

"And it looks like your first customer is already here." Kira stepped back hurriedly, making room for Quark to scuttle in to join them. "I'll start on those invitations right away, sir."

Dax laughed, seeing the exasperated glance Sisko threw after her. "I'll give you a hand with the traders, Benjamin, if you really need one."

"Be careful, old man. I may take you up on that." He gave in at last to the repeated tugging on his uniform sleeve, and looked down at the impatient Ferengi beside him. "What is it, Quark?"

The Ferengi cleared his throat, giving Dax an oddly respectful glance. "Did I just hear the lieutenant say that the wormhole's going to be closed for another day or two?"

Sisko rolled his eyes, but answered patiently enough. "Yes, you did. Do you want to register a protest now or later?"

Quark drew himself up to his full, unimpressive height. "In emergency circumstances like these, registering a protest is the last thing I would do," he declared with ringingly false sincerity. "I know how much strain a ban on wormhole traffic puts on this station."

"Do you?" Dax asked, curiously.

Quark threw her a glittering Ferengi smile. "You wouldn't believe how profits—I mean, alcohol consumption—rises at times like these. Now, Captain, it occurs to me that what you need is a distraction."

Sisko inclined his head toward the prismatic waterfall of

color pouring out into deep space. "You don't think the fireworks display out there is distracting enough?"

"Not to hardworking spacers looking for a profitable way to fill their time." Quark insinuated himself between Sisko and Dax, sliding a hand through both their arms. "No, what I had in mind was a little gambling tournament—"

After

Out here where sunlight was a faraway glimmer in the blackness of space, ice lasted a long time. The cold outer dark sheltered it in safety, preserving the last debris of the nebula that had birthed this planet-rich system. Inside that litter of dirty ice, the random dance of gravity sent one dark mass grazing too close to a neighbor, ejecting it into the unyielding pull of solar gravity. Unburdened by internal fragments of steel and empty space, no longer carrying memories of distant strife and blood and battle, the comet began its first journey toward the distant sun. It swung past the captured ninth planet, past the four gas giants, past the ring of rocky fragments and the cold red desert planet. Then, for the first time, it began to glow, brushed into brilliance by the gathering heat of the sun's nuclear furnace. By the time it approached the cloud-feathered planet that harbored life, it had become brighter than any star. Its flare pierced that planet's blue sky, amazing the primitive tribes who hunted and gathered and scratched at the earth with sticks to grow their food. They watched and wondered at it for a few days, until the comet's borrowed light began to fade. Then they forgot it, while the tumbling ice began its long journey back to the outer dark.

It would return to the sun again, regular as the turning seasons if more slow. As the centuries and millennia passed, it would trace its elliptical path fifty more times, growing smaller each time it neared the nuclear fire it orbited. It saw dim fires *glow to life on the nightside of the bluish globe that harbored life. It saw the fires brighten and spread, leaping across vast oceans. It saw them merge to form huge networks of light, outlining every coast and lake and river. And it saw them leap into the ocean of space. Out to the planet's single moon at first, then later to its cold, red neighbor, then to the moons of the gas giants. Finally, out beyond all of them, to the stars. . . .*

The
Invasion
Concludes
in

BOOK FOUR

The Final Fury

by

Dafydd Ab Hugh

There is no fear. There is no pain. There is no emotion . . .
let it fade and disappear. Pure logic; logic fills your brain.
Thought is symbol, and logic gives you complete power over
all symbols.

The meditation helped, but Lieutenant Tuvok still found himself caught in the grip of illogical emotion, the DNA memory of a hundred thousand years ago perturbing his endocrine system, triggering the release of Vulcan vidrenalase, which affects Vulcans as adrenaline affects humans. Tuvok trembled; he could not control the fine motor skills. It was the best he could do to maintain a veneer of logic and rationality across a sea of barbaric feelings and impulses.

He stumbled along behind the Fury, behind the captain and Neelix, through the warm, moist tunnel. Even in his nightmare state, he could not help but notice that it was like a return up the birth canal; but rather than fascinate him, as it should have, the image filled Tuvok with the unaccustomed *emotions* of loathing and disgust.

Like the impulse to kill the interlocutor, Navdaq, and every other demon on the planet, all twenty-seven billion of them. It was worse than the *pon farr*—at least the mating madness was carefully channeled by ritual. Tuvok had no ritual to deal with the primitive emotions that these creatures stirred in him. Only his meditation.

Tuvok was not bothered by the darkness of the corridor, nor by what the captain considered disturbing architecture: angles that did not quite meet at ninety degrees but looked as thought they ought to, tricks of perspective that made walls or ceilings seem closer or farther than they were, or strange tilts that threw off a human's sense of balance, which was tied so completely into visual cuing.

But he was disturbed by the sudden intrusion of a long-forgotten cavern in the Vulcan mind, the genetic memory of defeat and slavery so complete and remote it left no trace in the historical record, which was thought to have stretched back farther in time than the conquest.

Evidently not, thought Tuvok, clutching at the logical train of thought; *apparently, there are significant gaps in the historical record. I must write a report for the* Vulcan Journal of Archeology and Prehistory. Then he shuddered.

In our innermost beings, we are not very different from Romulans after all, he thought. With bitterness—another emotion; they came thick and fast now.

In fact, Tuvok realized they would never stop . . . not until he forced himself to confront the Fury. Gritting his teeth against the terrors, Tuvok increased his stride until he stood but an arm's length behind Navdaq; then with a quick move, before he could disgrace his race further by losing his nerve, Tuvok reached out and caught Navdaq by the shoulder, spinning the creature around to face him.

Tuvok looked directly into Navdaq's face—and felt an abyss open inside him deep enough to his hearts.

I know you! he thought, unable to keep excitement and emotion even out of his thoughts. *You are Ok'San, the Overlord!*

Ok'San was the most despised of all Vulcan demons, for she was the mother of all the rest. The mythology was so ancient that it was consciously known only to a few scholars; even Tuvok knew only dimly of the stories, and only because of his interest in Vulcan history.

But all Vulcans knew and—to tell the truth—feared Ok'San, for she represented *loss of control* and *loss of reason;* there was little else that a sane Vulcan feared apart from the loss of everything it meant to be a Vulcan: logic, control, order, and reason.

In demonic mythology, Ok'San crept through the windows at night, the hot, dry Vulcan night, and crouched on the chests of her "chosen" dreamers: poets, composers, authors, philosophers, scientists, political analysts . . . the very people whose creativity was slowly knitting together the barbaric strands of early Vulcan society into a vision of a logical tomorrow, who groped for shreds of civilization in the horror of Vulcan's yesterday.

She crouched on a dreamer's chest, leaned over his writhing body, and pressed her lips against his. She spat into his mouth, and the spittle rolled down his throat and filled his hearts with the *Fury of Vulcan.*

The Fury of Vulcan manifested as a berserker rage that flooded the victim and drove him to paroxysms of horrific violence that defied the descriptive power of logic.

Tuvok had tried to contemplate what must pass through a Vulcan's mind to drive him to kill his own family with a blunt stick, striking their heads hard enough to crush bone and muscle and still have force enough to destroy the brain. In one of the few instances of the Fury of Vulcan to be well recorded by the testimony of many witnesses, a Vulcan hunter-warrior named Torkas Torkas of the Vehm, perhaps eighty thousand years ago, grabbed up a leaf-bladed Vulcan Toth spear and set out after the entire population of his village. He managed to kill ninety-seven and wound an additional fourteen, six critically, before he was killed.

Tuvok had always believed Ok'San was the personification of the violent, nearly sadistic rage that filled the hearts of Vulcans before Surak. The Fury of Vulcan always seemed like a disease of the nervous system; yet it was curious that there were no recorded instances of the Fury within historical times . . . not a one.

Diseases do not die out; and it was unlikely in the extreme that primitive Vulcans who had neither logic nor medical science could have destroyed the virus that caused the Fury.

It was an enigma, until now.

Look for
STAR TREK® VOYAGER™
Invasion! Book Four
The Final Fury
Wherever Paperback Books Are Sold
Available from
Pocket Books

**It is the Day of Reckoning
It is the Day of Judgement
It is...**

STAR TREK®
THE DAY OF HONOR

A Four-Part Klingon™ Saga
That Spans the Generations

Coming Summer 1997
from Pocket Books

POCKET
B O O K S

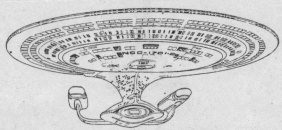